THE
KILLING
TIDE

COASTAL GUARDIANS // BOOK 1

THE KILLING TIDE

DANI PETTREY

BETHANYHOUSE

a division of Baker Publishing Group
Minneapolis, Minnesota

Published by Bethany House Publishers
11400 Hampshire Avenue South
Bloomington, Minnesota 55438
www.bethanyhouse.com

Bethany House Publishers is a division of
Baker Publishing Group, Grand Rapids, Michigan

Printed in the United States of America

Library of Congress Cataloging-in-Publication Data
Names: Pettrey, Dani, author.
Title: The killing tide / Dani Pettrey.
Description: Bloomington, Minnesota : Bethany House Publishers, [2019] | Series: Coastal guardians ; 1
Identifiers: LCCN 2018061274 | ISBN 9780764230844 (trade paper) | ISBN 9780764233432 (cloth) | ISBN 9781493418695 (e-book)
Subjects: LCSH: Murder—Investigation—Fiction. | GSAFD: Suspense fiction.
Classification: LCC PS3616.E89 K55 2019 | DDC 813/.6—dc23
LC record available at https://lccn.loc.gov/2018061274

Scripture quotations are from the Holy Bible, New International Version®. NIV®. Copyright © 1973, 1978, 1984, 2011 by Biblica, Inc.™ Used by permission of Zondervan. All rights reserved worldwide. www.zondervan.com. The "NIV" and "New International Version" are trademarks registered in the United States Patent and Trademark Office by Biblica, Inc.™

This is a work of fiction. Names, characters, incidents, and dialogues are products of the author's imagination and are not to be construed as real. Any resemblance to actual events or persons, living or dead, is entirely coincidental.

Cover design by LOOK Design Studio
Cover photography by Aneta Ivanova

Author is represented by Books & Such Literary Management.

19 20 21 22 23 24 25   7 6 5 4 3 2 1

To Karen

Thank you for your keen eye, for making my stories shine, and most especially, for the blessing of your friendship all these years. It's a joy to partner with you.

So this was how she was going to die. . . .

ONE

Fire ripped through Finn's right shoulder, ricocheting down his arm. Battling the eight-foot swells, he struggled to get his charge to the swaying basket and up into the Coast Guard helicopter.

Gritting his teeth, he swam backward. His right arm encircled her waist, but his grip kept slipping. "We're almost there," he hollered over the rumble of crashing waves.

She squirmed and flailed forward. "Stan!" she sobbed, lunging for the listing boat Finn had just dragged her from.

"I need you to be still, so I can get you to safety. I'll go back for your husband. You're going to be all right." He tightened his grip, ignoring the lancing pain.

Light faded to darkness. The storm was moving swifter than anticipated. The team would insist they go, but he wasn't leaving without the husband.

Finding strength he didn't think he possessed, Finn rolled the woman into the basket.

Tears streamed down her cheeks. Sloshing whitecaps slapped them away.

Gripping the edge of the basket, he strapped her in, the clips pinching his finger. Once she was secure, he circled his throbbing finger. Tony retracted the cable.

Buffeting winds rattled the basket as it swung up into the air. *Please, Father, let her reach safety.*

"We've gotta go," Tony yelled down. "Storm's moving in."

"Three minutes." *Please*. He'd never left anyone behind.

Lifting the basket into the bay, Tony hollered to the pilot, then turned his gaze back to Finn. "You got two."

Finn headed for the sinking boat as Tony lowered the basket.

The wind at Finn's back carried his failing strokes through the water. *Just one more, God,* he prayed. *Let me save one more.*

Spots clouded his vision, his right arm refusing to rotate. A torn rotator cuff?

Time ticking away, he dug in with his left arm but was barely crawling forward.

The man, according to his wife, was trapped belowdecks, his left leg broken and pinned beneath debris. The wife had tried to get him out but wasn't strong enough.

The wave-lashed boat listed nearly full to port. He had to swim faster, harder . . . ignore the pain.

The copter's blades swooshed almost silently over the ocean's roar as it rose higher above the heightening waves. The basket swung over the raging surface.

A fierce wave pummeled over him, dragging him under. He breached the surface only to be lashed by another wave.

Rising above the surface, he watched as the boat sank mere yards away.

The wife's piercing shriek echoed over the reckless, churning sea.

Tony hoisted the basket up and lowered the cable for him.

"No!" Finn hollered, shaking his head. He'd never left a man behind.

"Time," Tony insisted, "or you'll get us all killed."

His entire being sinking inside, Finn clipped in and rose above the angry sea.

TWO

Gabby Rowley drove through the nearly deserted downtown streets. The press-awards banquet had been a success, according to her boss at the *Raleigh Gazette*, but the local event was nothing like the press galas she'd attended before Asim Noren destroyed her international journalism career and nearly ended her life.

She glanced at the moonlight glinting off the faux crystal trophy she'd been awarded for excellence in journalism for her exposé on drug dealer Xavier Fuentes.

A shiver tickled her spine at the thought of their last encounter—his dark eyes boring into hers.

She jumped as her cell rang—her Bluetooth signaling a call from Noah.

She exhaled a steadying breath and answered. "Hey, bro."

"Hey, kid."

She glanced at the clock. 11:03. "You're calling a bit later than usual. Everything okay?" In his line of work, she never knew.

"Everything's fine. Just wanted to check in."

Since Fuentes's arrest and the confiscation of millions in cocaine, her brother's protective side had come out in force.

"How's Mom?"

9

"Good. I know she gets lonely at times, but the kiddos are keeping her busy."

Kenzie's son and daughter had brought so much joy to their lives, especially with Owen's birth just three months after Gabby's, Noah's, and Kenzie's dad—affectionately known as Poppy to Kenzie's daughter, Fiona—passed unexpectedly.

She slowed, making sure she was clear for a right turn, and the silver car behind her honked.

"Was that a horn?" Noah asked.

"Yep. Just on my way home from the awards banquet," she said, making a right. The silver sedan sped around her, disappearing into the night.

"How'd it go?" Noah asked.

"Fine. What's new with you?" She stopped at a signal, the red light refracting off her windshield, making an upside-down *L* across her dash.

"Just finishing up some paperwork. The games start tomorrow."

Every year the Coast Guard Investigative Service team went head-to-head with the NCIS unit from Camp Lejeune in a battle of strength, endurance, and all out-fun. "What kicks it off?" she asked, a strange uneasiness seeping through her. Why was the light not changing?

She glanced around as Noah said something that didn't even register. Sunday night in the business district left dark buildings surrounding her. Her sense of isolation heightened, despite being on a call with her brother.

Tapping her two-inch heel against the floorboard, she ticked off the seconds with no cars passing by, and yet the light remained red.

"Gab? Everything okay?"

"Yeah. Sorry. Just waiting for the light to change." And for the uneasiness sloshing inside to dissipate—an uneasiness she hadn't experienced since that day in South Sudan.

The guttural roar of a motorcycle reverberated behind her. Headlights glared across her rearview mirror as a Triumph slowed to a stop beside her. Relief at not being alone filled her until she glanced over at the black bike.

The man shifted toward her, raising his arm. *Is that a . . . ?*

Lunging over, she'd barely collided with the passenger seat when a *thwack* shattered her window.

"Gabby!" Noah said.

Clutching her hands over her head, she stayed low as glass rained over her.

Praying for protection, she scrambled out the passenger door, her hands and knees colliding with the pavement.

She crawled toward the alley only to be yanked back. Her heart racing, she turned to find her hem was caught on the car door. A quick tug tore the sequined fabric loose.

"Gabby!" Noah called.

She couldn't afford to give up her position, so she remained silent, sweat slathering her back.

Heavy footfalls hit the pavement.

He was coming for her.

Sucking in a gulp of air, she kicked off her heels, said a quick prayer, and darted for the alley.

Shots retorted, one pinging off the dumpster to her left.

Her pulse pounding, she dove behind it. The pavement scraped flesh from her flattened palms. Ignoring the stinging, she crouched low and prayed.

Please keep me safe, Jesus.

Footfalls grew closer.

Tears stung her eyes. With a deep breath, she darted for the next dumpster. A bullet whizzed past her, ricocheting off the container with a shrill ping. She flattened her back against the cool metal. The stench of rotting trash violated the air. An acrid taste skittered across her tongue.

Swallowing her upchuck reflex, she scanned the alley for a

way out. A dim light shone at the end. The Renaissance Hotel. If she could make it there, surely she'd be safe.

His footfalls nearly upon her, she broke into a flat-out run. Muscles heating, she stumbled into the road, headlights glaring into her eyes. Her heart sank.

What if the man had backup?

The car screeched to a halt.

"What are you—crazy?" the man yelled through the open driver's window.

She broke into a run as the car sped away. Refusing to look back, she flailed forward as fast as her trembling legs would carry her. Another bullet whizzed past her right ear, shattering the glass front of the hotel. She barreled into the revolving door, nearly tumbling into the lobby.

The front desk attendant lifted his radio. "Security!" He rushed to her side. "Are you okay, miss?" His attention darted to the door. Her gaze tracked with his, praying her would-be killer wouldn't be bold enough to enter. Thankfully he wasn't.

She collapsed into the employee's arms, winded and covered with damp, cold sweat.

THREE

Finn Walker woke from the night terror—or at least that's what the shrink the Coast Guard had made him see called them. It'd been six years since he'd last performed a rescue swim—the first and only time he'd lost a life on duty.

Rolling over in bed, he switched on his nightstand lamp.

Lightning jagged in the sky, followed by a thunderous clap.

A swift gust swept through the window screen, rattling the shade.

He stood and arched his aching shoulder. Just like he did every time it rained.

He inhaled, grateful he could still swim and surf, but his shoulder would never regain the range of motion he needed to be a rescue swimmer. Even if it did, he couldn't go back. Not after failing a man and destroying his family. He pinched the bridge of his nose. All because of a stupid torn rotator cuff?

He grabbed the half-full water bottle off the dresser and took a long swig of the room-temperature liquid.

Leaning against the pinewood bureau, he finished off the bottle. Every single storm, pain shot through his shoulder, and every single storm, the night terrors returned. Forever reminding him how he'd failed the man, and how God had failed him.

FOUR

Gabby thanked Officer Jensen, who'd escorted her from the Renaissance Hotel to the Sixteenth Precinct, a mere mile away from the attempt on her life. Her car was drivable but would need major bodywork.

The officer saw her settled, then left to grab her a cup of coffee. A chill still rippled along her sweat-drenched skin. Her sequined, floor-length evening gown clung to her trembling legs.

Her boss, Lawrence King, rushed into the bustling station. His gaze jetted about the precinct until it landed on her. Still in his tux, his bow tie loosened and draped about his white dress shirt's unbuttoned collar, he maneuvered his way through the jungle of people to her side.

"Are you all right?" he asked, kneeling beside her chair.

Other than a few scrapes and bruises, physically she was okay. *Mentally . . . ?*

It was the second time in less than a year a man had aimed a gun at her, but this time he'd pulled the trigger.

Before she could answer, Officer Jensen returned with her coffee and a blanket with *RPD* stamped in black across the muted gray fabric. The scent of industrial-strength detergent wafted along her nose as Lawrence stood and draped it across her shoulders, the material falling somewhere between soft and scratchy. He gave her shoulders a reassuring squeeze before

14

taking the seat beside her. Always the overprotective dad, but this time she supposed his concern was warranted.

"Any idea who your attacker was?" the officer asked.

"No," she said, shaking her head. "He had his helmet on the entire time."

"I've got a good idea," Lawrence said.

The officer's eyes widened. "Oh?"

"Gabby's investigative report on Xavier Fuentes resulted in a massive drug bust and seizure of thirty million in cocaine by the DEA."

The officer snapped his fingers. "That's why you look so familiar. You were interviewed on Channel 9 News. Good reporting."

"Thanks." She slipped a damp strand of hair behind her ear. When would the cold sweat stop?

"So we're likely looking at a hit by one of Fuentes's men." Officer Jensen exhaled. "Unfortunately, we'll never be able to link the man to Fuentes, even if we are able to determine who the shooter was." He rubbed the back of his neck. "So let's focus on getting him for now. Can you describe his height, weight, build?"

"I'd guess about five-ten, maybe one-seventy. I'd say average build. He was very fast on his feet."

"That's helpful." He typed her answers on his keyboard, the return key clicking with each tap. "What about his helmet or his bike . . . could you describe either?"

"It was a black Triumph, and an AGV Pista helmet."

Officer Jensen's brows arched.

"My brother's colleague owns a blue Triumph and a similar Pista helmet. It's easy to identify with the distinct fin on the back."

"Excellent. We'll pull all the traffic cams in the area for footage and run the make and model through our database. Hopefully we'll get a hit, though I doubt he had legit plates."

His phone rang. "If you'll excuse me," he said, standing and walking away as he answered the call.

Lawrence shook his head. "I told you that you were in danger."

She wouldn't let men like Fuentes and his thugs keep her from her calling. "It's my job, Lawrence."

Before they could say more, Jensen returned to his desk. "That was the crime-scene investigator. He pulled a handful of bullets from the alley's dumpsters. They're .45 caliber." He swiped his nose. "You're very lucky to be alive. Should I call the Marshals? I'm surprised you aren't already in WITSEC."

"She refused," Lawrence said, his gaze boring into her.

"Why?" Jensen's brows furrowed into a deeper *V*.

"She refused to give the DEA the information they wanted."

"I told you. I'm not giving up a source. I promised him or her anonymity, and I keep my promises."

Lawrence linked his arms across his chest. "Impossible, this one." He shook his head and directed his gaze back at Gabby. "At least get out of town. Noah said he'd come get you."

Noah had told her the same thing when she'd called him on the way to the station, but she'd refused. Apparently he'd moved on to Lawrence. "I'm not running home. No way I want to risk my family's safety."

"Your brother is a Coast Guard Investigative Service agent. He and his team can keep you safe."

Finn Walker's handsome face etched with pain flashed before her eyes. She wasn't sure which was more foolish—endangering her life by staying or her heart by going.

Two hours of questions and paperwork later, Officer Jensen followed Gabby and Lawrence back to the *Raleigh Gazette*, leaving Gabby's car at the police impound for the time being.

Lawrence insisted she was no longer safe at home, and the *Gazette* had security guards covering the office building.

The officer escorted them inside and didn't leave until the

doors were locked and the building's alarm reset. He'd remain outside for the rest of the night. Thankfully, she kept some basic necessities at the office—a workout outfit for when she used the building's gym, a change of clothes for when she spilled something—which happened far too often—a handful of toiletries, and an extra purse she kept on hand. Excusing herself, she headed for the restroom. She slunk out of her damp and torn evening gown and into a pair of gray yoga pants, a burgundy T-shirt, and her favorite black TOMS.

Lawrence gestured to his office sofa when she returned. "Get some sleep." He handed her the blanket and pillow he used when he worked too late. No wonder the man was still single. Fifty-five and married to the job. "I'll work at Joe's station."

"You need your rest too," she said, stalling. No way she'd fall asleep, not with her nerves vibrating through her limbs.

"I'm good." He lifted his chin. "Lots of work to do. We'll help the police identify whoever did this. I'm calling in some favors."

———

A hand shook Gabby's shoulder, tugging her from sleep. Her eyes flickered open, and she squinted in the dark.

"Wake up, sleepyhead."

Noah? She pulled to a sitting position, rubbing her dry eyes. Her contacts had stuck in place. She blinked, trying to moisten them but to little avail. "What are you doing here?"

"I'm taking you home."

"What . . . ?"

"Lawrence and I spoke, and we agreed. If you're not willing to give up your source, which I respect, then you need to come to Wilmington and let my team watch you. We'll keep you safe."

"What if Fuentes figures out where I am and sends another hit man?"

"He's going to find you for sure if you remain in Raleigh."

"I don't want to risk bringing Mom or Kenzie or the kids into this."

"We're your family. Let us protect you."

"I don't know." Shifting, she planted her bare feet on the thick carpet.

"You don't have a choice," Lawrence said from the open doorway, the fluorescent lights shadowing his tall stature.

"Why not?"

He slipped his hands into his trouser pockets. "If you don't go, I'm firing you."

She laughed. "You can't be serious?"

"Dead." His words matched his deadpan expression.

She grunted. He knew he had her. After her fallout with the BBC over her relationship with a turncoat source, no one in the news industry but Lawrence had been willing to hire her.

She raked a hand through her tousled hair. "You aren't playing fair."

He linked his arms across his chest. "To keep you safe, I'll play as dirty as I have to."

She released a long exhale. He was giving her no choice.

FIVE

NEW BERN, NORTH CAROLINA

Gabby kicked off her shoes and brought her knees to her chest, trying to stretch out as they entered the still-dark waterfront town of New Bern. Noah had insisted they stay off the highway, so the trip was taking longer than usual, but they only had an hour or so to go.

"Mom and Kenzie will be thrilled to see you," he said, tapping the wheel.

"Will Owen and Fiona be at the games?" She still couldn't believe her niece and nephew were four and two. Or that her sister was a mom.

"The challenge kicks off at seven thirty, so that's too early, but Mark said he'd bring them after they wake up."

Noah's CGIS team had beaten Lejeune's NCIS team two years in a row at the "friendly" triathlon challenge, but this was the first one she'd be attending.

"I'd take you to Finn's to get some sleep, but he'll be headed to work about the time we pull into town."

She narrowed her gaze. "Why would you take me to Finn's?" After the debacle in South Sudan, she'd spent the winter in his guest loft over his surf shack, but surely Noah didn't intend for her to stay there again.

Noah cleared his throat. "Finn's is the safest place for you to be."

"Why?" she asked, her throat constricting.

He glanced over as they entered New Bern's quaint streetlight-lit downtown shopping district but waited until they'd passed through before responding. "I know it might be . . . awkward . . . after . . . you know . . ." He shrugged.

Heat rushed to her cheeks. *Please don't bring up my relationship with Finn.* "Why do you think it's safer than with you?"

"Because he lives away from your family, where Fuentes would no doubt look first."

"Which is why I didn't want to come in the first place. If anything happens to you guys because of me, I'd never forgive myself."

"I can take care of myself, and Mark can protect Kenzie. He's a Marine, after all."

"Okay, but Mom's alone out in Topsail."

"She's going to stay with Kenzie and Mark on base."

Camp Lejeune wouldn't be breached, so that gave her a measure of peace.

"With Finn's house being on an outer peninsula, he can see anyone approaching from at least a half mile away. And"—he went on before she could argue—"there are multiple ways of escape should the need arise. By boat, dirt bike through his trails, or down one of three driveways leading off his acreage."

He'd left her with no argument . . . but with a heart very much in jeopardy.

WILMINGTON, NORTH CAROLINA

Finn raked a hand through his damp hair as he strode toward the CGIS office. He was late. He probably shouldn't have taken the time to surf before heading to work, but Noah's middle-of-the-night call, explaining what had happened to Gabby and asking if she could stay in his loft again, had kept him up for the rest of the night, and he'd needed the stress release. The swells had been awesome, thanks to the wicked September storm that had blown through during the night.

But judging by the tight expression on Caleb Eason's face, there was a far more sinister storm looming in the office.

"Glad you could join us," Caleb said with a tilt of his head.

Finn glanced at his watch. Four minutes. *Yikes.* He was tempted to say Caleb was being neurotic, but when it came to coastal rescues and, more specifically, CGIS investigations, even a minute could easily mean the difference between life and death, between solving the crime and watching the evidence dissipate before his eyes.

"Sorry, sir."

With Caleb being only two years older than he was, the title often felt weird in Finn's throat, but Caleb was the second in seniority of the unit, and the office was due his respect and promptness.

Caleb arched a knowing brow. "Let me guess," he said as he reached over and pulled the morning's bulletin from the printer. "Swells?"

Finn cleared his throat. "Yes," he said, taking the seat by Sam Foster, who graciously supplied the unit with much-needed caffeine every morning.

Sam grabbed a cup from the corrugated cardboard tray on the desk and handed it to Finn.

A blue tiki man trademarked the Hunga Bunga Java cup and also mirrored Caleb's frown. The strong scent of espresso swirled from the slit in the lid, wafting good vibes Finn's way in a room full of tension—the embodiment of which stood at the front of the room. He and Caleb didn't exactly jibe.

"As I was saying, before you decided to join us"—Caleb tapped his pen against the paper clutched in his hand—"we've got a call

21

to respond to. Finn, you're on the copter. I want you there before that ship is boarded to preserve any evidence if a crime has been committed. Sam, you're with me on the fast raft out."

"Out where, sir?" Finn asked.

"The Coast Guard found Master Chief Petty Officer Dennis Fletcher's boat adrift this morning after Tess Seavers called in that her husband, Will, hadn't returned from their fishing trip last night."

"Will *Seavers*?"

Caleb nodded. "I know he is a friend of yours," he said to Finn as his gaze swept the room. "Please be vigilant and heed the bulletin we received last week out of Miami . . . along with this update." He held up the sheet of paper. "Our Miami unit's recent clampdown on drug runners has not only pushed the drug runners up north, but this report indicates they were sighted off our shores last night. We're on high alert."

Five minutes later, Finn hurried to the helicopter's line edge and awaited the pilot's signal to climb aboard.

The *whoosh* of the rotor blades disheveled his hair as he climbed into the backseat. He buckled in behind the pilot, Dean, and next to Coast Guard medic Brooke Kesler.

Brooke lifted her chin in greeting. "You and Stu enjoy this morning's swells?" she asked over the headset, the roar of the blades whirring like a rush of seagulls' wings.

He was mentoring Brooke's younger cousin, Stu, in the art of surfing. The kid was a fast learner.

"I caught a glimpse of you two knuckleheads from above," she said as Dean guided the copter off the ground. Gliding out over the Coast Guard base and the shoreline's edge, Finn caught a glimpse of his home on the outermost peninsula of Wrightsville Beach.

They soared across the ocean, where his heart always longed to be—on a board gliding over swells and tunneling through the tubes when he was lucky enough to find them.

But today, in this moment, concern for his friend Will superseded the source of both his pain and peace.

"I figured you'd be late," Dean said with a chuckle. "I'm betting Caleb wasn't pleased."

Finn shook his head. "I thought I had it." A muscle in his jaw twitched. He wouldn't make that mistake again.

"You always think you've got it," Brooke said. "Stu is no different. Neither of you can shake the rush."

She'd hit the mark. There was something almost primal about the ocean's call to him. But he had higher priorities.

A swift gust rattled the copter, shaking Finn from his thoughts.

Dean countered the gust, balancing the copter with ease.

Finn sat forward, bouncing his knee as concern for Will's and Fletcher's safety rushed through him.

SIX

When they reached the site of the games, Gabby climbed from Noah's classic hunter green Jeep Sahara, her muscles feeling bruised after the night she'd had and the subsequent long drive.

The sun was only creeping over the horizon, but it was already seventy degrees. Unable to shake the chill gripping her, she needed to feel the sun's warmth on her skin.

Noah studied her as they headed for the main event tent. "You okay?"

She nodded—shaken but functioning. While she balked at Noah's brotherly concern, deep down she couldn't argue with the calming peace that rushed over her knowing he and his team would be guarding her.

Finn's face flashed through her mind—the hurt expression clouding his eyes as she drove away nearly six months ago. He'd been blindsided by her decision to take the job in Raleigh. But he'd stuck with her—his scent, his touch, his tender smile. How and why had she left him behind?

Unease at the thought of facing him rumbled in her stomach.

Noah chuckled. "Always hungry."

"Guilty." She shrugged, but hunger wasn't the cause of the gnawing. Easier to let Noah think that though. Rather than entering the main tent, Noah led her inside the food tent.

She went straight for a blueberry muffin and steaming cup of coffee.

Noah glanced at his watch. "We've got less than five minutes before the start. I better get ready. You gonna be okay?"

She arched her brows.

He lifted his hands, palms facing her. "Okay. Just asking."

"Gabby." Her mother rushed toward her, sand kicking up behind her bare feet. Her mop of red curly hair—hair none of them had inherited except Fiona—fluttered in the breeze.

Gabby exhaled, her breath lifting the hair across her forehead. Here came another burst of concern. "I'll be fine," she finally answered her brother.

He smirked and gave her shoulder a squeeze. "Remember, she does it out of love."

"I know." She did, and she appreciated her mother's love, just not her lectures.

Mom engulfed Gabby in a bear hug.

"Whoa!" She fought to stay upright with the impact. "Hey, Mom."

"There's my sweet girl," she said, not loosening her hold.

"I'm okay, really." Last night's attack had been far less scarring than Asim's.

Her mom stood back and slipped a strand of hair behind Gabby's ear. "It's a mother's right to worry." Her gaze landed on the gold locket hanging at Gabby's breastbone. She lifted her hand to the gift her mom had given her—with a duplicate to Kenzie—the day of her father's funeral. The locket held a picture of her dad, and Gabby never left home without it.

Her mom's gaze narrowed. "You sure you're okay?"

She offered a soft smile. "I promise."

Her mom shook her head with a sigh. "Such a brave girl." She shifted at the sight of Kenzie approaching. "Such brave girls, my daughters."

"Hey, Gabs," Kenzie said, greeting her with a hug, her locket bumping against Gabby's during the embrace.

"Hey, there." She hugged back, the tension gripping her limbs finally slackening.

It was good to be home.

Noah's gaze shifted from his survey of the water's edge to Kenzie, and without his saying a word, she nodded. He'd just transferred protection of Gabby to her, which was totally unnecessary.

At the shooting range, where Noah had taught them to use a gun, Gabby had always been the better shot. With her Springfield XD-S tucked in her cross-body purse, she was ready to adequately defend herself. Why she'd chosen the small sequined clutch for the banquet where her gun wouldn't fit was beyond her. It normally didn't leave her side, and the attack reminded her precisely why. Thankfully, it'd been in her lockbox at work, so she was packing once again, if the need arose.

Noah's coworker Rissi Dawson grabbed her pink SUP board and paddle and waved at Gabby as their gazes caught. She'd missed her friend. Maybe it was good she'd come back with Noah, after all, despite her hesitation to see Finn.

Logan Perry, another of Noah's coworkers, came up from behind her in vintage Jams. "Hey, Gabby."

"Hey, Logan." She chuckled at the '80s-style board shorts. He sure knew how to put a smile on her face.

"Good to see you," he said over his shoulder as he rushed past her with his SUP board and paddle. He lined up next to Noah and Rissi at the ocean's edge. Their competitors from NCIS stood in a row beside them—toes sinking into the water-drenched sand.

The whistle blew, and Gabby took a seat beside her sister on the tie-dyed blanket. She wished Fiona and Owen were there. She couldn't wait to see her favorite rug rats.

Rissi hit the water, balancing on her board and paddling out to sea. Moving up and over a cresting wave, she worked her way into a smooth rhythm. She didn't bother looking back to see who followed. Instead, she fixed her gaze on the buoys lining the course toward Surf City and then back down.

The ocean's breeze and rocking surface tested her balance as she paddled the arduous course. She was thankful she'd thought to tie back her hair in the gusting wind.

Reaching the northernmost point of the course, she maneuvered around the buoy and headed back for the finish line. The undertow tugged hard as she paddled, her arms burning with exertion.

"I'm gaining on you," NCIS agent Travis Jones shouted. He would be making the turn around the buoy in no time.

"Ignore him," Logan said as she passed by him less than a minute later.

"You got this," Noah added as he reached a speed indicating he had saved his strength for the homestretch.

Digging in hard against surging waves, she widened her stance, keeping her focus in the direction of the finish line, on the warmth of the sun as it rose in the sky.

"You're mine, Dawson," Travis called, not far behind.

Not this time.

The spectators came into view. Noah's niece and nephew skipped down the dune crossing, their dad, Mark, scurrying after them.

Paddling hard, she angled into shore.

Twenty more yards. Ten . . .

Her heart thudded in her chest, thwacking in her ears.

Travis's paddle smacked close on her heels.

"Come on, Ris, you got this," Noah hollered from nearby—the three now in a neck-and-neck battle for first.

"Go, Ris," Logan hollered, his baritone voice cheering her on.

The taste of victory overpowered the salty spray of the sea.

She thrust her paddle in, shifting to keep her board balanced as she rode a wave into shore. The tip of her board hit the sand seconds before Travis's and then Noah's.

"All right, Ris!" Noah rushed to her side, clapping his large hand on her shoulder. "Way to win the first event!"

She glanced at Travis and smiled at the pinched expression on his face.

She'd finally beat him. Adrenaline burned through her limbs as she moved for the refreshment stand, where a volunteer offered her a bottle of Gatorade. She took a long swig of the purple drink. She may have won the first challenge, but she had two more strenuous ones to go. Noting a buildup of clouds to the west, she hoped a storm wouldn't cancel the competition—and her chance to beat him again.

SEVEN

Finn spotted Fletcher's boat thirty feet below. There were zero signs of movement aboard the vessel's deck. He caught sight of a Coast Guard response boat idling in the distance.

The bay door opened and he hooked into the cable. He lifted his chin at Dean. "Ready to lower."

Dean nodded. "Lowering," he said. Sea spray misted Finn's face as he descended to the boat's deck. The swipe of the copter's blades swooshed above.

His feet secure on deck, he unclipped. Stepping clear of the cable, he circled his finger, and Dean retracted it.

Finn's gaze fixed on a blood trail running the length of the port side.

Pulling his SIG, he cleared the deck, careful to preserve the evidence.

Once the full ship was cleared, he'd photograph the upper deck first to try to preserve the evidence before what appeared to be oncoming rain could distort or destroy it.

He stepped down the narrow steps into the cabin, his muscles taut. "Seavers? Fletcher?"

No response.

The metallic scent of blood assailed his nostrils.

The handle of the SIG in his left hand was cool against his warming palm as adrenaline seared through him.

Blood splatter covered the aft cabin wall, and a tacky puddle pooled beneath the overhead storage compartment.

He cleared the rest of the cabin before returning to the compartment.

With a sharp exhale and a spiking pulse, he opened it. Will Seavers's body tumbled onto the floor with a thud.

Three shots to the chest and one to the head. Finn pinched the bridge of his nose. His friend was dead.

He swallowed. *Poor Tess.* Seven months pregnant and her husband murdered.

His chest squeezed. He'd had them over for dinner the night before last.

Pulling out his cell, he dialed Caleb.

"Eason."

It was too surreal to say. Finn swallowed. "Will's dead. There's no sign of Fletcher, but his outboard is gone."

"I'll notify the Coast Guard, and we'll start searching. You need assistance?"

"No. I've got this. I'll put in a call to the ME and process the scene in the meantime."

"If Fletcher is found alive, we're going to need answers."

"Yeah." Like why he left his fellow guardsman alone. Finn didn't want to even consider the possibility that Fletcher was somehow involved in Will's death.

"We'll head out with the search crew."

"Good idea." Slipping his phone into his pocket, Finn got to work. The way to honor his friend was to find his killer.

Notified he had a visitor, Xavier Fuentes was cuffed and escorted to the visitation area. Arturo sat on the opposite side of the glass. Taking a seat, he anticipated the news that Gabrielle Rowley, the woman who'd put him in this ridiculous orange jumpsuit and cost him millions, was dead. He picked up the phone on his side as Arturo picked up the other one. Arturo's usually dark skin held an odd pallor.

Xavier took a sharp inhale before Arturo spoke a word. "You don't have to tell me. I can read it on your face." Heat seared his limbs as he clasped the receiver. Arturo had failed him. Now he had two to kill, and he knew just the man for the job. "Where is she now?"

Arturo's face pinched, perspiration glinting on his forehead in the flickering fluorescent lights. "I don't know."

A muscle in his jaw twitched. "You. Don't. Know?" *Imbecile.*

"I followed her and her boss to their office building. No cars came out that I saw. Once they opened the building and lifted the garage gate for the morning, I went in as a deliveryman with donuts from the shop across the street. The receptionist said Gabrielle wasn't there, but I saw her boss. Someone else must have taken her out the rear entrance of the garage, because I was watching the front all night."

Xavier's knuckles paled and cracked as he balled his free hand into a tight fist.

"I broke in her apartment, but she wasn't there." Arturo's voice cracked. "I think she skipped town."

He slammed the phone onto the receiver and left without a second glance at Arturo. With an outside phone call, he'd send La Muerte to Arturo and then to Gabrielle Rowley. She'd be dead within days.

EIGHT

After a barely adequate rest period, Rissi once again lined up beside her competitors at the ocean's edge. Warm water rushed over her toes. Broken seashells tickled the soles of her feet as they sank into the wet sand.

The whistle signaled the start of the swimming challenge, and without a glance in Travis's direction, she bolted out through the knee-high sea to a depth where she could start her stroke.

Diving under a breaking wave, she swam freestyle deeper out to sea beyond the line of forming waves. The route followed Topsail Island's coast down around the southern tip and up a quarter of a mile along the sound side to where the finish line awaited them.

Halfway through, Travis hollered, "Gaining on you!"

She kept her focus on her strokes and the rhythmic movement of her legs—up and down in small flicks through the warm water.

A hand closed on her foot, and her throat squeezed shut.

"Got you now," Travis said. His deep voice . . . his harsh touch . . . his words . . . yanked her right back to Hank and the nightmare she'd survived.

Releasing her foot, Travis pulled ahead. Dizziness swept over her, and she rolled her head to the side for much-needed air. Gulping in an unsatisfying breath, she tried again. Why couldn't she get enough air?

Hank's hand clamped around her neck, his fat fingertips biting into her flesh.

She squeezed her eyes shut, waiting for him to choke the air from her.

Everything darkened, faded. . . . His words grew distant.

Another voice echoed. Mason.

No! *Tears burned her eyes.* Not again.

Hank released his hold, knocking what air remained from her lungs with a fierce elbow jab to her chest. She collided with the kitchen wall, slipped to the ground, and gasped for a breath that wouldn't come.

Her blurred gaze landed on Hank's fist hitting Mason's jaw. A splintering crack resounded as blood spurted in a fine mist from his mouth, but he refused to go down. Why did he always refuse to fall?

Instead, he widened his stance. Blood trickled over his lip, zigzagging around his chin dimple.

"You're going to pay, boy." Hank's knuckles whitened, his hands filled with blue webs of swollen veins. He pumped his fists, his jaw tightening.

Two more days and Mason would be eighteen and he could escape this hellhole. He was the lucky one.

She'd been here nearly as far back as her memory stretched. She had two more years to go in the torture chamber that was her life.

Part of her hungered to fight back like Mason, but the small shamed part of her only wanted to burrow deep inside where no pain could reach her—at least not the true her. The one she let no one see, except Mason.

One day she'd be free.

As she took a deep gulp of fresh ocean air, freedom reverberated through Rissi's aching limbs. Thanks to Mason's courage, it had been sooner than she'd expected.

The day he left was the day she'd freed herself.

She tugged herself from the decade-old memory and kicked her stroke into high gear. What had to be another eighth of a mile passed. Her limbs burned as she rounded the southern tip of the island, moving into the sound side and into its brackish, muddied water. The shift from pure seawater into the mix of bay and ocean took adjustment, her vision in the water not nearly as clear. Rolling her head to the side, she caught sight of a boat speeding directly for her. A man in a navy blue baseball cap, with a wide grin, lifted a beer can toward her. Within seconds the boat was nearly upon her.

She dove under the surface, kicking down toward the bottom. The boat's propeller spun above. The sound, like nuts and bolts rattling in an old coffee can, reverberated through the water as air bubbles popped. Her body shook at the rippling wake of the boat jetting over her—barely above the tips of her toes. She dove deeper.

Her hands hit the mushy sand on the bottom as the boat sped away. Short on breath, she darted up to the surface and lifted her head above the murky water.

"Hey," she hollered, waving her arms.

"Are you okay?" Noah asked, reaching her side.

She nodded. "Yeah. Just a little winded."

Noah swiped water from his face. "I caught the name of the boat."

"Then we've got them," Logan said, reaching their side as Travis treaded water several yards away, as if he thought they might start up the race again.

A beach patrol boat that had been bobbing out at sea in case any of the competitors needed help raced after the white-and-red-striped cigarette boat, which was setting an erratic looping course.

Moments later, a second beach patrol boat idled nearby. "Wanna ride?" Tim, the head of Topsail's beach patrol, asked.

"Definitely," Logan said.

Once they got in, the patrol boat skimmed over the burgeoning whitecaps in pursuit. Rissi held her stance, maintaining her balance. It took a few moments, but they gained on the boat. The guy in the navy blue cap had his back to them. It looked like there was only him and the driver, who was definitely under the influence.

The whir of copter blades echoed overhead. She looked up to see the Coast Guard copter rushing across the ocean. Off to her ten, two Guard fast rafts with sirens blaring cut across the sea in front of the vessel.

The boat made a swift hard to port, sending the man in the navy blue cap toppling overboard.

The first of the fast rafts sidled up to him, and a guardsman dove in the water as his shipmate covered him with a gun.

The swimmer circled behind the man and directed him to the boat. He hauled him into the fast raft and held him at gunpoint.

Rissi passed by, meeting his gaze. His eyes darted from the gun to her.

The cigarette boat made another hard turn to port, and collided with a wave. The bow dipped under the water, stalling the engine. The soaked man at the helm held up his hands, and the guardsmen took him into custody. She'd enjoy booking the pair.

NINE

The ambulance waited at the edge of the beach entrance, its motor running with a grumble. A white pickup with *Beach Patrol* painted across the length of its tailgate in bold red letters was parked on the beach. Two orange four-wheelers with patrolmen in red shorts and white tanks joined the grouping.

Rissi escorted the cuffed man who'd been in the blue hat, the cap now lost at sea. He struggled to walk straight, the smell of tequila and beer heavy on his breath.

She swallowed a gulp of air over her shoulder. The man reeked. She released him to the medics, and they assessed him for injuries. Noah escorted the man who'd been driving the boat past her, the strong whiff of tequila trailing behind him too.

Logan came up behind her. "You should let the medics take a look at you."

"I'm fine."

"I'm not giving you a choice," Noah said, handing off his charge to Cameron—one of Topsail's best medics.

"Let's go," the other medic, Martin, said, flagging Rissi over.

"This is overkill," she murmured but did as her boss ordered.

Sitting her on the edge of the lowered tailgate, Martin swiped a light across her eyes. "Pupils look good. How are you feeling?"

"Like this is totally unnecessary."

"Word is you were nearly run over by the cigarette boat."

"I made it down in time."

"How far?"

"To the bottom."

"Which is?"

"Thirty feet, maybe."

"That's a decent drop. It's worth checking you out." He slid the blood-pressure cuff up her arm and depressed the Start button. With a beep the lightly padded cuff swelled, the tightening pressure reminiscent of Hank's angry grip on her arm, yanking her to be punished for her perceived wrong.

Heat rushed up her throat, encircling her neck.

Martin's brown eyes narrowed. "You okay?"

"Yeah. Fine. Why?"

"145 over 90. That's high."

"It's been an intense morning."

"How is she?" Noah asked, coming up to sit beside her.

"She's okay, but I'd recommend the base medic reevaluate her later today."

Rissi dropped her head back. "That's not necessary."

"It's happening," Noah said.

She exhaled, knowing she didn't have a choice.

Logan strode up. "How is she?" he asked Martin with a lift of his chin.

"An obstinate patient, as usual." Martin chuckled.

"Cameron is wrapping up with the men," Logan said.

"Okay." Noah rubbed his hands together. "Can you take them into the station? I've got Gabby and Rissi in my car."

"No problem, though I'm going to have to clean my truck out after transferring two wet, alcohol-ridden drunks in it."

"Both men failed the Breathalyzer test," Cameron said. His black short-sleeve top and matching uniform pants had to be warm in the rising heat. The clouds in the west were holding off, and the sun was streaming across the stretch of beach surrounding them.

Beachcombers congregated at the edge of the scene, along

with Noah's family—concern etched deepest on his mother's face.

Noah swiped his hand over his buzz cut, water flicking off. "I better go let them know everything is okay."

Forty-five minutes after finding Will's body, the numbered yellow markers in place, Finn photographed the scene.

With a weight in his chest, he struggled to ignore the fact that the blood he smelled was his friend's.

The trajectory of the bullets, blood splatter, and damage to the body indicated the shots had come from close range. Had Will known his killer, to allow him or her to get so close?

And what did Fletcher's absence mean? Had he left the boat before or after Will's murder?

Exhaling, Finn studied the bloody handprint left on Will's white shirt. The chest shots had come first. He hadn't died instantly.

Father, please lead me to whoever did this. Let me, let Tess, see justice done.

Clenching his jaw, he followed the trajectory of the three chest shots to the aft wall, where he found three of the four bullets.

He photographed them, pried them out of their holes, and dropped them in an evidence bag.

He sealed it, labeled it, and coordinated it to the accompanying scene marker.

The fourth bullet was most likely lodged in the deck floor beneath the pool of blood. The chest shots had dropped him before the killer finished him off with a shot to the head.

The roar of a fast raft's motor along with the smack of the raft against the water sounded nearby. Finn moved on deck to greet Medical Examiner Ethan Hadley and a guardsman he didn't recognize driving the raft.

Hadley climbed the aft ladder of Fletcher's boat, *Off Fishing*, with gloves in place. Finn had already dusted for prints but appreciated Hadley's thoughtfulness.

Hadley's aging eyes anchored by wrinkles looked into Finn's with sympathy. "I'm sorry about Will, son."

Finn shifted his hands into his pockets and nodded, never one for emotion. Not since the summer of his fourteenth year.

He swallowed and looked back at the cabin. He inhaled, his breath shallow, and released a weak exhale.

Hadley tipped the brim of his straw hat. He always wore it, sun or rain, and Rissi insisted it suited his genteel southern charm.

"In there?" Hadley looked to the cabin's porthole windows.

Finn nodded and led him down the narrow stairs to his friend's body.

Hadley moved to kneel beside Will's body. "Poor man."

A muffled call crackled over Finn's radio.

He lifted it and depressed the button. "Walker."

"It's Sam." His voice was garbled. "We found Fletcher. Alive, but unconscious."

Crack. Crack. Crack.

Finn held the radio away from his ear. "Was that——"

"We're taking fire."

"Sam!"

No response.

Sweat beaded on his skin. "I gotta go. Can I use your fast raft?" he asked, the Coast Guard raft having left to search for Fletcher.

Hadley nodded intently, and Finn raced on deck.

"My team is taking fire," he hollered to the driver. "I need to get there ASAP."

TEN

Gabby rode in the backseat of her brother's Jeep, having insisted Rissi take the front. With the temperature rising to seventy-eight degrees, she had finally started to warm up after last night's ordeal, but the rain that had been threatening from the west looked to be moving in.

The wind riffling her hair, she settled deeper into the rear bucket seat and took time to look at her surroundings. She loved this place—loved the reeds swaying along the tops of the dunes, the rhythmic crash of the ocean waves, the sand skittering along with the breeze. The area held so many things she loved—her family, the beach, and . . .

Nope. She stiffened. She would not let her heart go there. Despite the relationship she and Finn had developed during her three-month stay in his loft . . . nothing could happen this time.

The position Lawrence offered at the *Raleigh Gazette* had been her only chance at a reporting job since the BBC fired her. Leaving Finn had been far harder than she'd imagined, and that was precisely why she had her guard in place this time. She couldn't allow a relationship to cloud her vision. Her career had to remain the focus.

Reminding herself of that would help strengthen her resolve when she saw Finn. She had disappointed him. Who was she kidding? She took a stiff breath. She'd crushed him. She hadn't wanted to, but she needed that job—and couldn't risk her heart anymore.

She didn't like the thought of living so close to him again, and yet it made sense. It kept her family as far away as possible, in case one of Fuentes's men showed up. Finn wasn't family, so it would be harder to trace their connection, and the way his property sat, they could see or hear anyone approaching from over a mile away.

Queasiness rumbled in her gut.

How would he react to her return?

How would she react to him and her brother watching her like hawks? And, it *really* didn't help to learn she wouldn't have a car to drive. Her family and Noah's CGIS team had made that decision. Noah insisted it was best that she be with one of them at all times, for her "safety."

While she appreciated their concern, she wasn't an orchid needing constant attention. She was more like a tumbleweed—sturdy and made to roam.

Noah's cell rang, distracting her from her thoughts. "Hey, Finn."

She swallowed at the mention of his name.

"Wait. What?" Noah's jaw tensed in the rearview mirror. "We'll be back as soon as possible and keep me updated. . . . Yeah . . . okay . . . be there soon." Worry and fear flitted across his face as he hung up.

"What's wrong?" Rissi asked.

"Finn found Will Seavers dead on Master Chief Petty Officer Fletcher's boat. And Caleb and Sam found Fletcher beaten and unconscious in his boat's outboard. They're under fire from drug runners right now—Finn's headed their way."

Rissi stuck the cherry on the dash and turned it on so other cars would see them as an approaching emergency vehicle and get out of their way.

Noah floored it, and Rissi grabbed hold of the roll bar. "I'd hang on if I were you," she said, looking back at Gabby.

Nodding, she grabbed hold of the small bar fastened on the back of Rissi's seat, thankful she had as they flew over a bump in the road, bouncing her several inches up from her seat.

She bounced back down, but only momentarily before the next hit came. Her mind finally absorbing what Noah had said, she leaned forward. "Did you say *Will Seavers*?" She'd become fast friends with Seavers and his wife, Tess, over the winter. They were good friends with Finn and often came by for dinner, and he'd always invited her to join them. Soon she and Tess had a standing weekly coffee date at the Coffee Connection in town. Tess had become Gabby's first close friendship after her fall from grace.

"I'm afraid so." Noah glanced at her in the rearview mirror, the spinning light casting a red hue across his skin.

"But . . . Tess. She's due with their first at the beginning of November."

Rissi shook her head, her long brown hair spiraling behind her in the wind. "That's crushing," she said, bouncing as Noah swerved around a car slowly puttering to the side of the narrow road.

"Does Tess know yet?" she hollered over the whipping wind flapping the Jeep's canvas roof.

Noah shook his head. "I'm sure she doesn't. Not yet. Finn will want to tell her in person."

As the impending rain finally let loose, Gabby prayed she could be there when Finn—poor guy—had to give Tess the devastating news that would forever alter her life.

ELEVEN

Sea spray mixed with the rain washed over Finn's face and soaked through his clothes as the guardsman guided the fast raft toward the melee, siren blaring. A handful of men in the drug runners' boat were firing automatic weapons at Sam on Fletcher's outboard raft, Caleb on the fast raft, and a Coast Guard craft.

The Coast Guard boat was positioned between the raft Sam was in and the shooters, but the presumed drug runners kept shifting, engaging and not backing down despite the mounting Coast Guard presence—with howling sirens, flashing lights, and orders over the megaphone to desist their gunfire and surrender.

Fletcher's raft had already taken fire and was deflating before Finn's eyes. Sam rose up over the edge to fire another round. The drug runners returned fire as they sped eastward, creating an opening between them and Fletcher's boat. Panic sloshed in Finn's gut at the open shot they now had.

Shots pinged out of the machine gun in rapid fire, one hitting Sam in the chest, followed by another. He flailed back, crumpling into the deflating raft.

"Noooo!" Caleb's cry echoed Finn's.

He'd been shot. Twice.

"Get me to that raft," he instructed the guardsman driving his boat.

The man nodded and raced forward.

Caleb shot one of the drug runners, and an exchange of gunfire rained heavily as Finn reached Sam.

The drug runners turned and fled. The Coast Guard boat followed, along with Caleb in the fast raft.

Finn climbed into the raft to find Sam lying beside an unconscious Fletcher. Sam's chest was doused in blood even though the falling rain was washing some of it away. He gasped, gurgling up blood as he struggled to take in air, his eyes wide with terror.

"We need a helo now!" Finn shouted over the radio as Sam lay dying beside him. "It's going to be all right," he said, kneeling on the raft. He lifted Sam into his arms. "Help is on the way. Dean, we need you here *now*!" he hollered over the radio.

"Two minutes out," Dean said.

"Send the basket down." They could cut through the time it would take to lower Brooke to make the assessment on site. He'd already made it. Sam needed an emergency evac.

"Hang on, Sam."

Sam tried to speak, but blood sputtered out of his mouth. Panic deepened in his darting eyes.

"Help's coming," Finn said, not making any promises he couldn't keep. He wanted to reassure Sam he was going to make it. He'd do everything in his power to save him, but it didn't look good.

The whir of Dean's copter whooshed overhead, and soon the basket was lowered. Carefully, he lifted Sam inside, strapped him in as Sam's eyes closed. "Hang on, friend," Finn said, swirling his finger for Dean to retrieve his buddy whose life hung in the balance.

"I'm coming along," Finn said over the radio.

Once Sam was in the copter, Fletcher was loaded on, and then Finn lifted by cable.

Climbing into the copter, he tried to stay out of Brooke's way as she tended to Sam. His blood pressure was dropping, his pupils unresponsive. She looked back to Finn and didn't have to say a word. Her expression said it all. They were losing him.

TWELVE

Fletcher lay unconscious as Brooke began CPR on Sam. While performing compressions, she looked up at Finn. "Can you check Fletcher's vitals?"

He nodded and moved his attention to the MCPO on the copter's floor next to Sam's bloody body.

Checking Fletcher's vitals would give Finn a purpose he desperately needed, and something to do, as he felt completely incapable of helping Sam.

Brooke continued CPR as she kept in contact with the trauma team waiting for Sam on the helicopter pad at Wilmington General.

Finn took time to study Fletcher's injuries—the bruising and swelling along his face . . .

He scanned down his neck and slid Fletcher's lime green short-sleeve shirt with bright pink flamingos to the side.

. . . his shoulder and . . .

He unbuttoned Fletcher's shirt.

. . . torso.

All indicated Fletcher had been severely beaten—his jaw and right rib cage appeared to have taken the brunt of the blows, though his left eye was about swollen shut. At least his blood pressure was stable, his pupils weren't overly dilated, and he responded to the small light Finn flashed across them. He read out Fletcher's vitals to Brooke.

"Thanks, Finn," she whispered as she stopped compressions on Sam. She smiled wearily. "He's back."

Gabby clasped her sweat-lathered palms together. Finn had gone to help Sam and Caleb, which meant he was *in* a gunfight. What if . . . ?

The muffler roared as Noah depressed the gas pedal, the street signs flying by. As they approached Wilmington, the storm's force increased, the sky growing ominously dark.

Shutting her eyes, she took a deep breath, trying to steady her racing pulse.

Please, Father, protect the men. Let them be okay.

Let Finn be okay.

What if she lost him?

Lost him?

He wasn't hers to lose.

A gust of rain rushed across her, the wind's wake flapping the soft-top roof. Her hair fluttering in her eyes, she fished a ponytail holder out of her bag and stuffed her hair into it.

Rain pounded against the windshield and flew in streams past the open doorframe. She tapped her foot along the metal floorboard. Noah hadn't wanted to waste time putting the doors back on when the rain started, and she didn't blame him. They couldn't get back fast enough.

She glanced at the speedometer. *Seventy-five.*

Normally a dangerous speed on rain-drenched roads with a storm-darkened sky, but she knew Noah wouldn't slow down. Nor did she want him to.

The opening riff of "Sweet Home Alabama" blasted in front of her. She jumped, her racing heart kicking up a notch.

Noah answered. "Rowley. Yeah . . . okay . . ." His face paled. "ETA fifteen." He flung his phone into the carryall cubby and released a shaky exhale.

"What's wrong?" Her chest tightened. *What if . . . ?* She swallowed hard.

"Sam's been shot."

Rissi took a sharp intake of air. "What? Is he going to be all right?"

Noah glanced over at her. "Emmalyne was only passing along the information she got from Finn. He just said Caleb and a Coast Guard boat are chasing the drug runners, and he, Sam, and Fletcher are in the copter on the way to the hospital. Sam is in unstable condition."

"Unstable?" Rissi's usually strong voice quavered.

Noah swallowed, his Adam's apple slipping down and back up. He nodded.

Gabby bit her bottom lip, clasping and unclasping her hands. *Please, Father.*

At least Finn was safe.

Heat rushed to her cheeks, and she sat forward. How could she think that when Sam had been shot?

Noah glanced back at her. "You okay?"

She nodded. Just ashamed at the relief that had filled her knowing Finn was all right.

Sam had been shot. Why should she feel anything but concern for him?

Headlights shown through the rain, sweeping across her face. *Headlights.*

She sat back, her muscles tightening.

The Triumph's headlight flashed through her mind. She blinked, the crack of bullets reverberating through her ears.

She exhaled. *That was last night. You're okay now. You're safe.*

She swallowed.

For now . . .

THIRTEEN

"ETA?" Brooke asked.

"Two minutes," Dean said, never once taking his eyes off the copter's windshield as rain battered against it.

"ETA two minutes," she radioed in to the trauma nurse at Wilmington General. "GSW victim's BP is dropping. He's losing blood and hasn't regained consciousness." She looked up at Finn, heartbreak in her eyes.

He swiped a hand through his wet hair, the reality of her dire expression settling in. Sam was in a battle for his life, and as of now, he was losing.

As the copter hovered over the helipad atop the hospital, Finn looked to where the trauma team stood waiting. Dr. Krystyna Blotny gripped the edge of the gurney. While he wasn't thankful for the circumstances, he was thankful to see Krystyna. She was the best doc on staff.

A second team with Dr. Graham, also an awesome doc, at the helm stood behind the first team, ready to see to Fletcher.

The copter settled on the pad, and Dr. Blotny's team rushed forward for a hot landing. Ducking under the still-whirring rotor, they moved in unison to strap Sam onto the gurney and raced toward the hospital doors. Dr. Blotny assessed Sam, calling out orders. Finn hopped out and hurried behind Sam, squeezing through the doors before they closed on him.

"Hang on, Sam." Finn clutched his friend's hand.

Dr. Blotny looked back at him with determination fixed firm in her blue eyes. She'd fight with everything she had to save Sam.

They wheeled Sam into the ER bay, and Krystyna rested her palm on Finn's chest. "This is as far as you go."

He didn't waste time arguing. It would only prevent her from tending to Sam. Instead, he stepped outside the glass doors as they slid shut.

"Come on, Sam," he whispered, cold perspiration dotting his brow.

After what felt like the blink of an eye, the constant blare of the heart monitor registering no heartbeat sounded through the glass. Having battled fiercely to revive Sam, Blotny stepped back—her gloves covered with Sam's blood, her eyes weary. She looked at the clock and after a brief moment said, "Time of death 11:37 a.m."

"No!" He punched the metal doorframe, ignoring the pain reverberating through his hand, the blood seeping from his cracked knuckles.

Sam was gone.

FOURTEEN

Gabby's gaze locked on Finn standing in the hospital hallway, shock plastered on his handsome face. Movement whizzed past her in a blur of white, but she couldn't take her eyes off him.

He just stood there—his eyes etched with heartache. He'd lost two friends—Sam and Will. She longed to hug him but didn't know . . .

How was she supposed to act in front of him after how *she'd* left things? After she'd left him? After she hadn't returned his call? Though he hadn't left a message, his number had shown up on her cell. She knew it was him. And, while curious about what he had to say, she'd been a chicken, refusing to answer.

Everything that had happened over their three months together flashed through her mind like a film reel scrolling through a projector.

Her chest tightened, her hands weighted and numb.

"Gabby." His whisper pulled her from the silent whirlwind tossing through her mind.

"Finn." She bit her bottom lip, shifting her stance. "I'm . . . so sorry." For more than she could voice.

He stepped to her, engulfing her with a hug. He was still damp from all he'd been through, but somehow he felt so warm, smelled so good. . . . She just wanted to hide in his embrace, but he stepped back, lowering his arms to his sides.

His left hand was bruised and bloodied.

"Finn, your hand. You should have it looked at."

"I'm fine. There isn't time."

"Are you sure?"

"I'm positive."

They stood in silence until Gabby whispered, "I heard about Will. Does Tess know?"

"I'm going to head to her house once Emmalyne brings me my car. I called her ten minutes ago."

"Do you mind if I go along?" Gabby asked.

"Of course not. I'm sure Tess will need a friend, will need you."

"I'm sure she will," Rissi said, stepping from the nurses' station where she and Noah stood, "but you don't need to go to her. Janice, the head RN, just informed me Tess is out in the lobby, and she's asking about her husband."

Finn rubbed his brow. "All right." He looked to Gabby. "You ready?"

How could she be ready to destroy her friend's dreams? Her seven-months-pregnant friend . . . How did she tell Tess she'd just lost her love?

"Rissi and I will head out to tell Beth about Sam," Noah said.

Two husbands lost. Two lives crumbled.

Please be with us as we tell them. Please spread your wings about them and wrap them in your shelter. You're the only One who can comfort them in the midst of this wretched storm.

Two men lost in the blink of an eye.

Noah's strong arms wrapped around her. "Be safe, kid." He pressed a kiss to the top of her head.

She swiped the moisture from her eyes. "I will."

He turned to Finn. "Take good care of her."

Finn nodded. "Always."

She swallowed. How could one word hold so much meaning?

Noah's cell rang, and his step hitched. "It's Caleb," he said, lifting his index finger, signaling for them to wait as he answered. "Rowley . . . We're all here." Noah's jaw shifted, his gaze lowering. "No, he didn't make it. . . . Yeah . . ." He listened for less than a minute and then said, "Okay. Rissi and I are heading to tell Beth. We'll meet you back at the station."

Noah hung up and slipped his phone in his jeans pocket. "They caught the drug runners. The one who was shot is being transported to the morgue. Caleb arrested the remaining three, and they are on the way to the station for questioning."

Rissi raked a hand through her hair, tears welling in her large blue eyes. "At least Caleb got them."

Noah nodded. "We'll head in to help interrogate them after we talk with Beth." Noah exhaled. "Speaking of Beth, we better be going. Rumors are probably already stirring."

"Same with us and Tess," Finn said. He looked to Gabby and held out his hand. "Ready?"

The day she'd left him radiated through her mind. Him standing on his porch with hand extended, asking her to stay.

And she'd walked away.

Pain echoed through her chest, spreading up her throat. Similar to the pain from swallowing wrong—deep yet sharp.

Struggling, she managed to draw in a shallow breath.

Finn wrapped an arm around her shoulder, directing her toward the ER doors. "It's going to be all right."

How could it be?

He pressed the button for the automated door, and the double doors swung in, allowing them passage out.

Tess turned as they stepped into the lobby, her eyes red and puffy, a bunched tissue clutched in her hand. "Is Will okay? I heard the Coast Guard found Dennis's boat. Heard one of them was brought in by copter. . . ." She paused for a breath. "Just tell me," she blurted, tears spilling from her brown eyes.

Finn's posture stiffened, his head tilting slowly. "I'm so sorry, Tess."

Tess shook her head, taking a couple steps back. "What are you saying . . . ?"

"I'm so sorry," Gabby added.

"We're having our boy in two months." Tears rolled down Tess's pink cheeks. "Eight *weeks*. He has to be here. He can't be . . ."

Gabby pulled her into her arms.

Tess's head rested in the crook of her neck, sobs bursting forth. "No!"

Gabby fought the urge to say "shh, it's okay," because it wasn't. And for Tess, it wouldn't be for a long time—if ever. "I'm here," she said instead.

Heaves wracked Tess's body, her cries breaking on hiccups.

Finn moved to hug her, one arm draped around Gabby's shoulders, one around Tess's. "I'm so sorry, honey."

Tess shifted, beating Finn in the chest. "How did this happen?"

Finn took it. "I don't know, but I promise you I'll find out."

Her shoulders dropped, tears rolling down onto her very pregnant belly. "I knew it. I just knew."

"Knew what?" Gabby asked.

The depth of agony when a wife or husband died was once described to Gabby as the spouse left behind literally feeling as if they were losing half of their soul. That feeling of once having wholeness was ripped away, never to return.

Tess choked on a sob. "I knew—" she hiccupped—"that when he left yesterday—" another hiccup—"something bad was going to happen."

"Why?" Gabby frowned.

"Is Dennis alive?" Tess asked.

"Yes. He's pretty battered and unconscious, but the latest update is that there's no cranial bleeding, so he should be fine."

"Then you need to investigate him." Tess swiped her tears away, her red-rimmed eyes now even puffier.

"Why?" Gabby said. "You think he had something to do with Will's death?"

"You and I need to speak privately," Finn said before Tess could respond.

Tess squeezed Gabby's hand. "I'm okay with Gabby being present."

"I'm not," Finn said. "This is an open investigation. No reporters allowed."

"I'm not just a reporter." Gabby's voice heightened in that squeaky, high-pitched way it did when she was stressed. "I'm her friend."

"I understand that, but friends aren't allowed during an open investigation's interview process either," Finn said.

Her jaw tightened, but before she could argue further, Finn placed a hand on the small of Tess's back. "Let's go talk." He ushered her toward one of the consultation rooms.

Heat swept over Gabby's face. He seriously wasn't including her?

FIFTEEN

Finn led Tess into a consultation room. He shut the door and pulled out a baby blue vinyl-upholstered chair. "Please, have a seat." He held her hand to steady her as she sat.

"Thanks." She leaned back, her belly protruding. "Pregnancy," she said with an attempt at a smile until tears sprang afresh in her eyes. "I can't believe Will Jr. is never going to meet his dad."

"I'm so sorry."

"I should have called you as soon as he left. I knew something bad was going to happen. It was like that feeling you get before a storm, knowing it's coming but being helpless to stop it."

He swallowed. He knew that helpless feeling well.

"Why didn't I call you?" she sobbed.

He moved around to the front of her chair and knelt on his haunches, facing her. "You couldn't have known this was coming. I promise you, I will bring whoever pulled the trigger to justice."

"Trigger?" She gulped. "He was shot?"

Finn nodded. He wouldn't go into detail, but she deserved to know how her husband died. Besides, when they released Will's body to the funeral home after his autopsy, she'd see for herself if she chose to look. Knowing Tess, she would want to see him one last time. "I'm afraid so."

"And Dennis?"

"He wasn't shot but was badly beaten." Pressing his palms against his thighs for leverage, he stood. "You said you believed I should investigate him."

"Yes."

"Why?"

"Because he and Will went out on the boat right after Will told me that he was too deep into something, and that he was getting out for me and Will Jr.," she said, stroking her belly.

"Did he say what he was into?"

"No. He didn't want me involved. He only told me because I could tell something was wrong and I thought . . ." She shrugged her shoulder, tears slipping down her cheeks.

Finn grabbed a handful of Kleenexes from the box on the side table and offered them to Tess.

She scrunched them up in her hand and then dabbed her eyes. "I thought he was having an affair."

Will? *Never*. He adored Tess.

"He swore he wasn't, and when I pressed about his weird behavior lately, he said he'd gotten in over his head with something."

"But he didn't say what?" If he was in over his head, why hadn't Will come to him? Maybe he could have helped.

"No." She shook her head. "Only that at first he'd believed that it—whatever it was—was going to help provide for me and Will Jr. But he quickly realized it was wrong, and he wanted out."

"Wrong, how?" As in illegal? Will?

"He wouldn't say," she wailed through a sob.

"I'm so sorry, honey. I know I'm only making it more difficult, but I have to ask these questions."

"No," she said. "I want you to ask." She reached for his hand, and he took hold of her cold fingers. Why did they have to keep hospitals so darn cold? "I want you to catch whoever did this to my Will."

Rissi stepped from Noah's Jeep, which he'd parked along the curb of Sam and Beth's Cape Cod–style home on the sound side of Wrightsville Beach. She followed Noah up the winding path Sam had installed just last year—Beth planting vibrant red and purple geraniums on either side.

Stepping on the front porch, Rissi spotted Sam's daughter, Ali, curled up reading on the porch swing. She looked so happy and innocent—something Rissi had never been as a child, thanks to Hank.

She swallowed, forcing her thoughts and attention back on Ali, terrified about what Noah had to share and how just a few words could ruin people's lives. She nibbled at her bottom lip. This was going to be painful.

Ali looked up at Noah and smiled. "Hi, Mr. Rowley."

"Hey, kiddo." His voice cracked.

"Hi, Noah . . . Rissi," Beth said from the screened porch door, a yellow Fiestaware bowl of sliced watermelon wedges—no doubt intended for Ali—in her hand.

Her pleasant smile faded as Noah removed his Boston Red Sox hat, clutching it in his hands.

"Can we talk alone?" he asked, gesturing in Ali's direction.

Beth's gaze darted to Rissi. "No . . ." She shook her head. The yellow bowl slipped from her hands, shattering on the wood floor.

Tears streaked down Beth's face as Ali raced over, bending to help pick up the larger shards surrounding Beth's bare feet.

"Ali, go to your room, please," she managed.

"Momma?" Her delicate face scrunched.

"Now, Ali," she said. "Sorry." She inhaled and released her breath through a narrow slit in her lips. "Please."

Rissi's chest squeezed.

"What's wrong?" Ali persisted.

"Allison Mae, upstairs now."

At the use of her full name, Ali said, "Yes, ma'am," and trudged up the stairs, looking back at Rissi with tears in her eyes as realization dawned. It was a crushing blow that would rock her young world, forever changing the happy family she'd known.

"Come in," Beth said, collecting her demeanor despite the sorrow clouding her. Noah bent, collecting shards, and Rissi knelt beside him to help.

"Thank you," Beth said, leading them into the kitchen.

Noah stepped to the tall white trash can and dropped in his handful with a clatter.

"No!" Beth darted past Rissi. She yanked the pieces out of the trash can, heedless of her bleeding hands. "Sam just bought that for our anniversary."

Rissi bit the inside of her cheek. Sam had been raving about the Fiestaware bowl he'd tracked down for his wife's collection. Their tenth anniversary had been a mere two days ago. To go from something so happy to this . . . Rissi's heart ached for Beth.

SIXTEEN

Pumping her hands in and out of fists, Gabby paced Wilmington General's lobby and down the sloping hallway. She strode back and forth by the room where Finn and Tess spoke.

While she understood Finn was just doing his job, frustration flared through her all the same. She'd make sure to find a way to talk with Tess after they finished. Tess was her friend, and she had every right to hear whatever her friend wished to tell her.

Movement at the end of the hall caught her eye. She squinted. It was Dennis Fletcher, awake on a gurney, being rolled out of the ER doors toward the elevator. Hurrying down the hall, she managed to squeeze into the elevator with the orderly and Fletcher.

The orderly, his badge listing his name as Wayne Ashe, greeted her with a smile. "Could you press three, please?"

"Absolutely."

She only glanced at Fletcher once, just to assess that he was still awake, and found him to be.

The elevator dinged, the number three over the doors lighting up. The silver doors slid open, and she gestured for the orderly to go first.

"Thanks," he said. "Have a good day."

"You too." She smiled.

She plodded behind them, keeping a fair distance as Fletcher was wheeled into Room 323. She exited the ward, giving the attending nurse who'd greeted Fletcher upon entry time to get him settled before she pounced.

She prayed it didn't take long, as she had no idea when Finn would appear. Once he was alerted that Fletcher was awake, he'd head straight up to question the only potential witness to Will's murder they knew of.

She took a seat on the couch in the waiting area. Before long, the orderly exited the unit and headed back for the elevator with the empty gurney.

Bouncing her knee, Gabby bided her time, not wanting to enter Fletcher's room while the nurse was still present. After a few anxious moments, she moved through the unit as if she belonged there.

Making a left into the ten-foot-long hallway, she spotted Fletcher settled in his bed through the open doorway. A nurse rounded the doorframe as Gabby approached the room, and her breath seized when the nurse looked her up and down. "May I help you?"

"Just here to see my brother, Dennis," she whispered, praying Fletcher didn't hear over the hum of the IV machine and the TV they'd turned on for him.

"He's only been awake a short while and needs his rest. So keep it brief, okay? You can visit longer tomorrow."

"No problem." Gabby smiled, thankful Fletcher's attention remained riveted on the small flat-screen TV anchored on the wall.

She waited until the nurse headed toward the nursing station, making a left, pushing her rolling cart with her. Once she was clearly out of sight and well out of earshot, Gabby took a calming breath and entered, shutting Fletcher's door behind her.

His bruised and lacerated head rested against the propped-up pillow, a hospital-issued blanket covering him from the waist down.

"Mr. Fletcher?"

He looked at her, confusion marring his brow. "Who are you?" He frowned, his face a swollen mass of varying shades of blue and purple. A handful of black stitches arched above his right eye and another row ran across his upper cheekbone.

"I'm Gabby." She scooted farther into the room, hoping he wouldn't turn her away before she got to ask at least a few of the questions dancing a curious jig in her reporter's brain.

"Am I supposed to know you?" Irritation sparked in his words.

"No, sir. I'm with the *Raleigh Gazette*."

"A reporter. I see. Look, I appreciate everyone saying I'm some sort of a hero for escaping to get help for Will, but the fact is I'm not."

"No?" So he freely admitted it?

"No. I went to get help for my friend, yes. It's the least anyone would do. But according to the doc who treated me, Will didn't make it."

"I'm afraid not."

Dennis ran his hand across his brow, careful to avoid the stitches. "Such a shame."

"Can you tell me what happened out there?"

"No."

"No?"

"That's for the Coast Guard to know. Not some reporter."

Some reporter? So he was one of those kinds of guys. She bet if she was a male reporter from the *New York Times* or CNN he'd be singing a different tune, getting his version of the story out among the public so they all heard what he wanted told.

Footsteps echoed down the hall. *Finn.* It was now or never.

"Do you know what Will was involved in?"

Fletcher's brow creased, his stitches bunching. That had to hurt, but he didn't flinch.

The footsteps drew closer. Definitely Finn's footfalls.

"What do you mean *involved in*?" he asked.

"Last evening before he went fishing with you, he confessed to Tess that he'd screwed up and gotten into something bad, but that he was getting out. Next thing, he's dead."

"Look, lady—"

Finn opened the door, his irritated gaze locking on hers. "You're not supposed to be in here, and you know it."

"I was just having a conversation with Mr. Fletcher."

"It's Master Chief Petty Officer Fletcher," Dennis said. "And we're finished." He looked to Finn, who moved to usher Gabby out with a self-satisfied smile.

"Don't bother," she said. "I can see myself out."

She looked back at Fletcher. "I'll see you again soon."

"I'm afraid not, sweetheart."

Sweetheart? Really? What a jerk.

"I'll be right back," Finn said as he followed Gabby into the hall. "The use of *sweetheart* was totally unacceptable," he said to her, "but you know you can't interview anyone involved in an open investigation. Understand?"

"Understanding and agreeing are two different things."

He raked a hand through his hair with an exasperated sigh. "How is it possible for you to drive me this crazy in under an hour and a half?"

She shrugged. "Just a gift, I guess."

With an exhale, Finn headed back toward Fletcher's room. When he reached the door, his cell rang. He looked at it, shook his head, and walked around the corner, presumably to answer.

Gabby was tempted to go back into Fletcher's room to get more answers but decided it wasn't the wisest move. Instead, she sighed and headed downstairs, hoping to find Tess.

It wasn't the first time she'd run into police—or this time, CGIS—lecturing her about an open investigation and the order for her to stay out of it. It was situations like this where the best stories lay, and her gut said there was a doozy of a story surrounding MCPO Fletcher—one her friend deserved to know.

She was doing this for Tess as much as for her insatiable need to uncover the truth and see justice done—even if it was only on the front page of a paper. Truth was truth, and it deserved to be told.

She found Tess crying in the hall outside the morgue where Will's autopsy would be performed. Yet another angle Gabby hoped to explore once the results were in. Finn had said Will had been shot but told them nothing else.

Her friend turned at her approach. "I knew something bad was going to happen," Tess said, not bothering to swipe away the tears streaming from her eyes.

Gabby's brow furrowed. "Why did you think something bad was going to happen?"

"Like I told Finn, something was wrong."

Finn. He'd probably be down any minute.

Gabby rested a hand on Tess's slender shoulder. "Why don't we go somewhere where we can talk?" *Without Finn interrupting.*

Tess sniffed. "Where?"

"How about our usual spot?" The Coffee Connection.

"Okay." Tess nodded, pinching her nose with a clumped-up tissue and blowing. Then she tossed the Kleenex in the silver trash can by the elevator doors.

The break from the hospital, and particularly the morgue level, would be good for Tess. There was nothing she could do for her husband now, and telling Gabby what she knew might lead to finding his killer.

"We'll have to take your car," Gabby said. Noah had driven her in, and she was supposed to ride back to the office with Finn when he was done. But hearing what Tess had to say was far more important. Not just for a possible new angle or insight into a potential story, but to be a listening ear for her friend.

Tess handed her the keys as they rode the elevator to the

lobby level. "You better drive," she said, her hands shaking at her sides.

The doors opened, and hoping not to find Finn, Gabby looked both ways as they walked toward the front parking lot as quickly as a very pregnant and distraught Tess could manage.

As the hospital awning ended, they stepped into the persistent drizzle. The damp heaviness held the oppressive feel of death.

Thankfully, both Tess and Will were believers, so Tess knew Will was living eternally with their Savior, but while that had to bring a huge measure of solace to her heart, it couldn't possibly stop the heartache tearing through her.

"Where'd you park?"

Her friend pointed to the yellow VW bug on the south side of the lot. "We can take Route 14 straight to the Coffee Connection."

Gabby winced at Tess's announcement in front of the valet who was walking back from parking a car. Knowing Finn, as soon as he realized she was gone, he'd be asking people who might have seen them leave, including the valet, about where they had gone.

Despite the fact that the valet didn't know her, a pregnant woman leaving with a brunette in a bright yellow VW bug would be pretty easy to remember. And he'd likely remember where they were headed.

Hopefully, Finn would be focused on Fletcher for a good while. Or would get caught up with the ME performing one of the three autopsies awaiting him.

SEVENTEEN

Finn knocked on the doorframe of Fletcher's room, clenching his jaw as his busted knuckles hit the metal. They'd be hurting for a while, but the physical pain would pass much faster than the pain of Sam's and Will's deaths.

"Yeah?" Fletcher said, bidding him entrance.

Frustration still flaring through him at having found Gabby in Fletcher's room, he inhaled and stepped inside.

"Who are you?" Fletcher slurred.

Finn pulled up a seat. While he knew Will well, he only knew Dennis Fletcher from Will's brief mentions of him. "I'm Special Agent Finn Walker." He held up his CGIS badge.

"Coast Guard Investigative Service. Good. Maybe you can catch the guys who killed Will and nearly me."

"About that . . ." Finn said, scooting closer to Fletcher, careful to avoid the IV stand situated by the head of the hospital bed.

"Are you up for answering a few questions?"

Fletcher sat up at an angle, looking more beaten up than he had in Finn's initial survey of his injuries. "I'll do my best. Whatever it takes to help find Will's killer, but I have to warn you, my head's fuzzy at best."

"We'll take it slow. How about we start with what you remember happening?" It was hard to restrain the massive flow of questions racing through his mind. Like how he managed to get away? What was the secret Will was keeping? And was Fletcher involved as well, as Tess believed?

"Will and I headed out at sunset for some fishing. We were about to head back when two men rushed us. We didn't even hear them board."

"What did they look like?"

"They were in scuba gear."

"Tanks and all?"

"No. Just full body suits. One knocked me to the ground with a hard crack to my head. He must have thought he knocked me out because he left me alone. Then the other man had a heated argument with Will."

"About what?"

"I don't know. He spoke Spanish."

"And Will? Did he respond in Spanish?"

"Yes."

"The arguing grew more heated. I stood and fought one guy, but the other pulled a gun on Will, and a shot rang out. Both men's attention focused on Will. I rushed up on deck and over to the outboard, nearly tripping over the men's scuba tanks and fins on the way. More shots rang out as I flopped into the outboard and then at least one more as I rode away."

"So the men dove to your location?"

"They must have." He slowly shook his head, as if trying to clear the cobwebs. "I think I hit my head again when I fell into the outboard . . . and banged my shoulder. I took off as fast as I could, anxious to get help for Will, but the next thing I remember is waking up here." He cleared his throat. "I heard what happened to your man trying to rescue me. I'm sorry."

Finn kept his thoughts focused on the questions for Fletcher. "Do you think they spent the night searching for you?"

Fletcher shrugged, then winced at the motion. "Must have." He coughed, wincing again.

"Any idea what the men wanted?"

"I don't speak Spanish."

"Anything else?"

"That's all I remember."

The doc entered. "That's enough for today," he said to Finn. "My patient needs to rest."

"Of course. I'll be back tomorrow."

Finn headed for the morgue. Hadley had texted, letting him know he was about to begin the autopsy on the drug runner Caleb had killed while trying to protect Sam. If only they'd reacted a moment faster, maybe Sam would still be alive.

He hadn't seen Gabby since he'd asked her to leave Fletcher's room. She clearly wasn't happy with him, and he worried she may be talking with Tess. . . . Come to think of it, he didn't see her either.

He stopped short.

"Gabby," he breathed as he turned around and rushed for the lobby. She wouldn't . . .

An extremely frustrating twenty minutes later, after searching the hospital, having Gabby and Tess paged, and trying both on their phones repeatedly, he'd concluded that he was right—she'd left the hospital. She and Tess were together, and they were gone.

Thankfully, it only took a minute with Reggie, the valet, to learn of their destination. The Coffee Connection on Market Street. He should have known. The two went nearly every day throughout Gabby's winter stay.

Climbing into his Nissan Rogue, he plopped the cherry on his dash, lit it up, and rushed for downtown.

EIGHTEEN

Rissi followed Noah into the station. The three surviving drug runners were being held in separate rooms. Caleb sat interrogating a man in the far right one, while guardsmen stood watch at the other doors.

Caleb looked back through the glass and nodded at them. He stood and stepped into the hall. "He's the one who killed Sam," he said, pointing at the man. "I talked plenty, but he isn't. Didn't even ask for a lawyer after we Mirandized him. None of them did."

"Let Rissi take a crack at him," Noah said.

"Of course." Caleb nodded.

Father, please help us get a confession. This man took our friend and teammate's life. Let justice be done, she prayed, pausing outside the interrogation room.

The team relied on her in these situations, relied on her knack for getting suspects to talk. She had no idea why God had gifted her in that area, but He had. As upsetting as it could be, she was grateful for her role in getting to the heart of a killer and bringing out the truth.

Taking a steadying breath and releasing it, she entered.

The man—midtwenties and Latino—didn't bother looking up.

Anger at his indifference for so capriciously taking a man's life sizzled through her limbs.

Taking and releasing another attempt at a calming breath,

she pulled out a metal chair and sat on the cool seat. She slid a legal pad and pen to the man.

"Write your confession."

"I want my phone call," he said, speaking for the first time since his arrest, his accent thick and heavy.

"All right." She sighed. He had the right, but it was frustrating that was the route he'd gone. Though she knew the chances of an outright confession had been slim-to-none.

Having no choice except to let him exercise his right, she watched as Noah walked in and unlocked his cuffs from the steel ring on the table. He escorted him to the phone at his desk and settled the man in his seat, cuffing one arm to the chair arm.

Rissi leaned against the doorframe, the metal cool against her bare arm. She hadn't had time to change into professional clothes since the competition, so she decided to change while the suspect made his call. In the locker room, she swapped her tank, swimsuit, and shorts for a pair of navy trousers, a white blouse, and navy Tieks.

Stuffing her shed clothes into her locker, she glanced over at Sam's.

Why, Lord?

She teared up at the thought of Beth without a husband and Ali without a father.

Exhaling a jerky breath, she shut her locker and rested her head against it.

Please be a shelter for Beth and Ali. Help me to anticipate any needs and to be there for them. Protect their hearts and mine in the sorrow.

She hated being vulnerable, and today had made her taste the sting of death. Sam was a believer, and according to Finn, Will was, too, so at least they were in a better place, but that didn't change the heartache those left behind had to endure.

After a brief knock and her call to come in, the door creaked open and she turned her head to find Caleb standing there.

He tapped the door's edge and then strode to her. "You okay?"

She lifted her head off the locker and linked her arms across her chest, rubbing the chill from them.

He pulled her into his strong arms. "It sucks."

Caleb was a man of few words, but he always got straight to the point, and she appreciated the brevity.

"It all happened so fast. I worked with Sam yesterday, and today he's gone."

"It always happens too fast. Even with long illnesses the end goes too quick." He cradled her head in his hand. "It makes me want to live differently."

She looked up, tears burning her eyes. "How?"

"To never put things off because you never know when it'll be too late."

Suddenly she felt very small and exposed.

"Ris?"

She looked around Caleb's shoulder to see Noah at the door. He rubbed his forehead. "He's done with his call."

She stepped back from Caleb's embrace. "Coming." Swiping the moisture from her eyes, she stepped around Caleb. "Thanks," she said, looking back.

"Anytime. I'm always here for you."

"And I appreciate it very much."

He nodded and followed her out.

"He spoke in Spanish on the phone—low and hushed," Noah said. "But I understood a few words. *Help* and *sorry*."

Noah stepped to his desk, uncuffed the man, and escorted him back into the interrogation room, recuffing him to the table.

Emmalyne Thorton appeared at the door, her poppy-patterned, flowing skirt and matching red blouse a bright spot in an otherwise dark day. "I found some information." She handed Noah a manila folder.

"Thanks," Noah said, shutting the door and skimming the folder.

Rissi retook her seat, but Noah remained standing—providing a level of intimidation as he brooded over the man. After reading the folder's contents, he handed it to Rissi and shifted into an at-ease stance. His military training lingered in a number of ways. He'd served in the Coast Guard a handful of years before attending CGIS A-school and becoming a civilian with the Investigative Service.

Rissi read the file. The man in front of her was Juan Cadarz, an illegal immigrant from Cuba.

"Juan," Noah said, "why don't you tell us what happened today?"

Juan swallowed at the mention of his name and shifted in his seat, but he remained frustratingly silent.

She couldn't help but wonder whom he'd called and what was said.

NINETEEN

Difficult as it was to ignore her reporter instincts, Gabby waited for Tess to begin. She didn't want to rush her friend or overwhelm her with questions.

They were nearly at the Coffee Connection when Tess finally spoke.

"I had the sickest feeling when Will left for his fishing trip with Dennis."

"When did you realize Will hadn't come back?"

Tess shook her head, kneading her fingers together, soft pink polish chipped from nibbling teeth. "Not until I woke up this morning. I feel so bad I didn't stay awake or wake up and notice he wasn't there. This pregnancy has me conking out by eight every night. Will and Dennis always stayed out until the last light vanished before heading back. He said it would be at least ten by the time they cleaned the boat and he hung out a bit. I didn't really expect him before eleven. Will was thoughtful but often lost track of time."

"So you called the Coast Guard when you woke and realized he hadn't come back?"

"I woke early, and when he didn't answer his phone, I decided to drive to Dennis's place. Every now and then Will would crash there, but he hadn't called me, and before he did something like that, he always called. His truck was still there, and the boat wasn't at the dock, so when no one answered the door, I panicked and called the Coast Guard."

"No one else lives at Dennis's place?"

"No. He lives alone. He and Val split about six months ago."

"He's divorced?"

Tess shook her head. "They're estranged. It's weird, if you ask me."

Finding a parking spot on the street outside of the Coffee Connection, Gabby decided to hold off on further questions until they were situated in the café. The scent of roasted coffee beans mingled with peppermint tea swirled in the air as they entered. The espresso machine whirred as they stepped farther in.

Paul Barnes, the owner, greeted them. "Hey, lovely ladies. It's been a while." He came around the waist-high counter to give Gabby a hug. "How ya doing, kid?"

She hugged the sweet, fifty-something man back, always loving the spicy scent of his cologne. "It's been a rough day."

"I heard there was some commotion with the Guard. I heard an officer was killed, but I don't know if that's true. You know how gossip runs."

"It's true," Tess said, her eyes welling with tears.

"No." He shook his head. "Not Will?"

Tess nodded as she broke into sobs.

"Oh, honey, I'm so sorry. I didn't know."

"Of course not." Tess dabbed her eyes with a scrunched-up tissue.

"What happened?"

"I don't know yet. Only that he was murdered." Tess sniffed.

"Murdered?" His gray eyes widened. "By who?"

Tess looked overwhelmed by Paul's questions, so Gabby decided to answer for her. "We don't know yet, but Finn said he would get to the bottom of it."

"Finn's leading the investigation?"

"Yes." Gabby nodded.

"You've got a good one there." She didn't know if Paul was referring to Finn's leading the investigation or her winter relationship with him. News spread fast in the Coast Guard community.

"Let's grab a seat," she said, placing her hand on the small of her friend's back—arched slightly to compensate for her protruding belly.

"Please, sit. I'll bring your usual," Paul said, hustling back around the counter.

"Thanks," Gabby said over her shoulder as she looked for an open table with some privacy. The brown leather chairs by the unlit fireplace were full, along with the tables lining the wide back hallway. Which left them either seats at the communal farm-style table running down the center of the shop, or a table in the front-window alcove.

She didn't want them talking so close to other people sitting at the farm-style table, but if Finn came looking for her, she'd be easier to spot in the window.

"Over there," Tess said through a sniff.

Gabby relented and moved with her friend to the table by the window.

The whir of the espresso machine heightened to a whistle, steam wafting over the bronze machine as Paul poured the dark brown liquid from the espresso glasses into their paper cups. Soon the sound and smell of frothing, steaming milk invaded her senses.

Tess fingered a straw she'd pulled from the jar on the table, twirling it between her fingers. She looked ready to talk, so Gabby started the conversation. "So you were saying when no one answered at Fletcher's place, you called the Coast Guard and . . ."

"They assured me they would look into it and told me not to imagine the worst, but panic set in. The guys had been out at sea all night. That wasn't like Will at all. He'd never stay out all night. Not without getting word to me. I knew then that the worst had happened. If I'm completely honest, I knew something bad was going to happen as soon as Will walked out the door."

"What did you fear happening?"

Tess leaned forward, then stilled as Paul carried their drinks over.

"Here you go, ladies, and some muffins on the house," he said, setting the plates down in front of them. The sweet, tangy scent of blueberries and butter swirled in the air.

"Thanks," Gabby said.

"I'm so sorry, Tessie," he said, giving her shoulder a squeeze. "You let me know if you need anything, ya hear?"

"Thanks." Tess nodded then remained quiet until he'd walked away.

She leaned forward and whispered, "I feared something terrible would happen to Will. I even had a nightmare about him dying."

"Why were you so sure something bad was going to happen? Was it just a feeling or something more?" She thoroughly believed in instinct—it's what kept her alive in the field . . . until it nearly didn't. She'd been played a fool once. She'd never be that vulnerable again.

"Before Will left he told me he'd gotten into something he shouldn't have and was in over his head. He promised me he was getting out that night, said he'd make things right for me and Will Jr." She ran her hand over her belly in soothing, rhythmic strokes.

Gabby tried her best not to go all-out-reporter. Friendship trumped story, even if her instincts and desire to uncover the truth were screaming to dive deeper. She paced herself while still proceeding forward. "Did he say *what* he'd gotten into?"

"No. But whatever it was, I believe Dennis has to be involved."

"Why do you say that?"

"Because there had been this weird dynamic between them lately."

"How so?"

"I don't know, exactly. It was like they were keeping a secret. You know the looks you share with someone when the two of you know something no one else does. The way you move off to the side to talk quietly to each other or how you shift the conversation when it touches on a subject you don't want others to overhear." She exhaled. "And it's not just that. The stress that comes from carrying a secret around—especially if it's not something you're supposed to be doing—hung heavy on Will. He was anxious, tired, worried. I could read it on his face. I asked him what was going on, but he just said work was hectic."

Gabby thought she'd been astute at reading situations and, more importantly, people, but she'd completely dropped the ball with Asim. Somehow she'd missed the red flags. Either he'd been a perfect liar, or she'd been too blinded by love. Had she totally misjudged Will too? How could sweet, faithful Will be involved in anything illegal?

Based on drug runners attacking Fletcher and the rescue team, she'd guess it was drugs. Had he and Fletcher been trafficking drugs on the side? It didn't seem real, or even plausible, yet here they were.

Had Will told the drug runners he was out, and it went very wrong? Had he told Fletcher? How had he reacted? Was he in on it, too, as Tess believed?

So many possibilities, but from the attention Fletcher was getting at the hospital, if anything, it appeared he was being treated as a hero for "going for help" and for surviving.

She had her next story—one she was doing for her friend's sake. She'd discover if Fletcher was involved or not. At this point, it really could go either way. It'd be her job to uncover the truth.

Gabby exhaled and looked up. She winced at the sight of Finn striding through the door, irritation sparking in his green eyes.

Tess turned to follow the direction of Gabby's gaze.

"Oh," she said, biting her bottom lip before turning back to Gabby. "I guess our time is up."

"You got that right," Finn said.

Gabby took a stiffening breath. "I have every right to talk to my friend."

"That's not the source of my frustration, and you know it. You have a drug lord sending hit men to kill you."

Tess's eyes widened. "You do?"

Gabby swallowed with a shrug.

"That's great. Shrug off a threat on your life." Finn released a frustrated exhale. "Noah entrusted you to my care, and you knew not to leave without me."

She tilted her head. "I never actually agreed."

Finn pinched the bridge of his nose. "Regardless of semantics, it's time to go. I'm needed back at the station."

"Tess can drop me off when we're done talking." There was so much more she wanted to ask her.

"Not a chance," Finn said.

"Contrary to what you and Noah think, I don't need a babysitter."

"Given your nonchalant attitude toward a professional hit on your life, I disagree. Maybe not a babysitter, but concerned family members and friends."

Finn still considered her a friend? She let that bounce around in her mind as she steeled herself for an intense argument. "I appreciate your concern." It was endearing . . . and frustrating. "But I can take care of myself." She'd been embedded undercover in South Sudan for nigh on a year. She knew how to take care of herself—Asim's lies and actions aside.

"I made Noah a promise." Finn pulled out handcuffs. "If you won't go cordially . . ." He let them dangle.

She arched her brows. "You can't be serious."

"As serious as I get."

She shifted to stand, but before she'd gotten to her feet, he'd cuffed her right arm to his left.

"Finn!" Embarrassment, mixed with anger, flushed her otherwise cool skin as everyone's gaze in the café shifted to her. "You're being ridiculous."

"I think it's the other way around."

He looked at Tess. "I'm so sorry about Will, and I'll be in touch. But please excuse us."

At Tess's nod, he placed his hand on Gabby's lower back to direct her out. She resisted, refusing to be dragged out like a criminal.

"Don't make this harder than it has to be."

"You can't really believe I'm going to make this easy."

"Of course not." He wrapped his free arm around her and hefted her over his shoulder, lifting their cuffed arms up to rest on her hip.

"Finn Walker! You cannot be serious." She squirmed, trying to wriggle her way down, but his hold only tightened as he strode to the door.

Pushing it open with the sole of his boot, he carried her outside into the rain and straight to his car. He dropped her with a tender hand onto his backseat and, uncuffing his wrist, quickly moved her hands behind her back and locked the free cuff around her other wrist.

"There." He moved to the driver's seat and started the engine.

"I cannot believe you just did that," she said as they pulled out of the parking spot.

"You didn't give me a choice." He made a right at the first stoplight, heading back to the office.

"I was having an important conversation." She wrestled to get comfortable with her hands cuffed behind her bum.

"Let me guess," he said. "She said you should investigate Fletcher? And that got your reporter senses going."

"Y . . . es."

"I knew it." He tapped the wheel. "You're willing to risk your safety for a story . . . anything for a story."

"It's what I do for a living."

"Trust me, I know. But I don't believe it's just for a living."

She narrowed her eyes. "What's that supposed to mean?"

"I mean that a story will always come first with you. Even before . . ." He took a breath, holding it as if weighing his next words. Was he about to say before *me*?

In all fairness, she *had* chosen the job in Raleigh over pursuing the feelings that had kindled between them.

His expression shifted to disappointment. "Even before your *safety*."

She kept quiet.

He drummed the wheel. "Before everything," he whispered.

She sat back, her fists bumping her tailbone. Was he right? Did she always put the story above all else? And did that include *everyone*? Did she put the story before God and His will for her life? She always assumed the pursuit of truth was what He wanted for her life, but she'd never actually prayed and asked Him to reveal His will. She preferred to assume the insatiable drive in her—the urge to discover the truth—was created in her from the start. What about family? Did she put following stories around the world before them?

She stood by the conviction of God first, family second, job third. But did her actions and not just her words prove that she lived out what she professed?

"Let us not love with words or speech but with actions and in truth."

Actions and truth.

In truth, she'd been so focused on exposing the falsehoods in

80

others—in those she didn't know or have a relationship with—that she'd been blinded to the truth of who Asim was.

She'd known that her relationship with a source was professionally wrong, but she'd focused on her feelings rather than her convictions or faith.

She swallowed, not wanting to go any deeper on those thoughts. Leave it to Finn to unsettle her. He always did—both in a good and in an extremely frustrating way.

TWENTY

Heat rushed over Rissi as Noah continued to question the detainee who shot Sam, and the man refused to answer.

Getting angry won't help. She repeated the words in her head, trying to convince herself, but it was useless. Her muscles tensed and her neck ached from the tightness gripping her. How could the man just stare blankly back at them, like they were wasting his time?

"You killed a good man today. A husband and father," Noah said. The vein in his temple flared purple.

Juan Cadarz remained silent, his gaze fixed on the ground.

"Who hired you?" Rissi asked, taking a different tack.

The man blinked, his dark lashes fluttering like butterfly wings.

She'd hit a nerve.

"Why were you ordered to kill Dennis Fletcher?" She'd continue in the one direction he'd responded to.

He swallowed, slumping deeper in his chair.

"Did you also kill Petty Officer Will Seavers?"

He shifted in his seat, stroking his thighs.

Finally, she was making him nervous.

"Why kill Petty Officer Seavers? Did it involve drugs?"

She leaned forward, her forearms braced on the black table, her legs crossed underneath. "So it involved drugs," she said, poking at the nerve she'd hit.

His gaze darted to the left, fixing on the corner of the room. "I'll assume your evasiveness means yes."

A slight smile curled in the corner of her boss's lips. His silent support spurred her on.

"Did Fletcher and Seavers catch you smuggling drugs?" Had they stumbled across the drug runners while out fishing? Had they been in the wrong place at the wrong time?

The man refused to respond verbally, continuing to show zero remorse for killing Sam.

Rissi fought the urge to throttle answers from him, but at least he was reacting, albeit only with bodily cues.

After another half hour of questioning met with silence, Noah stood, and she followed him out of the room. The door shut behind them with a thud.

"We'll let him stew overnight in the holding cell and try again tomorrow."

Rissi nodded. His bail hearing, all three of theirs, was set for 1400 tomorrow.

She prayed Caleb was having better luck with the other detainees, but the tense expression on his face as he entered the hall said otherwise.

"Let's hope Logan was able to trace the call," Noah said.

"Calls," Caleb said. "The man now identified as Alonso Garcia, thanks to Logan's digging, also made a call."

Rissi pursed her lips. *Interesting.* Two of the three made calls. Why not the third man?

Logan came around the corner and strode toward them, his broad shoulders the finishing touch for his toned physique. "The calls went to this number." He handed Noah a Post-it note.

Rissi arched a brow, looking around her boss at the numbers scribbled across the yellow square. "Calls? Both men called the same number?"

Logan rocked back on his heels. "That's correct."

"A lawyer?" Caleb asked.

"Surprisingly, no." Logan shook his head, his spikey, blond-tipped hair shifting with the swaying motion. "The number eventually traced to an offshore company called Litman Limited."

"Litman?" Rissi frowned. "Never heard of it."

"Neither had I, so I did some digging, and it looks like a front company."

"Front for what?" Noah asked.

"I don't know. That will take a lot more digging."

"Get on it," Noah said.

"Yes, sir." Logan turned around, heading back for his desk.

"Good work," Noah called after him.

Emmalyne approached. "I found some info on our third drug runner—Manuel Rodriguez. He's the only American citizen of the three but emigrated from Cuba like the others a couple years back."

She stepped forward. "I also have results on the bullet Finn retrieved. Three were .40 caliber rounds."

"Like Coast Guard standard issue in their P229 DAK, among other guns that use that caliber. And the other?" Noah asked.

"It's .45 caliber."

Why two different guns? Why such different ones? And had the .40 been fired from a Coast Guard issued DAK? When Finn searched the boat, he'd found no firearms, so what happened to them?

Exasperation flaring like ignited rocket fuel sizzled through Finn's veins as he pulled up to the station and shifted into Park. A man was trying to kill Gabby. How could she care so little about her own safety? How could she be so bold as to leave the team's watch and protection?

He knew from her career choice, risk drove her. She craved it, as he did.

There was something inside them both—a pulse reverberating through them—a longing for the adrenaline rush during that split-second when anything could happen.

Waiting on the precipice of a rush brought him to life—being in the dead calm of a storm waiting for it to cascade over him or standing with his toes on the edge of a plane before freefalling into a dive.

It was no different for Gabby, though he thought she tempted death far more readily than he did. It was like she enjoyed taunting it.

Cutting the ignition, he climbed out of the car. Reaching back in, he flipped open the child-safety lock on her door.

She stepped out and handed the unclasped cuffs to him. "Thanks for the ride, Sparky."

His brows hiked, a smile curling on his lips. How had she . . . ? The lady was impressive—frustrating as all get-out, but attractively impressive.

Gabby entered the office, Finn fast on her heels, fully expecting him to rat her out to Noah for bailing on him with Tess. Thankfully Noah didn't ask how the afternoon had gone, and shockingly, Finn didn't bring it up.

She wondered if he was trying to protect his own neck or hers.

"How is it going with the interrogation?" Finn asked.

Noah brushed a hand over his short-cropped hair. "The men refused to talk. But two of them placed phone calls to the same number."

"A number that leads to a front company," Logan said, striding toward them. "All I can find on Litman Limited is a false address in the Bahamas where it's registered."

"Okay, keep digging," Noah said.

"On it." Logan headed back for his desk.

"I got to speak with Fletcher," Finn said.

"He's awake?" Rissi asked.

"Yes. And I've got a lot to tell you both."

TWENTY-ONE

"All right," Noah said, in front of the team's case board. He lifted a bright blue marker and flipped the top off, setting it on the whiteboard's silver tray. The scent of blueberry wafted in the air. "Okay . . ." Noah's brown brows hiked. "Who bought fruit-scented markers?"

"Guilty." Emmalyne raised her hand. "If we have to write down awful details, the task can at least smell good."

Noah shook his head with a slight smile while Finn struggled to hold back a laugh. A smile curled on his lips. Typical Emmalyne—always looking to bring light to a dark situation.

Noah took a swig of his coffee, then asked, "What do we know?"

Finn sat forward and exhaled. "Fletcher said two men in dive suits and masks entered the boat. He said they argued with Will in Spanish and then shot him. Fletcher was able to escape and got away in the outboard. The next thing he remembers was waking up at the hospital."

He looked over at Gabby, beside him on the large cushy gray sofa. The air was cold, and she only wore a lightweight burgundy T-shirt. He slipped off his black windbreaker and offered it to her.

"Thanks." She slipped it on, her arms swimming in the sleeves.

He smiled. He liked the look of his friend bundled up in his jacket.

"We know that two of the men we processed called the same number, which as Logan discovered . . ." Rissi said, glancing back at him leaning against the far wall.

"Leads to what appears to be a front company registered in the Bahamas named Litman Limited," he said.

"The Bahamas are a known location for registering front companies." Noah added the bulleted points to the information Fletcher had relayed.

"A common place for laundering money through offshore accounts," Rissi said.

Finn glanced at the clock. The tired expressions of his teammates were evidence of the length and sadness of the day weighing on them.

"Tess said Will told her before he left last night that he'd gotten into something he shouldn't have, was in over his head, and was planning to get out," Gabby said, her hands interlaced around her knee as she leaned back.

Noah stared at his sister for a moment, and then his gaze settled on Finn, his brows arched.

"Gabby spoke with Tess while I was speaking with Fletcher," he said.

"Gabs." Noah's eyebrows hiked higher. "You know this is an open investigation."

"Trust me." Frustration sparked in her eyes. "Finn made that perfectly clear."

She was like a bulldog with a bone—ceaseless when she caught a whiff of a story.

"But you did it anyway," Noah said, his tone terse.

"She wanted to confide in a friend," Gabby said, her lips pursing to the side in that stubborn way they did when she'd pushed the boundaries. Which happened far too often for Finn's liking.

Noah's face softened. "I get that. I just don't want you getting involved in a delicate situation while you're supposed to be lying low."

She nodded reluctantly.

"Emmy, why don't you go over the results you've processed so far?" Noah said, switching his attention to her.

"Sure," Emmalyne said, sharing the information about the bullets again, then proceeding to say, "The fingerprints Finn collected show Will, Fletcher, and several dozen guardsmen, along with Fletcher's wife, Valerie, had been on Fletcher's boat."

"His estranged wife," Gabby added.

Noah's brows arched.

"I know. It's an open investigation. . . ." She released a stream of air.

"We'll need to run through all the guardsmen who'd been on the boat, but the possibility they were simply friends of Fletcher's who'd he'd taken out fishing or for a boat ride is high."

Noah added a notation to check into each man, or woman in Valerie Fletcher's case, who'd been on Fletcher's boat.

"If the men entered in full dive suits, masks, and gloves as Fletcher described," Finn said, "they didn't leave fingerprints."

"Unfortunately," Caleb said, shifting on Rissi's left.

"I'm still processing the rest," Emmy, Finn's CSI assistant and evidence-chaser extraordinaire, said.

"The ME's office called and said Will's autopsy is set for 1000, and the drug runners' bail hearing is at 1400," Finn said.

"Rissi and I will be at the competition, as it was postponed until tomorrow, after the incident. Which means, Gabby, you'll come with us."

"I'd rather stay in town so Tess can come hang with me if she needs a friend."

"Understandable," Noah said. "But I don't want you alone at the loft, even if Tess is with you."

"Agreed," Finn said.

"Fine. Then I'll stay at the office. Tess can visit me here."

Caleb raised his hand. "I'll be here."

Gabby exhaled. "I appreciate everyone's concern. Really, I

do, but I don't need a babysitter. Being away from Raleigh is safety enough."

"No, it's not," Finn said, his limbs heating.

"I agree with Finn," Noah said.

"Of course you do." Gabby took a shaky inhale.

"We're just trying to protect you," Finn said. They weren't trying to babysit her. They wanted her safe. She mattered so much to them. To him.

"Gabs." Noah inclined his head.

"All right," she said on an exhale. "The office it is."

"Thank you." Noah dipped his head before glancing back at the board. "Anything I'm missing?"

"I'll continue to dig deeper on Litman Limited," Logan said, pushing away from the wall.

"I'll follow up with the guys who nearly ran Rissi over," Caleb said, his jaw tight.

"Since their bail hearing isn't set until 1400 tomorrow, Rissi and I should be back in plenty of time for it," Noah said.

"I definitely want to be present for that." Rissi linked her arms across her chest.

"I still can't believe that happened," Gabby said.

"I can." Caleb stiffened. "You'd be amazed at all the drunk and reckless boaters the Guard deals with."

"I'm just glad you're safe," she said to Rissi.

"We all are." Caleb squeezed Rissi's hand.

"Thanks, guys." Rissi smiled.

"Okay. On that note, I think it's time we break for the night." Noah turned to Finn. "Not to invite ourselves over, but I can't think of a better way to honor Sam . . ."

"Than a bonfire cookout in his honor," Finn finished. "I couldn't agree more." The best way to celebrate Sam's life would be with his favorite pastime. "I'll grab the meat on the way home," he said.

"I'll get the drinks." Rissi grabbed her blazer. She flipped it over her shoulder, holding on to it with two fingers as she stood.

"I'll bring cups and plates," Caleb offered.

"I can hit the store with Finn on the way back to the loft and grab dessert—watermelon . . . and marshmallows for s'mores?" Gabby said.

"I'll bring potato salad," Emmalyne offered.

"I'll bring my famous baked beans." Logan raked a hand through his spiky hair.

Emmalyne arched a brow. "You mean Bush's?"

He shrugged. "If it tastes good, why mess with it?"

"All that sounds great," Finn said before the two started one of their oddly flirtatious arguments.

"I'll get ice," Noah said. "Meet up in an hour?"

Everyone nodded.

Finn said good-bye to the night guard watching the drug runners, his muscles coiling as he scanned their unremorseful faces. He'd never understand how they could take lives so needlessly and then show zero emotion.

Gabby helped Finn carry the groceries into his house.

The tap of nails rushed across the kitchen floor as they stepped inside the back door.

An adorable black-and-white dog skidded to a halt at Finn's feet, its tail wagging furiously. This was a new addition since she'd left in March.

"Who's this?" she asked, setting the bags on the counter and kneeling to pet the Australian shepherd.

"Layla."

"Layla?" Her brows arched as a smile curled on her lips. Not a name she'd anticipated Finn coming up with.

"What?" He cocked his head.

"Nothing."

He leaned against the kitchen counter. "Seriously, what?"

"It's just kind of a girly name for a guy like you to give your dog."

The dog looked up and grumbled before laying her head back on the terra-cotta tile floor.

His lips slipped into a smile, his green eyes narrowing. "A guy like me?"

Heat rushed to her cheeks. "I just mean you're . . ."

He took a step closer.

She got to her feet as he stepped directly in front of her. Lifting a hand, he swept the hair from her forehead, tucking it behind her ear. His skin was calloused, but his touch tender. "I'm . . . ?" he whispered. The deep timbre of his voice was beyond appealing as it resounded through her chest.

She swallowed, dipping her head with a soft smile. "You're just . . . a guy's guy."

Pleasure flashed across his sun-kissed face. "So I'm . . . *manly*?"

She scuffed the sole of her shoe against the ceramic floor. "I just meant that you're the opposite of feminine."

"Hmm," he chuckled. "I guess I'll take that as a compliment . . . ?"

"Trust me." She nibbled her bottom lip, yearning for his to be pressed against hers. She swallowed, hard. "It was."

He leaned in, his gaze shifting to her lips as if he'd read her mind.

She leaned in to him and . . . then shifted upright. What was she doing? "I . . . better go get freshened up before everyone arrives."

He straightened, shoving hands into his pockets. "Right." He swallowed, his Adam's apple bobbing in his tan throat. He always had the best tan—no doubt from all his time surfing. "I'll walk you to the loft."

"That's kind of you to offer, but—"

He shook his head. "Not up for debate."

She sighed. Of course he'd say that. "Okay."

They stepped out into the balmy twilight, fireflies flitting across Finn's yard, the lap of the ocean echoing up the slope from the beach.

"I forgot how beautiful it is here," she said.

He glanced her way out of the corner of his eye. "Definitely *beautiful*."

She forced her gaze to her feet.

He saw her up the stairs and cleared the loft before stepping back out on the landing. "Oh, about Layla's name—Mom's a big Clapton fan. Listened to him all the time while I was growing up." He braced his hand on the loft's doorframe.

"That's nice. You've never mentioned your mom before. You two close?"

A smile curled on his sun-weathered lips. "Curious is a state of mind with you."

She shrugged. "Goes with the job."

"To answer your question, yes, we are close."

"That's nice."

"Yep. It is."

His cologne was enticing. His presence alluring. All the feelings she'd developed for him over the winter rushed back in an encompassing swell. "I should probably—" She pointed over her shoulder.

"Right." He stepped back. "I'll see you at the bonfire." He looked at his watch. "You've got twenty."

Anticipation rippling through her veins, she shut the door and leaned against it. Staying at Finn's felt far more dangerous than Fuentes did.

TWENTY-TWO

Gabby dropped her leather bomber duffel on the queen bed in Finn's guest loft. After the pace of the last twenty-four hours, she was looking forward to freshening up a bit. Her clothing and toiletry stash from the office didn't provide many options, but Kenzie had offered to take her shopping at Bumblebee, their favorite store in town. They always had the best variety of eclectic clothing. Of course, Noah and Finn would insist one of them escort her and her sister. It was a kind gesture but, at the same time, suffocating. She wasn't exactly helpless.

She gazed through the open windows. The rain, which had come and gone for a good portion of the day, appeared to be over, and a nice southwesterly breeze fluttered the gossamer curtains. The beautiful scent of salt water wafted through the space.

Being near God's creation reminded her of His sovereignty and majesty. Setting the moon in the sky to control the tides . . . it awed her. Jesus walking on water, calming the storm . . . Knowing He tamed something so wild and free settled her soul in a way nothing else did.

She exhaled. Despite being run out of Raleigh, which she hated—she'd much rather face things head on—at least she was in a beautiful place surrounded by family and Finn.

Finn . . .

She didn't understand the depth of feelings he'd managed to

resurrect in her the minute she was back in his presence. Feelings her heart instantly understood but her mind refused to process.

She grabbed the new cell phone Noah gave her when he'd picked her up. Lifting the phone to her ear, she listened as it rang twice, then she hung up as instructed. She waited five minutes for Lawrence to get clear of the building in case any bugs had been planted in the news office. Lately, it seemed like Xavier Fuentes, a man whose reach appeared unending, had been one step ahead. Lawrence had swept the office and found nothing, but they still wanted to play it safe. It wouldn't surprise her if they found a *Gazette* staffer to be on Fuentes's payroll, disheartening as it would be.

When she called back, Lawrence answered. "Everything okay?"

"Yes."

"No indication that Fuentes's men know where you are?"

"No," she said, sinking onto the bed. "And I think I've found a story."

"Of course you have."

"It's what I do."

"Believe me, I know."

She explained the situation with Will and Sam.

"I'm sorry to hear that."

"Yeah." She didn't know Sam as well as the rest of the team, but he was, from what everyone on the team said, a good man who'd been ripped from his family.

"So the story is Will Seavers?" he asked.

"Yes. Before Will left for fishing, he had a conversation with his wife, Tess. She said Will was quite upset and confessed to her that he'd screwed up and gotten in too deep."

"In too deep with what?"

"He wouldn't say, but he promised Tess he was getting out for her and the baby they're expecting."

"She's pregnant?"

"Seven months."

"Oh man. That's messed up."

She swallowed, her throat tight. "I know." Not only had Tess lost her husband, but their baby would never know his father. "She said she believed Fletcher was involved, and wants me, in addition to Noah's team, to dig into it."

"Did Will tell her Fletcher was involved?"

"No."

"Then why is she claiming he is?"

"Her feelings."

"We all know how dangerous and misleading those can be."

She knew that better than anyone. Her feelings had almost gotten her killed in South Sudan.

"Regardless, I want to find out what Will was involved in, for Tess."

Lawrence sighed. "She may not like what you find."

"I doubt she will." Discovering what Will was into could be painful.

"All right. Work the story, but keep a low profile. I don't want you showing up on the news as investigating the situation or making too much noise. I don't want Fuentes discovering where you are."

"He's got to know I'd come to my family."

"I'm sure he thinks you're too smart for that. You're not staying with your family, and if he sends someone, you'll be well protected. Not as protected as you would have been with the Marshals."

"That was my call."

"Let's just pray it doesn't get you killed."

TWENTY-THREE

A knock sounded on the loft door just as Gabby finished freshening up. Her breath hitched.

Finn.

Was he coming back to finish what felt like a near kiss?

Taking a stiffening breath, she opened the door to find Rissi.

"Hey." She released a sigh of relief.

"Hey." Rissi held up an aqua bag with pink flamingos. "Since you didn't get to go home before rushing out of Raleigh, I brought you some toiletries and clothes. I think we're about the same size."

Both were about five-seven, and Gabby guessed around the same weight.

"Aww, thanks. That's sweet of you." Everyone had been so kind.

"No problem."

"Come on in." She stepped back, allowing Rissi passage inside.

Rissi glanced about. "I hope the place still feels cozy to you."

"It's amazing. Thanks for decorating it before my last stay."

"When Noah told me you'd be staying over the winter, I knew the place needed a major overhaul. Unfortunately, I didn't have any time today to run over and check it out, but . . ." Her sparkling blue gaze swept the room. "But it looks in good order."

"Yeah," she said, also sweeping the room. There were fresh flowers in the blue pitcher on the distressed white desk, fresh bedding, a covered plate of fresh fruit, and a large bottle of Fiji water.

"Looks like Finn got everything ready for you."

"Yeah." It did. He must have gotten up early to do so, because he'd been on shift all day.

"I know Noah doesn't want you and Kenzie shopping alone but maybe he'd go for it if I came along. I've been dying to see what Bumblebee has gotten in for their fall collection—or should I say, slightly more warm summer collection." She smiled.

"True." Raleigh was the same way. "That'd be fun."

"Great. It's a date. And we'll see if Emmy wants to join us. She loves Bumblebee's boho style."

"She dresses so adorably."

"I know, right?" Rissi slipped her hands in her back jean-shorts pockets.

"Hopefully Noah will be satisfied with the group of us going. He seems set on either him or Finn watching me."

"Trust me, Noah won't hear the end of it if he doesn't hold me on par with the guys in keeping you safe. . . . Not that you can't hold your own, but it doesn't hurt to have someone watching your back."

"Thanks."

"Don't get too frustrated with the guys' attitude. I have to deal with it on a daily basis, being the only woman and the youngest on the team. You'd think I was the little sister of the group."

"I noticed that." She nibbled her bottom lip, wondering if she should go there, but the reporter part of her couldn't contain her curiosity. "Caleb seems particularly concerned about you."

Rissi exhaled. "I know what you're thinking. . . . Everyone seems to think there's something romantic there. He took me under his wing when I started the job and was a huge help. I guess we've been pretty close since. But . . ." She exhaled. "I view him as a teammate and friend."

"Not sure he views the relationship the same way." She was probably overstepping her bounds, but it seemed so obvious in the way Caleb looked at Rissi with longing.

"I know, and I feel bad, but I just don't feel romantically about him."

"You can't force something that's not there." Or stop something that was, no matter how hard she tried to suppress her feelings for Finn. Not even a day in his presence and all the tingling was back. This was going to be much harder than she'd thought.

After a few minutes of chatting, Gabby followed Rissi down the steps into the firefly-filled night. The bonfire danced in the stone circle on Finn's shoreline. Ten colorful Adirondack chairs sat around the fire, a couple feet back from the flames.

"Grab a seat," Finn said.

"I put the sweet tea on the picnic table." Rissi sat, lowering into the cobalt blue chair.

Gabby chose the bright yellow one, pulling her knees to her chest, tugging the loose-weave cream sweater over the cute black beachy shorts Rissi had brought her.

Finn stoked the fire. Sparks flittered into the night sky, carrying on the sea breeze. "I think everything's about ready." He gestured to Caleb finishing up the burgers and barbecue chicken on the grill. He transferred the meat onto a large oval platter.

"Looks great," Emmalyne said, taking the platter from Caleb and carrying it to the faded white picnic table a few steps up the gentle slope from the beach. Wrightsville Beach was gorgeous—sloping dunes with wispy reeds, pristine sand, and crystal-clear waters. No wonder Finn chose to live there.

"Food's ready," Emmy announced.

"Now we're talking!" Logan bolted up the hill, sand flying in his wake. His blue Jams with a white hibiscus pattern brought a smile to Gabby's lips. He wore vintage well.

Gabby followed him up the hill. She placed a chicken breast in the center of the Chinet plate and scooped a spoonful of Emmalyne's homemade potato salad onto it. She added sweet-smelling watermelon and maple-bacon baked beans.

"Hey," Kenzie said, waving as she rounded the corner of Finn's house. Her hubby, Mark, walked beside her. Six-two and two hundred muscular pounds, he cut an intimidating figure.

"Hey, kiddo," he said, ruffling the top of Gabby's hair.

He was all of four years older than she was, but he insisted on calling her kiddo or kid, as Noah did. At twenty-seven she was the youngest of the three siblings, and it appeared she would never outgrow the moniker.

"How you holding up?"

"I'm doing good."

Finn's assessing gaze settled on her from across the picnic table. How did he always seem to know when she was bluffing?

"Where are my niece and nephew?" she asked, shifting the subject. Missing them growing up while on assignment was hard.

"With Mom," Mark said, taking the red plastic cup filled with sweet tea from Rissi. "Thanks," he said.

"It's already way past their bedtime," Kenzie said.

Gabby turned, nearly colliding with Finn's chest. Splaying her hand out to brace herself, her palm landed on his chiseled chest.

Heat rushed to her cheeks, and she yanked her hand back to her side. "Sorry."

His gaze lingered on her. "No problem."

Grabbing her drink, she hurried to her seat by the fire and dropped into it, hoping her racing heart would settle.

Logan sat to her left, and Finn took the chair on her right, his aftershave wafting on the breeze. The cedrat essential oil in it smelled of adventure and the outdoors.

Finn glanced over, flames lighting his gorgeous green eyes. A slow, soft smile curled on his lips.

She offered a gentle smile back, and his widened, creasing the corners of his mouth.

Don't look at his lips. Forget how soft they are.

A different kind of heat than the fire sifted between them.

Logan stood. "Either of you need a cool drink?"

Gabby swallowed. Was the connection between them that obvious? "What?" she managed.

"I'm grabbing a soda." Logan gestured over his shoulder at the galvanized-metal washtub full of drinks.

"I've got tea, but thanks."

"I'm good too," Finn said, lifting his cup.

Logan nodded.

She set her cup back in the sand, her head spinning. It was the smart and logical thing to stay in Finn's guest loft for her physical safety, but for the safety of her heart and her already-weakening resolve—it was proving a dangerous decision.

TWENTY-FOUR

"Let's pray," Noah said as everyone settled into their chairs, balancing their plates on their laps.

Gabby lowered her head.

"Father, we lost a brother today. Beth lost a husband and Ali a father. We know that Sam is your child, Jesus is his Savior, and he's up in heaven with you now, but that doesn't stop the pain and loss we're all feeling here. Please help us in the days to come, especially Beth and Ali. Let them know they aren't alone. That you are right there with them in their suffering and that we are all here for them and always will be. Help us do as Sam would want and celebrate his life tonight. In Jesus' name we pray. Amen."

Gabby added a silent prayer for Tess and her unborn son. And for Finn and his double loss.

Biting into her chicken breast, she tried to shift her focus off the heartache and onto the here and now. The meat was cooked just right—charred by the fire and lathered with vinegar-based Carolina barbecue sauce.

The meal progressed to making s'mores with roasted marshmallows and telling both funny and heartwarming stories about Sam before everyone, one by one, said good night and headed home.

Caleb offered to see Rissi to her house, but she assured him that, while she was thankful for the offer, she was good. Disappointment creased Caleb's brow, but he simply nodded and headed for his car.

Suddenly Gabby realized it was just her and Finn remaining, along with the constant heat emanating between them.

"Want to go for a walk?" He gestured to the beach stretching out before them.

"Okay," she said, against her better judgment.

He walked on the ocean side of her, the surf foam tickling her feet as they stepped in and out of the high tide—the waterline nearly reaching up to the dunes.

Moonlight rippled along the surf, skimming across the ocean's surface. She took a deep breath of the fresh air and gazed up at the nearly full moon.

"Wanna keep walking, or are you ready to head back?" he asked, hope filling his eyes that they'd keep going.

She hated to disappoint him, but . . . "We should probably head back. It's been a long day."

"Totally understand." He shuffled his feet in the sand. "When Noah called about the attempt on your life it . . ." He paused to take a deep breath. "It . . . jarred me."

"You and me both." It was the second time in less than a year that someone had tried to kill her. Thankfulness for God's provision and protection swelled through her.

"No," Finn said, hitching to a halt.

She stopped, facing him, nervous about what he might say but curious to hear it.

He reached for her hand, and without thinking, she placed it in his. His hand was warm as he intertwined their fingers.

It took him a moment to find his words, but he finally spoke. "I mean it jarred me to the core." He stepped closer, closing the small gap between them. With his free hand, he cupped her face, and while she knew she ought to pull away she couldn't seem to move—rooted in place by his consuming touch.

He caressed her cheek, the pads of his fingertips sending tingles spreading through her limbs.

His lips parted. "The thought of losing you . . ." He swallowed. "I couldn't breathe," he whispered before pressing his soft lips to hers. Ah, she remembered how good it felt to be held by him. He deepened the kiss, and she melted into it.

As the kiss intensified, his fingers spread through her hair.

Somehow the kiss eventually ended, though in her dizzy state she couldn't remember how. They walked back to his property hand-in-hand, and after a soft kiss, she entered the loft, said good night, and shut the door behind her. She leaned against the wall, her knees nearly buckling.

What had she just done?

Rage flared hot beneath his skin. The fools had called the number he'd set in place to be used in only the direst circumstances. At least he'd learned of it through the line of communication he'd secured.

As he paced the small space, heat flared hotter, breaking a sweat on his forehead. "No loose ends. Do. You. Understand?"

"Yes, sir."

"I want them in and out like ghosts," he said, his voice harsh.

"Yes, sir."

He disconnected the call, still gripping the phone, his knuckles whitening.

Cricking his neck, he headed to his bed. He'd find sleep tonight, but those who'd let him down wouldn't.

Finn stretched out on his bed, his hands tucked beneath his head, though he'd much rather be cradling Gabby's. Her hair was soft . . . silky beneath his touch. Their kiss had been light at first, his lips brushing over hers, and then it deepened.

He inhaled, releasing it in a stream. He looked at the empty white pillow beside him, wishing her head were there, her hair splayed around her beautiful face. Wished she was his in marriage. Yet that seemed so far from a reality that it squeezed his chest—choking the breath from his lungs.

The moonlight shone through the upper windowpane, a cool breeze sweeping through the lower screen. The air was growing heavy—the sign of another storm rolling in.

He turned onto his side, scrunching the pillow beneath his head. Layla jumped up beside him, her tail wagging. She rolled around on the bed until she got comfortable. Within minutes, she was snoring, but he feared it might be another sleepless night for him.

Finn shot up in bed, sweat drenching his skin.

The clock read 3:57.

He rubbed his brow.

When had he fallen asleep?

He stood, heading for the kitchen and a glass of sweet tea. Leaning back against the counter, he swallowed a cool sip, the chill spreading through his lungs.

He took another, then set the red Solo cup down. He'd lost two friends yesterday, one in front of his eyes. And there'd been nothing he could do to stop it.

TWENTY-FIVE

His board secure in his hold, Finn paddled over the cresting surf to where the tide was swelling into a sweet, curling row of waves. While keeping a protective eye on Gabby, which he didn't mind in the least, he hadn't expected to have the opportunity to surf, but Noah had dropped by to see his sister, who hadn't come out of the loft yet. He said he'd wait around for her, so Finn had taken the opportunity to hit the waves.

Thanks to the string of storms brewing off the coast, the sea was a churning vortex of killer barrels to surf through—just what he needed.

He reached the calm point where stillness resided between the swells. It was the perfect spot—quiet, and yet adrenaline and anticipation pulsed through him.

His thoughts flashed to Gabby, to the feel of her in his arms. He swallowed, focusing back on the wave cresting above him. Picking the line he'd take, he paddled up into its belly. His soul soared as he rode through the tube, carving out as it dissipated.

He shook his head, water flicking off his hair as he headed for shore. He was so tuned in, he hadn't even noticed another surfer at his three o' clock. She glided effortlessly over the arch of the swell and down along its foaming and bubbling surface before riding it in to shore. Was that . . . ?

Gabby.

He'd never seen her surf before, hadn't known she could. He'd thought about asking if she wanted to head out with him for a lesson, but he hadn't wanted to risk waking her after the long day and late night.

The sun cast into his eyes, making her a beautiful, curvy silhouette in its bright glare.

She shifted out of the sun's direct rays, and he could see her fully.

Her dark hair was down, wet along her shoulders. No makeup covered her radiant skin. She looked fresh and natural—the short-sleeve rash guard accentuating her womanly figure. He swallowed as her long legs glistened in the morning's rays, sand covering her calves, her toes squishing into the billowy caramel shore.

She shifted her stance, the sun spilling over the slope of her right shoulder and back into Finn's eyes. "Why are you looking at me like that?"

"I didn't know you surfed."

Her fingers curled around her Billabong board.

"Where'd you get the board?" She certainly hadn't brought it with her.

"It's Kenzie's. Noah brought it this morning."

"But where . . . ?"

" . . . did I learn how to surf?"

"Yeah."

"There is surfing off Maryland's shores. Granted not the best, but it's there and a good place to get a foundation while we were growing up in Annapolis. Then I picked up more through my travels—South Africa, primarily."

She'd covered a lot of stories across the world. He could only imagine the places she'd been.

"You're good," he said.

"Thanks." She tilted her head with a smile. "You're pretty good yourself. You grew up surfing in Melbourne, right?"

"Yeah." He hadn't realized she'd paid attention to where he'd grown up—at least for the first fourteen years of his life. Right up until life imploded.

"I got to surf Bells Beach in Victoria once."

"You never told me you have been to Australia."

She shrugged. "It never came up."

He liked the surprise.

"Noah left for the competition when I headed out to surf. He told me not to make you late for work, so I better grab a shower. What time do you want to leave?"

He narrowed his eyes. She willingly agreed to go into the office with *him*? Even if it had been decided last night, her going without a fight was far from the norm. Rather, he believed the woman lived to vex him.

"Earth to Finn . . ." She waved her hand in front of him.

"Right. How soon can you be ready?"

"Fifteen. Twenty-five, if I grab breakfast."

"Take your time. I'll make breakfast."

"Great. I worked up a good appetite."

He watched her cut a swath across his lawn, her bare feet skimming along the grass. Man, she was a sight to behold.

Finn glanced at Gabby in the passenger seat beside him. She'd chatted during breakfast and was relaxed as they drove into work. He'd half anticipated she would withdraw after their kiss last night. They'd need to talk about it at some point, but for now he just wanted to hold her hand. He reached toward her, sliding his fingers between hers, caressing her silky skin.

She bit her bottom lip, and her hold tensed.

He knew it was coming, but he wasn't going to be the one to bring it up.

"I'm sorry," she began, sliding her hand out of his, leaving it cold. "I'm so sorry. I . . ."

He swallowed. He had no intention of arguing. "I understand."

She pulled her bottom lip into her mouth, then released it, her shiny lip gloss still on.

He gripped the steering wheel, not wanting his disappointment to show. She wasn't ready, wasn't in the same place as him, despite the kiss.

"It's not fair to you for me not to make up my mind." She swallowed. "To kiss you when I'll be leaving again." She turned to look out her window.

He focused on the road, letting the subject drop, like his heart. He'd tried before to reach that part of her that cared about him romantically, but in the end, she'd left. He wasn't interested in round two—not if he was setting himself up for the same brutal ending.

She remained silent the rest of the ride, nibbling on her bottom lip, her arms linked over her chest.

Arriving, he cut the ignition, got out, and opened her door for her.

"Thanks," she said. So much emotion welled in her eyes. Why couldn't she let a little spill out?

Quite pleased at being first to the office, Finn unlocked the office door, switched on the light, and turned off the security system.

Gabby set her bag on her brother's desk, feeling like the biggest jerk in the world. What was wrong with her? Giving in to her feelings for Finn meant being vulnerable and ultimately having to give up the job she loved in Raleigh. The former had sent her packing to Raleigh in the first place, and now she had the latter to consider as well.

She cared about Finn. *A lot.* She just wasn't ready to be back in that place again. She'd fallen hard over the winter. And against her hopes, it hadn't eased up. Her heart was still attached to his.

She sank down into Noah's chair.

Who was she kidding?

She was in love with the guy.

She exhaled, so many words dancing on the tip of her tongue. *Just tell him.*

She stood, ready to say . . . what, exactly? That she was wrong to pull back, that her heart screamed to jump in fully?

Fear held her back. Fear her heart would get broken again. But Finn was nothing like Asim. Why was it so hard to wrap her head around that?

Finn stood from his desk. "I'm going to let Hal know he can go."

"Hal?"

"The night guard. I'm surprised he hasn't checked on our entry."

"Gotcha. I'll go make some coffee." She stood and moved for the small kitchen.

Finn nodded and disappeared down the hall. She'd barely slipped a clean filter into the basket when he came tearing into the room, his gun drawn.

"What's wrong?" she asked as he pulled her close and moved her behind him.

"They're dead," he whispered close against her ear.

"What? Who?"

"Hal and the drug runners. I need to clear the office."

She kept in step with him, leaning against the wall just behind his shoulder before they rounded the corner.

She grabbed her purse as they stepped past Noah's desk, retrieving her Springfield 9mm. "I'll help."

Finn arched a brow but didn't ask.

The steel cool in her palm, she helped him clear the office.

"Where'd you get a gun?" he asked, slipping his into the back of his pants.

"I bought it years ago."

"I didn't even know you knew how to shoot."

"Please. With an older brother like Noah? He taught me and Kenz before we'd even graduated high school."

The front door opened, and Gabby aimed her gun at it as Finn retrieved his.

Emmalyne entered and hitched midstep.

"Sorry," Finn said, returning his gun to his back waistband.

Gabby lowered hers and slipped it into her purse. She always carried it with her, except the night of the gala. That little sequined clutch had nearly ended her life.

Emmalyne didn't move. Her gaze fixed on Finn. "What's going on?"

"They're dead."

"Who?"

"Hal and the prisoners." Finn lifted his phone.

Emmalyne's round eyes widened. "What?"

"I need to alert the rest of the team," Finn said, dialing and excusing himself.

Five minutes later, he returned to her and Emmalyne. "Caleb is nearly here. But I had to leave messages for Logan, Rissi, and Noah."

"Rissi and Noah are at the competition in Topsail," Gabby said. "Where's Logan?"

Emmy leaned against the edge of her desk. "It's his day off, and he's on a deep-water fishing expedition. Most likely out of cell range for the day."

"What happened?" Caleb asked, striding in, his shoulders rigid.

"Hal's dead in the hallway, and the drug runners are dead in their cells."

"How?"

"No clue how they got in here, but it looks like a professional hit. All with a single shot to the head. And the weird part is . . . the way the bodies are lying, it almost looks like they all lined up at their cell doors and . . ."

"Just took it?" Caleb's brown eyes narrowed.

"I don't know." Finn shook his head. "I'm basing it off my first glance at the crime scene. I'll know more after I determine the bullets' trajectory, study the blood splatter, etc., but that's what it looks like."

"Was the security system on when you came in?" Caleb asked.

Finn nodded. "Yes."

Caleb released a heavy exhale. "That makes this even more frightening."

"I agree. They either knew the code, which is a terrible possibility, or they figured out a way to bypass it."

Caleb raked a hand over his cropped hair—quite similar to Noah's, except for the tinge of blond. "I'm hoping the latter," he said, pushing off the desk he'd been leaning against and moving around to sit at his desk. "I'll get started on the video footage."

"I'll help." Emmy moved to Caleb's side. "Two pairs of eyes are always better than one."

"Agreed," Finn said. "I'll put a call in to the ME's office before I start processing the bodies. Then I'll do a full sweep of the office. Maybe we'll get lucky and find a fingerprint on the security system, the door handle, the windows . . ."

"Need any help?" Gabby asked.

"Sure," he said. "I never turn down an extra pair of hands. Unless you feel it might be too upsetting."

Too upsetting? This crime scene couldn't possibly be worse than some of the atrocities she'd witnessed in South Sudan.

TWENTY-SIX

Rissi's heart raced as she settled into her waist harness, spreading her kite out in front of her in the water. The wind was perfect and should fill the kites quickly once the race started.

"You and me, Dawson," Travis said, wading farther out against the oncoming tide.

"Don't count me out," Noah called.

The three were frontrunners for bragging rights and the coveted challenge trophy.

At the starting horn, the wind quickly caught her kite. It billowed and lifted. Her board skimmed over the restless seventy-degree surf. Spurts of water streaked over her toes, tickling them as she glided over the ocean's surface on her kiteboard.

She caught a glimpse of dolphins off to her nine. Their fins arched above the waterline, then dipped below as they swam alongside the competitors.

Pulling on the right string, Rissi shifted to grab the best stream of air, gliding in front of Noah.

"Let's see what you got," he said with a playful smile.

Her board rushing over the cresting waves powered by the kite's tug was nothing short of the best adrenaline rush she'd ever experienced.

Glancing over her shoulder at Travis falling farther behind both her and Noah, she smiled. It would be so satisfying to beat him and his obnoxious attitude.

An earth-shattering roar quaked across the water. Fire flashed high in the sky. A boat? *Dear Lord.*

Heightened waves rippled under her board, nearly tossing her into the churning sea. She shifted her stance, just barely managing to stay upright. A cold weight settled over her, queasiness in the pit of her stomach.

Red-hot flames mingled with charcoal plumes of smoke on the horizon. The boat had to only be a handful of nautical miles away.

Please let whoever was on board be all right.

Her muscles rigid, she jumped at the sound of Noah's voice. "Beach patrol will have seen the explosion and called it in," he said.

Her throat tightened. "We need to get out there." Needed to help.

"Agreed." Noah nodded.

The hum of a boat's motor rumbled, the water choppy in its wake.

Beach patrol.

Thank you, Lord.

"Get in," Tim said as he idled the boat beside them.

Rissi unhooked from her kiteboard and swam to the boat's starboard side. Tim extended a hand, and she grabbed hold, letting him heave her in. He reached for her board and rigging, lifting it into the craft behind her.

Noah followed. "I need to radio the Guard base," he said, setting his gear and board in the vessel.

"We put in a call straightaway. They said the copter's ETA is ten, and they'll have rescue swimmers," Tim said, relaying the information.

"Thanks." Noah swallowed, concern etched across his

pinched brow. "I'm going to call the station, let the team know."

"Of course," Tim said, gesturing to the radio at the ship's helm.

A chill tingled along Rissi's limbs, gooseflesh rippling up her arms.

Please let everyone be all right.

"Caleb," Noah said.

"I heard." Caleb's voice crackled over the radio. "I hate to tell you this, but it's Mo's boat."

"Mo?" Rissi's heart thudded in her chest.

Noah's face paled.

"He called in the Mayday. Said there'd been an explosion and they were abandoning ship."

"He say how many on board?"

"Ten."

Which, with his usual crew of four, meant he had six passengers on board.

Please let them all be okay.

Noah lowered his head, his softened gaze sweeping over Rissi before he asked Caleb, "Did he say if everyone survived the explosion?"

"He didn't . . ." Caleb paused for the beat of a breath. "The call dropped before Mo finished talking."

Rissi balled her hands into fists as the boat sped toward the flames and Mo Tucker's boat. She'd always liked the old seadog. The whole team, save Emmy and Logan, often took dive charters with him and his crew. Young Braxton, a mere nineteen, flashed through her mind. And Marv, the stalwart one of the crew. Her last wreck dive, they'd all been laughing and merry. How would she find them now? *Would* she find them?

She swallowed, her throat swelling. Couldn't the boat go any faster?

What felt like an eternity later, the two bright yellow life rafts came into view. She spotted Mo's ash-covered face and sighed with relief. He was battered but alive. As were Jack, Braxton, and Marv.

She did a quick count. *Nine.*

Heaviness sank in her chest. Mo had said ten on board.

TWENTY-SEVEN

Rissi's muscles coiled. Had someone been left behind, or were they lying in the bottom of one of the life rafts?

Noah's jaw tightened, a muscle in it flicking. He was clearly wondering the same thing.

"Good to see you guys," Mo said from one of the yellow-and-black octagon life rafts. The charter passengers were secured in orange life vests as the rafts bobbed in the arriving boat's wake. Slack faces and dazed expressions stared back at her as she assessed each passenger for obvious signs of injury.

The chop of helicopter blades cut through the air above.

Rescue *swimmers*. Hopefully they could retrieve the missing passenger. She looked back at the *Calliope*. Half-ablaze and half-submerged—she was going down fast.

How did a lifelong seadog lose his vessel?

Rescue swimmers jumped out of the helicopter, fins first. They splashed into the water five yards north of the life rafts.

"Please," a forty-something woman with wet curly hair cried. "My husband is still on the boat."

"Do you know where?" the brown-haired swimmer asked as the blond swimmer turned and headed for the sinking ship.

"He's dead," Mo said. "Don't risk your life trying to get him."

"Dead?" Rissi's chest squeezed.

"Please." The woman sobbed. "Please don't let John sink with the ship."

A young woman wrapped her arm around the sobbing woman's shoulder, rubbing her trembling arms.

The blond rescue swimmer halted twenty feet from the boat, waiting at the outside edge of the debris field.

The second swimmer reached his side, assessing the ship.

A horrible crack emanated from the *Calliope*. Rissi watched in horror as the boat split in two. The aft bobbed upright in the sea, then rapidly sank below the surface.

"No!" The woman shot to her feet, hollering.

The rescue swimmers held at the edge of the debris field as the boat fully submerged below the surface as the ocean swallowed it whole. They turned and, with sad expressions, swam back to the rafts.

"I'm sorry, ma'am," the blond swimmer said. "It sank far too quickly. It wasn't safe to enter. I'm very sorry," he said, bobbing in the wave-churned water.

Wailing, she crumpled into the raft.

Finn finished placing the scene markers at all the pertinent spots in the second dead prisoner's cell.

Sitting on his haunches, he surveyed the space to double-check his work, then glanced over at Gabby. Possessing a strong constitution necessary to work a bloody crime scene without losing her breakfast, she was proving to be a great help.

"Ready for the next round of pictures?" he said, getting to his feet.

She nodded, her cheeks losing their color.

"You okay? I can take it from here if you'd like—no problem."

"No." She shook her head, lifting the camera. "The distraction is good." Color rushed back to her face. "I'm so sorry. That came out wrong." She lowered her hands, holding the camera at her side. "It's just . . ." She bit her bottom lip.

He stepped to her side, warmth radiating through his chest with love and compassion for her. "You're worried about Noah."

She swallowed, glancing at the floor. "I know he'll be all right. . . ."

"It's natural to worry."

She shrugged. "Yeah. I suppose so. I just heard *explosion* and . . ."

He rested a hand on her shoulder. At first she tensed, but then her coiled muscles softened beneath his touch.

She blinked, her long lashes fluttering as she looked up at him. "Thanks."

He brushed a stray hair behind her ear, letting his fingers linger a moment longer than he should, but he couldn't help himself. He was drawn to her like the tides were to the moon.

She blinked again.

"Hey, guys," Caleb said, rounding the corner.

He halted a few steps in, his gaze falling over them. "Sorry. I didn't mean to interrupt."

She took a pronounced step back and swiped her nose. "It's fine. What's up?"

Finn's hand still tingled from her touch.

Caleb exhaled. "You're going to want to see this."

Rissi clasped the woman's trembling hand, helping her from the raft up into the patrol vessel. The Coast Guard ship out of Wrightsville Beach gave an ETA of fifteen minutes. A second out of Wilmington would arrive shortly after.

In the meantime, they'd deemed it best to secure the passengers on the beach patrol vessel.

Noah gave Mo, the last to board, a hand onto the ship.

He was covered with ashes, his short-trimmed hair thickly powdered.

"What happened?" Noah asked.

"I'll tell you what happened." The woman broke from Rissi's grasp and hurried to Noah's side, lunging at Mo.

Noah's eyes widened as he moved to restrain her.

She flailed in his hold. "He"—she fixed her gaze on Mo— "let John die."

"Whoa!" Noah said. "Take a deep breath and tell me what happened."

"My husband died from a blow to the head."

Noah's brows arched, his gaze darting to Mo.

Mo exhaled. "Mr. Layton was in the bathroom, not feeling well after his dive. We were headed back to the marina at a good clip. The boat was rocking. He must have lost his balance and hit his head on the sink."

Mrs. Layton shook her head. "It's your fault he was sick in the first place." She lunged back at Mo, but Noah's grip held firm.

"It's your fault he's dead."

TWENTY-EIGHT

Finn watched the video footage with a mixture of shock and, though he loathed the crime itself—four men were dead because of it—an odd sense of appreciation for a masterful plan.

"As you can see," Caleb said, pausing the footage as the men entered the building dressed in wet suits, "they kept their heads down and averted their gaze. It's like they knew where the cameras were."

"Juan was quite glance-y while he was on the phone," Emmy said. "Do you think he relayed information about the cameras?"

"Like he knew they were coming?" Gabby asked. "Why would he give their murderers that kind of information?"

"Maybe he thought they were coming for another purpose," Emmy said.

Gabby shifted to Finn. "You said based on the bodies' positions it looked like the men lined up at the cell doors."

Finn's sandy blond brows hiked. "What if they thought the men were coming to rescue them?"

Mrs. Layton flailed at Mo, who took a step back as Noah again wrapped his arm around her waist. She was a feisty lady, seriously struggling to break free of his arms.

"You are responsible for John's death, and don't think I won't pursue this."

Mo's face flushed. "John ignored our instruction regarding scheduled stops on the way up to avoid the air bends. He panicked and shot for the surface. That was *his* decision."

"There's no way the impact necessary to cause such damage to his head could occur from a bump on the sink."

Mo snorted. "What, are you a doctor?"

"As a matter of fact, I am."

Mo's shoulders straightened. "It doesn't change the facts. He hit his head. End of story."

Her eyes narrowed. "I think you killed John. Whether by accident or on purpose, I don't know."

"Why on earth would we kill your husband?" Mo swiped his hand in the air. "I'm sorry for your loss, lady, but it's gone to your head."

Was there any chance that what Dr. Layton claimed was true?

Noah saw the same question in the glance Rissi sent his way.

He wished they could discuss an approach to this mess, but after another heated argument with Mo, the woman collapsed into Noah's arms, sobbing.

"It's going to be okay," he said, hoping to calm her.

He escorted her to the port side of the ship, but Mo followed.

"Her accusations are ridiculous. My crew did everything by the book."

That had been his experience with Mo and his crew whenever he'd wreck dived with them.

Rissi stepped in front of Mo. "I need you to return to the starboard side."

"I understand she's upset, but this isn't right," he called over Rissi's shoulder as she pushed him away. "She can't blame my crew."

Dr. Layton attempted to bolt from Noah's hold yet again, but he tightened his grip.

She wrestled, squirming in his arms. "Stop doing that. I want answers. I want the truth."

"I need you to calm down," he said in a gentle-yet-firm voice.

She looked over her shoulder, her back to him. Eyes red-rimmed and puffy blinked up at him. Anger and fear brewed in her gaze. "Calm down? My husband is dead, and you expect me to calm down?"

"I'm extremely sorry for your loss, but your attempts to lunge at Mo aren't helping anything."

Mo shuffled, trying to step past Rissi, but she held her ground, blocking him from Dr. Layton.

"You need to listen to me," Dr. Layton said, tugging at Noah's arm.

"And I will. After you're cleared at the ER, you can tell me everything you'd like to."

"That goes for me too!" Mo yelled from the starboard railing, pacing like a caged lion behind Rissi's blockade.

TWENTY-NINE

Noah and Rissi stood at the ship's bow, glancing back at the pair of medics examining the passengers.

Cool sea spray tickled her face as they sped to the waiting ambulances, which would transport everyone to the nearest hospital.

Rissi took a calming breath and released a slow exhale. "What do you make of all this?"

Noah glanced at Mo, then shifted his gaze to Dr. Genevieve Layton on the opposite side of the ship. "I'm not ready to pronounce judgment. We'll question everyone as soon as the ER clears them. But Dr. Layton seems genuinely convinced the crew is to blame for her husband's death."

Rissi sighed. "I agree." She shifted, leaning against the boat's edge. "I just can't see Mo or any of the crew being anything but one hundred percent cautious on Mr. Layton's dive."

Noah rubbed his chin. "Maybe there's another reason she blames them."

Rissi's brows arched, surprise riddling through her. "You think foul play *was* involved?"

Noah leaned next to her. He linked his arms across his broad chest. "I can't help but wonder at the odds of Mr. Layton having a problem with his dive and then a ship so well run as Mo's exploding."

Accidents occasionally happened on boats—people getting

injured, tanks rupturing, fires starting—but as fast as the *Calliope* sank, the explosion had most likely ripped all the way through the keel. The odds of both happening at the same time were unlikely. Was it possible John Layton's "accident" had been no accident at all?

The heavy menthol odor of Vicks tickled the base of Gabby's nose. It was a trick Finn had shared for masking crime-scene odors, or at least making them less pungent. And he was right.

She'd been exposed to death many times on her BBC assignments, and the memories of death always lingered. As did the sight of the night guard's shocked expression plastered on his face. He'd died in horror.

The office door opened, and she glanced to it. Finn's hand rested on his gun, as did Caleb's. Her chest tightened, then relaxed as a short man, best described as petite, entered. Mid-fifties, graying hair, wearing a brown houndstooth jacket, wide-brimmed straw hat, and taupe trousers. He tipped the brim of his hat. "Afternoon. It's far from good, given the circumstances."

"Agreed." Finn released a slow exhale. "Ethan Hadley, this is Gabby. Noah's baby sister."

Gabby sighed. Did he always have to add *baby* when he introduced her? Yes, she was the youngest of her siblings, but at twenty-seven she was hardly a baby.

The man's chestnut eyes settled on her. "You can call me Hadley," he said, crossing the room toward her. "A pleasure to meet you, my dear."

So this was the medical examiner the team had spoken about with admiration. She stood and extended her hand. "Same."

"I'll escort you back," Finn said, striding around the desk to Hadley's side.

"Ladies," Hadley said, dipping his head in her and Emmy's direction. "Lovely scarf, Emmalyne."

Her hand reached to it, her fingers tracking the beautiful yellow leaves artfully arranged on the sheer white background. She wore matching sunshiny yellow dangly earrings and necklace charm, hanging low on a silver chain. Emmalyne carried an air of whimsy with her, and Gabby was thankful for the dash of light in an otherwise bleak and startling morning.

Swirling red lights marked the marina parking lot just above the boat ramps.

Rissi was ready to be back on land. Keeping guard over a pacing Mo and a lunging Genevieve Layton had required her and Noah's constant attention for the majority of the ride back.

Rissi tried to talk to Genevieve, but she'd asked to be left alone.

They'd given the woman space, but Rissi was anxious for her and Mo to be cleared for questioning after being checked out at the local ER. She needed answers to the rattling questions inside.

THIRTY

Hadley emerged from the cells and lifted his chin at Finn as four paramedics rolled the dead men in black body bags out the front door.

Gabby swallowed.

"I'm finished here and will conduct the autopsies tomorrow—at least two of them," Hadley said. He took a stiff inhale. "Speaking of autopsies . . ." He fingered his earlobe. "I don't mean to be insensitive, but I figured you'd want to at least know, if not attend . . . given the circumstances." He rocked back on his heels. "This incident threw me off my schedule a bit, but I'll be performing Petty Officer Seavers's autopsy upon my return to the morgue."

"I want to be there," Finn said.

Gabby reached for his hand. "Are you sure? He was your friend, with a personal connection—"

"I *need* to work this investigation like any other. I owe it to Will."

She nodded, self-conscious as Caleb's astute glance shifted between her and Finn. "Okay." She cleared her throat. "I'll stay here. I've got some work to do."

"All right." Finn looked at Caleb, and he returned a firm nod.

She rolled her eyes. He was transferring babysitting duty to Caleb. While she appreciated their concern, she was a skilled and capable woman, though it seemed everyone was ignoring that fact. "Can I use your computer while you're gone?" she asked.

Finn's brow arched. "Sure. . . ."

The curiosity dancing in his green eyes was obvious, but he didn't need to know her purpose.

Gabby snuck into the bathroom and called Tess on the cell Noah had given her.

"Hey," she said, whispering just in case Emmalyne entered.

"Why are you whispering?"

"I'll explain later." She peeked over the stall to make sure she was still alone. "I'm working Will's case, and I'd like to start with Fletcher's estranged wife. Do you know where she is?"

"No . . . I've only heard a few rumors about what went on." She was quiet for a moment. "I guess I could ask around . . . if you want me to."

"No, that's okay. People might wonder what's going on if you start asking questions. I'll check into it."

"All right. Call me if you find anything."

"Absolutely." She tucked the phone in her pocket, washed her hands well. Trying to look as nonchalant as possible, she settled back into Finn's desk chair to do some research on Valerie Fletcher while Finn was at the morgue attending Will's autopsy. She was worried about him and said a prayer for God to protect his heart during it.

It might take her a while to find what she needed on Valerie Fletcher, but she wouldn't stop until she did. Thankfully, uncovering information was her gift from God.

THIRTY-ONE

Rissi paced. She clenched her hands into fists, then shook her fingers out. Glancing at the clock, she exhaled.

It'd already been two hours. "How much longer do they expect it will be?" she asked Noah as he entered the private consultation room—one of two they'd been given by the co-operative hospital staff to question everyone after they'd been released from the ER.

Noah handed her the can of Coke he'd grabbed from the vending machine.

The can was cool in her palm. She tapped the top after the tumble it no doubt had taken dropping into the bay of the outdated vending machine in the nurses' station.

He set his coffee cup on the small table between the stacked magazines and the short brown lamp. "They said Genevieve is still pretty upset, understandably. They don't want to release her until she's calmer."

"That might be a while." She felt for the poor woman, but the best way to help her was to encourage her to share what was brewing inside. To let her get all her concerns and fears out.

"They said they might keep her for overnight observation."

"Really?"

"She's having dizziness and nausea that won't abate."

"They think it's dive related?"

"No. Just stress induced, but they aren't comfortable releasing her. They said most likely she'd be placed under a twenty-four-hour observation."

"Poor lady." Rissi slid her hands into the pockets of her white shorts, once again not having anything to change into since the challenge. It felt odd to be working in such casual clothes and under the chilly AC. Gooseflesh, alternating with heat, flushed her skin.

She popped open the soda, a burst of carbonation releasing. She took a sip, thankful for the sugar rush. It'd been hours since she ate, but she was too preoccupied to bother seeking out food.

"They'll grant us access to her as soon as she's either stable and released or settled in her room," Noah said.

The analog clock mounted on the wall ticked the time away.

Rissi plopped into one of the chairs lining the wall, releasing a puff of air as impatience pricked at her. Was there any way what Genevieve Layton claimed could be true? She hated to ponder the implications if it was.

Noah's tight jaw said he feared the same.

THIRTY-TWO

The information Gabby had been searching for popped up on her screen twenty minutes later. *Bingo*. The address of Dennis Fletcher's estranged wife.

She looked around. Caleb was replaying the video feed for Emmalyne while zooming in to see the wet suits' brand, which might be possible to track to a local scuba shop.

As stealthily as possible, Gabby placed a call to Tess Seavers.

"Hey," she said in a hushed tone when Tess picked up. "It's Gabby."

"Did you find her?"

"Yep. Could you pick me up at Noah's office?" she whispered, thankful Caleb and Emmalyne were so fixated on their work.

"Sure. I can be there in five, but you really think Noah's just going to let you out of his sight?"

"He's on a call, and Finn's at the morgue. I'll fill you in when you get here. Pull up on the south side. I'm coming out the bathroom window."

"Seriously?"

"Seriously." She switched back to speaking at normal volume as Caleb's inquisitive gaze shifted to her. "Yeah, my stomach's off. Breakfast must not have settled right."

"Good play," Tess said.

"Thanks. I'll talk to you soon," Gabby said.

"Grabbing my purse now," Tess said.

"Bye." Five minutes after hanging up, she excused herself for the bathroom. Finn and Noah would be as mad as all get-out, but something was going on. She could feel it, and she wasn't wired to ignore a story. She'd be safe. She was with a friend. There'd been no sign someone was after her here, and she'd be back within the hour. Finn could berate her afterward.

She waited until she saw Tess pull up in Will's truck. Flipping open the window, she popped out the screen and crawled out. She hurried to the truck and jumped in the passenger seat.

Tess pulled out of the lot. "Hey, girl. So where are we headed?"

"Val Fletcher's house," Gabby said, looking over her shoulder, thankful to find no one following for her. "Let's hope she can provide some answers." She gave Tess the address and exhaled with relief once they were off the base and out on Route 14.

She glanced about her, surveying Will's truck. Tess had driven her car yesterday. "So . . . Will drove his truck the night he . . . disappeared," she said, thinking that might hit a little softer than *died*.

"Yes, he did," Tess said as she turned onto Magnolia Lane.

Gabby's brows pinched. "Then, where'd you get it?"

"It was still parked at Fletcher's when I went to look for him. My brother helped me pick it up this morning. I wanted it back."

That's right, Tess had mentioned that. Gabby realized she hadn't asked many details because she'd been too focused on the *why*s rather than the *how*s.

"I think you said they launched from a dock on Fletcher's property?"

"Yep." Tess nodded, chewing her minty-smelling gum.

She needed to check out his place, his dock—see if any clues had been left behind. "You said Valerie Fletcher is his *estranged* wife. Do you remember anything else about what went on with them?"

Tess's chipped pink nails tapped the wheel. "Let's see. Val left, and I heard she's living with another man. They had an affair. I think his name is Kenny . . . if I remember right. Anyway, the two of them supposedly ran off together, but neither she nor Dennis has filed for divorce. At least not last I heard."

"If that's the case, then I'm guessing Val technically is still part owner of the house."

Tess frowned. "I suppose. . . . Why does that matter?"

"Because if Val gives us permission to search Fletcher's house and vehicle, as long as they're still legally in her name, then we aren't breaking any laws."

"Man, you *are* good at this."

"Thanks. Now, would you mind if I look through Will's truck while we drive to Val's?"

"No problem, but what are you looking for?"

"Anything that might provide a clue—or better yet, an answer—to what Will might have been involved in."

Gabby started with the glove box, pulling everything out and flipping through the registration and car manual. Halfway through the latter, she pulled out a red-and-white entrance pass of some sort.

"What's that?" Tess asked, her gaze darting to the pass, then back to the road.

Gabby held it up. "You've never seen this before?"

Tess shook her head. "Nuh-uh."

"Let's ask Val about it. Maybe Fletcher had one, too, and if so, maybe she'll know what it's for."

Anything that would give her a clue about what they'd been up to.

THIRTY-THREE

After an unexpected meeting with a colleague, Hadley signaled Finn into the autopsy room as his coworker exited. Finn pushed off the wall he'd been leaning against.

"Sorry about that," Hadley said as Finn followed the ME into the sterile autopsy room.

"No problem." He was anxious to get back to Gabby though. It was impossible to stop himself from worrying about the girl. It was rather frustrating, but also warming, to realize how deeply she'd burrowed into his heart.

Finn paused at the sight of his friend on the steel table, a paper sheet covering him from waist to knees. The sanitizer scent emanating from Hadley's tools and the sight of the gleaming sink and spotless counter space were a stark contrast to the heavier odor of decay thick in the air.

Hadley slipped on his blue paper mask and settled his protective glasses in place.

Finn swallowed. This was going to be harder than he'd thought. He took a moment to swipe Vicks under his nose, then folded a stick of cinnamon gum into his mouth. He hoped to prevent the odor of death from seeping into his mouth and settling on his tongue. It was the strangest sensation to taste death, but it was similar to the way the scent of buttery popcorn seeped into one's mouth, lingering on the taste buds and causing one's mouth to water—obviously the latter a far better sensory experience. The former was beyond unsettling.

"James, my colleague, needed to confer on a case," Hadley explained.

"Everything okay?"

"Just some peculiar findings."

Finn didn't prod any further, knowing Hadley couldn't share details about a case that wasn't his. Shifting his thoughts to the case at hand, Finn stared at his friend's prone body as he strode to the steel table. Will's eyes were closed, the bullet holes prominent on his body.

"I took photographs from head to toe while James and I were discussing his case. Now it's time to examine the wounds and interior damage." Hadley inhaled and released the breath in a whoosh, his gaze fixing on Will's body.

He didn't have to expound. It was time to cut into his friend.

Finn's muscles tensed further, unease raking through him. Maybe this wasn't the best idea after all, but he owed it to his friend to work the case as he would any other.

Hadley switched on his headlamp and directed the adjustable overhead light onto Will's forehead wound. He ran his gloved hands around the edges, then measured the wound. "You said there were no guns retrieved on the boat?" he asked as he proceeded.

"No. Will must not have been armed."

"Probably thought it was unnecessary for an evening fishing trip."

Maybe if Will had brought his service weapon, as Finn did everywhere, he would have been able to defend himself. Maybe he would still be alive. Though *maybe* was a dangerous word. He had to stick to the facts rather than conjectures.

Hadley moved to the first of the chest wounds.

Finn still couldn't help but wonder why two different weapons were used. Had there been two different shooters? Fletcher claimed two men had boarded his boat. Had both shot Will with different gun models?

Hadley retrieved his bone saw. "Now for the messy part." He narrowed his eyes, his gaze fixed on Finn over the edge of his paper mask. "Are you sure you want to be in here for this?"

Finn nodded. "Positive."

"While I begin . . . the file on John Doe's autopsy is on the counter." Hadley gestured across the room with a lift of his chin. "Thought you'd want to take a look at it."

Finn was thankful for the distraction as Hadley made his first cut into Will's sternum. The saw buzzed. The scent of burning bone trailed after Finn as he strode to the counter. He flipped open the cover of Hadley's report on the drug runner still identified as John Doe.

The sight of Sam being shot, his body flinging back with the impact, the shock radiating in his dimming eyes reverberated through Finn.

Please, Father, help me through this torrent of emotions. I feel like I'm sinking. Please lift me above the water. Help me to keep my eyes on you. Don't let me drown in this case.

Two friends were dead, and now *all* the drug runners responsible for the shootout were dead. Who'd killed them? And why?

Perhaps to keep them quiet, to get rid of any loose ends? Maybe even to punish them for failing to kill Fletcher or for getting caught?

Whatever the reason, they were dead, which just left the evidence. Finn prayed the clues were enough to solve the case.

After scanning the autopsy report, he flipped to the photographs and paused. The man had numerous scars—the one near his rib cage the work of a serrated blade. Hadley's notation confirmed Finn's assessment. He had a healed bullet wound to the right of his heart. He'd clearly seen some action.

Finn's cell rang. "Sorry," he said to Hadley over his shoulder as the saw stopped.

"No problem. We'll be here."

Finn nodded and stepped into the hall, thankful for the fresh air as he answered the call. "Hey, Caleb. What's up?" He prayed there'd been a break in the case.

Caleb cleared his throat. "Gabby's gone."

Finn's muscles coiled. "What?" A chill crept up his spine.

"I'm sorry. I was tracking down info about the wet suits from the security footage. I was on the phone pretty much constantly." He cleared his throat again, tension tight in his tone. "Gabby said she was heading to the restroom. When she didn't come back, I sent Emmalyne in. Turns out Gabby popped out the window screen and left."

Without a car of her own, she must have gotten a ride with someone. "Any idea where she went or with who?"

"Don't know the *who*. But despite the fact that she'd erased the history off your computer, Emmalyne was able to retrieve the intended location. Looks like she was searching for Valerie Fletcher's place."

"Valerie Fletcher, as in Dennis Fletcher's estranged wife?"

"Yep."

"Got an address?"

"She did a fair amount of searching, but yeah, she found her."

The girl was good.

Caleb relayed the address.

"Got it. I'm on my way." Finn hung up, apologized to Hadley for having to leave, and darted for his Rogue.

When he found Gabby, it was going to take every ounce of his restraint to keep from strangling her.

THIRTY-FOUR

Tess pulled Will's truck to a stop in front of the trailer. The double-wide sat along the marsh-lined river about a half hour from Wilmington. Aged pine trees dotted the landscape, their needles cushioning the path to Val's front door.

Tess opened the storm door and knocked.

A man with a wrestler's build—tall but stout, with wide shoulders, bulky arms, and a wide stance—answered. His questioning gaze shifted from Gabby to Tess, whom he studied as if he were trying to place her.

"Hi, I'm Tess. I think we met a while back. I'm here to see Val."

He continued appraising her for another moment before recognition dawned. "Right." He snapped his fingers. "Hang on." Keeping the door open, he called Val's name into the house, his deep voice echoing through the trailer.

Val Fletcher stepped to the door. She was brunette and petite. "Tess! I heard some ladies in town talking about Will. I'm *so* sorry."

"Thanks." Tess nodded, her fingers fidgeting with the small white pom-poms decorating the fringe of her maternity top. "Could we chat for a minute?"

"Sure." Val stepped out to join them in the warm September air. She gestured to the wooden picnic table nestled beneath a giant pine tree. "How about over here?"

"Great," Tess said. "Thanks for chatting with us."

Val nodded and led the way across the pine-needle-covered yard. She took a seat at the well-worn table and gestured for them to do the same. Tess sat sideways to avoid pressing against the table's edge with her baby belly. Gabby sat beside her, eyeing the silver double-burner grill standing on the concrete slab to the right. She bet Val and Kenny spent a good many nights out here. And with the incredible view of the river, she didn't blame them.

"So what did you want to know?" Val asked.

"Anything you can tell us about Dennis," Gabby said.

Val's arch-shaped brows hiked. "Who are you?"

"I'm sorry," Tess said. "This is my friend Gabby. You may remember her brother, Noah Rowley."

"Sure. The handsome one." Val smiled, glancing back to the trailer to make sure Kenny hadn't overheard them. "So what specifically do you want to know?"

"Honestly, anything you can tell us could be a huge help."

Val chuckled, but there was no humor in it, more like an edge of bitterness. "I could tell you a lot."

"Start anywhere you'd like," Gabby said, knowing they needed to learn all they could about the man lying in a hospital bed.

Val's brown eyes narrowed, her fake lashes fluttering with each blink. "What's this all about?"

Tess twirled one of the pom-poms on the fringe of her shirt through her fingers. "I'm . . . we're . . ."

"Trying to determine what kind of man Dennis is. Is he an upstanding guardsman, or is there another side to him?" Gabby said, her gut indicating the latter, but she had nothing concrete to base that on.

"Another side . . ." Val snorted. "Dennis is the kind that likes to punish women. Infer from that what you will."

Tess's widened gaze fixed on Val. "What? Are you saying . . . ?"

Her lips thinned. "That man took pleasure in knocking me around."

"I'm so sorry," Tess said. "I had no idea."

"No one did." Val shrugged a shoulder. "And I wasn't saying anything."

"Why not?" Gabby asked, not trying to be rude but truly curious. Had Dennis held something over Val to keep her quiet? Or was he just that scary? Maybe she thought she had no place else to go.

Gabby looked back at the trailer . . . thankful Val had gotten out alive. Many women didn't.

Val leaned in, lowering her voice. "Kenny gets enraged if he hears Dennis's name. Not with me," she clarified. "With Dennis."

"Understandable," Tess said.

"It was all I could do to keep Kenny from killing him when I finally told him."

Gabby understood his anger.

"Here's the thing. Dennis knew how to hurt me in a way that didn't readily show. It's my fault for not leaving sooner, but . . ." She glanced down, spinning the silver knotted ring on her index finger. "My old man was a mean drunk too. It was all I knew—until I met a good man, that is."

As if knowing he was being discussed, Kenny popped his head out of the trailer, his protective gaze fixing on Val. "Everything okay?"

Val nodded. "Just girl talk, babe."

"That's my cue to leave." He gave a friendly wave and let the storm door shut.

"Kenny's a big teddy bear," Val said with the smile of a sixteen-year-old smitten with her first big crush.

Tess squeezed Val's hand. "I'm happy you escaped Dennis."

"Thanks. Me too."

Tess raked a hand through her long, layered blond hair. "I'm still so sorry that I missed what you were going through. Maybe if I'd paid more attention . . ."

"Trust me. No one had a clue. We were good at hiding it—both my scars and his angry outbursts. I thought I was stuck in that life forever, but then I met Kenny at the gym." She smiled. "He's a keeper."

"I'm glad you found someone you can trust," Tess said. "But I can't help but wonder . . . I mean, now that you are out . . . why not file charges against Dennis?"

Gabby was thinking the exact same thing.

Val looked up, nervousness flickering over her up-until-now calm demeanor. "I just wanted out. Kenny had a short talk with Dennis, and he agreed to let me go. That's all I wanted. Out."

Gabby studied Val, curious how she would have handled the same situation. Her instincts said she'd have gone to the cops the first time he'd touched her. At least that's what she hoped she'd have done. Though she'd learned long ago that it was easy to judge, but until you were in someone else's place, you never knew for certain. Her heart ached for the life Val had endured until Kenny, but she was glad she'd found a kind, protective man.

She shifted her attention back to Val and realized she and Tess had still been chatting while *she'd* been ruminating in her thoughts.

"We were hoping we could ask you some questions," Tess said. "I'm just trying to find out what happened to Will."

Val's eyes softened. "I'm so sorry about Will, honey." Her gaze slipped to Tess's very pregnant belly.

Tess bit her quivering lip. "Me too."

"Not sure I can be of much help since I'm not part of that life anymore, but I'll give it a shot."

Not part of what life? Gabby wondered. Did she just mean she no longer lived with Dennis or that she didn't participate in the Guard life? Or was she saying she'd been part of something more? Something that had ended with Will's murder?

"Anything you can share might be helpful," Tess said, shifting her gaze to Gabby. "She's an investigative reporter and is helping me find out what happened to Will."

"A reporter?" Val's jaw tensed.

"Don't worry," Gabby assured her. "Anything you say is off the record."

The tightness in Val's shoulders relaxed. "Okay. Ask away."

"Will told Tess that he was into something too deep," Gabby began.

"Like what?" Val asked.

"I have no idea," Tess said. "It floored me when he said he was into something questionable. I mean, he'd been stressed for a while. Money was tight, and with Will Jr. on the way . . ."

Tess rubbed her belly, and she took a deep breath as tears welled in her eyes. "I told him I could get a part-time job and find a friend to watch the baby when he came, but Will knew how badly I wanted to be a stay-at-home mom. He told me it'd be okay, that he'd take care of things. And then a couple days later, it seemed like everything was all right. He was relaxed and happy for about a month." Her hands knotted into fists. "Then he got really stressed again."

"Worrying about money again?" Gabby asked, not having heard this part yet.

Tess shook her head. "No. It was different, like something heavier was weighing on him. I kept asking him what was wrong. Then right before he left for the fishing trip, he told me that he'd gotten in too deep." She shifted. "I asked him what he was talking about, what he'd gotten too deep into, but he wouldn't go into specifics." Tears streaked down her face. "I think he was trying to safeguard me by not sharing, you know?"

"Of course he was, honey," Val said. "Will always looked after you."

Tess nodded, tears rolling off her chin. "Right before he left, he also told me he was getting out of whatever he'd gotten himself into." Her voice cracked. "Next morning, he was found murdered on Dennis's boat."

"We were wondering . . ." Gabby said, "if perhaps Dennis knew what Will was involved in, or if . . . ?"

"Dennis was involved?" Val said.

"Yeah." Gabby nodded.

"Wouldn't surprise me at all," Val said, her hands fluttering about as she spoke. "In fact . . ." Val leaned closer across the table. "I'd bet Dennis was the one who got Will involved in the first place."

"Really?" Gabby asked. Now they were getting somewhere.

"Pish," she said. "Dennis was *always* into something."

"Do you know any specifics?" Gabby prayed for a concrete lead.

"Nah, he never shared anything with me, but I ain't stupid. I could tell when he was running a scam."

"A scam, huh?"

"I'd wager money on it."

Gabby fished the red-and-white access tag from her purse. "Any idea what this is? We found it in Will's truck."

Val studied it, then shook her head. "Sorry. Never seen it."

Which brought Gabby to the big question. "I'm guessing your name is still on the house and car?" she asked, clearly pressing her luck with such a personal question.

"Ye . . . ah." Val's eyes narrowed. "Dennis believed that I'd come running back at some point. That's never gonna happen, but I didn't know what he'd do if I filed first."

"I don't suppose you still have a key to the place?" Now she was beyond pressing her luck, but Val clearly had no love lost for Dennis. If she might be of help in bringing him down, Gabby felt Val would jump on the chance.

"No," she said, "but he keeps a key in a lockbox on the doorframe—inside the screen door."

"Do you remember the code?" Assuming it was still the same.

"Last code he used was 1942—the year his dad was born, but why are you asking about the house and Dennis's car?"

Here went nothing. "Any chance we could have your permission to search them?"

"Sure." She shrugged. "What do I care?"

Finn pulled into Val Fletcher's driveway and banged the steering wheel at finding Will's truck not present. He'd asked the guard at the base's exit gate who he'd seen leaving at the approximate time of Gabby's exit, and the guard said he'd seen Will's truck drive on and then quickly off base. Tess was driving and a pretty brunette was with her.

So Gabby was off with Tess, which equaled nothing good.

He looked at the blue Maxima in the driveway, praying it belonged to Val and that she had some idea where Gabby and Tess had gone.

At his knock, a woman opened the screen door, eyeing him warily.

"Hi." He flashed his badge. "I'm Finn Walker with CGIS."

"I heard what happened with Will and Dennis. You the one looking into it with Gabby and Tess?"

So they had been here.

"Yes," he said, thinking that bending the truth might gain her cooperation more readily than explaining that Gabby and Tess were not supposed to be meddling in the investigation, period.

Val scrutinized him.

"Please. It's very important I find them. Their lives could be in danger."

Val's eyes widened, but surprisingly, she didn't ask for details. "They went to Dennis's place."

Great. Now they were breaking and entering.

"After I told them my name is still on the house and car, they got really excited and hightailed it out of here."

Smart, ladies. Though he'd still need to throttle Gabby for sneaking out of the station.

"Thanks so much," he said, rushing back down the porch steps, praying with all his might that they were safe. He'd been doing a lot more praying lately. Praying for Gabby and her safety.

He climbed into his car and released a shaky exhale. The woman worried him to no end.

THIRTY-FIVE

Rissi finally got the go-ahead to talk to Genevieve Layton in the hospital room where she'd be spending the night.

She knocked on the door of Room 341.

"Yes?" Genevieve called.

Rissi opened the door and popped her head in. "Hello, Dr. Layton. Is it okay if I ask you some questions?"

"Yes, but please, call me Genevieve," she said, sitting up in bed. She tucked her hospital gown beneath her legs. "I don't know why they insisted on my wearing this lovely frock." She rolled her eyes. "I'm not injured or sick—at least not physically."

Rissi looked to the reclining mint green armchair. "Do you mind if I sit?"

"Please." She gestured to the chair. "I'm glad you're here."

"Oh?"

"Yes. I have so much to tell you, and I didn't want to say anything about this in front of the crew. Didn't want them trying to explain it away or blame John, like they did with the dive."

Rissi scooted to the edge of her seat.

Please, Father, help me get to the bottom of this.

The last thing she wanted was to discover that Mo or his crew was responsible in any way for John Layton's death. But she wanted the truth wherever it led. "Can I get you anything? Water, perhaps?"

"I have a hot cup of tea on the way, but thank you." Genevieve's eyes were still red-rimmed and puffy, a slight daze lurking there. No doubt from the calming medicine she'd been given.

"All right," Rissi said. "How about you tell me everything you remember about the day—starting with when you arrived at the marina this morning?"

Genevieve swiped her fingers across her cheek, wiping a tear away as she licked her swollen bottom lip. She'd spent the majority of the return trip nibbling it.

"John . . ." She cleared her throat. "We arrived at the marina at six, as instructed. Since we'd gone over all the instructions and questions at an orientation prep class the afternoon before, we headed straight onto the boat. Once everyone finally arrived, we cast off. That was right around six thirty. Why the Thompsons kept us all waiting a half hour, I don't know. I find that sort of behavior rude, and so does . . ." She caught herself but couldn't prevent the fresh tears from tumbling down her cheeks. "John," she finally squeaked out.

Rissi handed her a box of Kleenex from the side table. "I'm so sorry for your loss." She waited as the woman sobbed, giving her the time she needed. "Would you like me to step out and give you some privacy?" she asked.

Genevieve pulled a Kleenex from the box, swiped her eyes, and blew her nose. Tossing it in the round metal trash can in the corner of the room, she grabbed another. "No. It's fine. Thank you for asking, but I want to tell you what I know about what happened. Though I wish I knew more."

Rissi frowned. "What don't you know?"

"What happened on the dive."

"I thought he ascended too fast?"

"Yes, that's what they claim, but I wish I knew *why*."

What was she getting at? "It's not uncommon for people to panic during a wreck dive, especially if they're new to it."

"It was his second qualifying dive." Genevieve sniffed.

So he was still working on his wreck-diving qualification, which made the likelihood of his freaking out far higher than that of a well-established wreck diver.

"It's not uncommon for people to panic from the claustrophobic nature of swimming in such tight quarters."

She thought of her experience exploring the same wreck. The *St. Marie*, an eighteenth-century Spanish galleon, had been found and subsequently looted a handful of years ago, before the discovery became public knowledge. They'd never found the person or persons responsible, but it was a *very* tight dive. Even she'd gotten claustrophobic. Had Noah's soothing presence not been with her, she could have very easily panicked.

"John didn't get claustrophobic, and yes, he was a novice, but he loved wreck diving."

"Then, any idea why he panicked and bolted to the top?"

"All I can think is that something made him fear for his life."

That seemed a little extreme. "Why do you think that?"

"Because of what John said when he came back on the boat. He was upset. . . ."

"I think we're getting a little ahead of ourselves, Genevieve. How about we go back to the beginning? You made it to the dive site, and . . ."

"My dive was an easy thirty-foot dive with the other people on board. John was the only one working on his wreck certification. He and Marvin were still getting ready when we entered the water."

"So Marv went down with John?" The way Genevieve had attacked Mo, Rissi assumed that *he* had been the one diving with John.

"Yes." Genevieve nodded.

"Then why blame Mo?"

"Because it's his charter. Marvin is his employee, and Mo's the one who'd taught John to wreck dive. He's the one ultimately responsible for every passenger, and that includes John.

Either he didn't teach him right, sent John too deep and in too complicated a wreck, or his employee wasn't a good enough diver to take him. And he's the one claiming John lost his balance and hit his head."

"But you don't believe that?"

"No." Genevieve shook her head.

Rissi needed to run a timeline, beginning to end, so she could see the whole picture. "Let's get back to Marv taking John to dive."

"Right. I surfaced from my dive and saw the two jumping flippers first off *Calliope*'s aft deck."

"And then?"

"Our group—including Mo and Braxton, who'd accompanied us and instructed our dive—headed back on board. We all went down to change. When I returned on deck, Braxton was carrying a tray of fresh fruit and a variety of snacks over to us. I joined the group at the stern, but I had an anxious stomach."

"From your dive?"

"No. I just felt nervous for John. It was a big dive for him, and . . . I don't know. I was worried about him. He hadn't quite been himself lately."

"How do you mean?"

"He was stressed."

"Any idea why?"

"I think work has been extra busy. Plus we totaled our car last month, and the insurance has been a nightmare to deal with. Just annoyances, really. But when we won the trip, I thought it was the perfect opportunity for us to get away from it all for a while."

Rissi's eyebrows pinched. "You won the trip?"

"Yes. Mo said he puts the names of all his charter customers in a bag, and twice a year he chooses a name to win a follow-up dive or cruise or whatever you want out of his services."

"Wow. That's nice." She wouldn't mind winning one of those.

"It was. . . ." Genevieve swallowed. "Until today."

"How long before John returned?"

"Maybe a half hour."

"What happened upon his return?"

"He surfaced alone, and I asked him where Marvin was. He mumbled something I couldn't understand. I could tell by the edge in his voice that something was wrong."

"But nothing to indicate what it was?"

"No."

"He yanked off his fins and dropped them on the deck. Braxton helped remove his tanks, and then he ripped off his mask. He looked pale, peaked. He said he needed to head to the bathroom. I hurried after him, catching him on the galley stairs, and asked what had happened."

"He said something had gone very wrong. They were in the wreck and . . ."

"And?" Rissi again scooted to the edge of her seat, balancing her weight on the balls of her feet.

"He cut off his words there. Told me to go above deck and stay with the group. 'No matter what, stay with the group,' he said."

"Did you ask him why?"

"I didn't have a chance. He ducked into the bathroom with panicked eyes, said 'I love you,' and shut the door." Tears spilled down her eyes. "I knocked, but he continued insisting I go up and stay with the group." She shook her head. "Something was obviously very wrong, but I had no idea what, so I did as he said. Marvin was back and talking with Mo in hushed tones at the stern."

"Any chance you overheard what they were saying?"

She shook her head. "I wish I had. Maybe then I'd know what happened down there."

"Did you ask Marv about it?"

"No. John told me to stay with the group, so I did. I assumed he'd be up soon, so I could ask him, but . . . he never came up."

Rissi reached out and clutched Genevieve's cold hand. "Do you need an extra blanket?"

"No."

"Knock, knock," a woman said from the doorway.

"Come in," Genevieve said.

A full-figured woman with a cheery smile entered with a tray. "I've got your tea, and I brought you some shortbread cookies. Fresh from the cafeteria kitchen."

She set it on the tray table on the right side of Genevieve's bed.

"Thank you," Genevieve said, wasting no time in lifting the Styrofoam cup, wrapping her long fingers around it.

"Is there anything else I can get you?"

"I'm fine, but thank you," Genevieve said.

She turned her gaze on Rissi. "How about you?"

"I'm fine. Thank you."

"Okay, you take care now, Miss Genevieve."

Rissi felt like a heel continuing the questioning, but it was the job and the best way she could help a grieving wife. "I know this isn't easy, and I hate to prod. . . ."

"I'm glad you're asking. It means you're interested in finding out what happened to my boo."

Rissi warmed at the special name Genevieve had for her husband.

"When John didn't come up to join us, I went to check on him."

"And?"

"And the bathroom door was locked. I knocked, but he didn't respond. I called out his name, but no response." She took a couple deep breaths. "I started to worry. He hadn't looked well, and now he wasn't responding. That wasn't like him. He never ignored me.

"I called his name louder. Another crew member—I think his name was Jack—must have heard me, because he came rushing downstairs. He tried the door and then told me to stand back, and he kicked it open. I looked in. John was on the floor, his head gashed and bloody. I rushed for him, but Braxton held me back."

"Braxton was there too?"

"At that point, yes. He must have heard the door break down or my scream. I don't know. I just wanted to get to John, but Jack rushed in and tried to rouse him. He checked his vitals and then looked at me, and I knew." She rubbed her neck. "I got sick. . . ."

"That's a perfectly normal reaction."

She nodded. "Mo rushed in and asked what happened."

"What about Marv?"

"No." She shook her head. "He wasn't there. When we headed back up, he was at the helm. He must have been covering for Jack while he was down with me."

"What did the crew do then?"

"Braxton got me a towel to wipe my face. And Mo instructed him to escort me up. I didn't want to leave John, but he insisted—said I didn't need to see John like that. Braxton took me to the bow for some fresh air, and next thing I knew there was this jarring quake and heat rushing at us. Mo came running up, saying we had to evacuate. It was all a blur from there."

"The crew started evacuating everyone to the life rafts?"

"Yes, but I stood my ground, not wanting to leave John behind. I tried to get Mo to get him, but he kept insisting they needed us in the life rafts. That it was too late. Water from the cabin was spilling out onto the top deck."

So many questions were swirling through Rissi's mind. She

needed to speak with Marv next. And once the *Calliope* was deemed safe to dive, Noah and most likely Finn, now that Sam was gone, would dive down and retrieve John Layton's body so he could be autopsied.

"Did you tell any of the crew what John said to you when he came up from the dive?"

"No." She bit her bottom lip and inhaled. "I just had this feeling not to. That's why I was so anxious to speak with you away from the crew." She leaned forward, her small blue eyes tinged with fear. "Do you think they killed my John?"

"I don't—"

The door pushed open, and a woman who looked like Genevieve, only a couple decades older, rushed in.

"Mom." Genevieve reached out her arms, her face crumpling in pain.

"Oh, honey." She rushed to Genevieve's side, enveloping her in a hug.

"John . . . is—" she hiccupped as sobs burst from her lips—"dead."

"I heard. I'm so sorry, baby."

Rissi stood. "I'll let you two have some privacy."

Genevieve reached for her. "Will you talk to them? Find out what happened?"

"I will make sure we look into everything." She nodded. "I'm going to set my card with my cell number on it on the table, just in case you think of anything else."

"Thank you."

She greeted Genevieve's mom with a dip of her head and saw herself out.

It was times like these, seeing a mother love on her daughter, that the realization of being an orphan tugged hard at her heart.

She'd dealt with years of heartache and loss of a different kind, but there'd been no one who could truly comfort her. Not since Mason.

THIRTY-SIX

Gabby and Tess pulled up to Dennis Fletcher's house, a two-story Cape Cod on the outskirts of Wilmington. It was situated on the Golden River. Though, on closer inspection, dark brown was probably a more apt description. Tess told her the unique coloring was a result of the tincture of the trees leeching into it. Whatever the reason, it gave Gabby the willies to think that alligators were lurking just below the murky surface.

They pulled to a stop beside Fletcher's burgundy SUV and found it unlocked. Gabby started with the glove box but had no luck in finding a matching pass to Will's. She searched the passenger-side door pocket as Tess did the same with the driver's side.

She was just about to give up hope of finding anything when Tess flipped down the visor to find a zipped compartment with a red-and-white pass inside.

"Good job."

"I think I'm getting the hang of this."

Now they had to figure out where the passes led to. Perhaps a garage or a storage unit? Wherever they led them, Gabby prayed it was one step closer to whoever was behind Will's death.

What Will and Dennis were involved in kept tracking through her mind. And how were the drug runners tied to Litman Limited?

Why had Will gotten involved with any of this mess in the

first place? She'd gotten to know him well during her three months in Wilmington last winter, seen how deeply he loved Tess. How he doted on her. How proud he was when she first announced her pregnancy. Gabby had been there for that happy occasion. Now, six months later, he was dead. His baby would grow up never experiencing his daddy's love. Will must have been seriously strapped financially and worried about providing for his wife and baby to get involved in anything illegal, which was most likely the case.

"You ready, Gabs?" Tess asked.

"Yeah, sorry. Just running things through my head."

Tess offered a smile—or at least the tug of a small one—though sadness still welled in her eyes. "I figured. Does that mind of yours ever stop?"

She shook her head. It made finding rest interesting at best. "Nope." She exhaled, blowing a strand of hair from her face. Gooseflesh ripped up her forearms at the memory of Finn's touch, of his fingers slipping the same loose strand—the one that always was unruly—behind her ear. How he'd lingered there, his face inching closer to hers . . . and . . .

She took a deep inhale. That was a place she couldn't return to, couldn't dwell in. She couldn't risk her career for another man, even one as good as Finn. She'd risked her reputation for Asim, and he'd destroyed it along with nearly ending her life. If the SEAL team hadn't come running over that desert mound, firing shots when they did, she'd be dead. The sight of Asim dropping lifelessly to caramel sand, granules puffing up in the wake of his collision, flashed through her mind. Gunfire resounded in a series of pops through her ears as her heart thudded—

A hand landed on her shoulder and she jumped.

"Sorry," Tess said. "You just looked off."

Gabby smoothed her hair back. "I'm fine. My mind's just racing today." She straightened her shoulders, pushing the memories to the back of her mind, where they lived. "I'm good. I'll head in, and you wait in the truck. And lock the doors."

Tess frowned. "What?"

"I don't think there's any chance of anyone coming by with Fletcher still in the hospital, and we're legally here, but just in case, I'd feel much better if you'd wait in the car and keep the doors locked. Any sign of trouble, get out of here."

Tess pursed her lips. "Pleeease . . . not happening."

"Tess. I'm serious."

"Just as I'm sure Finn and Noah both were when they told you to stay put."

"Perhaps."

"And just as you ignored them, I'm ignoring you." She shut the driver's door and strode toward the house. "Let's go."

Tess was just as stubborn as she was. She'd come in one way or another.

"Fine. But stay by me. Deal?"

"Deal."

They crossed the lawn smattered with patches of grass and dirt. Climbing the front steps, Gabby opened the storm door. The lockbox was right where Val said it would be.

She punched in the combination Val had given, and it slid open as she depressed the button. Fletcher hadn't changed it since his wife left.

Opening the main door, they entered the foyer. The living room sat to the right, and they moved into it. A cocoa brown reclining sofa and matching loveseat with burgundy pillows took up the majority of the space. An easy chair angled to face the large flat-screen TV.

"What are we looking for?" Tess asked, glancing around.

"Anything that might tell us what illegal activity Fletcher and Will . . ." Gabby bit her lip. She was pretty sure all they had learned indicated Will's involvement, but she hadn't meant . . .

Tears welled in Tess's brown eyes.

"Oh, Tess. I'm so sorry. I didn't mean to say Will was into something illegal."

"It's probably the truth. It's just . . . until you said it out loud, it didn't really register. But the way he spoke about it and the stress he was under . . . he was clearly involved in something very bad, most likely illegal." She rubbed her belly, tears falling.

Gabby wrapped her arm around Tess's shoulder. "Will loved you fiercely. If he did anything illegal, I'm sure it was just as he said—he'd been trying to provide for you and the baby. He just went about it in the wrong way."

Why had she spoken before thinking? Her mind had just been wound around the case so tightly. She hadn't even considered her friend's feelings before the word *illegal* left her mouth. She *had* to stop doing that. She feared Finn was right—that she put tracking down a story before everything and everyone. She hadn't believed it when he said it, but now . . . What was driving her so hard? Her desire to be there for Tess or her desire to crack a story?

She felt like the greatest heel in the world. "He was getting out for you and Will Jr., because he loved you. He told you he was getting out."

Tess sniffed and nodded. "You're right." She brushed back her tears. "Let's get to searching."

"Hang on," Gabby said, pulling out two pairs of latex gloves she'd snagged from the box at the station. "We want to make sure we don't contaminate any evidence, just in case the investigation leads here."

"Right." Tess slipped on the pair Gabby handed to her before sifting through the mail stacked on the hallway table.

Gabby surveyed the space. "I wonder if Fletcher has a study or home office?"

Tess nodded. "Spare bedroom upstairs."

Right. With Dennis being Will's superior and fishing buddy, it was only natural Tess would have been to Fletcher's house before and spent time with him and Val.

Tess followed Gabby upstairs. "First door on your right."

"Gotcha." Gabby jiggled the handle. *Locked.* A smile curled on her lips. Rarely did one lock a home office unless one was hiding something.

Lifting up onto her tiptoes, she ran her gloved hand along the top of the doorframe. Her fingers clasped a slender bobby pin–like key. She lifted it down and smiled. Nearly every house came with several, in case a kid accidentally locked themselves in one of the rooms and was too little to open it. Popping it open, she stepped inside, Tess behind her.

Two matching bookcases lined the far wall, with a five-drawer black file cabinet in between. She strode to it, and as she'd expected, the drawers were locked.

"See if the key is in one of the desk drawers," she said to Tess, who was already rooting through them.

"On it."

She turned to the bookcase to the left. Mainly books—most on guns, ammo, and fishing—but a few knickknacks. One of Val's touches, no doubt. Gabby's favorite by far was the crystal duck on the third shelf. She lifted it up, surprised at its weight, and smiled at the key taped to the shelf underneath.

As she reached to pull off the key, a creak sounded below. Tess's gaze flashed to hers. "Was that—"

"Shh." Gabby held a finger to her lips and moved for the door, the heavy duck grasped in her hand. She'd been so distracted by trying to get Tess to stay in the truck, she'd forgotten her purse—and thereby her gun—in Will's cab.

Footsteps pounded up the wooden stairs.

Gabby signaled for Tess to hide behind the desk, and after a moment of flurried hand gestures between them, Tess ducked beneath it.

Gabby's breath hitched in her throat, her heart racing. She pressed herself against the wall. Whoever it was paused a moment in the hall, then moved closer. *One, two, three* . . . She swung with all her might at the sight of a gun pointing through the doorway.

The man fell backward, slamming into the floor. Gabby looked at the blood dripping from the base of the duck, then to the man with a nasty gash on his head. Then her gaze tracked to the Glock on the floor beside him.

"Gabby!" a male voice called from the back of the stairs.

Finn? "Up here."

His footfalls echoed up the steps, and he rounded the corner with fear in his eyes. His gaze shifted from her to the duck to the man on the floor. He kicked the man's gun away. "Are you okay?" he asked, looking up at her as he bent to cuff the man.

Gabby nodded and turned to find Tess rounding the desk toward them. "Are *you* okay?"

Tess, trembling, nodded. "Are you?"

Adrenaline burned through her limbs, her heartbeat still spiked. Otherwise, she was fine. "I'm good."

Finn glared at her, his face tinged red. "*Good* is the last thing you are. And I'm probably not half as mad as Noah's going to be."

She swallowed. "Wait a minute . . . how'd you know we were here? I mean, I'm assuming Caleb told you I was missing, but how'd you figure out—"

He rubbed his hands together. "I'm just that good."

Gabby rolled her eyes. "Uh-huh."

He shook his head. "It's a long story. One best saved for later."

He pulled out his cell and, after explaining everything, requested Caleb's presence. "I need you to escort the suspect into the station while Gabby and I see Tess safely home. Yes, he is still out." Finn studied the man. "But I think I see some movement. I'd order a medic too. . . . Thanks." He hung up and turned back to the man.

The man's eyes opened, and anger flashed across his face.

He yanked on the cuffs as an expletive slipped from his gritted teeth.

"Easy now," Finn said, aiming the muzzle of his gun at the man's bloody forehead. "There are ladies present."

"I don't care if the bloody"—a second expletive, crasser than the first, spewed from his mouth—"queen of England is present."

"Let's get you downstairs until Agent Eason arrives." Finn hauled the man to his feet and headed for the stairs.

The man looked over his shoulder at Gabby. "I'll be seeing you again, if you don't let this drop."

"You won't be seeing anything outside a jail cell for a good long while," Finn said, his hand gripping the man's upper arm.

The man snorted. "How little you know."

Gabby's gaze narrowed. "Let *this* drop?" she hollered down the steps after the man. "What do you mean?"

The man strained his head back, creepy pleasure dancing in his eyes.

Gabby followed them into the living room, where Finn read the man his rights, before moving into questioning. "Did Fuentes send you?"

The man's face pinched, confusion filling his eyes. "Who's Fuentes?"

THIRTY-SEVEN

Rissi found Marv Lewis in one of the ER rooms, stitches lining the gash on his forehead.

"How you doing, Marv?"

"Can't complain. I survived an explosion."

"I need to ask you a few questions when you're done here."

"As busy as they are, it'll probably be a while before they discharge me. I'm fine with you asking me now."

"Okay, great." She turned and shut the glass door behind her.

"So what do you want to ask me?" Marv said, flattening out the sheet around his legs.

"Can you walk me through your day? Specifically, your dive with John Layton?"

"Sure," he said, being oddly pleasant. Marv had always been polite but had never come across as friendly. "Everything was going fine. It was a normal day, a smooth dive, until he panicked on the ascent."

"Panicked, why?"

"I don't know. I can only assume the depth had gotten to him. It was only his second wreck dive, and as you know, the *St. Marie* has tight corridors. As soon as we exited, he shot for the surface. It's no wonder he was disoriented and hit his head on the sink."

"You saw him disoriented?"

"No. I made the required stops on the way up, so he was

already in the bathroom by the time I surfaced. With that rapid of an ascent, he'd be feeling the effects. Not to mention, it was a bumpy ride back to the marina. A strong wave, the ship bouncing, it'd be easy enough for anyone to lose their balance. Poor guy just got knocked the wrong way."

"Where were you when he was found?"

"I was talking with Mo at the stern about the dive and what happened and then we heard Mrs. Layton scream. Jack handed the helm to Braxton and raced down. Then we heard a huge crash, and Mo instructed me to take the helm and Braxton rushed down. Mo checked to make sure all the topside passengers were okay, then he headed down as well. Next thing I know, Braxton is escorting an extremely pale Mrs. Layton topside."

"Is that when you learned Mr. Layton had died?"

"Yes. Mrs. Layton was crying. Braxton explained everything and then sat with her. Jack came up and said Mo wanted to see me, so we swapped places and I headed down."

"And what did you find when you got down there?"

"Mr. Layton laid out on the floor. Next thing I knew there was a loud explosion and we were abandoning ship."

"Before the dive, did you thoroughly instruct Mr. Layton about the necessity of dive stops during the ascent?"

Marv's shoulders tensed and broadened. "Of course. He'd already had the training, but we always go over it just to make sure people understand the importance. I explained that because of the depth, we have regular hold spots on the way up to avoid decompression sickness. I also explained that occasionally folks got freaked out about having to ascend slowly, but it was absolutely imperative for the client's safety. John said he understood."

"So let's backtrack. You see John Layton on the floor, and then how long would you say it was until the explosion occurred?"

He shrugged. "From the time I got downstairs, maybe five minutes."

His initial comment suggested it had happened almost instantly. "Five minutes?" she confirmed.

He shrugged again. "To the best of my recollection."

"And what happened during those five minutes?"

"Well, Mo and I double-checked that Mr. Layton was deceased. Then he started to go to call the death in, but the explosion nearly knocked us off our feet. Water came rushing in, and Mo and I moved Layton's body to try and get him out of the water. We didn't know the ship was beyond rescue yet."

They'd moved the body—that would have greatly compromised the crime scene, but with the *Calliope* underwater, it was destroyed anyway, which made an explosion so soon after . . . suspicious at best.

"Where'd you move his body to?"

"Mo's cabin up front."

"His office or bedroom?"

"Office, on the couch."

"Did you not consider that you were destroying evidence?"

"Evidence?" Marv frowned.

"It's a crime scene." Or it was until they corrupted it and the explosion had sunk the ship.

"Crime!" Marv's brow furrowed. "What crime? It was an accident."

"How can you be certain?"

"He was in the bathroom with the door locked. He slipped and hit his head."

It was very possible that was what happened, but given their inability to process the bathroom and examine the body, she couldn't be sure—they might never be sure. "Tell me more about the explosion," she said.

"I don't know." Marv shrugged. "We heard a loud blast and water flooded in. We moved Mr. Layton's body, then went topside. The stern was on fire and already dipping below the waterline, so we immediately evacuated the passengers into the life rafts. We made sure everyone had a life vest, sent a distress call with our coordinates, and abandoned ship. You guys arrived, and then the Coast Guard showed."

"So Mo didn't initially call the death in because . . . ?"

"Because of the explosion."

So why hadn't he said anything about it when he'd called in the Mayday, and what had happened during those five minutes? Had they really just talked and inspected the body?

Mo had been great during their charter dives, but something was definitely off.

THIRTY-EIGHT

Finn glanced at Gabby as she waved good-bye one last time to Tess. They'd taken her home, helped her pack, and dropped her off at the tiny airport outside of Wilmington. She'd agreed it would be a good idea to stay with her brother and his family on Norfolk's Navy base.

"She'll be safer there," Finn said, resting his hand on the small of Gabby's back and directing her outside to his Rogue. He opened her door and saw her in before moving around to the driver's side.

The warmth of the sun-heated car only heated his limbs more. He'd been burning up since he'd seen a man enter Fletcher's house. Parking the car maybe only forty-five seconds later—it had seemed like an hour—he'd raced up the steps, his heart in his throat, fearing he'd be too late. He was doomed to be late, or so it had seemed. But thankfully, God had spared him this time. Spared Gabby and Tess.

He reversed out of the parking spot, shifting the SUV into drive. "Gabby . . ."

"I know what you're going to say."

He highly doubted that.

"What I did was stupid—I agree."

"That's a first." Gabby never admitted she was wrong.

"I should have never taken Tess with me."

"Tess? No, you shouldn't have, but what about you? You should have never gone, period."

"But I had a lead."

How many times had he heard her talk about leads? What had he learned from all her stories about time in the field? That a lead appeared, and she dropped everything. Just as she'd dropped him and their growing relationship. She'd gotten the job offer from the *Raleigh Gazette* and was gone the next morning. He doubted she'd even given *them* a thought in that rapid turnaround. He tapped the wheel. "Today could have ended very differently."

She flipped her hair over her shoulder, running her fingers through it. "Well, it didn't."

"But it could have. You shouldn't have taken the risk."

She propped her forearm along the window frame.

A warm breeze riffled through the cab, the scent of black-eyed Susans lingering as they passed the open fields outside of town.

"There was no way for me to know that would happen."

"Exactly." His voice hitched up a notch. "That's what I'm saying. You don't know what will happen when you go poking your nose around."

"Poking my nose around? And what are *you* doing?"

"My job."

She linked her arms across her chest. "So am I."

"According to Noah, you're off the job right now."

"No. I'm not."

Stubborn woman. "Don't you care about your safety, your life?" Heat raked through his limbs at her silence. He gripped the wheel tighter. "You might not care, but I do." He swallowed as his throat narrowed. Had he really just said that? To the woman who didn't care about breaking his heart?

What was it about her? She'd barely been back in town, and all the feelings he'd shoved down, or tried to, were back and raw on the surface.

"I . . ." She struggled for words. "Of course I care about my safety. I didn't think anything was going to happen."

He raked a shaking hand through his hair as the wind ruffled it. "You never do."

She looked at him, then back out the window. "The fact that someone was there should tell you there's something important in Fletcher's house."

Finn frowned. "Why would you think that?"

"Why else do you think that armed man was there?"

He tapped the wheel. "Fuentes sent him."

"Please, no way you missed the genuine confusion on his face when you mentioned Fuentes. He had no clue who Fuentes is."

She was right, but the man had gone after Gabby. Or . . . had gone to Fletcher's to get something and was caught off guard by her and Tess's presence. "Regardless. It was a dangerous move."

She arched a brow. "You aren't even going to admit I'm right?"

"Right about what? Unless he confesses his motives for going to Fletcher's, you have no way to know why he was there for certain."

She exhaled in a long stream.

But there was a way for him to find out if Fletcher was hiding anything connected with the case. He instructed his Bluetooth to call the office.

"CGIS, Wilmington office," Emmalyne answered.

"Hey, Emmy. Can you work on getting a warrant to search Dennis Fletcher's house? We think there might be something inside that ties to this case." He relayed the rest of the information.

"On it," she said. "Gabby okay?"

"I'm fine," Gabby said.

"Glad to hear it."

"We're on the way. ETA fifteen," Finn said.

"See you then." Emmy disconnected the call.

Gabby looked over with a smirk.

He shook his head. "You don't even know if you're right."

She cocked her head, linking her arms across her chest. "We'll see."

///////////////////////////

Gabby and Finn entered the station to find Caleb pacing. "What's up?"

"The man asked for a phone call during processing . . ." Caleb said.

"And?"

"He called Litman Limited," Emmy said.

Finn shook his head. "What is it with this company?"

"I covered the basics, then left the interrogation for you, since you were the one on-site," Caleb said.

"Thanks." Finn looked at Gabby and then his watch. "When are Noah and Rissi due back? Do they need help with the new case?"

Caleb swiped his nose. "They are investigating as we speak, and Noah said they've got it covered."

Gabby looked at Caleb, unease stirring inside. The last thing her brother needed while working a case was to be worrying about her. "Did you mention . . ."

"Your Houdini trick?"

She swallowed. She hadn't meant to make Caleb look bad by leaving the office. "I'm sorry. I . . ."

Caleb held up a hand. "You don't have to explain to me. That's between you and your brother. But if I'm ever on sister watch again, you aren't going anywhere on your own."

She nodded. "Got it."

Finn smirked and headed for the interrogation room. "I'll be back in twenty. She's all yours," he said to Caleb.

Great . . .

THIRTY-NINE

Noah paced the hall outside the Wilmington General's ER. He understood Mo wanted all the passengers and even the rest of his crew to be tended to before him, but why was it taking so long for them to get to Mo?

He took a sip of coffee and looked at the clock.

Once the *Calliope* was deemed safe to dive, he and Finn would go down and retrieve Mr. Layton's body—if it hadn't been decimated by the explosion. He hoped the two ship sections had settled relatively close to where they went down, making it easier for the Coast Guard to find and assess the stability of each for diving.

His gut tightened. Doing an investigative dive without Sam would feel awkward at best. With his passing, they'd have to modify. He knew that, but it didn't make it easier. On the plus side, Finn was a talented diver and would be a great help in the interim, but Noah had already put in a request for a new dive investigator. No one could replace Sam, but they needed to fill the role.

Dizziness swirled through Noah's head. He took another sip of cold coffee, hoping it would ease the constant thumping in his head. He rubbed his brow.

"You okay?" Mo said, entering the room.

"I should be asking you that." Noah gestured for him to sit. "Are you?"

Mo sank into the cushioned chair, running a hand across his bald head. "Other than heartache over my girl sinking . . ."

Noah asked the question still burning in his mind. "What happened out there?"

Mo looked up, his shoulders hunched. "It was all going well. We had the regular crew—me, Marv, Braxton, and Jack." He propped his elbow on his knee and cradled the weight of his head in his hand. "Everyone aboard was working on their basic open-water dive certification except John Layton. He was doing his second wreck dive."

Noah nodded. It was just as he'd heard from the others he'd interviewed.

"Marv took John Layton, Braxton and I took the others, and Jack had the helm. Our dive went flawlessly. We were back on board and the clients were having a snack when Mr. Layton returned, and then Marv."

He shifted, repositioning himself in the chair. "Mr. Layton went to the head as soon as he got back. Braxton and Marv put their dive equipment away. Next thing I know, Mrs. Layton is hollering for help. I head down the galley steps, Jack's busted into the bathroom, and Mr. Layton is laid out on the floor, his head all banged up and bloody."

"He was . . . ?"

Mo exhaled out a long stream of deflating air. "Dead."

FORTY

After reading the file Emmalyne had put together, indicating the intruder's identity and last-known address, Finn entered the interrogation room. "Mr. Bashert, Isaac Bashert. That is your name, isn't it?"

The man nodded, a sullen, irritated expression on his face.

Finn leaned across the table and released his cuffs from the hook. He didn't seem like a threat, and it'd make it easier to read his body language if his hands were free.

The man was blond with blue eyes, about Finn's six-one height. In coloring and physique, they were quite similar, but he doubted they were alike in any other way.

"So why don't you tell me why you were at MCPO Fletcher's house?"

Isaac slouched in his chair. "I was going to check on him. I heard he'd been in an accident."

"So you and Fletcher are friends?" Why didn't he believe that?

"Uh-huh." The man picked something out of his teeth. *Charming.*

"How do you know each other?"

"From bowling," the man said, not missing a beat.

Finn arched his brows. "Bowling?"

"Yeah. He's in a league at Wilmington Lanes, and I drop

by occasionally. We picked up a conversation a while ago and enjoy a beer together when we're both there."

"Okay." He wasn't buying it, but it was easy enough to check out. "How'd you learn about Fletcher's injury?"

"At the bowling alley. Besides, the town is all abuzz about it."

"Why'd you go to his home instead of the hospital?"

"I thought he was recuperating at home."

"You always visit your friends with a firearm?"

"I have a legal permit for it."

Unfortunately he did. "Why rush up the stairs holding that gun?"

"I saw a strange car in the driveway, heard rustling upstairs. It felt like something was wrong, so I ran up to check it out."

"What did you think was happening?"

"I thought Fletcher might be in danger. I was trying to protect my friend."

"Did you call for Fletcher when you entered?" Gabby said he'd never identified himself or said a word.

He stalled a moment, then said, "No."

"Why not?"

"You don't announce your presence if you're checking out a possible break-in."

"Why'd you suspect a break-in?"

"I just had a bad feeling."

"A bad feeling?"

"Yes."

How was he supposed to argue with that? "And when you saw the woman in the office . . . ?" He didn't need to learn Gabby's name.

"I didn't have time to ask who she was or what she was doing there. I rounded the corner, saw something glass in her hand. Next thing I know, she bashes me in the head. I wake up and find I'm on the floor in cuffs. I want a lawyer because I'm going to sue."

"Sue for what?"

"Assault."

"You entered a home that's not yours, didn't identify yourself, and ran at a woman with a gun. It was self-defense, and she has witnesses."

"I want to talk with my lawyer."

"Is that who you were calling at Litman Limited?"

The man's blue eyes narrowed. "You traced my call?"

"You're using our phone. We're allowed to monitor all calls."

He leaned forward, resting his intertwined hands on the Formica tabletop. "That seems like an infringement of my rights."

"It's legal."

"We'll see about that. Like I said, I'm requesting a lawyer."

"So that isn't why you called Litman Limited?"

"I don't have to answer that."

"What is Litman Limited?"

"Again . . ." He slouched in his chair with a satisfied smile. "I don't have to answer that."

Gabby watched Finn emerge from the interrogation room with irritation sparking in his eyes, lips tight.

"Went that well, huh?"

He exhaled. "He claims he's a friend of Fletcher's and that he thought you were an intruder."

"That's ridiculous."

"You and I know that." He dropped the case folder on his desk. "But he has no priors, and he's requested a lawyer."

"Great."

"I do have a couple leads to check out—his home, if we can get a warrant based on the evidence we have, and Wilmington Lanes."

Gabby frowned. "A bowling alley?"

"He claims that's where he knows Fletcher from." Finn pulled the man's mug shot out of the folder and tucked it in his pocket. "I'll go see if anyone recognizes Mr. Bashert."

"You might want to check this out first," Emmalyne said, handing Finn a piece of paper.

"What's this?"

"An address where Litman Limited received a package."

Gabby smiled. Finally, they had a local connection to the mystery company.

"I'm on it."

"Can I go with?" Gabby asked.

"I'd rather you stay put with Caleb."

"I'm on my way out to check out the drug runners' homes." Caleb stood from his desk. "Warrants just came through."

"She can hang with me," Emmy offered.

"Nah," Finn said. "She can come with me."

Emmy inclined her head. "I'm quite capable of keeping Gabby safe."

Gabby linked her arms across her chest. "I'm quite capable of keeping myself safe." Not to dis Emmalyne's ability, but they were talking about her as if she was inept. She'd protected herself just fine with Bashert.

"Clearly," Finn said. "The duck move was impressive, but with two attacks—first in Raleigh and now with Bashert, regardless of his concocted story—you're safer with a trained agent."

She opened her mouth to argue, then quickly shut it. Why was she arguing? She was getting what she wanted, to accompany Finn on the investigation. "Fine," she said.

Finn narrowed his green eyes. "You agreed way too easy."

She simply smiled.

FORTY-ONE

Finn led the way up the front stairs of 4564 Shore Lane, the way-too-eager-to-accompany-him Gabby on his heels. Regardless of what he or Noah said to try to get through her thick skull, she was working this case just as much as he was. He could either accept that and partner with her—in a manner of speaking—or he could continue to worry about her investigating on her own. His muscles tensed at the thought of her poking around on her own.

Exhaling, he knocked on the front door and waited for an answer.

Wind blew, rustling the weeping willow in the front lawn, which appeared a tad overgrown.

Gabby rocked back on her heels, her hands in her back jeans pockets. Her brown hair wisped on the wind, fluttering about her shoulders.

He knocked again. "CGIS," he announced. "Please open the door."

He turned the handle but found it locked. They wouldn't have been able to enter without permission anyway. Though he'd called for a warrant, it hadn't come through yet.

"Let's check out back."

Gabby followed him through the waist-high side gate and around to the back stone-and-concrete porch.

They climbed the back steps and moved for what appeared

to be the kitchen door. He knocked, and once again, no one answered.

Gabby peered in the window. "Kitchen is empty, and it looks like it's dark throughout this level."

The bungalow-style home Emmy had sent them to sat eerily quiet.

"Who are you?" a woman asked.

Finn turned to find a woman in her early sixties, with short gray hair and a quizzical eye, standing on the opposite side of the chain-link fence.

"Who are you, young man?"

Gabby followed as Finn strode over and flashed his badge. "Agent Finn Walker, and this is—"

"I'm Gabby Rowley."

"What are you doing on Mr. Bowen's lawn?"

Finn explained the pertinent details.

"Well, you aren't going to find Mr. Bowen around here."

Finn frowned at her confidence. "Why not?"

"He died six months ago."

The breeze fluttered through Rissi's open window as she and Noah drove back to the station in his Jeep, her head still spinning from her talk with Dr. Layton and then Marv. Noah's spicy aftershave mixed with the salty scent of the ocean, only a hundred yards to their left.

He looked over at the stoplight. "What did you learn today?"

Rissi relayed everything she'd garnered, starting with Marv's version of the events. "He said the dive went well, but that John Layton panicked and shot to the surface, bypassing the compression stops."

"So Layton could have been suffering from decompression sickness?"

"Very possible, but Genevieve Layton told a different version of the story."

Noah arched a brow. "Oh?"

"She said that after her husband returned to the boat, he headed to the bathroom immediately after shedding his gear. He was agitated and said that something had gone very wrong."

Noah frowned. "Did he say what?"

"No. He just told her to get atop deck and stick with the group. Then he locked himself in the bathroom."

"Did you ask Marv what went wrong?"

"No. I wanted to see what he had to say with no lead-in."

"Smart."

"And he said other than Layton's rapid ascent, everything went fine."

"So either Marv or John Layton lied."

Rissi nodded. "My thoughts exactly."

"As we can't ask Mr. Layton, let's get back with Marv tomorrow."

"Sounds like a plan. How long do you think it'll take for the *Calliope* to be cleared to dive?" she asked.

"A day, maybe two."

"Hopefully we'll get some answers from the ship and Layton's body, which they moved."

Noah's brows hiked. "They what?"

"Marv said he and Mo moved Layton's body to the couch in Mo's office."

"Why? Didn't they know they were compromising crime-scene evidence?"

Rissi exhaled. "Marv said there was no crime. That it had been an accident."

"Even so . . . why move the body?"

"He claimed that after the explosion, water was rushing in. Before they realized it was too late to save the *Calliope*, they wanted to prevent Layton's body from being underwater."

Noah tapped the wheel. "It sounds reasonable."

"I hope that was their intention."

He gave her a sideways glance. "But you don't think so?"

She shifted in her seat, weighing what she was about to say. "I hate to think Mo or Marv or any of the crew could do anything wrong, but . . ."

"There are a number of questionable issues—the discrepancy between Marv's and John Layton's versions of the dive being the most glaring."

"Along with the odd timing of a man dying and then an explosion occurring. I'm sure it's possible. . . ."

"But not probable."

"And the fact they moved the body. I suppose they could have simply not thought it through. . . ."

"True, but there's more than enough there to be investigated."

Rissi nodded. "Agreed."

He tapped the wheel in a sharp beat.

She narrowed her eyes. "You're worried about Gabby."

He exhaled. "Yeah. I appreciate Finn keeping an eye on her, and I know if anyone comes looking for her, it's better if she's not right with me, as they'll look to me and the family first, but still . . ."

"You're a good brother. We both know it's good for Gabby and Finn to spend time together."

"True. I just hope it doesn't end the same way as last time. With Finn hurt."

"Me too." Rissi bit her bottom lip. "I don't think he's up for more heartache."

Noah sighed. "Neither is Gabby."

FORTY-TWO

Rissi followed Noah into the station, glad to be back. It'd already been a long day.

"How is everyone holding up?" Emmy asked, her long dark brown hair pulled up in a ponytail, her high cheekbones a soft hue of pink.

Noah sank into an open desk chair. "Shaken, for the most part."

"I was so sorry to hear about the passenger's death."

Rissi exhaled, sinking into her office chair and rolling over to Noah's desk. "His poor wife. She was heartbroken."

"What happened, exactly?" Emmy asked, looking at Noah. "You didn't get into specifics when you called in."

He raked a hand over his buzz cut. "It's complicated. Take a seat so Rissi and I can bring you up to speed."

Emmy rolled her pink-cushioned, specially ordered office chair over to join Rissi and Noah. After all the questions had been answered, Rissi rolled her chair back to her desk. She was more than ready to change out of the shorts, tank, and flip-flops she'd worn to the competition. "I can't believe we're investigating Mo and his crew. It's surreal."

Emmy leaned against her desk, her arms linked over her white silk blouse, her flowing claret skirt matching the claret flower pattern on her scarf. Rissi wished she had half of Emmy's fashion sense. She was more a T-shirt and jeans kind of girl. She'd never had a mother to teach her those things. Well, she'd technically *had* a mother, but since she'd died of a drug overdose at twenty-five, when Rissi was five, she definitely didn't qualify as a parent.

Noah glanced around the office. "Where's Gabby?"

"With Finn," Emmy said.

"How'd it go today? She stay put without much protest?"

Emmy nibbled her full bottom lip. "Um . . ."

Noah's dark brows lifted. "Em?"

She inhaled. "I think you should ask Gabby."

"Where are she and Finn now?"

"Finn called in and said they were going to grab a bite to eat at the Coffee Connection. He asked if I wanted them to bring anything back for me."

He inclined his head toward Rissi. "You okay handling the paperwork until I get back?"

"No problem."

The door shut behind him and Rissi turned to Emmy. "Pray for Gabby."

"I know." Emmy cringed. "I felt bad saying anything."

"You didn't have a choice. Noah asked you a direct question, and even if you didn't say anything, we both know Finn would have. But you're right. It's better if he hears it from Gabby."

Emmy exhaled. "Still feel bad. I get Gabby's point of view. It's gotta be hard being asked to sit on the sidelines when there's a story unfolding right in front of her."

"I agree." But it was nice she had a brother and friends who wanted to protect her. "I'm going to change before I dig into the paperwork."

Emmy lifted a pile from the printer tray and headed for her desk. "Let me know if I can help."

"Thanks. I'll get started and see where I'm at."

"Sounds good. I'm going to make a pot of coffee after I drop this at my desk. Want a cup?"

"Please." She'd been up since five thirty to check in at the competition by seven.

Rissi moved into the locker room. She changed, slipping into the black pants and turquoise blouse she'd left in her locker for after the competition.

Sitting on the bench that ran half the length of the lockers, she slipped on her turquoise Tieks flats. Since she spent most days on her feet, they were definitely worth the price.

Pulling her hair out of the ratty ponytail she'd thrown it up into during the rescue, she ran a brush through the dried saltwater tangles. Finally, it regained some softness and shape after a spray of leave-in detangling conditioner. She pulled it into a smooth side braid and flipped it over her left shoulder. A quick splash of water on her face, a little mascara, blush, and lip gloss, and she returned to her desk. She didn't want to think of the mound of paperwork she was about to dive into.

She'd just settled into her desk chair when the front door opened. Logan strolled in wearing a hot pink Hawaiian shirt with white and yellow hibiscus, and white board shorts.

A smile curled on her lips. It took a confident man to wear bright pink, but Logan was nothing if not confident. Perhaps borderline cocky at times, but he pulled it off without the usual accompanying arrogance.

A strong whiff of fresh fish wafted across the room as he approached. "Whoa!" Rissi said. "What's with the smell, Logan?"

"Amber threw her fish at me."

"Amber? Let me guess . . . your latest conquest?"

"The women I date aren't conquests."

"Right." Rissi tried not to laugh.

Logan unbuttoned his shirt, flipped it over his shoulder, and headed for the locker room.

Emmalyne's lips twitched, amusement dancing in her eyes. "Why'd she throw a fish at you?" she asked as he paused at the locker room door.

"Smacked me with it is more like it."

Emmalyne burst out in laughter. "What'd you do?"

"I love how you assume *I* did something."

As he stood there shirtless, Rissi had to admit his washboard abs were impressive, but she never looked at Logan that way. He was the office player—though the term was probably a bit too strong. He possessed a heart of gold. He just had to learn to get out of his own way. He was swimming in the shallow end and needed to take the plunge into the deep with a woman of substance.

"I'm with Emmy on your being to blame," she said, linking her arms across her chest. "So let's hear it."

A resigned expression crossed his handsome tanned face. "She may have interpreted my helping another charter guest with her casting as a tad flirtatious, but I was just being polite."

"Uh-huh." Emmy shook her head. "Please, when you flirt, you go all out. Don't try to sell a 'tad' flirtatious."

"Yet I still seem to have zero effect on you."

Emmy smirked. "Because I know your type."

"And . . ." He dropped his shirt at his desk, strode over to Emmy, and sat on the corner of her desk. "What type is that, beautiful?"

"A serial player."

"Just because I like to spend time with a beautiful woman like you doesn't make me a player." He leaned forward with a smile, and Emmy cast her glance away.

She focused on the pile of papers before her, but Rissi didn't miss the rose flushing Emmy's cheeks. "It's the sheer number of women you date that makes you a player."

"Excuse me, I'll have you know, I never date more than one woman at a time."

"No." Emmy rolled her eyes. "You just cycle through them at warp speed."

He tilted Emmy's chin with his finger, his gaze meeting hers. "Trust me. When I find the right woman, I'll commit."

Emmy swallowed, and after a silent moment between the two, she shifted back from his touch. "Now shoo. You need a serious shower, and I have work to do."

Logan retrieved his shirt and moved toward the locker room, a soft smile tugging at his lips.

Emmy dropped a note on Noah's desk and sighed. "I swear, the man's impossible."

Rissi spun her chair back to face her desk with a smile. Logan's love life may be a comedy of errors, but that really could change. She truly believed no one was hopeless.

Please, Father, let Logan accept our offers to come to church one day. Let him hear your Word. It can change hearts and transform lives. As good of a guy as he is deep down, he desperately needs you. We all do. Help Logan see there's more to life than looking for distraction in empty relationships. Help open his eyes to the beauty of women fully committed to you . . . like Emmy.

There was something there, but as things stood, it would never move beyond that unless Logan did some soul searching.

FORTY-THREE

Finn pulled out a brown wooden chair for Gabby, having chosen the square table on the back wall of the Coffee Connection.

The scent of corn bread and fresh chili swirled in the air, mixing with the burnt coffee smell that Gabby insisted was the worst way to describe the wonderful smell of roasting coffee beans emanating from the gold roasting machine.

During her winter stay, he'd often seen her sitting at the glass separating the restaurant side from the kitchen, watching the roasting machine at work. She claimed there was something soothing about the whir of the grinding. To Finn, espresso smelled like burnt coffee, but he couldn't get enough. He started nearly every day off with a quad macchiato.

Smitty, Paul Barnes's manager and second-in-command, greeted them with a smile. "Here you go, my dear." He handed Gabby the chalkboard menu—fresh and different every day depending on Paul and Smitty's whims.

"Ooh," Gabby said, her eyes skimming over it. "The roasted green tomato soup sounds delicious."

Finn's brows hiked.

"What?" A smile flitted across her lips. "You're not nearly adventurous enough when it comes to food."

"I'm just a man who prefers the basics—a piece of southern-style corn bread and that chili I smell cooking."

She shook her head. "What is it with you and chili?"

"I can depend on it to be good."

She huffed and handed Smitty the menu. "I'll have the roasted green tomato soup and the Gruyère grilled cheese."

Smitty tucked the menu at his side and bent forward from the waist. "Excellent choice." He smiled and headed for the kitchen.

"Not even going to ask about Gruyère," Finn said.

"It's earthy and nutty and tastes delicious."

"And good old American cheese doesn't work because . . . ?"

She rolled her eyes. "I don't know who's worse at trying new stuff—you or Noah."

He leaned forward. "I'm always up for new stuff. I just like my food to be standard."

She shook her head, reclining against the back of the chair. "You mean boring."

"Is there anything you don't argue about?"

"With you . . ." She smirked. "Not much."

He chuckled. "At least you didn't argue about that."

She stuck her tongue out.

"And I'm the immature one?"

"I never said you're immature. I said when it comes to food you don't have a mature palate."

His lips twitched into a smile. "And what kind of palate do I have?"

"That of a teenager."

He weighed the idea. "I'm okay with that."

She rolled her big blue eyes. "Of course you are."

He lifted his chin, not willing to let this playful moment go. "Food snob."

"Child." She swished her hand toward him.

He grabbed hold of it, circling the pad of his thumb down her palm.

She swallowed, her gaze locking on his.

When he spoke, it was low and intentional. "I promise you, I'm very much a man."

She opened her mouth to speak, then closed it again.

His smile widened. He'd rendered Gabby Rowley speechless. He never thought he'd see the day.

The service bell on the counter rang in fast succession, and Gabby pulled her hand back, lowering it to her lap and smoothing the napkin she'd laid across it.

Pink flushed her cheeks as warmth spread through his chest.

He'd never met a more vibrant woman. The way he responded when she walked into a room . . . He reached for his glass of water, debating which was better—guzzling it or dousing himself in an attempt to temper the heat rushing through him.

Gabby smiled, casting her attention to the counter as "Sweet Caroline" rang out.

The Paul and Smitty show was beginning.

Finn angled his chair for a better view.

"Order up," Smitty said.

"Ring it out." Paul grinned.

"A triple cinnamon soy latte, triple nonfat mocha, grande iced quad macchiato . . ."

Paul started juggling cups as Smitty called out the orders in quick succession.

Someone in the crowd whistled.

Finn glanced at Gabby, her eyes wide with enjoyment.

"Keep 'em coming," Paul said, juggling faster and higher.

"Grande cocoa nitro with steamed cream and three stevia, tall hot chocolate with whip, green tea, and a blueberry smoothie."

Paul worked in three more cups, juggling half a dozen.

People got to their feet, clapping and singing along with the chorus as Paul and Smitty juggled the cups between them—tossing them in loops from one end of the counter to the other.

Gabby started clapping and Finn joined in as they really got into it.

Paul tossed one cup after another under his leg, across the open space to Smitty, who tossed it back to him. Then one by one he flipped the cups under the syrups and started pumping while Smitty positioned himself on the other side, grabbing the cups and sliding them under the espresso machine.

Steam rose as everyone got to their feet, belting out "Sweet Caroline," as Rissi said they did in the middle of every eighth inning at Fenway Park in Boston, where she, and apparently Smitty, had ended up in Wilmington from. Milk poured, the blender whirled, and Smitty and Paul sang as they performed their dance routine. Finally, it concluded to a roar of applause.

Gabby sank back in her chair, practically doubling over with laughter. "Those guys are the best."

"I think they've watched the hippy-hippy-shake one too many times." He laughed with her, his smile widening as his gaze fixed on her.

"What?" She tried to stop herself from laughing, but it seemed futile.

"I like it when you smile."

She bit her bottom lip, her smile alight.

Noah entered the Coffee Connection, the bell over the door signaling his presence.

Spotting Finn and Gabby in the rear, he strode for their table.

Gabby's gaze met his, and she paled. So she *had* pulled something.

He arched a brow as he reached her side. "Do I want to ask?"

She straightened her shoulders. "Nope." She lifted her oversized yellow mug and took a sip of her frothy drink.

He squeezed Finn's shoulder and pulled up a chair, settling it between them. "Let's hear it."

Gabby looked to Finn.

He held up his hands. "Your story to tell."

"Fine." She exhaled, shifting to face Noah.

"On that note . . ." Finn stood. "I should head back to the station. I've got a ton of paperwork to fill out. I'll take my food to go."

Noah nodded. "Sounds good."

Finn smiled at Gabby in a way not lost on Noah. "Gabby."

She waggled her fingers at Finn, then shifted to face Noah again. "Let's get this over with."

Noah rested his hand on her shoulder, dipping his head to look her in the eye. "This is your life, Gabs. Someone tried to kill you."

"Not for the first time, and I doubt it'll be the last."

He leaned forward, the scent of yeast and freshly baked bread swirling in the air. "What happened today?"

She bit her bottom lip.

Noah stiffened. This wasn't going to be good.

He listened while she relayed the day's events to his horror. He rubbed his brow, praying for wisdom and restraint. "Seriously, Gabs? You're lucky Finn came when he did."

"I had it. I knocked the guy out."

"You shouldn't have put yourself in that position in the first place. And what about Tess—a pregnant woman who lost her husband yesterday?" He sighed. *Please let her hear me, Lord.* "I'm just trying to keep you safe."

She looked to the side and exhaled as she always did before she softened her reply. Maybe he was getting through to her. "I know you're just looking out for me and I appreciate it, but . . ."

There was always a *but* with her.

"*But* you can't ask me to give up being me. Hunting down stories is my calling. It's what God created me to do. I don't like to cause you or Mom or Kenzie worry, but I can't stop doing what brings me alive. If I do, I won't be me."

Noah let his shoulders drop. How did he argue with that?

"Your job isn't exactly one of safety," she said, lifting her cup and taking a sip as he pondered that. She looked up with a frothy mustache clinging to her upper lip.

He couldn't help but smile.

"There," she said. "I haven't seen you do that since you hijacked me at the office."

"I'd hardly call it hijacking."

She tilted her head. "Then what would you call it?"

He shrugged. "I commandeered you."

"I'm not a ship."

"You're as obstinate to maneuver."

She punched his arm.

He grimaced. She packed a wallop. Then again, he'd taught her how.

"All levity aside . . . I'm just trying to keep my baby sister safe."

She clapped her hands over his. "I know, and I appreciate it, but I'm not a baby anymore."

He exhaled. "Well, it was much easier keeping an eye on you then, but you were always into mischief."

She straightened. "I prefer to call it *exploring*."

"You can prefer what you want, but we both know it's true. And you've never changed."

"So why do you think I'm going to change now?"

He leaned his head back, staring at the ceiling. She was right, but why did she have to be so obstinate?

Noah pulled out of the on-street parking spot and merged into the flow of traffic. He draped his left arm across the wheel. "How's it going with Finn?"

"Fine. . . ." Where exactly was her brother going with this?

He swallowed, his Adam's apple bobbing. "You know he's crazy about you."

Warmth spread up her neck, flushing her cheeks. "Awkward alert. I am not talking about guys with my brother."

"Guy," he said, holding up his index finger. "Just one."

He was seriously going there?

"I'm just saying." He shrugged. "It's painfully obvious."

"Dude, I'm not talking guys with my brother," she reiterated, praying he took the very unsubtle hint. She straightened, preparing to jump from the moving vehicle if he didn't cease and desist. Didn't he get how awkward this was?

"When you left last winter, he was in bad shape."

She bit her bottom lip. Had Finn really been that bad off? To be honest, she hadn't been much better. She just hadn't been there for them to witness her heartache. Yes, it'd been her choice—or rather, her flight mode kicking in—but it'd crushed her all the same.

"I'm sorry I hurt him. That wasn't my intention." It'd been self-preservation, definitely not the intention of harm, that had fueled her decision to take the job Lawrence offered.

His fingers danced rapidly on top of the steering wheel. "This isn't exactly a comfortable conversation for me, but—"

"Then stop." *Please.*

"Okay. Give me one more comment, and I'll stop."

She exhaled the nervousness ticking through her heightened pulse. "Do I have a choice?"

"No."

"Fine. One and you're done." She clenched her teeth, the heat of embarrassment raking over her skin.

"As his boss, I need Finn fully functioning for the team, but as his friend"—he glanced over at her—"watching his heart break was painful to see."

FORTY-FOUR

Noah stood by the whiteboard as they all found seats on the couches facing it. "Let's start with Finn"—Noah looked to her with resignation fixed on his brow—"and Gabby. Where are you guys at?"

"Litman Limited had a package delivered via UPS to the home of a Craig Bowen. He passed six months ago, and his family lives overseas. His neighbor, Mrs. Dolores Finksburg, keeps an eye on the place."

"And has she seen anyone enter the home?"

"She said the mailman still comes and slips the mail through the door slot," Gabby offered.

"And occasionally a UPS driver," Finn added.

"Right," Gabby continued. "We're thinking maybe the person retrieving the package either posed as one or the other. Or came at night while Mrs. Finksburg was sleeping."

"Did she say what happens to packages left on the stoop?" Noah asked. "I'm assuming the UPS driver leaves them out front since there's no one there to take them."

"She said she's never seen packages on the stoop."

Noah arched his brows. "Then what is UPS delivering?"

Gabby looked at Finn, and he nodded for her to continue. "We're thinking only packages that fit through the mail slot. It's wide enough to fit a nine-by-eleven padded envelope. I looked in and saw letters fanned across the floor as well as a padded UPS envelope."

Noah wrote *UPS Packages* on the whiteboard underneath the facts they'd amassed thus far.

"I put in for a warrant," Finn said. "It's taking longer than I expected, but given Litman Limited's tie to three of our prisoners, I'm confident it'll come through."

"In the meantime, Litman might send someone to make a pickup," Noah said, glancing around the room. His gaze landed on Logan. "Logan, I'm putting you on watch at the house until morning."

"Roger that," Logan said. "Should I head out now?"

"Yes," Noah said.

Logan had just exited the office door when Emmy said, "I'm going to take him some of the leftover food on my way out. I'm sure he didn't stop and think about needing food, being the man-child he is."

Gabby laughed. "That's one way to describe him."

"I've got a batch of chocolate oatmeal cookies in the oven," Rissi said.

"Is that what smells so good?" Caleb asked.

Gabby had been wondering the very same thing. It smelled of cinnamon, chocolate, and brown sugar. Though, when had Rissi had time to whip up a batch of cookies?

"I think best when I bake," Rissi said, reading her thoughts.

"Gotcha. I hate cleaning, but it's when my mind best processes clues and stories," Gabby said. "For some reason, it helps me put the pieces together. That and surfing."

"Kenzie's board worked well for you?" Noah asked.

"I'd say." Finn smiled.

Everyone shifted their gazes to Finn and then to her.

She pulled her lips into her mouth, warmth kissing her cheeks. "We were both out this morning."

Noah smiled but didn't say anything.

"I can swap out with Logan in the morning," Caleb said, thankfully shifting the focus off of her and Finn. She considered mouthing a thank-you but wasn't sure if he'd taken the heat off her on purpose or if it'd been a happy accident. Caleb didn't seem the most astute when it came to emotional subtleties.

"Thanks." Finn nodded. "That'll free me to speak with Fletcher tomorrow about his supposed friend who's sitting in our cell and check in with Hadley about Sam's autopsy."

A hush of silence blanketed the room.

"Sorry," he said.

"No . . ." Noah cleared his throat. "We all knew he'd need one performed, given he was murdered."

Rissi curled up her legs on the gray couch, grabbing the toss pillow and fiddling with the cream fringe surrounding it. "I still can't believe he's gone."

Noah released a slow exhale. "I don't think any of us can." He rested his hand on the top corner of the silver-framed whiteboard. "I talked with Beth today, and she's planning a service for the day after tomorrow."

"How are Beth and Ali?" Finn asked.

"Struggling," Noah said.

"It'll be that way for a good while . . . as happy as they were," Emmalyne said.

Gabby picked at her sparkling gray nail polish. In her experience, it was when she was happiest that the bottom dropped out.

Noah tapped the dry-erase marker against his palm. "Let's shift to the death of John Layton. Rissi, what did you find out about him?"

"He was the senior customs agent at Wilmington International in the ILM international office. Worked there for twenty years."

"Customs, huh?" Noah said, writing it down in black marker under John Layton's picture. "Okay, until Finn and I can dive down and inspect the *Calliope*, let's keep digging into Layton.

See if there's any tie between him and Mo, or his crew, that might cause them to want to harm Layton."

"On it," Rissi said. "I'm also pulling Layton's financials, and I'll head to the airport and interview his coworkers."

"While you're there, ask to see the manifests for the last month. Let's find out what he's been letting in and make sure everything was accounted for."

Rissi nodded. "So you're thinking foul play was involved with Layton's death?"

Noah sighed. "There's enough there to warrant a full investigation. I'm hoping we will know more once we retrieve his body and an autopsy is performed. But the longer his body is down there, the more compromised it becomes. We also need to retrieve Layton's dive gear, make sure everything was working properly. Of course, that is if we can find it, and if it wasn't damaged in the explosion."

Noah cleared his throat. "While we're on the subject of diving . . . you all should know I put in a request for a new agent with a specialty in dive investigation."

"Already?" Rissi sat forward.

Noah's shoulders dropped. "I know it's hard to think of replacing Sam, but we need an investigative diver on our team."

Everyone nodded, but based on their tense expressions, the news was clearly difficult for the team to hear. Gabby understood. It was so very soon after Sam's loss, but Noah had made the right call.

The front office door opened, and everyone's attention flashed to it.

"Hey, Kenz," Noah said.

Her puffy, red-rimmed eyes blinked back tears.

Noah's brow creased. "What's wrong?"

"Mark's being deployed."

Gabby rushed forward, enveloping her sister in a big hug.

FORTY-FIVE

"I can't imagine being in Kenzie's place, my husband being sent to who knows where, for who knows how long," Gabby said as Finn drove toward home.

"You've been deployed all over the world as a reporter."

"Yeah, but it's different."

He narrowed his eyes and glanced toward her. "How?"

The oncoming headlights glinted off the green flecks in her otherwise blue eyes.

"Because she's losing her husband." She swallowed. "I didn't leave anybody behind for South Sudan."

She *had* left him for Raleigh. Though their relationship hadn't been fully defined over the winter, his feelings were fixed. But she'd cut it off at the roots. Taking the job in Raleigh, she'd left him and the budding relationship in the dust.

He understood journalism was her passion, what she was made to do, but she hadn't given any indication she wanted to continue things over the distance. Instead, she'd simply said she had to go and wished him well. Wished him well? That was something you said to an acquaintance, not a man you were falling in love with.

Maybe he'd read the signals wrong. Maybe their talks hadn't been as deep and significant for her. Maybe . . .

He inhaled and released it. He'd spent enough time chasing down that rabbit trail. It was time to accept the fact that they were never going to happen. But being back in her presence, knowing she'd never be his . . . It was like losing her all over again.

"I just can't imagine losing my other half." Gabby shook her head. "It's how Kenzie said she's feeling. I can't imagine any part of that."

"What do you mean? Having another half or being in love?"

She bit her bottom lip, then looked out the window. "I mean . . ." She turned back to face him, vulnerability instead of weariness radiating in her eyes. "I understand being in love, but to the extent of someone being my other half, it . . ."

"Scares you." He called it like he saw it.

"No." She released a nervous laugh. "It doesn't scare me." She rested her arm along the windowsill, her fingers tapping the tan lining. "I don't get scared."

He arched his brows. "Everybody is scared of something."

She linked her arms across her chest, clinging tightly to herself. "Well, I'm not scared of that."

He tapped the wheel. "You sure about that?"

His Bluetooth rang at the most inconvenient time. "Hey, Logan."

"We had a visitor at the drop spot. I have him in custody, along with the package he collected."

"Excellent. Where are you now?"

"Standing outside my car with him cuffed in the backseat. I thought I'd take him into the station and you could meet us there."

"Be there in fifteen." He hung up. "Hang on," he said to Gabby as he pulled a U-turn.

FORTY-SIX

"I'll run you to Noah's before I head to the office," Finn said.

"I'm fine going with you."

"It could be several hours."

"I'm fine waiting at the office. It's been a long day for Noah, and I can find something to do."

Finn tilted his head, glancing over at her.

"I'll stay put."

He arched his brows. "Promise?"

"Promise."

"Okay." His shoulders relaxed.

She leaned against the door, ducking her head to gaze up at the nearly full moon. A couple of days and it'd be a super moon. She couldn't wait. Big, full, and round—a super moon made her feel as if she could practically reach out and touch it.

It was a beacon of light in an otherwise dark world. Finn had been her beacon during her winter stay, and now he and Noah were her promise of safety and protection. As much as she balked at it, and at times felt smothered by the constant attention, it was out of concern and—if she was honest—love for her on both their parts. Looking at Finn's eyes made her feel safe, at least from physical danger. Emotional danger was an entirely different matter.

Finn glanced at the clock as he strode to the interrogation room—9:13. Another long night faced him.

He wished Gabby had agreed to go to Noah's and gotten a good night's sleep. After the last couple days, she had to be running on empty. Regardless of what she said, a man rushing her gun in hand had to shake her. She always put on such a brave front. She was brave, but even the brave felt fear.

The girl was real, vibrant, and made for his arms. Every memory of her lingered—her scent, the feel of her touch, the sound of her voice. . . . He was falling hard and fast all over again.

He pulled himself from his thoughts, entered the interrogation room, and dropped the file on the table. "Mr. Jacobs," he said with an exhale.

The man before him didn't fit the mold of the men he'd come across thus far in this investigation.

Eric Jacobs was sixty-nine, five-seven, graying, and he'd wager around one hundred and six pounds soaking wet. He wore a charcoal paddy cap, matching blazer with suede elbows, and a maroon sweater vest. He reminded Finn of his great-uncle Al, whom he hadn't seen since he and his mum left Australia well over a decade ago.

"I've got to say, Mr. Jacobs, you aren't what I expected. What is a gentleman of your age doing mixed up with Litman Limited?"

Jacobs's bushy gray brows twitched. "I was simply picking up a package, as I was told, and waiting for instructions to drop it off."

"Told by whom?"

"Excuse me?" Jacobs pulled his glasses case out of his blazer's interior pocket and slipped on black-rimmed glasses.

"You said you were picking up a package as told. Who told you to pick it up?"

"I run a delivery service to supplement my retirement from UPS. I pick packages up, I drop them off."

"Did you know what was in the package you picked up to-night?" It was just an old book, of all things. How that fit in with the case he had no idea. He hoped Mr. Jacobs could shed some light.

"Of course not. I never look."

"It was a book."

Jacobs's brow arched. "Really?"

"Yes."

"As I said, I never look."

"Any idea how a book fits into all this?" The seemingly out-of-place item nagged at him.

"I have no idea."

"I assume you at least know who hired you to pick up the package."

Jacobs clasped his hands in front of him on the table. "I received a call a half hour before I headed to the house. The man said he needed a package retrieved from his house. He gave me the address, said the key was under the mat, and told me he'd call later with instructions of where to drop it off."

"You didn't find that strange?"

"What . . . strange?" He shrugged, cupping his hands palms up.

"You don't find the fact that the delivery address wasn't pro-vided at all suspect?"

"I pick things up as I'm told, and I drop them off when and where I'm told. It's that simple."

Finn leaned back in his chair. "Let me guess . . . you don't ask questions."

He smiled. "There's no crime in that."

FORTY-SEVEN

Wrapping up his phone conversation, Xavier Fuentes sat back on his bunk. It paid to have guards in his pocket—always paid to have avenues to get what he needed done. And he'd paved those avenues well.

Gabrielle Rowley's location had been found. He knew La Muerte was worth the money. He was tempted to give him the go-ahead to do away with her, but with his own freedom imminent, he withheld the order. He wanted to strangle the life from Miss Rowley himself, to feel her pulse stop beating beneath his fingers. No, she was his, and he'd repay her well— showing no mercy.

His cellmate, Antonio, snored on the bottom bunk.

His jaw tightened. How he abhorred snoring.

He wished he could snap Antonio's tattooed neck midsnore, but he couldn't do anything to jeopardize his plans. He had to refrain from anything that might prolong his current incarceration. Murdering his cellmate would fall in that category, unfortunately. Besides, he needed Antonio for his escape.

He reclined onto the subpar mattress that reeked of Antonio's nicotine habit and pickled eggs. Of all the items to get from the outside world, Antonio requested his girlfriend bring him pickled eggs on her visits.

Everything about this place was disgusting, but freedom and

Gabrielle Rowley's death were rapidly approaching. And that brought a smile to his face as the overhead lights clicked off.

Needing to unwind before trying to sleep, Gabby and Finn went out to the swing on his back porch. They sat in a comfortable silence, simply listening to crickets chirping and the rhythmic lapping of the water.

It'd been a long, emotional day, and Finn's interrogation of Mr. Jacobs had been more frustrating than helpful, but at least they had a concrete tie to Litman Limited—though Jacobs claimed this had been his first pickup for them. On the way home, she and Finn considered that possibility. But it seemed far more likely that Eric Jacobs was lying.

Not providing the drop address until after the pickup was brilliant. That way if the pickup person was caught, as Eric Jacobs had been, he couldn't tell them what he didn't know. Though, they likely used random drop spots that wouldn't lead directly back to them anyway.

Kicking off her shoes, Gabby relaxed into the sway of Finn's porch swing, although hanging sofa was probably a better description. The white wooden frame cradled an outdoor twin mattress. Oversized pillows in turquoise and jade with designs that reminded Gabby of the flow of ocean waves lined the back wooden slats. White rope fastened the swing to large metal eye-hooks screwed into the porch ceiling.

The lap of the water grew closer as the high tide swept in. Fireflies sparked in the darkness.

Finn arched his right shoulder, a crease of pain furrowing his brow.

The air held the damp moisture of coming rain, which she'd learned really affected the torn rotator cuff that he stubbornly refused to have surgically fixed. Plus, the morning's surfing couldn't have helped his shoulder either. And he claimed she was the stubborn one.

Only a man as bullheaded as Finn would, one, refuse surgery and, two, continue to swim, surf, and even dive with a torn rotator cuff. He'd adamantly made up his mind not to even consider surgery to repair it. Frustration flared through her whenever she thought about it. She exhaled. Why was he so hard on himself in refusing to get it fixed, to take the constant pain away?

He'd suffered *one* loss on the job as a rescue swimmer. Surely, he had to know there'd be losses going into that field. As strongly as he'd reacted to the loss, she couldn't help but wonder if there was more to the story. During her years in journalism, she'd found there was almost always more to a story than met the eye.

Would Finn ever feel comfortable enough with her to share what lurked beneath his pain?

"Are you hurting?" she asked.

"It's fine." He shrugged his shoulder, pain again creasing his brow.

He *was* hurting.

She set down the glass of lemonade Finn had offered her and wiped her pants with damp palms—condensation from the heat lingering in the stale September air.

Standing, she moved behind the sofa swing.

Finn glanced back at her, a question forming on his face.

She wrapped her hands over his warm, broad shoulders, massaging his tight muscles.

He swallowed, an entirely different expression dancing across his brow.

His sandy blond hair edging his neckline tickled her fingers as she kneaded his corded muscles.

God had most definitely made a masterpiece with Finn Walker. Combining his stellar physique with green eyes, a strong jaw, and chiseled cheekbones made it hard not to sigh when he walked in a room.

"That better?" she asked after a while.

"Y . . . eah," he said in a choked whisper.

The friction between her fingers and his skin as she'd slipped her hands under his loose tank top shot warmth up her arms. Maybe this wasn't such a good idea after all.

Lying awake at half past one, Gabby wiggled her still-tingling fingers.

Swallowing, she rolled over, bunched the feather pillow beneath her head, and kicked the white comforter from her feet.

Rubbing Finn's shoulders had been an innocent action coming from the purest of motivations—relieving his pain. She never could have anticipated such a powerful reaction coursing through her.

She climbed out of bed and slipped the cream terry robe Rissi had lent her over a Washington Caps T-shirt and matching knit pajama shorts. Planting her feet on the driftwood floor, she marveled once again at its unique beauty. According to Rissi— who'd decorated the place before Gabby's winter stay—Noah and Finn had purchased the driftwood from a local landscaper, then planed, sanded, and laid the floor before sealing it with clear varnish to protect its natural, rugged coastal beauty.

Stepping to the half-open window, she breathed deeply, her sleeves ruffling in the storm-brewing breeze.

Shafts of moonlight streaked across Finn's lawn. She followed the beams up along the wood-shingled house, straight up to Finn's bedroom window.

She leapt back at the sight of him standing there shirtless.

Her heart pounding in her throat, she pressed her back against the beadboard wall, praying he hadn't seen her.

Her room was dark. Surely, he couldn't have seen her.

Chuckling at herself for overreacting, she stepped back to the window, only to find him still standing there.

His piercing gaze shifted directly to hers, and a soft smile curled in the corner of his lips.

Mason found her crying in the crawl space behind her closet. She'd taken refuge there again. Hugging her knees to her chest, Rissi rocked back and forth, trying to soothe her fight mechanism. She'd tried fighting back once, but it'd only resulted in a stiffer beating.

Finding the crawl space while playing hide-and-seek years ago had proven such a blessing. Either Hank didn't know it existed or he chose not to bother her there. Knowing Hank and his horrific lack of boundaries, evidenced by the hidden bruises and out-of-sight scars littering her body, it had to be the former.

She'd hid the crawl-space entrance behind her laundry basket, knowing Hank would never bother touching something so far beneath his role as "ruler" of the children's home. It had been her place of refuge for a long time, but now the spot belonged to her and Mason.

She listened as he shimmied through the hidden entrance on his hands and knees, shifting the laundry basket back into place.

He'd only been living in the home for a few months, but for some reason they'd jibed. She trusted him. It was an odd sensation, giving her trust to someone, but he had hers.

He sat cross-legged beside her and leaned over, brushing his shoulder against hers. "Want to talk about it?"

She fought back the tears pricking at her eyes. Please don't cry in front of him.

How did he even know? The assault had been in Hank's office, and she'd been as quiet as a mouse. She always was or it only prolonged the torture.

How no one discovered Hank's abuse over the years, she had no clue. None of the kids talked, not even after getting out of the hellhole. And the minimal staff Hank oversaw . . . They all just looked the other way. All five of them. She'd love to know what he had over them . . . or maybe they just didn't care. Most people didn't. Not in her world.

He pulled a bag of ice from his pocket. "I snagged this for you. Thought it might help."

"Thanks."

"Where is the worst?" His hands gripped the bag tighter.

Hank always left bruises on her skin, a hidden trail of his inflicted pain.

"My back."

Mason reached for her shirt. "May I?"

She nodded, knowing it'd hurt more if she had to angle her arm back. Everything was so tender.

He lifted the back of her shirt up above her waist as she clasped the front tightly to herself.

A swear leaked from his lips. "It'll be cold."

She nodded, too embarrassed to look him in the eye.

The cold hit the raw gashes on her back with a frigid sting. She winced, embarrassed by the weakness of her reaction.

"I'm sorry. I know it stings."

She swallowed, focusing her gaze on the attic rafters, faint wisps of sunset slipping in the drafty cracks.

He held the ice bag in place until the smarting dulled and her back grew numb.

He didn't badger her with questions. Just sat there as day bled into night.

Rissi lurched up with a jolt. Sweat slickened her skin as her heart skittered in her chest. Swallowing, she clicked on the bedroom light.

Just a nightmare.

She forced herself to take a deep inhale, then released it slowly through her mouth, as her counselor had taught her. It settled her body but not her mind.

Climbing from the bed, she strode to her dresser, retrieved her Penn State sweatshirt, and slipped it over her pjs' tank and knit shorts. Glancing about her bedroom, her gaze darted to the closet, the sound of Mason's voice echoing through her mind.

Two nightmares in less than seventy-two hours. What was triggering them? And why was Mason living in her mind so much lately?

She stepped into the front room, grabbed her copy of *W is for Wasted* by Sue Grafton, and curled up on her Yogibo bean bag chair. There'd be no more sleep tonight.

FORTY-EIGHT

The steady patter of rain bouncing off the pitched metal roof roused Gabby from slumber. Opening her eyes, she fixed her gaze on the still half-open window, thankful the rain was streaking sideways across the screen rather than pelting in.

A knock sounded on her door.

Extricating herself from the tangle of covers about her legs, she stood, glancing at the clock on her bedside table. 6:16.

"I brought breakfast," Finn said from the other side of the door.

A very sweet and thoughtful gesture, especially so early.

"Hang on a sec," she said, throwing her robe back on and knotting it about her waist. Taking a quick second to run her fingers through her hair, and inhaling a steadying breath, she opened the door, praying Finn hadn't seen her gawking at him last night. A sudden rush of embarrassment washed in a wave of heat over her cheeks. Finn stood holding a white wicker breakfast tray loaded with goodies, the homey scent of bacon swirling about her.

"May I?" he asked, lifting the tray.

"Of course." She stepped back, suddenly feeling very self-conscious and hoping she didn't look an absolute mess from a restless night's slumber.

"Over here okay?" he asked, walking over to the distressed aqua desk nestled in the far window nook. Rissi had done an amazing job refinishing the piece. "We've got a busy day ahead of us."

"Oh?"

"Yep, I figured you needed better sustenance than those cardboard-tasting bars you're always eating on the go."

"Protein bars are good for you," she said with a tilt of her head, taking in his casual morning attire—black running pants and a yellow T-shirt with the Endless Summer logo screened across the front.

"Eggs, bacon, toast, and fruit are much better," he countered.

"So what's on the agenda for today?"

"Time to follow up on Bashert—check out his home and the bowling alley he supposedly knows Fletcher from. We need to find out if anyone there can corroborate his claims."

"Hopefully we'll get some answers," she said, picking up a slice of bacon that was crispy to the point of nearly being burnt—just like her momma made it. She took a bite. "Mmm."

"Applewood smoked, and maple-syrup cured."

It really was like her momma made it.

"Nana Jo did a local market run-through with me when I moved here." He chuckled.

Of course she had.

"Said single men needed all the help they could get." A soft smile curled on his lips, and she worked not to get drawn into the appealing expression.

She bit back a smile of her own. For not being a North Carolina native, Finn sure had southern charm down.

He arched a brow. "What has you on the verge of smiling?"

"Nothing." She swallowed as heat rushed to her cheeks again. "Want to join me?" she asked, curling up on the window seat as rain drizzled outside. Her simple question was probably far more dangerous than she'd intended, given how strongly she suddenly longed for him to stay.

His smile grew. "I'd like that." He took a seat beside her.

She handed him the fork and lifted the spoon for herself. "Thanks."

She reached for the Texas Pete sauce. "Thank *you* for this." She jiggled the glass bottle before sprinkling its contents over her half of the eggs.

"I remembered you're a hot-sauce lady."

She took a bite of the spicy eggs, wondering what else he remembered about her.

What she recalled most from their three-month time span together was how special he'd become to her. So much so, that she'd actually—for a nanosecond, at least—considered turning down the job in Raleigh. But Asim's treachery had taught her a valuable lesson. She needed to trust her head and never her heart.

She blinked, realizing Finn was studying her.

"Must be thinking about something serious," he said, snagging a half slice of wheat toast and slathering it with butter. "Your brow is furrowing in that deep concentrating way of yours."

She swallowed, irritated he could read her so well, especially while many facets of him remained a mystery. Finn was a man of secrets. Just as Asim had been.

FORTY-NINE

Noah and Rissi pulled up to Marv's house first thing in the morning.

Stepping up to Marv's front stoop, they opened the screen door and rapped on the main one with a gold anchor knocker.

A miniature version of the black-and-white Cape Hatteras lighthouse stood between the two high-back white rockers on the small square porch. The brief early morning rain had broken up quickly, and Rissi now reveled in the warm sun on her back. It was going to be a beautiful day.

While she occasionally missed her hometown of Boston, the weather in Wilmington was a definite plus.

She was still stoked about the Wilmington Sharks' victory last night—seven to four. She had tickets to next week's home game against the SwampDogs. She just had to decide whom to take with her other ticket. Caleb had been itching to go, but she didn't want to lead him on and feared he'd view it as a date.

Noah knocked again, and she tapped her foot while they waited.

"Coming," Marv finally responded, and Rissi slipped her fidgeting hands into her tan trouser pockets.

Marv opened the door. His gaze shifted to Noah and then Rissi, his brow furrowed.

"Hey, Marv. Can we talk?" Noah said.

"Sure." He stepped outside and gestured to the picnic table. "Loraine," he called back at the house.

His wife popped her strawberry-blond head around the screen door. "Yeah?"

"Why don't you get us some of your sweet tea?"

She smiled. "Be right out."

They made pleasantries until Loraine brought them the sweet tea and poured them all a red Solo cupful.

Rissi took a sip and smiled at the hovering Loraine. "Delicious."

Loraine smiled. "Y'all let me know if you need anything else." She headed back into the ranch-style house.

"So what's up?" Marv asked, lifting his cup to his mouth.

"I want to run through your dive with John Layton," Noah said.

Marv's brow creased, his gaze darting between them. "I already told Rissi everything."

"I'd like you to go through it again with me," Noah said.

Marv's blue eyes narrowed. "Why?"

"We're just trying to be thorough."

"Ok . . . ay." He clasped his hands together on the tabletop, his thumbs shuffling atop one another.

He proceeded to relay the same story he'd told Rissi yesterday.

When he finished, Rissi said, "Genevieve Layton said her husband told her something had gone very wrong on the dive." She left the statement open-ended.

"I told you the guy panicked. It was only his second wreck dive, and the *St. Marie* is a tough dive. When we got almost to the far end, he signaled that he wanted to head topside, but we still had to work ourselves back through the wreck. When a dude's panicking, you know it can actually slow things down rather than speed things up. By the time we made it out of the wreck, he bolted for the surface. I did the necessary stops, and when I surfaced he was in the bathroom."

"So why didn't you tell us he panicked in the wreck itself?"

Marv swiped his nose. "I thought I had."

"You said everything went smoothly."

"Yesterday was a blur, and I suppose at the time I didn't want to embarrass the guy's memory. I mean, his overreacting had nothing to do with his accident, so why bring it up?"

"It's vital to the investigation that we understand everything that happened."

"Investigation?" Marv frowned. "Why do you keep talking like that? The guy had an accident. He ascended too fast and was probably experiencing decompression sickness. Dizziness is one of the common symptoms. The ride back was rough. He probably lost his balance when the boat rocked over a wave and hit his head on the sink. It's unfortunate, but there's nothing more to it."

Rissi narrowed her eyes. Why did it sound like they had Layton's death all wrapped up in a neat bow?

Noah cleared his throat. "It's our job to determine that, and we can't jump to conclusions without having all the facts."

"You have them," Marv said, his tone clipped.

"Not yet," Rissi said.

Marv linked his arms across his chest, his white T-shirt stained with black grease.

"What were you doing before we arrived?" Something told her to ask.

Marv's brows pinched. "Working on my car. What does that have to do with anything?"

"Just curious," Rissi said, feeling far too much irritation lingered in his voice for such a simple question.

"What's wrong with it?" Noah asked.

Marv tucked his chin. "It needed an oil change and grease. Seriously, guys, why are we talking about my car?"

"Just curious, as Rissi said," Noah explained, looking past Marv's shoulder at the freestanding garage with closed doors.

The same question raced through Rissi. Why keep the garage doors closed on such a warm day?

"Mind if we take a look in the garage?" Noah asked.

"Actually, I do. And if this is it for questions about the accident"—he rose from the table—"I'm going to get back to it."

"Just a couple more questions about the dive," Noah said.

"Fine." Marv sat back down with a sigh. "Let's get this over with."

Noah's eyes narrowed. "Why the rush?"

"Because I have plenty to do today, and I don't like wasting time."

Rissi wanted to inquire what exactly he had on his agenda but didn't want to push him away. Without a warrant they had no legal authority to search the garage, and Marv had the right to refuse to answer questions.

"What about Layton's tank?" Noah asked.

"What about it?"

"Did you inspect it before and after the dive?"

"We always inspect all our gear before setting out."

"And after?" she asked.

"Why would I check it after?"

"Maybe Layton panicked because his air wasn't flowing properly. Or maybe he was dizzy because his mixture was off," Noah said.

"He didn't signal anything was off. Only pointed to the surface. I think the enclosed space got to him. It happens."

Rissi pondered his statement and wondered why Marv hadn't brought that up yesterday.

Frustrated with Marv's defensive and borderline rude attitude, she followed Noah to his Jeep. She climbed up into it as Noah held the door for her—always a gentleman, like the rest of the guys on the team. Their mommas had raised them right.

Noah settled in the driver's seat. "He was far too defensive," he said, echoing Rissi's assessment of Marv's demeanor.

"Agreed."

As they pulled out of Marv's drive, Rissi glanced in the side mirror to find the man standing at the top of the drive, staring at them. Worry creased his sea-and-sun-weathered face.

What had really happened below the surface?

Rissi and Noah showed their badges and handed over their service weapons to the security guard upon their entrance to the ILM international customs office, which serviced Wilmington International Airport.

They were told the new acting supervisor, Mr. Stewart, would be out as soon as possible, so they sat down on one of the silver benches lining the waiting area's walls.

Almost thirty minutes later, a man entered the lobby through the side door and strode toward them. "Sorry about the wait," he said, rubbing his hand along his combed-over, thinning brown hair.

"No problem," Rissi said, standing to shake his extended hand.

"Thanks for seeing us," Noah said.

"Security said you're with the Coast Guard Investigative Service."

"Yes, sir. Agent Rissi Dawson." She flashed her badge.

"And Noah Rowley." He did the same.

"Jeremy, please."

Rissi nodded. "Jeremy it is."

"Kind of far from the water, aren't you?" He said it with a smile that suggested he was anticipating laughter.

She humored him with a smile, as did Noah.

"We're here investigating John Layton's death," Noah said.

"John's death?" He slipped his hands into his brown pants pockets. "I can't believe it. We've worked together for fourteen years. What happened?"

"He died on a dive charter."

Jeremy shook his head. "He was so excited about winning that dive excursion for him and Genevieve. I can't believe he died, but I warned him wreck diving was dangerous."

The adrenaline rush of pushing the limits was addictive—seeing how deep you could go . . . what all you could get into.

"We'd like to ask you some questions about John's work here," Noah began.

"Sure." Jeremy rocked back on his heels. "I'm happy to oblige, but what does John's work have to do with a dive accident?"

"We just have a few questions. It shouldn't take much of your time."

"All right, let's head to my office."

Forty-five minutes later, Rissi and Noah left the customs office with a headful of knowledge and a handful of the last two months' manifests, thanks to the very-eager-to-help Jeremy Stewart.

Climbing in the Jeep, Rissi laid the manifest pile on her lap, grabbed a highlighter from her bag, and set to work.

She prayed that, if anything on the pages was related to John Layton's death, God would help it stand out. It was a long shot but definitely worth checking.

Noah pulled onto the highway leading away from the airport and back to town. An incoming plane roared overhead as it made its final descent into Wilmington International. The drive to Dockside took a half hour with traffic backed up on the Wrightsville Beach bridge, which gave her lots of time to comb through the manifest pages.

Slipping into a shaded parking lot in front of the waterfront restaurant, Noah cut the ignition.

"I only have a few pages left," she said. "Why don't you go on in and grab a table, and I'll finish up here, since I'm on a roll?"

"No problem." Noah reclined his seat and lay back, resting his hands behind his head. "I'll just chill."

"You sure?"

"Absolutely. Lunch can wait until you're done."

"Cool." Reaching for the Arnold Palmer she'd brought, she took a long sip, then set the glass bottle back in the cup holder. She turned on the radio and found Sam Cooke's "Bring It on Home to Me" playing. She always worked better with music.

"Nice," Noah said, closing his eyes and smiling as the music played.

The tunes soothing, she reclined her seat back as well. Settling in, she turned back to the work in front of her.

She continued highlighting every incoming airport shipment that John Layton processed.

Three-quarters down the list, her yellow highlighter slid across what she was searching for. On August 10, a package arrived via Delta flight #1350 addressed to Litman Limited. And it was signed for by Eric Jacobs. *Bingo!* "Got it."

Noah opened his eyes.

She read off the find.

"Excellent work," he said. "And now that we know John Layton handled customs approval for Litman Limited packages, it's a pretty good bet our cases are connected. We'll have to pay Mr. Jacobs a visit when we get back to the station."

"Agreed. Two more pages to go, and I'm done."

"Take your time. It's been a chaotic few days. I don't mind a few down minutes." He leaned back and closed his eyes again.

She continued through the remainder of the records, finding three more packages processed—all by John Layton, all belonging to Litman Limited, and all signed for by Eric Jacobs. Seemed the man Finn interrogated last night knew far more than he admitted to.

FIFTY

Rissi and Noah entered Dockside—the waterfront restaurant at the edge of a marina. It boasted a dock where folks could tie up and enter the restaurant via the pier.

The smell of briny water wafted in the air as seagulls' cries echoed overhead.

They headed inside.

"Hey, Kim," Noah said, greeting the hostess.

"Hey, guys." Kim grabbed two menus and two sets of napkin-rolled silverware. "Your usual table?"

"That'd be great," Noah said, stepping back. With a sweep of his hand, he indicated for Rissi to go first. They followed Kim to a table in the outer right corner, giving them a great view of the sound and marina.

Kim set down the menus and silverware and with a smile said, "Amber will be right with you."

"Thanks, Kim." Rissi took the south-facing white plastic chair, and Noah took the one opposite her. Both preferred to sit facing the restaurant entry, but Noah conceded to her because, as he and Caleb always said, she was a lady.

Part of her wanted to be treated like one of the guys, but the other part enjoyed their polite and caring attitude. Being treated like a lady hadn't been part of her experience until she'd started with the unit a little over two years ago.

Logan entered and walked to the takeout counter.

"Hey, Logan," she called.

He waved, grabbed his takeout bag, and stepped to their table.

"Join us," Noah said.

"Sure." Logan set the white plastic bag with his takeout down and pulled up a chair from a nearby table.

"Smells like fried tomatoes and pulled pork," Rissi said of Logan's bag.

"You nailed it." Logan winked. "How'd your morning go?" he asked, opening his food containers. The scent of fried green tomatoes wafted in the air, mingling with the ocean air carrying on the breeze.

A couple of kayakers in a red-and-green kayak paddled by as seagulls squawked overhead.

"It's been interesting," Noah said, squinting in the high-noon sun. He slid his aviator sunglasses on.

Rissi popped a hush puppy in her mouth from the complimentary basket Dockside served each table upon arrival. Southern hospitality at its finest.

She looked at the two-sided menu, despite having it pretty much memorized, then set it down, waiting for Amber to bring their drinks so she could ask her about the day's fresh catch—always the best thing on the menu.

Amber came over, and as Noah was ordering, Rissi spotted Paul and Smitty sitting three tables over. She waved with a smile.

Paul gave her a wink in response.

Noah turned, following her gaze. "Hey, guys." He lifted his chin in greeting.

Paul lifted his mojito, while Smitty raised a long-neck bottle.

"Can we send you guys one?" Paul asked, jiggling his glass. "Looks like you could use it. Rough day?"

"Rough week," Noah said.

Paul stood and strode to their table. "I want to offer my condolences about Sam. Word spread quickly through town."

He raked his hand over his short dark hair. "I'm sorry. He was a good lad."

"Thanks."

Paul signaled Amber over. "Hey, lady, could you get these fine agents a round on me?"

"Thanks," Noah said. "But we're working."

"You sure? Smitty and I won't tell anybody." Paul smiled.

"Thanks, but we're good. Though we appreciate the gesture," Rissi said.

"But maybe you could still be of help," Noah said, pulling two more chairs up. "Could you join us for a minute?"

"Sure."

Smitty carried his and Paul's drinks over and took the empty seat in the scrunched-up circle Noah had fashioned with the extra chairs.

"How can we be of help?" Paul asked, taking the last seat.

"You both know just about everyone in town," Noah began.

"We know our fair share," Smitty said.

Just about everyone in town had stopped by the Coffee Connection at one point or another. It was always bustling.

"Do you by chance know a man by the name of Eric Jacobs?" Noah asked.

"Sure," Smitty said. "Always orders a vanilla soy latte."

"What do you know about him?" Rissi asked.

Smitty's wrinkles creased as his eyes narrowed. "What's this all about?"

"Let's just say he's a person of interest." Noah sat back, his arm draped across the back of Rissi's chair.

"I couldn't tell you much," Smitty said, his gaze shifting to three women who'd just entered. They stood at the hostess counter, waiting to be seated. All three were decked out in white tennis skirts, neon polo shirts with matching socks, and tennis shoes.

Smitty's eyes widened. "Hiya, Phyllis."

The one in the hot pink shirt waved as a coy giggle escaped her lipstick-slathered lips. "Hiya, Francis."

The other two women covered their mouths to whisper.

Smitty grabbed his drink and stood. "If you'll all excuse me." He didn't bother giving them a chance to reply before he scurried across the weather-worn deck to the gaggle of ladies and wrapped his arm around Phyllis's shoulders.

"Don't pay him any heed," Paul said. "He's a ladies' man. Always has been. You should see him at the town-hall dances. Different lady every night."

"Francis?" Rissi asked, never having heard him called that.

"His given name," Paul said. "Took on or was given the nickname Smitty in the Navy. Last name's Smith."

She'd never known that. Then again, she'd never asked.

Smitty and the ladies chatted a moment, then left without saying good-bye.

"What's that all about?" Rissi asked, surprised they'd left so quickly, especially when it had looked like the ladies were just arriving to eat.

"I don't think Smitty took too kindly to you asking about Eric. I'm assuming it made him uncomfortable."

"Why's that?" Noah asked.

"Because the two are friends."

Noah's brows hiked up. "Really?"

"Why wouldn't he tell us that?" Rissi asked.

"I have no idea." Paul shrugged. "Now," he said, standing, "I've got to get back to work. It was nice chatting with you all."

Amber arrived with their fresh-catch mahi-mahi tacos with mango slaw layered on top.

"Thanks," Rissi said.

Noah said a blessing over lunch, and they dug in.

"What's the latest with you?" Noah asked Logan.

Logan set down his glass of water, perspiration drizzling down the outside of the glass. "Emmy and I have been running

Marv's records. Me on financials, and Emmy his home phone and cell."

"And?" He took a sip of his drink.

"I discovered Marv has an offshore account in the Bahamas with several hundred thousand in it."

He gulped the remainder of his drink down. "Marv?"

"Yep."

"Any idea where the money came from?"

"Litman Limited deposited a hundred thousand a little over a month ago and another large deposit went in yesterday."

"Seriously?" Noah looked to Rissi. "I'd say our case connection is definitely established."

With a nod, Logan continued, "The deposit was made yesterday late afternoon, about twenty minutes after Marv placed a call, and ten minutes later that same person called Marv back."

"Why do I have a bad feeling about this?"

Logan cleared his throat. "He called Mo."

FIFTY-ONE

Rissi tried to wrap her mind around all the facts. First, they'd been told two conflicting stories of what occurred during John Layton's wreck dive—one from Genevieve Layton and one from a very defensive Marv. Not long after the dive, Layton died, and then minutes later an explosion shredded the stern section of the *Calliope*, causing everyone aboard to abandon ship before it sank.

Then after returning home, Marv called Mo. That in itself wasn't all that unusual, given what had just occurred and the fact that Mo was his boss and friend of many years, but the timing of what had to be illegal funds being deposited into Marv's offshore account shortly after the phone exchanges between Marv and Mo was too curious to ignore.

Noah asked Logan and Emmalyne to pull Mo's financial and phone records while he and Rissi headed out to once again press Mo on his story.

Fifteen minutes later, Rissi and Noah hopped down from his Jeep and approached Mo's front porch. Rissi cocked her head to the side, following the sound of water spraying. "I think he's around back."

They stepped around to the rear of the house, which sat directly on the ocean, and headed to the dock.

Mo was washing off the exterior of a burgundy-and-white Tahoe fishing boat.

Mo's gaze tracked up to them. "Hey, darling." He cut off the hose and reeled it up as they stepped onto the deck. "How you guys doing today?"

Rissi waited for Noah to begin the conversation.

"We need to ask you a few questions," he said.

"About *Calliope*?" Mo swiped his damp hands across his flowered board shorts. "Sure."

"Actually, about Marv," Noah said.

Mo's gray-tinged brows furrowed. "What about Marv?"

"Can we talk at the table?" Noah asked, gesturing to the black wrought-iron patio table and chairs situated on the terraced brick patio.

"All right." Mo followed him up the well-worn path that snaked through the grass up to the patio.

Noah pulled a chair out for Rissi, then took a chair for himself.

Dark clouds filled the recently blue sky. The dense air held the fresh scent of rain's imminent return.

Mo rested his hands on the table and intertwined his calloused fingers.

Rissi eyed the scrapes and bruises along his knuckles.

"What happened to your hands?" she asked.

"What?" Mo lifted his hands, inspecting them. "Huh. Hadn't noticed. Must have been during the evac."

Not knowing all that occurred during the evacuation, Rissi couldn't be totally sure, but those scrapes and bruises looked far more like . . . like someone had been struggling to break free of his hold.

Noah got straight to it. "Marv called you yesterday afternoon. What did you two talk about?"

Everything they'd discovered today tossed violently through the storm emerging in Rissi's mind.

Irritation sparked in Mo's eyes, as if the answer ought to be obvious. "What do you think?"

"I don't know," Noah said with an edge of authority. "That's why I'm asking you."

Mo bristled. "We talked about the explosion, the evac, about losing a passenger and the *Calliope*."

"Let's focus on losing John Layton," Noah said.

"All right."

"What did Marv tell you about the dive?"

"We already went through this, Noah. You know the answers."

Noah folded his arms against his broad chest. "Humor me, Mo."

He threw up his hands. "Fine! He said it went well, but that John panicked on the way up and didn't make his decompression stops."

"But the dive went fine as far as you are aware?" Rissi asked.

Mo arched a brow. "Yeah." The word came out more as a question than an answer.

"John Layton told his wife something had gone very wrong on the dive. She said he acted concerned for both of their safety. He insisted she go topside and stick with the group of passengers. Then he locked himself in the head. Next thing she knows, her husband is dead from what looked to her—a medical doctor—like blunt-force trauma to the head."

"Okay," Mo said. "Just say she heard correctly, and what John told her was true and not some story he concocted to explain away why he'd freaked out rather than just admitting he'd panicked. What does any of this have to do with me?"

"That's what we're trying to determine," Rissi said.

Mo angled his head and lifted his brows. "You can't seriously believe any foul play was involved in John Layton's death?"

"It's beginning to look like a strong possibility," Noah said.

Mo released a guffaw. "You've got to be kidding. Layton made up a story because he didn't want to admit he'd freaked out on the dive."

"You really believe that's what happened?" Noah said.

Mo nodded. "I do."

"Let's say you're wrong and Layton's story was true. Why would Marv lie about it?"

"He didn't lie. It didn't happen." Mo's jaw tightened.

"How can you be one hundred percent certain?" Rissi asked.

"Because I've known Marv for twenty years. He wouldn't lie to me."

"No," Rissi said, "I suppose he wouldn't." She looked at Noah—both realizing if Layton's story was true, then both Marv and Mo had lied to them.

"Why'd you call Marv back?" Noah asked.

Mo frowned. "What?"

"The afternoon of the evac, Marv called you at 3:10. You talked for eight minutes, then at 3:48 you called him back and talked for three minutes. What did you talk about?"

"I wanted to make sure he was all right." Mo's eyes narrowed. "How do you know that we spoke?"

"We had reason to look at your phone records."

"What reason is that?"

"We're investigating John Layton's death, and right now Marv is a possible suspect if foul play is involved."

Mo stood. "I can't believe this."

"Please sit down," Noah said. "We have a few more questions."

"That I'm done answering."

"We'd hate to pull you into the office."

Mo's jaw shifted, and after a moment of contemplation, he said, "Fine. Let's finish this."

"Thank you," Noah said. "Now, you said you called Marv to make sure he was all right. All right in what way?"

"We'd just lost a passenger to an ac-ci-dent," Mo enunciated the last word. "And lost the source of our livelihood. The whole crew was upset."

After pressing Mo on a few more details, it was readily apparent he was sticking to his story, so they thanked him for his cooperation, such as it was, and excused themselves.

"What do you think?" Rissi asked as they climbed into the Jeep.

"I think we need to keep digging. Everything seems too wrapped up in a neat package of explanation. And I doubt there is an innocent reason for that deposit into Marv's offshore account."

"Mo didn't even show an ounce of concern at the possibility Marv had lied."

"That's what concerns me." He sighed.

"Me too." Though she hated to think it.

"Hopefully, Logan or Emmalyne calls shortly with Mo's financials."

"I half pray we don't find anything—for Mo's sake—and half hope we have our next clue in Layton's death."

"We also need to check into Layton's phone records and financials," Noah said as the first drops of rain fell.

Rissi took a brisk inhale. "What do you want to bet we find calls to and payment from Litman Limited?"

FIFTY-TWO

Finn entered the interrogation room where Eric Jacobs sat waiting.

"Thought you might like a glass of water." He slid the glass across the table.

Mr. Jacobs lifted it. "Thank you."

Finn couldn't wrap his mind around the fact that a guy who appeared to be a sweet middle-aged man was picking up and delivering what he assumed were illegal shipments for Litman Limited. It was the delivery part—where Jacobs dropped the packages—that interested him most.

He started with a statement. "I'm disappointed to discover you lied to me."

"Lied?" Mr. Jacobs tilted his head, his eyes wide with false innocence.

"You said when you picked up the package on Shore Lane you didn't know where to drop it."

"Correct."

"Where have you dropped Litman Limited's other packages?"

"Other packages?" His tone remained calm.

"Yes." Finn slid the list Emmalyne had put together based off the manifests Rissi obtained from the customs office across the black Formica tabletop.

Jacobs leaned forward, his eyes scanning it. Beads of perspiration sprung on his wrinkled brow.

"That is a list of documented pickups you made for Litman Limited from the customs office at Wilmington International. Where did you deliver those packages, or are they still in your possession?"

"No." Jacobs coughed. "Of course not."

"You may as well tell the truth now, as we'll soon discover it for ourselves."

"Oh?" His fingers clutched the list, the paper shaking slightly in his hold.

"Two of our agents are searching your home and property as we speak."

Color rushed to Jacobs's face. "You have no right!"

"Actually, we do. Warrant came through just before they left."

"On what grounds?" His knuckles whitened.

"We only have to provide the reasons for the warrant to the judge." Finn lifted his pen and straightened the legal pad in front of Jacobs. "Do you have anything to confess?"

The blue vein on the side of Jacobs's temple twitched.

He'd hit a nerve. Curiosity and adrenaline warmed his body at the thought of what Logan and Caleb might discover at Jacobs's house.

"Where have you dropped the other packages you retrieved for Litman Limited?"

Jacobs shrugged. "It varies."

Finn's brows arched. "Such as?"

"I meet a man. I don't know his name, so don't bother asking."

"Meet him where?"

"At the park, in the public beach access parking lot, at the library—if it's a smaller package."

"And if it's larger?"

"More secluded places. I park where I'm directed. A white

painter's van pulls up and we load the container into the back of the van. I get paid and go my way."

"What kind of payments are we talking?"

"My finances are my business."

"Not since we obtained the warrant to check them." He pulled out the last three months of Jacobs's bank statements Emmalyne had given him—the questionable deposits circled in red.

Jacobs pushed his tongue up under his top lip, bulging it out momentarily before licking his lips.

"Looks like you've made some large cash deposits over the last few months."

Jacobs shifted in his chair. "I get paid in cash for most of my deliveries. I have a lot of customers."

"Of course." Finn slid the copies of Jacobs's bank statements in front of him. "Were these circled deposits payments from Litman Limited?" Unless he confirmed Finn's suspicion, it would remain just that—a suspicion.

"I can't recall each transaction," he muttered.

"But some were from Litman?"

"I imagine."

Finn rubbed his chin, then interlocked his hands on the table. "Mr. Jacobs, it only takes one call to the IRS if you choose not to cooperate."

Jacobs swallowed, audibly. "What do you want?"

"The van's license plate number, which I feel confident a man like you noted. Along with a description of the man you meet. And a list of all the drop locations." Finn slid the legal pad and pen to him. "You had best get started."

With fear and anger clouding his eyes, Jacobs lifted the pen and began scribbling.

Finn sat back with a satisfied smile.

Close to half an hour later, Jacobs slid the pad back to Finn.

"I'll review this and let you know if I have any questions." Finn stood, grabbing hold of his pad.

Jacobs rubbed his brow. "I'm sure you will."

"Oh," Finn said, pausing at the door, "I nearly forgot." He turned back and retook his seat. "Tell me about your relationship with Smitty."

Jacobs's brows puckered. "Who?"

"From the Coffee Connection."

Finn emerged from the interrogation room with a yellow legal pad in hand and a curious smile on his lips.

"Let me guess," Gabby said. "You got him to talk?"

"Yep."

"And?" Rissi asked, leaning forward in her chair.

"We're going to want to case board this."

"All right, people," Noah said, heading for the board. "Grab a drink or snack, and let's circle up. Rissi and I have a lot to cover. And it sounds like Finn has even more."

Gabby followed Rissi into the kitchen, where they made up bowls of trail mix—dark chocolate chips, dried cranberries, walnuts, and almonds.

"Want a Coke?" Rissi asked, pulling one out of the fridge.

"Yes, please."

She pulled another out and handed it to Gabby.

"Sounds like everyone is making good progress."

"Yeah." Rissi opened her Coke—the fizz releasing—and leaned against the counter. "The more we dig, the more intertwined things become."

She'd been thinking the same thing based off what she knew, and Litman Limited appeared to be the common denominator.

Gabby followed Rissi out to the couch and took an open spot. She hoped Noah would let her stay. It wasn't easy eavesdropping from the desks in the front room.

"Let's start, folks. Who wants to go first?" Noah opened the red dry erase marker and shook his head. "Seriously, strawberry scented?"

"I thought it'd add a nice touch to some tough topics," Emmy said.

Gabby smiled. She was coming to adore Emmy.

"Fair enough. Moving on," Noah said with another shake of his head. "Who wants to start?"

"I'll go," Rissi said. She quickly ran down everything she and Noah had learned.

Noah wrote down the key points in a neat column beneath Layton's name and his blown-up driver's license picture.

"While we're on John Layton . . ." Emmy said. "Logan ran his financials and located an offshore account in his name. He received wire transfers from . . . one guess."

"Litman Limited," Rissi said, tucking her legs beneath her on the sofa.

Emmy tapped her nose.

Gabby knew better than to comment or she risked Noah shooing her off to the front room while they finished discussing the leads, but she couldn't help but wonder what all Litman Limited had its hooks in, and how many people were in its pocket. But more importantly, who was hiding behind the front company. Someone had to be pulling the strings.

"Look what we found at Eric Jacobs's house," Logan said as he entered the station with Caleb close behind. He held up a large evidence bag with a padded envelope inside.

"What do we have here?" Finn asked, sitting forward as Logan slipped on a pair of gloves while Caleb hunkered down beside Rissi on the couch.

Logan opened the evidence bag along with the padded envelope, slipping his gloved hand in and pulling out a stunning diamond necklace.

"Whoa!" Rissi said.

"This package wasn't sent through UPS. It came through

232

customs at Wilmington International, so it looks like Litman Limited was using Mr. Layton to pass their stolen goods through customs," Caleb said, "and then acquired the stolen jewels or whatever else they've been smuggling using a courier like Eric Jacobs."

Finn tapped his notepad. "I've got a list of drop spots from Jacobs. All of which appear to be near the water. I'll map them out, see if there's a pattern."

"I think Rissi and I may have found a possible motive for John Layton's death, if foul play was in fact involved," Noah said, going on to explain the money found in Marv's account.

Gabby's mind was racing. It sounded like Marv had been paid to take Layton out, but Layton survived long enough to reach the ship. The question was, why? If Layton was helping Litman Limited smuggle contraband, why kill him?

"Where are we on Mo's financials?" Noah asked Logan.

"He received deposits in an offshore account from Litman Limited too. He's been getting them over the past two years. The last deposit was made the day before Layton's death."

Noah raked a hand over his head. "So it's pretty clear Mo, Marv, and Layton all worked for Litman. I'm assuming the necklace you found"—Noah looked to Caleb and then Logan—"is in fact stolen."

"Definitely stolen," Caleb said. "After finding the necklace, I made some calls to friends in a few different agencies—sent a picture. The necklace was stolen two weeks ago from a private collection in Florence."

Rissi retrieved and flipped through the manifest. "Layton processed a package from Naples on August twenty-fifth."

"Two days after the necklace was stolen," Caleb said.

"And Jacobs retrieved the package, but for some reason he didn't deliver it," Finn said. "I'll try to find out why."

Gabby knew she should remain quiet, but she didn't have it in her. "Two of the drug runners who attacked you . . ." She looked to Finn. "And who killed Sam . . . called Litman. Looks like whoever's behind Litman is smuggling more than stolen goods."

Finn propped his elbows on his knees and rubbed his forehead. "Which most likely provides the answer to what Will Seavers was in too deep with."

"Drug smuggling." Rissi shook her head. "I can't believe it."

"Trust me." Finn exhaled. "I don't want to believe it, but I'm guessing he was either actively smuggling drugs or giving up Coast Guard patrol schedules so the drug runners could move freely without fear of being caught."

"What about Fletcher?" Rissi asked. "And do you think the intruder you and Gabby encountered at his house also works for Litman Limited?"

Finn retrieved a folder from his desk and sat back down. "Let's start with the intruder, Isaac Bashert. He's definitely connected to Litman because he called that same number when Caleb brought him in, but my interrogation gave no indication of how he fits into the bigger picture. Gabby and I checked out his house this morning. We found Litman's phone number in a small notebook that's being processed by Emmy in the lab."

"It's got an interesting code or possibly a personalized shorthand throughout," Emmy said, sitting on the couch's padded arm, a cup of cinnamon-smelling tea in her hand.

"We're thinking it's a log of his work for Litman," Gabby said. "Or hopefully something that will allow you to keep holding him."

Rissi exhaled. "If not, we're going to have to release him."

"If anyone can decode it, it's Em." Logan lifted his cup of coffee with a smile.

"Thanks," she said. "As soon as we're done meeting, I'll get back on it."

"Since Bashert claimed to have met Fletcher several times at Wilmington Lanes, we checked that out too," Finn said. "One of the bartenders recognized Bashert's picture, and he thinks he remembers seeing him talking with Fletcher a time or two."

"Wow. I'm surprised that one paid out," Logan said.

"Me too." Finn took a sip of his Mountain Dew. He offered Gabby a sip, and she took it.

"Thanks." She wondered what Fletcher and Bashert had been talking about.

Finn got to his feet to stretch. "Fletcher's involvement could go one of two ways. It's possible he is in on whatever Will was into, and when Will tried to get out, as he told Tess he was going to do that night, Fletcher either killed Will or had someone tied to Litman do it."

"And the other option?" Noah asked.

"Fletcher is innocent. He was a witness to Will's death, and the drug runners tried to kill him to keep him from talking."

"So assuming Bashert is involved in this Litman thing, why would he break in to Fletcher's house?" Logan asked, tapping the rim of his mug.

"Maybe he thought he was home from the hospital and was ordered to take him out," Finn said. "I can see Litman wanting to kill Fletcher, regardless of his connection to them."

Gabby leaned forward. "If Fletcher *is* innocent, why isn't he saying more?"

"Maybe his head injury is affecting his memory," Finn said.

Noah lifted his chin. "What does your gut tell you?"

"I hate to say it." Finn exhaled, clearly disheartened at the thought of a corrupt guardsman. "I'm betting Fletcher is involved."

Noah nodded. "Then run with that theory."

"I'll head back over to the hospital tomorrow. The fact that Will was shot with two different guns leads me to believe there were two shooters." Finn swallowed. "My gut says Fletcher was one of them."

FIFTY-THREE

"You know what's still bugging me?" Noah said as he and Gabby drove to Kenzie's for dinner.

"What's that?"

"I get that Layton and Jacobs helped whoever's behind Litman smuggle jewels and whatever else through the airport. It makes sense that Seavers and—I'm almost positive—Fletcher were helping him smuggle drugs. But how did they reach Layton once he was locked in the bathroom?"

"We can't know for sure, but it could be as simple as the way I opened the locked office in Fletcher's home. There's almost always a pin key in case a kid locks themselves in."

"Right." Noah snapped his fingers. "I'll check out the lock style when we're cleared to dive *Calliope*." He took a deep inhale and released it. "Speaking of Fletcher's house . . ."

She shifted in her seat. Where was this headed?

"If Finn hadn't showed up when he did, you or Tess could have been seriously injured, if not killed."

"Must I remind you that I'm the one who knocked the guy out?"

"I know, but it had to be terrifying for Finn . . . and Caleb and Emmy until he located you. They all feared Fuentes had or could find you while you were away from the team's protection. I know you are very capable but . . ."

"But, it wasn't considerate sneaking out on their watch." She bit her bottom lip. "I was trying to be helpful."

"I know, but I need to know where you are at all times and that you're safe."

She narrowed her eyes. "What are you suggesting?"

He pulled a small silver disc from his shirt pocket.

"Is that what I think it is?"

"It's a tracker."

She sat up higher, squaring her shoulders. "You've got to be kidding."

"You worry us all—me, Mom, Kenzie, and the team." He inhaled and blew it out slowly. "*Please*. Just slip it in your locket for all our peace of mind."

"You don't think that's overkill?"

"Even if it is, what can it hurt?"

"Fine." She reached out her hand, and he dropped the small tracker into her cupped palm. She slipped it in her locket and clasped it shut.

He squeezed her shoulder. "Thank you."

She nodded. "Now back to the case. There's actually one other thing that's bugging me. . . ."

Noah arched a brow in the oncoming headlights. "Oh?"

"Besides killing Layton, what does Litman pay Mo and Marv for?"

"Excellent question."

Finn parked behind Noah in Kenzie and Mark's driveway. Climbing from the car, he stared at the one-story brick rancher in Camp Lejeune's base housing. He hadn't been to their home for dinner since Gabby left for Raleigh, but Noah insisted he join them.

Shutting his car door, he headed up the drive with a bouquet of mixed flowers in his hand for his hosts.

He glanced in Noah's empty Jeep—he and Gabby had already gone inside. Queasiness tumbled in his gut. It was just a friendly dinner, so why were his nerves taunting him?

Knocking on the door, he held his breath. Seeing Gabby with her family was one of the reasons he'd fallen in love with her. Watching her play Chutes and Ladders with Fiona while Owen kept trying to teeter on his newly walking legs onto the board to steal their game pieces. Watching Gabby unreserved, laughing unabashedly at Fiona's four-year-old attempts at jokes that usually ended in an animal sound. Seeing her smile at Owen as he tumbled over her while she lay on the floor, head propped on a pillow, watching *Peppa Pig*.

Seeing her filled with joy had stoked the embers even more fully alive inside of him.

Swallowing, he knocked again. A moment later, the door opened and Kenzie answered. "Finn, so glad you could join us. It's been too long." She held the door open as he stepped inside. "Sorry for making you wait. We were out back. I thought I heard the door, but I wasn't sure until you knocked again."

"No worries." He followed her along the hallway, pausing with her as she bent to pick up discarded toys, Fiona's princess shoes, and Owen's "uh-oh." According to Gabby, every time he dropped it, Kenzie had said "uh-oh," and as soon as he'd learned to talk, Owen started calling his pacifier "uh-oh." It was flipping adorable.

Kenzie set the pile of discarded items in the oversize wicker basket beside the sofa. "I'll deal with that later." She smiled. "We're all out back."

He stepped outside to the sound of chirping crickets and meat sizzling on the grill.

"Walker!" Mark said, raising his spatula. "Good to see you, man."

"Same here."

"What can I get you to drink?" Kenzie asked as Nana Jo moved in for a big hug.

"Lemonade would be great, thanks. *Ooof*," he muttered, releasing a puff of air as Nana Jo squeezed him tightly.

"You don't come around nearly often enough, young man." She released her hold and looked up at him. "Are you getting enough sleep?"

"Mom, let him be," Gabby chided.

"It's fine," he assured her and turned his attention back to Nana Jo. "Yes, ma'am."

She rested her hands on her hips and studied him. "All right. Make sure you do. A good night's sleep—"

"Makes for a good day," the three siblings said in unison.

"At least you three have listened to *something* I say."

"Momma." Kenzie sighed. "You know we listened to most of what you said." She winked at Gabby.

"And then you just ignored it?" Nana Jo looked over her purple-framed glasses sitting on the edge of her nose.

"Not all of it," Noah said with a teasing chuckle as he squeezed her shoulders.

Nana Jo pursed her lips, trying to bite back a smile, but the crinkles in the corners of her eyes gave her away. "You go on and get." She swatted Noah with the dishrag she'd tucked in the Kitchen Queen apron the grandkids had given her last Christmas, and he scooted.

"Now, now, adults. Let's behave," Mark said, loading a blue platter with steaks from the grill.

"Mom," Fiona said, "Owen's throwing sand again."

Kenzie inhaled. "Excuse me." She strode to the turtle sandbox, where Fiona was building castles in her princess tiara and Owen was chucking fistfuls of sand.

"Take a seat." Mark gestured Finn to the table.

As he lowered into the chair beside Gabby, she brushed her hair back from her face.

He wondered if she was remembering the nights they'd spent at her sister's playing games in front of the fire, the flames illuminating the amber highlights in her hair.

"I'll say the blessing," Mark said, lowering his baseball cap to his side. "Thank you, Father, for this bounty of food and all who are here to share it. We pray for everyone's safety and for your continued protection and provision. In Jesus' name I pray. Amen."

"Amen," Finn said, laying his napkin across his lap.

After dinner, everyone moved inside for Fiona's production of *The Princess and the Pea*.

While awaiting the set to be put in place, Nana Jo took a seat between Finn and Gabby.

"You know, when the kids were little they, too, put on plays."

He leaned over, smiling at a blushing Gabby. "Is that right?"

"Yes. They were always the same characters, but they had many different adventures."

Finn's lips twitched as Gabby's blush grew.

"Mom, I'm sure Finn doesn't want to hear about our silly plays."

"Of course I do," he said, stretching out his legs. "They sound interesting."

"That's a good word for it." Nana Jo chuckled.

"Mom . . ."

"Gabrielle, I'm telling the story."

Noah chuckled.

Gabby turned on him. "What's so funny?"

"How flustered you're getting."

Her cheeks tinged crimson.

"So what characters were they?"

"I was a valiant knight," Noah said, his shoulders broadening.

"And I was a princess," Kenzie called over the top of the cardboard castle. "As you can see, the apple didn't fall far from the tree."

"And . . ." Finn nudged Gabby's socked foot. "Who were you?"

"It really doesn't matter who—"

"Oh, come on, Gabs," Kenzie said. "Just tell him you were Carmen Sandiego."

Finn's lips curled into a smile. "Carmen Sandiego, international spy?"

"What?" She jabbed her foot into his as he laughed. "She was cool."

"Absolutely." Of course Gabby would be an international spy. Her love of adventure, mystery, and exposing evil ran deep.

Xavier settled in his bunk. Before long, he'd be back in a real bed and Gabrielle Rowley would be dead.

It'd taken more time than anticipated, but his freedom was on the horizon, the gears in motion.

He nestled into the thin, bumpy mattress with irritation. Soon thoughts of Gabrielle filled his mind. All the possible ways to kill her danced through it.

Fast? Slow? Brutal? Intricately brilliant?

So many methods. He'd stay his hand until the perfect one fixated in his mind.

She'd nearly ruined his life. He'd take the time to ruin hers, watching her suffer as everything she loved was destroyed. And when she had nothing left, when despair filled her eyes, he'd strike. He'd end her pathetic life. But not before looking her in the eyes as the life drained from them. He wanted his smiling face to be the last thing she ever saw.

He rolled over, punching the pillow beneath his head. One more day.

FIFTY-FOUR

Finn headed upstairs, where Gabby had gone to put the kiddos to bed. Owen's room was dark, save for the green turtle-shaped lights spinning on the ceiling from the round toy on his dresser. The green light bounced off his chubby cheeks.

Please, Father, keep Mark safe where he is going. Bring him home safely to his family. Comfort Kenzie and the kids while he's away.

He'd grown up without a dad since he was fourteen, lost him for good when he was sixteen after two years of being nearly a world away. He didn't wish that on anyone.

His chest squeezed at the thought of Will Jr. on the way and Sam's daughter, Ali, and the loss they and their moms had suffered mere days ago. He said a prayer for protection, for God to wrap His arms around them and hold them up in the rough days ahead.

He moved for Fiona's room at the end of the hall, decorated in sparkling pink. Gabby's back was to him. She sat by Fiona's side on her twin bed.

"I know it'll be hard," she said. "But how about you write notes and draw pictures, and we can send him a care package every week?"

Fiona nodded with a smile.

"You write the letter or make him one of your super special drawings, and I'll get a box with some goodies."

"Cheetos are his favorite."

Gabby laughed softly. "And Lucky Charms?"

Fiona nodded, her attention fixed on Gabby—not even noticing his presence as he leaned against the open doorframe, his thumbs hooked in his belt loops.

"And Snickers bars."

"Wow." She tickled Fiona, and the little girl squealed and squirmed with joyous laughter. "Your daddy eats so healthy."

"Finn!" Fiona said, her gaze slipping to him.

Gabby spun around. "Oh, hi."

"I didn't mean to interrupt."

"Are you ready to go?" she asked.

"Nah, take your time." He loved watching her with her niece and nephew. She'd make an amazing mom.

Gabby turned back to Fiona. "All right, lady. I should probably get going. If Finn doesn't get his sleep, he walks around like a zombie all day." Gabby stretched her arms out in front of her and wobbled side to side.

Fiona giggled. "Like the zombies on *Scooby-Doo*?"

"Exactly like that. Now . . ." She tucked Fiona's pink Minnie Mouse comforter in tighter. "Just one more thing to do." She held her pinkie crooked and extended it to Fiona. "Pinkie swear we'll take good care of your daddy with packages?"

Fiona smiled, interlocking her small pinkie with Gabby's. "Promise."

They swung their intertwined pinkies about, then unhooked them and slid their hands along each other's, and then finished the secret handshake with jazz hands. "All right, missy, time for bed."

"Night, Aunt Gabby." She snuggled deeper under the covers.

"Night, sugar bean." She leaned over, pressing a kiss to Fiona's forehead. "Sleep tight." She clicked off the light. "Love you a million red jelly beans."

Fiona yawned. "Love you a billion sour worms."

Gabby smiled as she headed to Finn's side, and with one last loving glance at Fiona, she shut the door save for a small crack.

Finn couldn't help but smile.

"What?" She tilted her head to the side, her gaze intense.

His smile widened. "Nothing," he whispered, lest he wake the babes.

She tugged his arm, halting him. "Seriously, what?"

"You're a good aunt."

"Thanks. It's easy with those two sweethearts."

"You'll make a great mom."

"You think so?"

"I do. You're a natural with kids."

Gabby stood barefoot in Finn's kitchen, eating strawberries and feeding every other one to Layla. She'd never known a puppy to like fruit, but Finn's Australian shepherd gobbled them up, her tail wagging feverishly.

"I see she's decided who the easy mark is." Finn smiled, hopping up on the counter, his legs dangling down.

"Look at that face." She pointed at Layla's big puppy-dog eyes. "You'd have to be heartless to ignore her cuteness."

"Like I said." Finn swung his legs back and forth. "Easy mark."

Gabby rolled her eyes. She'd seen him being just as much a sucker for Layla's charms. Finn's comments about her being a good mom still tossed through her mind. She'd never really stopped to think about her life after chasing stories around the world. She didn't want to live the traveling life with kids, and if—or rather, when—she had kids, she wanted to be with them and work smaller, local pieces.

A life with Finn at her side and a couple little rug rats danced through her mind. She popped a strawberry in her mouth and leaned against the counter for support. Now she was idealizing a life with Finn? She took a stiff inhale, realizing she feared not being with him far more than she feared an idyllic future like that. What was going on with her? How had he gotten so deeply ingrained in her mind and heart already? She'd known coming back was dangerous. . . .

"What's got your attention?" he asked, hopping down to give Layla a good rubdown. She licked his face and he laughed.

She shrugged. "Just daydreaming."

He got back to his feet.

"About anything in particular?"

You. She cleared her throat. "Nah," she said, biting the inside of her cheek as the word left her mouth. She hated to lie to him, but she wasn't ready to tell him . . . wasn't ready for any of it. Or at least that's what her fear told her.

He leaned against the counter next to her, a grin tugging on his lips. "So . . . Carmen Sandiego?"

She turned her attention and her hands back to hulling another strawberry. Best to keep preoccupied as gooseflesh rippled up her arms at Finn's close proximity. She tossed the stem in the small white bowl to the side. "She was very cool."

"Yes, she was," he said with sincerity. "I can see why you picked her."

"Really?"

"It's basically your job in a nutshell."

Her face pinched. "I think you're confusing a spy with a reporter."

"You were undercover in South Sudan, right?"

"Yes."

"So there are similarities."

"Perhaps similarities . . ." She shrugged a shoulder. "But there's a key difference."

He lifted his chin. "What's that?"

"The objective. A spy's mission can be a wide variety of things, but a reporter's is always the same."

He waited for her to answer.

"To find the truth."

"That's what drives you, isn't it?"

She gave Layla the strawberry in her hand. "Yes, and what drives you?"

"I'll think on it and get back to you." He pressed a kiss to her cheek. "We better get to bed. We've got a rough awakening tomorrow."

She swallowed. Sam's funeral.

Rissi retrieved the storage box from the back of her closet. She carried it to her bed, curled up in the covers, and opened it. It only took a moment to find what she looked for. Her hand clasped the binding, and she lifted her diary.

Blowing off the soft film of dust that had crept through the cracks, she wiped her hand over the burgundy cover, fingering the raised Aslan crest. She smiled at the memory of the day Mason gave the diary to her. He'd smuggled it into the house and up to their secret hiding spot. And she kept it concealed in the rafters until the day of her emancipation—the day she broke free of Hank's ironclad hold on her.

She flipped to August 17, 2009, and her heart winced. The day Mason left the home. He had no choice upon turning eighteen, but that day it felt as though she'd lost half her heart and the entirety of her hope.

She scanned the page, the words written with an unsteady hand.

With wings wide, we soared above the clouds, above the grime into the blue sublime.

The sweet smell of freedom touched my soul for a

blissful moment until the grip of violence clasped me
hard, dragging me back under as he soared.
    A prisoner again, I see nights with no end.

Swallowing, she closed the diary and set it on her nightstand. Her chest heavy, the breath squeezed from her lungs.

Why was the past resurrecting itself now?

She clicked out the light, her breath hitching tighter.

Maybe just for tonight, she'd dig back in, remembering the good times with Mason—flip to those pages.

She reached out and switched the light back on.

Finn pressed his hand against the turquoise tile, letting the hot water stream over him, rolling off his aching shoulder.

Steam filled the bathroom and Gabby his thoughts.

He'd done exactly what he vowed not to do. He'd fallen in love with her all over again.

After another moment of indulging in the warmth spreading over his skin, he shut off the water and stepped out to find Layla waiting for him, her body pressed against the tub.

"Hey, girl." He grabbed his towel off the hook and wrapped it around his waist. Tucking in the corner to secure it, he took a wide step over the dog.

Feet planted on the cool floor, he moved for the bedroom.

Changing into his boxers, he climbed into bed, and Layla jumped up beside him.

He turned out the light and settled in, wondering which nightmare would fill his dreams tonight—the agony of losing Stan Larson to the ocean waves or the horror of Fuentes finding Gabby. As much as he wished otherwise, he feared it was only a matter of time before the drug lord did.

FIFTY-FIVE

Finn looked at Gabby, surprise shooting through him when she reached for his hand, interlacing her fingers with his. They followed the rest of the gang down the winding, sand-packed path between the dunes, rushes fluttering in the breeze. At the end of the trail, the ocean spread far and wide. The rhythmic lapping of the waves lulled as they headed barefoot across the warm sand for Sam's memorial service.

The people gathering took a seat in a large circle on beach blankets spread out across the sand. Flowers in vibrant oranges and yellows lay in a large pile in the center of it all.

Coconut suntan lotion wafted on the salty sea breeze.

"Hi, guys," Beth said as they approached.

"Hey, lady." Finn hugged her. Then he knelt in front of Ali. "Hey, kiddo. I'm praying for you today."

Ali nodded, tears welling in her sweet eyes.

His chest tightened, choking the breath from his lungs at the injustice of it all.

Beth clasped her daughter's hand and wiped the tears from her eyes. Then she stood and sniffed, not bothering to hide the tears rolling down her own cheeks. Her yellow sundress fluttered in the breeze blowing over the heightening tide. "If everyone will take a seat, we'll get started," she said.

Finn did as instructed, sitting on the yellow and jade tie-dyed blanket. Gabby sank beside him, tucking her legs to the side and securing her blue-and-white sundress beneath her knees.

Chris Tomlin's "I Will Rise" played on the iPad nestled on Beth's blanket.

Tears misted in Rissi's eyes across the circle—Noah on one side of her and Caleb on the other. Logan and Emmalyne sat on the blanket beside Beth and sweet Ali.

Beth leaned forward and began in a trembling, yet somehow strong, voice. "Sam wouldn't want us mourning at a funeral parlor. He'd want us out here celebrating his life by the sea that he loved so much. So today I'd love to have anyone who'd like to share a story about Sam speak. And then instead of placing flowers on a coffin, we'll send them off to sea in his memory."

Finn's chest warmed. Sam wouldn't have wanted it any other way.

Rissi took a shaky inhale as she climbed into her Fiat. Noah wiped the sand off his feet before climbing in the passenger side. He pulled his Sperrys on and unrolled his khaki Dockers until they met the top edge of his shoes. His light-blue dress shirt highlighted his tan skin. All the men had worn similar attire to the memorial service, while all the women had worn sundresses.

"I'm guessing we should go by the station, so I can change before we head to Marv's?" Rissi said, hoping to get back into real clothes.

"We aren't far from his place. If you don't mind, let's just stop on the way, and then we'll head to the station."

"No problem," she said, lowering the convertible top.

Noah ducked slightly, the top of his head nearly bumping the black collapsible roof.

She shifted the car into reverse, feeling silly in the jade sundress—in any dress. And especially when headed to work. Where would she keep her gun?

Knowing what they now did about Marv and Mr. Layton, they had a good deal of questions for him, and a warrant to search his house and property. Rissi wasn't sure exactly what they were looking for but hoped the search would uncover something that explained what he and Mo had been doing for Litman Limited—other than killing John Layton. The payments went back months, long before Layton had been killed, so what were the payments for? Drug running as well?

She was itching for Noah and Finn to get clearance to dive the *Calliope*, and she prayed it offered the clues they needed to tie everything together. It was hard to wrap her head around a replacement coming for Sam. Mere days ago, they had been ribbing each other during their pickup baseball game.

The warm September wind ruffled her hair, tousling it about her head as they made the ten-minute drive to Marv and Loraine's place. She hoped Loraine was out and about. Rissi hated that they might have to search the house while she stood by, watching as they went through her things. Hated to question her husband in front of her.

Unfortunately, they weren't that lucky.

Loraine answered the door. Her freckle-smattered face frowned. "You guys again. Haven't you already done enough?" She moved to shut the door.

Noah interceded, catching it before she could shut them out. "I'm sorry, Loraine, but we need to speak with Marv."

"He ain't here. Hasn't been since you all left yesterday."

Noah cocked his head. "What?"

"He headed out not long after you two did, and I haven't seen him since." Annoyance filled her tone, but concern showed in her chestnut brown eyes.

"I assume you've tried calling him?" Noah asked as her hands settled on her hips.

"Gee. I didn't think of that." She rolled her eyes. "Great detective, you are."

"Look, Loraine, we want to find him as much as you do," Rissi said.

"I doubt that, and if so, it's only because you want to pester him. He didn't do anything. That guy on the boat had an accident. Accidents happen all the time. I don't know why you're making such a big deal about it."

So Marv had worked his spiel with her. Much as he'd tried with them.

"Have you called Mo?" Noah asked.

"Of course I did, but he hasn't seen him. No one has."

"Did he take anything with him?" Rissi asked.

Loraine tilted her head, leaning against the doorframe with a look of resignation. "Like what?"

"A bag of clothes? Anything that might suggest he was taking off for a while?" Rissi asked, adding the *for a while* for Loraine's benefit.

"Nah. He just said he had to run an errand. He kissed my cheek, jumped in his truck, and took off. Haven't heard a peep from him since."

Noah handed Loraine the warrant. "I'm afraid we're going to need to look around."

Loraine flipped the paper open and shook her head. "Of course you do."

Gabby stepped through the hospital's front sliding door, Finn's protective hand on her lower back.

They moved for the elevators, intending to question MCPO

Fletcher before his discharge, but the murmur of a crowd echoing across the arched ceiling caught their attention.

Camera flashes popped over the hallway separating the elevators from the main lobby sitting area.

"You don't think . . . ?" Gabby said.

Finn sighed. "Yeah, I do."

They rounded the front desk and stopped short at the plethora of people—guardsmen clapping, reporters shouting questions, cameras flashing. In front of it all, with a bashful smile that Gabby would bet was as fake as a three-dollar bill, sat Dennis Fletcher in a wheelchair.

"What happened out there?" the brunette female reporter in the front row asked.

"I'm afraid I can't answer that while Petty Officer Seavers's murderers are still at large." He looked at Finn, disapproval etched on his stern brow.

"I thought Coast Guard Investigative Service already made arrests?" another reporter asked.

"And they were massacred in their cells," someone in the audience said.

The crowd erupted into a frenzy of murmurs and questions.

"Agent Walker," Fletcher called. "Agent Walker." He waved Finn forward.

The noise of the crowd lessened as gazes shifted to Finn.

"Why don't you come up here and answer these good folks' questions?"

"I'll be back," Finn whispered before striding to Fletcher's side.

"Agent Finn Walker," Fletcher said.

"What's happening in the case?" the brunette reporter asked.

"Sheila Murphy with the *Post*," a tall woman on the right side of the room said. "Why hasn't Petty Officer Seavers's murderer been brought to justice?"

Finn held up his hand, and the questions ceased—at least

momentarily. "I am not at liberty to discuss an open investigation." He looked at Fletcher. "Back to you," he said, striding off the stage.

A tall man with broad shoulders and a mop of dark curly hair, who'd stood behind Fletcher for the duration of what could only be described as a full-fledged press conference, stepped in front of Fletcher.

"Master Chief Petty Officer Fletcher appreciates your concern and well wishes, but it's been a trying time for him, and he needs his rest."

More questions flew, but the man simply strode behind Fletcher, took hold of his wheelchair, and rolled him toward the main entrance to the hospital.

Those still sitting in the audience joined those already on their feet clapping and saluting Fletcher as he passed by.

"They're treating him like a hero," Gabby said, leaning into Finn.

"If what he said happened did, then the fact he went to get help for Seavers does make him a hero."

"But if he's lying . . . ?" she whispered as Fletcher approached.

"Then he's a murderer," Finn said, his gaze locked on Fletcher.

Fletcher held Finn's stare, then shifted his gaze to Gabby. "Miss." He tipped his hat.

They followed Fletcher and his guardian out, and as the tall man rolled Fletcher to the back door of a black sedan, Finn said, "Master Chief Fletcher."

"What is it, Walker?"

"I need to ask you some more questions. We have new information."

"And I'd love to hear it," Fletcher said as the man helped him into the car. "But the doc ordered rest, and I'm listening."

"It will just take a few minutes of your time," Finn said.

The still-unidentified man shut the door. "As he said, he needs his rest."

Finn tilted his head. "And who are you?"

"Not anyone of consequence." The man moved to the passenger door and climbed in.

Finn held up his badge. "I asked you a question."

"Scott Caldwell," the man said as he shut the door, and the vehicle sped out of the lot.

"We going to chase them?" Gabby asked as adrenaline heated her skin. It'd been a while since she had been in a decent car chase.

"Not near a hospital. Besides, I've got a better idea." He pulled out his phone and dialed. "Hey, Em. I need you to run a name and a license plate for me."

FIFTY-SIX

Frustration seared through Rissi at finding nothing useful to the case in Marv and Loraine's house. She headed out to the shed, pumping her fists in and out, while Noah stepped into the free-standing garage.

After taking in the bigger contents of the shed—lawn mower, trimmer, weed whacker, and the like—she turned to the metal shelf lined with old, lidded coffee cans. There had to be at least forty of them. She sighed. She had her work cut out for her.

Eight cans in from the right, on the third row up, she opened the lid expecting more screws, nails, washers, or some other building essential. But instead she found a white handkerchief—surprisingly fresh, like it had very recently been placed there—wrapped around the can's contents.

She scooped her hand underneath, and whatever it was slid into her palm. Her eyes widened as she peeled the handkerchief away to find barnacle-encrusted coins. *Doubloons.*

"Noah," she called.

"Yeah?" His voice echoed across the concrete pad between the garage and the shed.

"You're going to want to see this."

Noah entered. "What's up?"

She held up the handful of doubloons. "I think I just discovered what Marv and Mo have been doing for Litman Limited."

Finn entered the station with Gabby at his side, his thoughts wrapped up in her. He was falling even deeper in love with her.

He exhaled. How long until he had to watch her drive away again?

Lost in the moment, he didn't realize Logan and Emmalyne were present until Logan cleared his throat.

He looked up to find the two of them leaning against the front of Emmalyne's desk, both grinning.

"So where are we at on the license plate?" he asked, hoping if he got straight to it, they'd stop smiling.

Logan's lip twitched, but he shifted his focus onto the case. "They're stolen plates."

"Who were they stolen from?" Finn asked.

"Mr. Bowen's Buick."

"Mr. Bowen?" Gabby frowned. "The deceased owner of the drop-spot house?"

"One and the same." Emmy nodded.

"Let me guess," Gabby said. "Right after he died?"

Emmalyne tapped her nose. "Two weeks after—his family who'd been in town at the time reported it."

Gabby rested her hands on her womanly hips. "What do you want to bet whoever is behind Litman pays attention to the obituaries?"

"Smart," Finn said. "He—"

"Or she," Gabby said.

"He or *she*," Finn said, "finds empty houses and uses them as drop spots while they remain empty. I'm guessing they've already moved on to a new place, given the bust of Mr. Jacobs at Bowen's place."

He turned back to Emmalyne. "Have you checked on the man who identified himself as Scott Caldwell?"

She shook her head. "No one by that name in the area. I'm guessing he made it up."

Finn exhaled. "I'm going to have another talk with Mr. Jacobs. Maybe I can get some more information out of him."

"And Fletcher?" Gabby asked. "And the mystery man who left with him?"

"I'd say you stay here, and I'll go question them, but . . ."

She smiled. "You know that's not going to happen. Not when Fletcher holds the key to this story or at least one very important one."

"We'll go after I talk with Jacobs."

She sat at Finn's desk. "I'll be waiting."

He shook his head and headed for Eric Jacobs.

Having gotten nothing further out of Jacobs, Finn and Gabby headed for Fletcher's place.

There was no sign of the black sedan that had picked him up at the hospital.

"Looks like Fletcher's bodyguard left," Gabby said.

"Or they went somewhere else."

"Like where?"

"No place good, I imagine."

After knocking on the door several times without answer and peering in the window to find the house dark and still, Finn decided there was no point sticking around. "We may as well head out."

They walked to the car, and he opened the passenger door for Gabby.

"Thanks," she said, her voice as bottomed out as he felt.

He nodded and, with one last look at Fletcher's house, climbed in the car.

"He's got to come back sooner or later," she said.

Finn sighed. "We can hope."

FIFTY-SEVEN

Noah knocked on the Laytons' door as Rissi tapped her foot.

She hated having to be the one—ones, since thankfully Noah was with her—to inform Genevieve Layton that her husband was a thief when she was so crushed by his death. "This is going to devastate her," she said, rocking back on her heels as uneasiness shot through her.

Noah rubbed his hands together. "Unless she knew about his extracurricular activities."

She arched her brows. She hadn't even considered that, but it was possible. The way things were going, anything was possible.

Genevieve opened the door. "Agents," she said, her eyes red and puffy. "Have you found evidence to prove John was murdered?"

"Not yet, ma'am, but I've been told we will be getting approval to dive the *Calliope* tomorrow, so we should be able to gather helpful evidence, or so I pray."

"Good." She wrapped her arms about herself, snuggling into an oversized gray cardigan Rissi was betting was John's.

"I'm afraid we have to ask you some difficult questions," Noah said.

Dr. Layton's bloodshot eyes narrowed. "Such as?"

"May we come in?" Rissi asked, not wanting to do this on the porch.

She stepped back, permitting them entrance. It was always

easier to ask permission rather than to barge their way in, despite the fact they had a warrant. Maybe by chatting first they could cushion the blow.

"Please, have a seat." Genevieve gestured to the floral-print sofa in the front room.

Rissi took a seat on it beside Noah.

Genevieve sat in the matching armchair catty-corner to them. "Can I get you anything? Tea or lemonade?"

"I'm good, but thank you," Noah said.

"I'm fine too," Rissi said.

Genevieve crossed her legs, fuzzy slippers on her feet despite the low eighty temperatures. "Now, what's this about difficult questions?"

"First, I want to apologize for having to question you about this, given your loss, but it's vital to our investigation."

"If it helps you discover what happened to my John, I'm happy to answer."

Rissi inhaled, wondering if Genevieve would keep that sentiment after the questions began.

Noah leaned forward, his hands braced on his thighs. "We have found that John was receiving payments from a company called Litman Limited. Do you know anything about his work with them?"

She shifted, her gaze darting to the side. "I've never heard of them."

Rissi tensed. She was lying.

"John worked at the airport."

"He worked at the customs office," Rissi said, at Genevieve's generalization of John's job.

"Correct." Genevieve nodded. "Not for some company I've never heard of."

Noah handed her the copy of the financials they'd pulled from John and Genevieve's joint account, the deposits from Litman circled in red.

She clutched the paper, her face tightening. "Where did you get this?"

"We had a warrant," Noah said.

"This is our private business." Genevieve's voice heightened.

Rissi sat back. So, she *did* know.

"We believe Litman Limited was behind your husband's accident," Noah said.

Genevieve's face pinched. "How is that possible? We were on a dive."

"You won a trip on a dive charter," Rissi said.

"Correct."

"Had you had any connection with the dive charter prior to that?" she asked.

"We'd gone on it once before."

"Did you know that Mo and Marv are also in Litman's employ?"

"What . . ." Her eyes narrowed. "What are you saying?"

"We believe Litman ordered Mo and Marv to kill your husband by making it look like a dive accident."

Her thin fingers clasped together, her hands balled in her lap. "Why would they do that?"

She was no longer acting as if she didn't know who Litman Limited was. Rather, she was asking what they'd done. Rissi stiffened. She hated when people lied. "We believe there's a chance that John kept something he shouldn't have," she said.

Noah cleared his voice. "We have a warrant to check your home and property."

FIFTY-EIGHT

Rissi studied Layton's office. It was the last room in the house to check. Was it possible her hunch was off? That morning she'd studied the customs' manifest for a second time and had found one item Jacobs had supposedly signed for but which had different handwriting. What if Layton had forged Jacobs's signature and kept whatever was in the shipment?

However he explained a missing package to Litman probably wasn't good enough, because that's probably what had gotten him killed.

Rissi searched every drawer and file cabinet while Noah kept the now-belligerent Genevieve Layton sequestered in the front room.

As she shut the top file door of the third chin-height cabinet, something rattled behind it.

Rissi pulled the drawer open and slammed it shut again. The cabinet rocked, and something hit the wall behind it.

She tried moving the cabinet, but it wouldn't budge. Pulling the desk chair over and balancing on the spinning chair, she hoisted herself atop the row of cabinets and peered down.

A brown-paper-wrapped package three feet wide and she was guessing four feet high was wedged between the cabinets and the back wall.

Lying on her belly, she reached between the cabinets and

the wall. She fished for it, her fingers finally clasping hold of the upper edge.

She lifted, and as soon as the top crested the cabinets, she sat up and, with both hands, lifted it the rest of the way up. "Noah," she called.

He entered, Genevieve behind him, her face ashen.

"Let me help you," Noah said, taking the painting-shaped package from her, then offering her a hand.

She clasped it and hopped down.

Genevieve sprang forward. "You have no right."

Noah held her back. "Yes, we do. I prefer not to pull my weapon on you, but if you don't step back, you'll give me no choice."

She swallowed and took a step back.

"Thank you," he said, then turned to Rissi. "Go for it."

With her gloves still in place from the search, she carefully peeled back the paper to reveal an oil painting underneath. Her eyes grew wide. "It looks like . . . the Rembrandt that was stolen from that exhibit in Holland."

Genevieve Layton rubbed her brow, her eyes downcast.

"I remember reading about that in the news," Noah said. "I'll call Emmy and have her bring in the FBI's art-theft team. They will have to authenticate it, but I'm guessing from the look on Dr. Layton's face, it is."

Noah cuffed her and escorted her out to the car. "The FBI will be handling this part of the investigation from here on out. Whoever is behind this has quite the smuggling ring going. He must be selling to collectors across the U.S."

Rissi nodded. "Or someone is amassing a collection of their own."

FIFTY-NINE

The Collector stepped to Fletcher, handing him a three-finger glass of rum, neat. It was the least he could do before killing him. And a much cleaner way to extract the necessary information than torture, which would only destroy his pristine white carpet. From the outside, his fishing shack looked ragged, but once past the staged front room, it'd been crafted down to the last detail. It was his refuge.

"So no one knows?" He circled Fletcher's chair, preferring not to ruin the leather with something as crude as a bullet to the head. Such things were for his hired men. Men lacking intelligence. He had far better plans. He tossed back his own rum, the liquid burning sweet down his throat. "You haven't confided in anyone about the nature of our business?"

"I'm not stupid," Fletcher said.

There he begged to differ. If the fool had simply brought Seavers to him so *he* could dispose of him directly, rather than making the asinine decision to stage a drug runners' raid with *his* men, without *his* consent . . . Heat seared through him.

Fletcher let his bringing Will Seavers into the fold—having one man under him—go to his head, giving him the illusion that he was higher up in the pecking order than he was.

"You cost me four men, five if you count your being unable to keep Seavers in line."

"I had no idea they'd get caught, and Seavers was getting

ready to confess to our lieutenant what he'd done. There was no talking him out of it. He suddenly grew a conscience, saying he needed to do right by Tess and their boy. I had no choice but to kill him before he made that call."

He took another swig of rum, staring at Fletcher squirming over the crystal rim of his tumbler.

At least he knew enough to squirm. They all did eventually.

"So let me see if I have this straight. Your answer for a simple problem was to stage a drug-runner attack, have my men beat you, put you in the outboard, and set you adrift, thereby portraying yourself as a hero escaping to get help."

"Yes." Fletcher swallowed, downing the rest of his drink.

The Collector signaled with a wave of his hand for Philippe—who'd picked Fletcher up from the hospital—to refill his glass. One more drink before the fool died.

"Your foolish actions forced me to send Juan and his crew back after you when they informed me of the night's activity. Do you know why I did that?"

Fletcher took his crystal tumbler from Philippe, a slight tremor to his grasp. He was fearful. *Excellent*. His babies sensed and fed off fear.

"To add to the ruse?" Fletcher swallowed, his face reddening.

"No." He shook his tumbler—the ice realigned exactly the way he preferred, settling on the bottom rather than stacked up on one side. "I sent them to kill you. Just as I sent another crew to kill Juan and his team in their cells."

The blood drained from Fletcher's face.

The Collector smiled and gave Philippe the nod to proceed.

Philippe pulled out his gun and motioned for Fletcher to stand.

Perspiration clung to his paling brow. "You don't have to do this."

"Yes," he said, his smile widening. He took great pleasure in watching his babies feed. "I really do."

After searching a few places in town for Fletcher, Finn got a call from Noah that he and Gabby should head back home and get some rest. They cooked up a light dinner and brought it down to the shore. Finn lit a fire in the pit, and Gabby settled onto a beach blanket. Finn refilled Gabby's watermelon lemonade. It had sounded like the oddest concoction when she'd insisted on making it, but it was delicious—surprising and sweet—just like the woman herself.

He sank down beside her on the beach blanket and, stretching out his legs, crossed one ankle over the other. The flames spread warmth along the soles of his feet, the orange flames highlighting the amber strands in Gabby's hair, glistening off her beautiful blue eyes.

She reclined, propping her weight on her elbows, her toes barely an inch from his. Sparks flittered up toward the star-filled sky, burning bright for a second before fading to nothingness.

She stared up at the sky. "There's supposed to be a super moon tomorrow."

"Yep."

"I love super moons. They make it seem like the moon is a giant ball sitting on the ground outside my window."

"Like you can just reach out and grab hold."

She looked over with a smile. "Yeah."

"Yeah," he said, the breath leaving his body at the sight of her, her hair long down her back, the ends almost touching the blanket. Her eyes wide with delight. Her skin bathed in moonlight. If he could freeze a moment, it would be now. The two of them right here.

She licked her lips. "I should probably get to sleep."

"Of course," he said, hopping to his feet and extending a hand.

She grabbed hold, and he lifted her to her feet. "Thanks."

They stepped on the lawn, dewy and cool.

"I can see myself to the loft," she said, pointing over her shoulder.

"I don't mind walking with you."

She nibbled her bottom lip and nodded. They strolled past the picnic tables and sycamore tree beside the surf shack.

He led the way up, the sand on his feet scrubbing against his skin with each step.

Gabby stepped around him, the scent of the bonfire swirling about her, and reached for the knob. Her hands stilled, and she turned to face him, her weight against the door. "I know I don't say it often . . . or at all . . . but I don't want you to think . . . I mean, I want you to know . . ."

She cleared her throat and started over. "I just want you to know how much I . . ."

He took a step closer.

———

Gabby swallowed, shifting to take a step back, and realized she was as far back as she could go.

"How much you . . . ?" Finn prompted, his voice a throaty whisper.

The moonlight glinted off his green eyes.

She swallowed again, her throat suddenly parched. "I . . ." What had she been about to say? Something about . . . *Oh, right.* "Just how much I appreciate your concern."

He lifted his hand to her cheek, his thumb caressing her jaw. "You know it's much more than concern."

"I . . ." Why couldn't she speak? Better yet, why couldn't she feel her legs?

"So much more," he said, cupping her face and lowering his lips to hers.

His touch was slow, featherlight, and searching.

She shifted, her right foot rolling to the side. She didn't pull away. Just stayed there, his breath lingering across her lips.

Move away! her head screamed, but she remained rooted in place. She parted her lips ever so slightly.

With a groan, he captured her mouth in his.

Thank goodness something solid was holding her up.

His long, sturdy fingers spread through her hair.

She slipped her hands behind his neck, the edge of his hair tickling her fingers.

"Gabby," he whispered raggedly, pulling back just enough for his breath to dance across her lips.

She pressed her lips together, struggling to find her stance. "Mmm-hmm?"

He shook his head. "Never mind," he breathed, lowering his lips back to hers. The kiss was strong and warm and dizzying.

Rising up on her tiptoes, she kissed him deeper.

He groaned, then pulling his hands from her hair, braced them on the door on either side of her.

Her breath quickened.

He hung his head, inhaling in a shaky breath. "We . . ."

She raked a hand through her hair, missing his touch. "Shouldn't be . . ."

He nodded. "I should . . ."

"Go." The words left her lips in the weakest of tones.

He pressed a kiss to her forehead and rushed down the steps, her heart aching for him to stay.

She stumbled into the loft, closing the door behind her. Moving to the window, she watched Finn stride across the lawn. A handful of feet from his porch, he stopped and turned, looking up at her, his gaze hungry and heartfelt.

Biting her bottom lip, she waved good night.

She slumped to the floor, her heart still thudding in her chest, and closed her eyes.

Please, Father, I need your guidance. My head and heart

are merging into the same place—here with Finn—and it ter-
rifies me.

Lieutenant Russet, who commanded his prison sector, slipped him the pill in passing. Xavier held it tightly until he was back in his cell. Only moments to go, and then Antonio would be his witness, calling the guards for help.

It'd been a simple thing to get Antonio on the payroll. All he'd had to do was convey messages to the outside through his girlfriend during their visits. Every message sent out that way saved Xavier having to use the burner cell Russet had slipped him his first day in. The more he used it, the stronger the chance he'd get caught. Antonio had come in handy, and today he'd be his key to freedom.

Slipping the pill in his mouth at the appointed time, Xavier fell to the floor, thrashing and jerking as it foamed inside. The white foamy liquid spilled over his lips, dripping onto the floor in a puddle around his face.

"He's having a seizure," Antonio hollered. "We need help!"

The lights clicked on, and Sergeant Beauford came running.

"Oh, dang," he said. "Open cell three-seven-two and call an ambulance. Fuentes is having some sort of seizure."

Xavier clenched his teeth, swishing his eyes about.

Beauford and two guards kept watch over him as the paramedics rushed in, rolling him onto the stretcher and strapping him in before raising it up to roll out.

"Hang on," Beauford said. "He needs to be cuffed." He moved, clicking the handcuff in place on Xavier's flailing hand, securing him to the stretcher rail.

"Officer Trent will accompany the prisoner in the ambulance," Lieutenant Russet said, "and I want a follow."

"I'll go," Officer Garret volunteered, not realizing he'd be slaughtered.

They rolled Xavier out. Prisoners rattled and banged on their cell doors as he passed.

He was transferred to the ambulance and sighed with relief as the bay door shut and they pulled out of the prison.

Ten more minutes and he'd be free.

SIXTY

Xavier braced for impact, feeling fairly secure in his restraints. He couldn't say the same for Officer Trent. Tonight was not his lucky night.

The ambulance jolted hard as the truck rammed into its side as planned. Tires squealed, and the horn blared. Officer Trent's head collided with the side of the vehicle, knocking him out. The crunching sound of metal crumpling beneath the impact resounded through the otherwise still night.

Sliding sideways with skidding tires, they slammed into something else. The impact heaved him up, but he clamped onto the stretcher railing as the rocking vehicle tipped onto its side and stopped with a screeching thud.

Glass shattered in the front cab, gunfire retorting.

Two swift thwacks sounded on the other side of the wall separating the back from the cab.

The paramedic glanced up at Xavier from the floor, her eyes wide with fear. She scrambled to her feet.

The doors opened, and he smiled at the sight of his right-hand man, Max.

"Please," the paramedic cried.

Max didn't hesitate. Two swift shots and she fell to the ground.

"You okay, sir?" He stepped in, kicking the dead paramedic out of his way.

"Better than ever. Now get me out of these." Xavier rattled his restraints, the cuff cutting into his wrist.

Max moved to assist.

"The paramedics up front taken care of?"

"Yes, sir." Max removed the thick straps binding Xavier, then picked the cuff lock—the metal bracelet falling open.

Xavier rubbed his wrist, then climbed off the stretcher and out of the ambulance.

The follow police car was smashed into the concrete divider, the windshield shattered. Officer Garret wouldn't be volunteering for any more follows.

"This way, sir." Max led him to the waiting green minivan, a baby-on-board sticker on the back-hatch window.

His brows arched. "A minivan?"

"A good cover until you're out of town."

Xavier climbed inside.

"Hello, sir," Hector greeted him.

Max lowered the hood—the "broken-down" vehicle had provided an excellent roadblock. He climbed in behind Xavier and shut the sliding door. "Ready," he said, and they drove into the night.

Now to finish Gabrielle Rowley.

Finn kicked off his flip-flops and lay back on his couch to watch a rerun of *Everybody Loves Raymond*, trying to distract his mind from their kiss. But there was no way his mind would stop replaying it. The feel of her warmth against him. The featherlight touch of her lips . . .

He bunched his hands into fists, scrunching the couch pillow into a distorted mess. Releasing a shaky exhale, he tossed the remote on the coffee table and stood. Layla padded after him. Time for a cold shower.

His cell rang.

He glanced at the screen as Layla licked the back of his leg and he bent to pet her. *Noah*.

He answered, but before he even uttered a hello, Noah blurted, "I need you to get to Gabby *now*!"

His chest squeezed the air from his lungs. "What's wrong?"

"Gabby's boss called. Fuentes escaped."

Tossing his phone, he grabbed his gun and a flashlight. The dew-covered grass soaked his bare feet as he sprinted for the loft, praying Gabby was okay.

SIXTY-ONE

Gabby let the hot water stream over her, rinsing the jojoba shampoo from her hair. Then she applied a thick lather of conditioner—to counteract the ocean's salt water drying her ends—let it sit for a few seconds, and rinsed it out. Turning off the water, she stepped onto the plush bath mat and rubbed herself down with an oversized fluffy white towel.

She had just pulled on her pj's when she heard footsteps racing up the outside steps. Her chest tightened. Rushing for her purse, she pulled out her Springfield and positioned her back against the wall, aiming the gun at the door. It swung open and she jumped out, gun in hand.

"Whoa!" Finn held up his hands, a gun gripped in his left, a flashlight in his right.

"Finn!" Her heart thwacked in her chest. "You nearly gave me a heart attack."

"I could say the same. You mind putting the gun down?"

She looked at the Springfield 9mm still clutched in her hand. "Sorry." She lowered it to her side.

Finn lowered his hands, sliding his gun into the back of his faded jeans.

"Wh . . . what are you doing here?"

"Fuentes escaped."

She swallowed, her heart constricting. "What? When?"

"I don't know, exactly. Noah just called and told me to get to you."

"Do you think he knows I am here?" *Please don't let anything happen to my family.*

"I don't know, but I imagine it's only a matter of time."

She shook her head, moving for the closet.

"What are you doing?"

"Getting my bag."

"What?" Confusion marred his brow.

"I'm leaving."

"Why?"

"I can't stay here." She moved to the dresser and started throwing the few clothes she had in the bag.

He gently laid his hand on her arm. "You don't have to run, Gabby. I'll keep you safe."

She bit her bottom lip. "Tell Rissi I'll bring her stuff back as soon as this is over."

"Over?" He shook his head. "What are you talking about?"

"I have to leave." She finished shoving things in the duffel— leaving out a shirt and pair of jeans.

He tightened his hold. His voice dropped an octave as he said, "I will protect you with my life."

She swallowed. "I know you will. That's why I have to leave."

"Come again?"

"You will all give your lives to keep me safe, and I can't endanger you all like that."

"So you're just going to run in the hopes he doesn't catch you?"

"Yes." She clutched her outfit in her hand, trying to move into the bathroom, but Finn held her tight, not letting go.

"And if he catches you?" His jaw tensed along with his shoulders.

"Then at least you guys will be safe," she said.

He shook his head. "You can't do that."

Her shoulders dropped. "I don't have a choice. I won't let him hurt the people I love."

He stilled. "You love?"

She nodded. "My family and the team."

"Of course. The team." He swallowed.

"And . . . you." She might be dead come morning. She might as well tell him the truth.

He stared down at her, and she swallowed.

He cocked his head, his brow furrowing. "And me?"

She nodded.

"You *love* me?" He closed the gap between them.

Tears bit at her eyes, and she nodded.

He pulled her hard against him and lowered his mouth to hers. She kissed him with all the feelings she'd been holding back. Everything dissolved except the feel of his arms holding her tight, and—

"Seriously!"

Gabby jerked her flustered gaze to the door.

Noah gripped the doorframe, half panting.

"Noah." Gabby swiped her mouth. "What are you doing?"

"I just ran every light getting here, fearing you were in danger, and meanwhile you two are making out."

She swallowed. "We weren't . . . I wasn't . . . I'm okay."

"Yeah. I can see that." Noah stepped inside, his breathing uneven. "Do me a favor? Answer your phones!"

Gabby bit her bottom lip. "Sorry. I was . . ."

"Yeah." He linked his arms across his chest. "I saw."

Heat rushed to her face.

"I . . . can explain," Finn said, raking a hand through his hair.

Noah arched a brow. "And I look forward to hearing that

276

explanation, but for now let's focus on the fact that Fuentes is loose."

"I heard, and the best solution is for me—"

"Is not for you to leave," Finn said.

"Leave?" Noah's brows shot back up. "You have got to be kidding."

SIXTY-TWO

Gabby changed, and they managed to calm Noah down somewhat. Finn insisted for Gabby's safety it would be best if she stayed in his guest room rather than being alone in the loft, and Noah agreed. While both acknowledged she was well able to protect herself, this was Xavier Fuentes—a ruthless drug lord and killer.

After fifteen minutes of arguing, she'd relented, and Finn helped her move her stuff into his guest room, happy she'd be where he could keep a better eye on her—to know she was safe and near. Noah was bunking on his couch, not wanting to leave his sister, period.

Finn tried to focus on her as his friend's younger sister—his *boss's* younger sister, but after that kiss and her declaration of love it was nigh impossible.

The heat of it all simmered beneath the surface, making it excruciating to say good night. His lips and heart longed for just one more kiss. But this was not the time to get distracted. His sole focus had to be on protecting her.

He doubted he'd sleep with so much energy coursing through him, but before he knew it, his eyes fell shut.

He rode through the tube, streams of sunlight reflecting off the water in rainbow prisms.

Cody had ridden along the wave, instead of in it. He had

yet to ride inside one. Catching it just right was hard, but it was also the best feeling in the world. It was addictive to be in the center of something so powerful and beautiful. But he had no doubt his younger brother would master the skill one day soon. He was a fast learner.

Seafoam tickled Finn's toes as he glided out of the tube into the open air.

Cody offered a chin lift of congratulations as he headed back out for the next gnarly line of mounting waves.

The surf was rougher than expected. Its churning and swelling made for sweet rides. Having a half hour before their mom would wave them in for breakfast, Finn swam back out. Sitting on his board beside his brother, he waited for the perfect wave. Then he spotted it.

Gripping his board, he swam for the oncoming swell. Cody swam beside him. They dipped their boards, diving under the thrashing wave.

Surfacing, Finn looked over to Cody, but he wasn't there. He spun around, searching—waiting for his brother to surface, but there was no sign of him.

"Cody?"

Nothing.

"Cody!" His chest and throat squeezed. He scanned the sea. No sign of him. He rode up on the next wave to gain height. Finally, he spotted his brother's feet tumbling in the midst of a crashing wave, but Cody was at least fifty feet to his right.

The undertow yanked Finn out to sea, and he swam hard against it, trying to reach his brother. The harder he pushed forward, the tighter its grasp yanked him back.

Finally reaching the general area he'd seen Cody's feet, he glanced frantically around, searching. Surely Cody would have worked his way to the surface by now. Finn scanned the surface, his heart pounding in his ears over the ocean's roar.

Cody was nowhere to be seen.
"Cody!"

Finn jerked upward, perspiration sticking to his skin in a thick layer.

A warm hand landed on his forearm. "It's okay," Gabby's sweet voice said.

He tried to shake himself awake, to catch his bearings in the dark room. "Gabby?"

"You were having a nightmare," she whispered.

He flipped on the bedside lamp, his heart thwacking in his chest.

Gabby stood over his bed, concern creasing her brow.

He rubbed his eyes, confusion marring his vision. "What happened?" Why was she in his room? He certainly didn't mind her presence, but what had pulled her to him?

"You screamed, and I wanted to make sure you were all right." She wrapped her arms across her chest. She looked adorable in her maroon tank top with a multicolored elephant in the center, her black sports bra straps sticking out from under the thin tank straps, and a pair of black knit shorts.

She shifted her stance, shuffling her feet along the floor. "I wanted to make sure you were okay."

"Thanks." He propped his back against the surfboard headboard. "Sorry I woke you. Everything's okay. I was just . . ."

"Having a nightmare?"

He swallowed, heat rushing to his cheeks. "Noah?"

"He's still asleep." Gabby rubbed her hands along her arms. "I have them too."

He climbed out of bed, grabbed his Panthers T-shirt off the chair in the corner, and slid it on, the edge hitting halfway down his gray sweat shorts. He moved to stand in front of her, cupping her face, his gaze soft and searching. "What wakes you up at night?"

She sighed. "Memories of the moment I thought my life was over."

"By Fuentes's man?" He caressed her cheek.

She shook her head. "By Asim."

———

Gabby never talked about it, not even with family, barely even with God. She knew she had to release the hurt, anger, and terror of that moment to her Savior, but she feared if she did, she'd be vulnerable again. And that was a place she never wanted to return to.

But somehow Finn eased those anxieties. Maybe it was the way he looked at her or the utter genuineness of his words. Or perhaps it was the realization that something haunted him in the depths of night too.

He was waiting for her to say more, but she couldn't quite go there yet. "What about you?" she asked.

Loss clung to Finn like a dry suit on a cold November day.

"What were you dreaming about?" she asked, not wanting to prod but wanting to be a listening ear and a place of support.

He looked down, raking a hand through his tousled hair. "Losing my brother to the sea."

"Your brother?" She did a poor job of hiding the shock. She hadn't even realized he'd had a brother.

He sank down onto the corner of his bed and rubbed his hands along his thighs, his gaze fixed on the floor.

"Cody." His voice cracked. He looked up at her, a torn-up, bittersweet smile on his lips. "I haven't said his name out loud in years."

Just as she hadn't spoken Asim's in months.

He exhaled and, with a look of utter vulnerability, reached out his hand. She took hold, and he pulled her to sit with him on the bed.

"I was fourteen," he said, the words coming out hoarsely. "Cody was twelve. We went surfing every morning before

281

school. The ocean was our backyard. One morning we were out, and the waves were swelling great." A tiny muscle in his jaw flickered, and she moved her hand to his face, caressing the spot, trying to ease him as he continued.

"We went under a wave, but Cody never came up. I spotted him a good ways away, his feet kicking above the surface. The undertow must have pulled him down." He shook his head, his gaze fixed on the floor. "We never found him."

"Oh, Finn." Her chest squeezed, tears burning her eyes. "I can't even imagine . . . I'm so sorry."

He clasped his hands, tightening his grip until his knuckles were white. "He was my responsibility, and I failed him."

"You didn't fail him. It was an accident." She rested her hand atop his.

"That's what everyone said, but I should have saved him. He's gone because I wasn't watching him closely enough."

She laid her head against his chest, praying for him, praying for them both.

"Is that what propelled you to become a rescue swimmer?" she asked.

"I lost my brother to the sea, and I believed being a rescue swimmer would help me make sure the sea took no one else's life. At least not on my watch. But I failed again."

"Noah told me he read your file. What happened with the rescue wasn't your fault. He said you had a torn rotator cuff, the copter was in jeopardy of going down if it stayed any longer, and the man was pinned in a sinking ship. He said you did everything right."

"If I had, Stan Larson would still be alive, and his wife, Margie, wouldn't be a widow."

"It wasn't your fault, and I'm sure Mrs. Larson knows that."

He inhaled. "How could she not blame me?"

"Have you asked her?"

He pulled back, his brow furrowing. "What?"

"Have you talked to Mrs. Larson since that day?"

"No. Of course not."

She rubbed his clutched hands. "Maybe you should."

After a moment of silence, he said, "I'll think about it."

"Good." She prayed that would be a healing experience for him and the widow.

He brushed the hair from her forehead and gazed at her with love. "Want to talk about what happened in South Sudan?"

She inhaled. It was time she fully shared it with another, and who better than the man she loved?

"The BBC hired me because of my work with the *Post*, and because I spoke Arabic and served in missions there numerous times during college and the years following. I was a journalist who already had inroads in the country and lots of contacts, along with a good cover in place with the mission group."

She exhaled an unsteady stream. Here came the shame of it. "I was only there a handful of months when I met Asim Noren. He was a local who volunteered with Doctors Without Borders. I believed him to be a good man. He knew the area well and made an excellent source. That's how it started." She hunched her shoulders, fighting the urge to curl up into a ball.

He wrapped his arm around her, rubbing her back in soothing circles.

"He became my main source of information. We spent increasingly more hidden time together to cover the fact he was feeding me information. After a while . . ." She swallowed, her throat tight. "I knew it was wrong. I was a journalist and he was my source, but I thought I loved him and he loved me."

Her skin heated with embarrassment and shame. "He was using me, feeding me false information. But I only learned that the day we were supposed to be searching out a terrorist cell that had set up camp outside of the village's boundaries. We went so I could take pictures, so I could find out who was involved."

Finn rubbed her back in long strokes as her heart raced. The terror—the adrenaline burning through her, her skin flushing as sweat broke on her brow and body—ricocheted through her as it had that day.

"I had no idea Asim was involved with the terrorists until he handed me over to the leader of the cell, who ordered him to kill me. Even after learning he worked with the terrorist cell, I was sure he wouldn't hurt me. But he didn't even hesitate, just pulled his gun on me without a second thought."

She squeezed her eyes shut against the memory of the gun muzzle mere inches from her face and the hatred in Asim's dark brown eyes. "I heard a gunshot and thought my life was over. After a moment of paralyzing fear, I opened my eyes to find Asim dead at my feet, a bullet in his head."

She swallowed the bile burning up her throat. "SEAL Team 7 raided the camp that day. If they hadn't been there, I would have been dead. If the Navy didn't have a satellite watching the team and the camp as they infiltrated it, I would have been considered a traitor. They saw what happened, saw I was innocent, but . . ." Her muscles coiled. "I still crossed the line. I got involved with a source. And with the Navy's footage of that day classified, rumors and questions about my loyalty swelled. The BBC promptly fired me, and no one would offer me a job . . . until Lawrence."

He hugged her to him—his solid body nestled against hers. "No wonder you felt compelled to take the job."

"That was part of it," she said, nibbling her lip before looking him in the eye. "The other part was I was scared to be vulnerable again, to choose a man over my career as I had with Asim. I'd vowed never to do that again."

Finn nodded. "I understand."

She lifted her hand to cup his scruffy face. "You need to shave." She smiled, thankful for the brief moment of levity.

"Every morning," he said, cupping his hand over hers, holding her hand against his cheek.

Summoning the courage to continue, she cleared her throat and said, "I don't . . ."

His brow furrowed.

"I'm torn. I love what I do, but I love you too."

He nodded. "Let's keep you safe and get Fuentes back behind bars, and then we can talk more."

She nodded, knowing that was where the focus had to remain, and to be honest, she wasn't ready to make a decision, though she knew her heart already had.

SIXTY-THREE

Xavier pulled into the ridiculously small town of Wilmington, where Gabrielle Rowley's family lived. It'd taken a lot of searching and calling in of favors, but he'd finally found her, thanks to a phone call from a man who assured him of not only Rowley's death—and a spectacularly brutal one at that—but also a fresh start for him. All in exchange for helping the Collector expand his drug trade. Xavier possessed the skills to do so and to make a hefty profit in the process. Fate had smiled on him.

He followed the directions the Collector gave him, parking his car far off the main road and following the river.

Biting flies landed on his forearms, and he smashed them with his hands, flicking what remained of their bodies to the ground. He gazed at the marsh surrounding him.

A boat's motor hummed, idling by the old dock about thirty feet ahead of him. The man driving it signaled for him to climb aboard. It took him to another dock upriver, on the end of a peninsula. He stared at the ramshackle shed of a house.

What a dump.

Why would a man supposedly as powerful as the Collector live here? Probably to remain hidden. No one would think to look for a smuggling kingpin in this wreck of a place. He'd never have found him if the Collector hadn't sought him out. Even with Xavier's extended reach the man was a ghost.

The Collector smiled, knowing his men were about to pick Fuentes up. What a patsy. The fool had agreed to his terms for a stake in his business.

He took a sip of cuba libre, the ice jiggling as the liquid slipped down his throat.

As if he'd give anyone a stake in his business. People worked *for* him—not *with* him. But he'd said what he needed to say to lure Fuentes to his territory.

With Fuentes on the loose in the area, attention would divert to the fool from Raleigh playing the wronged drug lord out for revenge—giving the Collector time to relocate his operation. And if anyone died along the way, Fuentes would be the natural scapegoat.

No one would even know *he* existed. Like the puppeteer pulling the strings, he'd make everyone and everything move to his will, all while remaining hidden behind the curtain.

A satisfied smile curled on his lips.

It was a brilliant plan. One he couldn't wait to execute.

SIXTY-FOUR

Finn stood outside the single-story brick home with a black roof. He turned and looked at the giant oak tree with a tire swing swaying slightly in the breeze.

He swallowed, remembering the young girl standing beside her mother at the funeral. He'd attended, but from a distance, using another oak tree to shelter his presence. He'd refused to cause any more pain but needed to witness the totality of what he'd done—of the lives he'd destroyed by his failure.

There'd been no coffin—just a memorial square in a mausoleum where the people laid mementos and flowers at the base of the marble wall. It gave them a tangible place to mourn the loss of Stan Larson when his body, like Cody's, had never been recovered from the sea.

For years he'd struggled to reconcile the beauty of the ocean, and the joy it brought, with the turmoil of its destructive power—with the anguish the sea had brought him and so many others.

The front door opened, and Finn swallowed at the sight of Margie Larson.

Her hair had changed from the blond at the funeral to light brown. She looked a little older but in a good, grown-into-her-own-skin kind of way. Her almond-shaped eyes locked on his, and after a moment of clearly trying to place him, recognition dawned. Instead of the hurt and hatred he'd anticipated and deserved, he thought he saw . . . grace.

"Mr. Walker," she said, stepping out.

"Finn, please." He swallowed, clearing his throat and the cobwebs of memories clogging it.

"Finn." She nodded.

Her little girl, Kaylee, now school-aged, stepped outside. Her head was level with her mom's waist. Her hair was longer, too, pulled back in blond braids. Her face was bright and dotted with a smattering of freckles, and she wore a blue skirt and white blouse—no doubt a school uniform.

Tugging at her mom's navy skirt, she asked, "Who's this, Mommy?" and stared up at Finn with a smile, a top front tooth and a bottom one missing.

Finn smiled. She was adorable.

He looked to Mrs. Larson, waiting for her response, anxious to see how she introduced him. Dreading it, actually.

"This," Margie Larson said, resting her hand on her daughter's shoulder, "is the man who saved my life."

Finn exhaled in shock. Had she just said . . . ?

He stood dumbfounded and rooted in place as Mrs. Larson placed Kaylee on the yellow school bus, waving good-bye as the vehicle chugged away.

She turned and stepped back to face Finn. "Want to come in for a cup of coffee? I just made a pot."

"Thanks," he said, still trying to wrap his mind around her statement and her kind reaction.

Margie held the screen door open, and he stepped inside, pausing at the family picture in the entryway of Mr. and Mrs. Larson and their daughter around age two—the age she was when standing beside her mother at her father's funeral.

He swallowed, guilt washing over him. He'd destroyed another family. First his, then the Larsons.

She paused in the kitchen doorway. "Kaylee's really grown, hasn't she?"

He nodded, his eyes locking on Stan Larson's in the picture. "Thanks to you, I'm here to see her grow up."

He slouched his hands into his pants pockets. "I'm so sorry your husband isn't."

"I am too," she said, her appraising gaze studying his face. "You still think it's your fault, don't you?"

Here it came—the ugly truth. "It was my fault. . . ." He couldn't save Stan Larson. He'd failed him as he had Cody.

"No," she said, standing in front of him. "It isn't. You tried your best to save him, despite the fact you were injured."

"It wasn't enough." *He* wasn't enough.

"You did everything you could. You rescued me under extreme circumstances—circumstances in which I should have gone down with that boat. I owe you my life. It's because of you that my daughter isn't an orphan."

He looked at the kindness and gratitude in her eyes, and it undid him.

Fifteen minutes later, still reeling from the mercy and grace she'd extended during their short time together, Finn pulled away from the Larson home.

"My grace is sufficient for you."

The Bible verse scrawled across the small wooden sign his mom had placed in every home they lived in as they bounced around after the divorce reverberated through his soul.

It had been so long since he'd felt awash in God's grace, let alone his mom's, who never once blamed him for not watching his brother better—for not doing more. *Being* more. Rather she, just as Margie Larson had done, had shown him nothing but grace—reaffirming he'd done everything he could. That the loss wasn't his fault. That accidents, tragic as they can be, happen.

Maybe he really had done all he could.

A liberating breath filled his lungs, his body finally releasing the death grip of guilt and shame he'd carried for so many years.

He just had to make sure he kept Gabby safe. He couldn't lose her too. The smallest fraction of a thought of her being hurt, of her being . . .

His muscles seized.

The mere thought was breath stealing. He *couldn't* lose her. He loved her, which he'd known all along. The fact that she loved him back floored him.

SIXTY-FIVE

Finn grabbed his usual quad macchiato on the way to the station. A call came in over his Bluetooth while he was still twenty minutes out.

Noah.

"Walker," he answered, praying Noah wasn't calling about another of Gabby's escapades. When he'd dropped her off at her sister's earlier that morning, she'd promised to simply ride along to the airport to be a comfort to Kenzie after dropping Mark off for his deployment. Then Kenzie was bringing her back to Noah at the station. He hated being away from her, but she'd be with Mark, a tough Marine, except for the short ride back. And, she'd insisted on being there for her sister. But he was counting the minutes until she was back at his side.

"Sorry for the pause. Hang on one more second. I'm getting some news," Noah said.

"No problem." He waited, bouncing his left leg, his right depressing the gas pedal a little heavier.

What news was coming in? If something had happened with Gabby, he wanted to be there as fast as possible.

"Sorry about that," Noah said. "Had to take an incoming call."

"No problem. What's up?" His knee bounced faster.

"We just got clearance to dive the *Calliope*."

"I'll be there in . . . fifteen." Maybe they'd finally get some answers to Noah and Rissi's case.

"Perfect."

Less than an hour later, Finn sat on the bow of the CGIS powerboat, waves bobbing in its wake.

He pulled on his dive boots and zipped up his suit.

Noah idled near the orange buoy the Guard had used to mark *Calliope*'s resting spot, anchoring about ten yards due east.

He joined Finn at the bow and got fully suited up—head-to-toe coverage for evidence protection, though Finn feared most had been cleansed away by the sea.

He gathered the metal light poles they'd erect by the wreck.

Noah anchored the rope they'd use for off-loading the necessary gear below. "We're set," he said.

Finn nodded, turning on his headlamp. He jumped flippers first into the sea. Water gushed around him as he dropped below the surface.

The weights secured on his dive belt helped him descend straight and fast to the seabed.

He unclasped and tugged the rope before swimming clear. "Clear," he said over the comm.

While waiting for Noah to clip in and lower the first load of equipment, he turned in a one-eighty.

The stern portion of the *Calliope* rested five yards away, while the bow portion was three yards in the other direction.

"First load down," Noah said, and Finn got to work off-loading. Ten minutes later, Finn had erected the light poles around *Calliope*'s stern, concentrating the focus on the engine room hatch and the ripped-open center of the cabin. He switched them on, illuminating the wreck as Noah approached.

"Good work," he said over the comm.

Finn nodded his thanks.

"Let's run the length of the deck first," Noah instructed. "I'll take port and you're on starboard."

"Roger that." With his camera looped around his neck, Finn swam to the farthest point of the ship's stern and started photographing what remained of the *Calliope*.

Bursts of light popped from either side of the ship. Smaller details sprung to life in the camera's concentrated flash.

Finn stopped over the engine room hatch and signaled to Noah he was going in.

Noah responded with a thumbs-up as he continued his forward motion.

Snapping the first of three light sticks, Finn shook the glowing liquid throughout the casing.

He dropped the green stick into the engine room and repeated the process with the next two.

The room was now aglow in hues of green and yellow, and Finn swam into the confined space.

The first thing he saw was a ruptured nitrox tank tattered into shards of metal shrapnel. Either it exploded, starting the fire, or the fire exploded it. Either way, what was a dive tank doing in the engine room?

He swam up to retrieve a mesh evidence bag. As he crested the hatch, one of the long light poles swung toward his head. He ducked back into the engine room, his heart racing.

"Noah?" he called over the comm, his breath quickening. "Noah?"

Pulling his knife from its sheath, he swam out the interior engine room door, praying he wasn't diving himself into a dead end. Thankfully, the interior entrance wasn't cut off. He swam past fish already claiming the wreck for a home and headed for the main cabin.

A few more feet . . .

At the base of the stairs a man in full black dive gear waited for him. Finn lifted his knife, and the man rushed him with a knife of his own.

Finn struck first, and the man bobbed just out of his reach.

He swiped back, and Finn ducked, lunging for the man's legs, knocking him off balance.

He drifted back, and Finn swiped his blade at the man's hose, slicing it in two.

The man jerked, grabbing at his mask. He sliced his knife through the water while he yanked off his mask with his free hand.

Marv?

Marv shoved his secondary regulator into his mouth and lunged back at Finn. Finn sliced, and his movement ceased as the knife jammed into Marv's shoulder.

Blood floated in a red funnel cloud between them.

Marv kicked him in a debilitating place and, dropping his weights, swam out.

Finn watched him jet upward, quickly fading past the visibility range. His chest squeezed. If he wasn't careful, he'd use up his own mixture before he surfaced.

Movement flickered to his four—another diver headed to the surface. He spun around, his gaze darting about for Noah.

He spotted Noah. His mask was off, no goggles on. Finn's gaze tracked down. Blood streamed from Noah's right thigh.

Please, Father, don't let it be his femoral artery.

SIXTY-SIX

Finn handed Noah his extra set of goggles and Noah slipped them over his head while Finn kept guard, making certain no one else attacked. Noah had his auxiliary regulator in his mouth, but his leg was bleeding at a fast clip. Finn needed to get him to the surface *now*.

Grabbing a bungee cord from his dive bag, he fashioned a tourniquet. Signaling for Noah to keep his leg still—he needed as little blood pumping through it as possible—he slipped it around Noah's thigh and signaled for the surface.

Noah nodded, and Finn moved behind him, the light from the light poles glaring in his eyes.

Securing his arm underneath Noah's shoulder, he wrapped his right arm tightly around Noah's chest as he'd done so many times as a rescue swimmer. Fifteen saves and one loss. He prayed Noah remained in the former. He *would* remain in the former.

Biting back the pain that ripped through his torn rotator cuff, Finn carried Noah toward the surface. He'd refused to get it fixed—wanting the pain to be a constant reminder of the life he lost, lives . . .

Please, Father, let me save Noah.

He swallowed.

Please save Noah and me.

Reaching the first decompression stop, he kept his arm

cinched around Noah's torso. Blood eked out of the wound, and he prayed the sharks stayed at bay.

They had two more stops to safely ascend. He would have blown by them and gladly taken the decompression sickness if it would help, but in Noah's compromised state, the harm would far outweigh the benefits of the faster ascent.

Finn's shoulder throbbed all the way to the surface, fighting each rotation, but he pushed through. The larger the strokes, the faster the ascent.

Finally breaching the surface, he lifted his mask off and gulped in a fresh breath of air.

He stilled at Noah's dead weight in his arms.

"Noah?"

His head lolled forward, his body limp.

"No! No! No!" Finn placed two fingers on Noah's neck, searching for a pulse. *Come on.* His chest tightened, his breath ragged. *Come on!*

SIXTY-SEVEN

Finally, Noah's pulse throbbed beneath his fingers.

His head lolling, Noah murmured something Finn couldn't make out.

"I'm getting you to the boat and to safety," he assured him.

Noah managed a loose nod.

Finn turned toward the boat, but it was gone.

He spun around and spotted it disappearing in the distance— another boat at its side.

Heat seethed through his cold limbs. *Marv and the man with him.*

"It's okay," he assured Noah. "When we don't check in with Caleb and he can't reach us, he'll send help."

Finn switched on his rescue strobe—the light flashing white. He reached for Noah's and clicked it on. Two were better than one.

He lay back in a modified float, keeping Noah's back to his chest. Maintaining their heads above the frothy waterline, they bobbed with the waves.

Please, Father, let the rescue team come soon.

~~~~~~~~~~~~~

After a tearful good-bye between Mark and Kenzie, Gabby and her sister made their way along the airport road toward the exit. Passing the entrance to the commercial hangar area, Gabby spotted a red-and-white pass hanging from a truck's rearview mirror as it entered through the gated area.

She pulled the pass she'd found in Will's truck out of her purse, thankful Tess had allowed her to take it, and quickly hung it on Kenzie's rearview mirror.

Kenzie's brow furrowed. "What are you doing?"

"Follow that truck into that area." She pointed at the commercial hangar lot.

"Why?" Kenzie frowned.

"I'll explain in a minute. Just drive past the guard shack like you belong."

Kenzie tapped the wheel as they passed the guard and drove along the row of hangars. "Now explain?"

"I found that pass hidden in Will Seavers's truck. Tess didn't know what it was for but said I could take it. Then we found the same pass in Dennis Fletcher's truck."

"And clearly the passes give access to this area. . . ." Kenzie's blue eyes narrowed. "So what were two Coast Guard guys doing with passes to commercial airport hangars?"

"Excellent question, which hopefully we can find the answer to," she said as they passed one large steel hangar after another—several open with small private planes sitting inside, while other hangar doors were closed.

"Where to?" Kenzie asked.

Gabby looked at the pass swinging from Kenzie's rearview mirror, her gaze fixing on the black *19* on the square white sticker in the upper right corner, both on the back and—she flipped it around—on the front. She looked at the hangars and noted that each one was consecutively numbered. "Hangar nineteen," she said, praying her hunch paid off. It was the farthest hangar out.

Pulling up to it, they found it still—no cars parked out front.

"Park on the side, so you aren't directly in view from cars

driving by. Park at an angle that allows you to still see if any cars approach."

Kenzie did as requested and shifted the tan '90s Range Rover into Park. "Now what?"

Unbuckling, Gabby opened the door and hopped out. She leaned back in to grab her purse and said, "I find a way in."

Kenzie leaned toward her, resting her palms on the passenger seat. "You know that's probably the last thing from safe."

"It'll be all good. You stay here and keep watch. If you see anyone, call me and I'll get out."

"How are you going to get in?"

"I'll find a way." She always did.

Shutting the door quietly, she hurried to the back side of the hangar, leaning against the building and scoping out the area to be sure no one had seen her.

The hangar door most likely had an alarm, so she needed to find an alternate way in.

She spotted two large rectangular windows lining the rear. Unfortunately, she needed help reaching them.

She scurried back to Kenzie's car and opened the door.

Kenzie jumped. "Sheesh. You scared me. I was so focused on the road I didn't see you. Or hear you . . ." She narrowed her eyes. "You've gotten stealthier with age."

As a kid, she'd been dubbed the "loudest child on earth" and had been the reason she and her siblings had gotten busted midescape by their mom more often than not. Silence and stealing Momma's homemade oatmeal–chocolate chip cookies from the counter jar hadn't gone as hand in hand as she'd hoped as a kid, but she'd learned. She had to in her profession.

"I need you to pull around back for a minute," she said, sliding into the passenger seat.

Kenzie cocked her head, her wavy blond hair slipping over her shoulder. "Dare I ask?"

Gabby smiled, loving being in her element. "You'll see."

Kenzie shifted the car into Drive and did as Gabby asked, positioning the Rover parallel to the hangar and centered under the first window.

Kenzie shook her head. "Not even going to ask."

"That's why I love you." Gabby winked. Exiting the car, she hopped up onto the hood, then onto the roof. She lifted up on her tiptoes and managed to push the window open. Stretching to her full length and clasping her fingers over the windowsill, she heaved herself up and in. Ungracefully, she dropped. Her elbow and entire left side collided with the concrete floor. Pain ricocheted up her arm.

Kenzie's motor hummed as she moved back around to the side of the building. Gabby smiled despite the pain as she got to her feet. Her sister was still a great partner in crime.

Swiping the dust from her hands across her jeans, she turned her attention to her surroundings, rotating her now-stiff shoulder and shaking out her achy arm.

A Cessna sat in the center of the hangar, its nose facing the front sliding hangar doors. The rest of the space was lined with tall metal shelving units filled with blue Rubbermaid tubs, their lids fastened in place.

She walked the length of the shelves, curious why they stood so far out from the wall. Pulling out a tub, she found another behind it. The tubs were lined in double rows. Setting both on the floor, she inspected the back of the shelf. Corrugated cardboard lined it.

She narrowed her eyes. The shelves looked exactly like the ones Kenzie and Mark had in their garage, but theirs had nothing nailed to the back.

She studied the backing again. It'd most certainly been added postpurchase.

It took some finagling, but she found a small wedge between the last shelf in the row and the one perpendicular to it.

Gabby nibbled her bottom lip, then tugged on each metal

shelf, hoping she'd find one that moved. She'd nearly given up hope when she tugged at the bottom shelf and it slipped out of place, opening the unit like a hidden door. She stepped into the narrow passageway between the two sets of shelves. Her jaw slackened at the sight before her.

SIXTY-EIGHT

Finn prayed the Coast Guard rescue unit arrived soon—and that they would easily see their beacons strobing. It was his first time on the other side of a rescue.

"Hang on, Noah. I've got you," he said. Gritting his teeth, Finn cast his gaze on the horizon.

Soon he heard the sweet chop of copter blades thwacking through the air. A slight measure of relief washed over him. Help was on the way, but with the amount of blood Noah had lost, he feared greatly for his welfare.

A cable lowered the rescue basket. It swung back and forth inches above the rocking waves. Finn swam Noah to it, praying his shoulder held out. Rolling Noah into the basket, he secured him into place. He circled his finger, and they retracted the cable, lifting Noah up.

Once Noah was safely inside the copter, they lowered the basket back down for Finn. He climbed inside, the experience new as he'd always been lifted by cable after rescues.

Swinging up over the ocean, the cable retracted until he was level with the copter's open bay door. Brooke pulled him in and slid the door shut.

Hurrying to unbuckle, Finn rolled out of the basket and rushed to Noah's side as Brooke knelt to assess him.

Blood and water soaked through his wet suit, and Brooke

swapped out the makeshift tourniquet for a sturdier, more sanitary one.

She lifted her chin at Finn. "You did good. You saved his life."

He prayed so. Prayed they weren't too late in reaching the hospital, where Noah would no doubt have to undergo surgery for what Finn was betting was a severed femoral artery.

Still shaken that Marv had been the man who'd sliced Noah, he worked to restrain his rage, focusing on his boss instead. An occasional wince and tense jaw were the only outward signs of pain Noah expressed.

"Hang on, boys," Dean called back. "It's going to be a bumpy ride. Wind shears have intensified. We're looking at gusts up to eighteen miles per hour."

Reaching the helipad of Wilmington General for Finn's second time in a matter of days, with yet another teammate on the brink of death, weighed heavy in his chest. They'd lost Sam, but they wouldn't lose Noah. They couldn't.

Dr. Blotny was once again the one to greet them with a gurney. "It's going to be all right, Noah," she said, shifting her gaze to the medic. "Thanks for the call in, Brooke."

Brooke nodded, having conveyed Noah's vitals and status via radio prior to their landing so Blotny and her team could jump right in. "Trauma room one," Blotny ordered as the team rolled the stretcher across the roof and into the hospital.

Brooke remained at Blotny's side, apprising her of Noah's status, and Finn followed closely behind as a sense of déjà vu washed over him. He'd walked through these very doors with Sam just minutes before they lost him.

Fear tracked through him.

He prayed for a very different outcome.

SIXTY-NINE

Magnificent jewels lined the black velvet trays running nearly the full length of the wall. Gabby stepped to the first tray. Emeralds, sapphires, and rubies donned the various earrings and rings. In the center of the display sat a stunning diamond necklace.

She longed to hold it, but knew she had to leave everything untouched to preserve the forensic integrity.

She reached for her phone to call Finn and snap pictures to text to him, but her back pocket was empty. Either she'd left her phone in the car or dropped it on her climb into the warehouse.

Dropping to her knees, she slid out the tub closest to her and lifted the lid. Inside were doubloons, like Rissi and Noah had discovered at Marv's, and . . .

She used the edge of her sleeve to lift the lid of a large cherrywood jewelry box. Nestled inside was a decadent, old-world gold crown, embedded with jade and ivory. She gently shut the lid and slid the tub back into its spot. What was going on here?

Footsteps shuffled, voices emanating from the front of the hangar.

The doors cranked open and light spilled through the narrow cracks between the shelving.

It was only a matter of time before whoever it was saw the sliding shelf unit ajar.

She moved away, tiptoeing around the corner opposite where she'd entered, praying there was another way out.

Hurrying, she scampered down the corridor as light spilled over the top of the shelves.

Footsteps padded on the other side of the shelving, the men's voices growing louder . . . *closer.*

"I want this shipment ready to go tonight," a man said.

Gabby stilled. She knew that voice. It couldn't be.

"Do you think that's a good idea, when—?"

"Excuse me?"

"Sorry, sir. I just thought—"

"Leave the thinking to me. You understand?"

"Yes, sir."

"Better. Now, all the jewels from the *Santa Allegra* go to the buyer. Except the crown. That I want for my collection."

"And if he asks . . . ?"

"He has no idea what Marv and Mo found out there. Any piece of the treasure is mine to keep if I decide so."

"Of course, sir. I'll prepare the shipment for transport."

Footfalls moved toward the back of the hangar.

"Kill him and handle the shipment yourself," the man who was clearly the boss said to a third man. "*No one* questions me."

Certain she recognized the man's voice but unable to believe it, Gabby crept forward, leaning over a waist-high crate to peer between two crates in front of her.

"Yes, sir," the third man said. "Consider it done."

"Then prep the rest of my inventory for transport. I'm relocating the operation."

"Yes, sir."

Gabby peered through the slit. A dark-haired man moved toward the rear of the building, walking slowly toward the man who had been ordered to the back of the hangar. He approached, raised his gun, and two hushed shots dropped the man.

The dark-haired man stood over him and fired again for good measure.

The light shifted, and she blinked as the man who'd ordered the hit moved into her line of sight.

Paul? She gasped. It had sounded like him, but she hadn't believed it could actually be.

His head whipped in her direction.

She pushed back from the crates and stumbled.

"Someone's here!" Paul yelled. "In the back row!"

Pounding footsteps rushed down the jewel-lined aisle toward her.

Scrambling to her feet, she turned and started running. *Please let there be a way out.*

A horn blared out front. *Kenzie.*

"Get her!" Paul roared.

Gabby rushed for the row's end, praying for a way out.

"I hear you," Paul said. His voice sent chills rippling in waves along her skin as a cold sweat beaded on her brow.

She ran, tripping over the edge of a large metal crate. She tumbled forward, bracing her hands on the front door of the black crate. A low growl—or was it a deep purr?—resonated inside.

She swallowed as the shadow of movement crept toward her. Two yellow eyes stared out as the panther lunged for her.

Dear God.

She flung herself back, knocking into the shelf unit behind her. A small crate tumbled down, its door popping open as it collided with the floor. A needle pierced her calf. Scorching heat burned up her leg. She looked down at a green-and-black snake slithering at her feet, poised to strike again.

The dark-haired man rounded the corner, and she ran straight for the shelving unit, barreling into it shoulder first. The unit rocked.

The man lifted his gun, and she rammed into the unit again.

A bullet whizzed past her as the unit crashed forward. She fell with it, crates of animals falling around her.

The horn honked again. The engine roared.

Her gaze locked on Paul coming around the Cessna, and then he blurred as searing pain spread through her chest.

She fumbled out the hangar doors, gasping for breath.

She managed to tumble into Kenzie's car before her vision blackened.

"Sn . . . ake."

Kenzie's eyes widened at that, but Gabby had to tell her more.

"Diii. . . .d yoo . . . u see . . . hhh . . . i . . . m?" she slurred. Why was her tongue so thick?

The world spun as Kenzie floored it and tore out of the lot. "See who?"

She tried to say Paul's name, but her tongue wouldn't cooperate, so she tried something else. "Co . . . Co . . ."

Her world went black.

SEVENTY

Finn paced the hall connecting the ER with the trauma operating rooms, where Dr. Blotny performed emergency surgery to stitch up Noah's femoral artery and hamstring. Finn had tried entering the room as they rolled Noah in, but Dr. Blotny wasted no time in ordering him out.

If there was one woman he didn't mess with—well, two—it was Dr. Blotny and Gabby. Neither was to be trifled with. Both were brilliant, driven, and fascinating in vastly different ways.

Slumping against the wall, he braced his hand on his throbbing head.

Please, Father, bring Noah through this.

The chill of the ER seeped through his wet suit. Brooke had draped a blanket across his shoulders in the copter, but it must have fallen off when he'd leapt from the copter.

Dean had patched him through to the station so he could apprise Caleb of the situation. He and Rissi were en route to the hospital now, but where was Gabby? Caleb said she and Kenzie had yet to return. He really needed to send someone to pick up Noah's phone from the marina parking lot. Then he'd be able to track Gabby's whereabouts.

Caleb and Rissi burst through the ER doors, racing down the linoleum floor toward him.

"I brought an extra outfit," Caleb said. "I figured you could use it." He handed him a T-shirt, sweat pants, and running shoes. "I hope they fit all right."

"Anything's better than a wet suit or the hospital gown the nurses offered."

Caleb arched a brow.

"Don't ask." He'd change as soon as he sent Caleb to the marina.

An ER nurse approached, the squeak of her shoes giving her away before she reached them.

Finn turned in time to see her frown.

"We need to keep this hall clear," she said.

Not happy, but understanding, Finn led the way to the double doors leading out of the ER. He moved to hit the square silver button that opened the doors but was too late. They swung open from the other side and a gurney pushed through.

His eyes widened at the sight of Gabby laid out on the stretcher. *What on earth?*

A very panicked Kenzie followed inches behind.

"What happened? Is she okay?" he said, realizing the stupidity of his question. Of course she wasn't okay or she wouldn't be in the ER on a stretcher being rushed toward a room.

He rushed alongside her and Kenzie, his pulse quickening. Gabby's pale skin was covered with a damp sheen of perspiration. She was unconscious. A lump caught in his throat, adrenaline burning through his veins.

"She got bit by a snake," Kenzie said.

The nurse pushed the gurney into an open room. Dr. Kent rushed in, examining the bite on Gabby's leg. "Snakebite," he said. "Let's get some antivenom in her ASAP."

Finn gripped Gabby's limp hand. "It'll be okay, sweetheart," he said over the nurse's shoulder as she directed him out of the room. He swallowed, warmth flaring through his body, sweat moistening his skin.

Please, Lord, let her be okay. I love her so much.

"We're going to need you to stay out in the waiting room," the nurse said, shutting the glass doors and pulling the privacy curtain closed.

A fear he hadn't known since Cody disappeared into the sea shook him.

SEVENTY-ONE

A weary-looking Dr. Blotny entered the room where they'd been pacing.

She pulled off her surgical cap, clutching it in her hands.

Finn's muscles tensed. *Please be good news.*

"He came through surgery fine," Blotny said, and Finn's tight muscles relaxed a bit. "He's a strong one," she continued. "He's still under anesthesia in post-op. As soon as he wakes and we get him transferred to a room, I'll let you see him."

Shaking with adrenaline despite the good news, he asked, "Gabby Rowley came in with a snakebite? She's with Dr. Kent."

"I'll see what I can find out."

"Thank you."

Heaviness sank into his bones, and he struggled to gulp in a solid intake of air.

Thank you, Lord, that Noah is okay. Please let Gabby be too.

"It's going to be all right," Rissi said, rubbing his nearly numb arm as the room spun.

He nodded.

"We should pray," she said.

They stood in a circle, holding hands.

"Caleb, will you pray?"

"Of course. Father, thank you that Noah came through surgery strong, and that he's going to be okay. Let Gabby respond well to the antivenom. Please let her come through this. Be with her and with us. In Jesus' name we pray."

"Amen," Rissi said. giving Finn's hand a squeeze before letting go. "Logan and Emmalyne send their love. They wanted to be here. . . ."

"They are needed at the station so they can work on tracking down Marv." Finn shook his head. "I still can't believe he attacked Noah."

"Any idea who the second man was?" Caleb asked as he took a seat.

"It was hard to see. It happened so fast, but based on build, it could have been Mo."

Caleb shook his head. "I can't believe they would harm you guys."

Rissi raked a hand through her hair. "It's unreal."

Finn swallowed. "I know."

"I'd better call Mom," Kenzie said. "She's staying with Fiona and Owen."

Finn rested a hand on her arm. "Can we run through what happened first?"

"Of course. Gabby was investigating a commercial hangar at the airport."

Finn frowned. She'd violated her promise to him, but he probably should have expected it if she found a new clue to investigate.

"What was in it?"

"I don't really know, but when I pulled up in front, the doors were open and I saw a plane and a bunch of crates and plastic storage containers."

"Did she say anything about what she found?"

"She was babbling by the time she got to the car, but she said 'Snake,' asked me if I saw *him*, and then mumbled something like 'Co' before she blacked out."

"Co?"

"It could be the name of the person she saw," Rissi offered.

Kenzie continued, "I briefly saw a man—tall, dark hair—but I was so focused on Gabby, I didn't really get a good look."

Finn raked a hand through his hair. "Cole Nelson or Dr. Cohen . . ." He rattled off the names Gabby might know from town, but none made sense given the circumstances.

"I'll head to the warehouse," Caleb said, his shoulders stiffening. "Kenzie, can you tell me where to go?"

"I'd be happy to."

"Thanks, Caleb," Finn said. "Keep me posted."

Caleb nodded. "You too. Let me know as soon as you get an update on Gabby."

"Rissi . . ." Finn looked to her. "You should go too."

"Are you sure?"

"Positive. I want whoever's responsible for this caught."

"Okay." She nodded. "I'll be back as soon as I can."

"Watch out for snakes."

Rissi tensed. "I don't even want to think about it."

Everyone had a thing, and snakes were Rissi's. Just like rats gave him the heebie-jeebies. It was embarrassing but true.

Finn paced the ten-by-ten room after his teammates left.

Fear and a chill swept through him as he waited with Kenzie. The second hand ticked on the round wall clock in sync with his palpitating heart.

Please, Father, it's been so long without much change. Please let her pull through. I can't lose her.

SEVENTY-TWO

An hour passed before Dr. Kent entered the waiting room. "Gabby's stable," he said.

Kenzie squealed and thanked Jesus. The adrenaline that had gushed through Finn's coiled muscles, pumping his heartbeat through his ears and chest, released with a painful whoosh.

Thank you, Jesus.

He fought the urge to drop to his knees in gratitude—at least until Dr. Kent was done talking.

"Can we see her?" He needed to be near her.

"Once she's settled in her room, but I should warn you, she's still unconscious."

He swallowed, the motion feeling like jagged shards scraping his raw throat. "Is that . . . ?"

"Normal," Dr. Kent said before Finn could finish. "Her body has been through a lot. Between the effects of the pain meds and the antivenom to counteract the poison, it's not surprising. Her body needs rest, but she should wake before too long." Dr. Kent lowered his clipboard by his side. "I'll have Pam, the head RN in the ward Gabby will be in, notify you when you can visit her."

"Thank you." He shook the doc's hand. Gratitude flowed inside, nearly to the point of tears. The man had saved the woman he loved.

After a brief visit with Noah, Kenzie decided to head home to relieve Nana Jo. She said her mom was anxious to get to the hospital, and her children wanted her to be there when they went to bed.

Finn went down to the cafeteria, his stomach growling. It was after seven, and he hadn't eaten since breakfast.

The cell phone Rissi had brought to replace his, which was still on the stolen dive boat, rang. "Walker."

"It's Caleb."

"Did you find anything?"

"Try the jackpot. You should see this place. Jewels like the necklace we found at Eric Jacobs's place, artwork like you found at the Laytons', salvaged treasure like you found at Marv's . . . And here's where it gets really funky—exotic animals."

"Like the snake that bit Gabby?"

"And a panther."

"Seriously?"

"Seriously. Looks like he's been slightly sedated. Probably in an attempt to keep him subdued."

"Any idea who the warehouse belongs to?"

"Logan found the lease. It's under Litman Limited."

"Shocking." Finn shook his head on an exhale.

"Emmy is also working the scene. Hopefully, we'll soon get prints."

"Keep me posted."

"Will do. We called in the FBI's art-theft department, as this is really their jurisdiction, but given its ties to our case, they're playing nice."

"Good."

"Rissi decided she should take a Coast Guard dive contingent and retrieve Layton's body before the sun went down. They just transferred his body to Hadley."

"Excellent."

"He said he'd perform the autopsy first thing tomorrow."

Maybe the Layton case was finally wrapping up so they could shift all their focus to catching Fuentes. "Any sign of Marv or Mo?"

"Looks like Marv is in the wind, but we've got Mo in custody."

"Has he talked?"

"Not yet, but I think we'll get there. I sicced Caleb on him."

Next to Rissi, he was the best at reading people and getting under their skin.

"How are Gabby and Noah doing?"

Finn updated him.

"That's a relief."

It'd be even more of one when she woke.

After eating, Finn finally got the okay to visit Gabby. He bought a bouquet of flowers, so they were the first thing she would see. The name or word she'd muttered still ticked through his mind. No one with either a first name or last name that started with *Co* made any sense. He was anxious for her to wake up so she could elaborate and they could get the person responsible. He was anxious for her to wake, period.

He knocked on her door just in case she'd awakened, but upon no answer, he stepped inside. The room was dim and quiet. He moved around the corner and found an empty bed.

Bathroom?

He strode to the dark restroom, praying she'd gone in and skipped turning on the light. His heart thumped in his chest. He knocked on the bathroom door. "Gabby?"

No answer.

He knocked harder. "Gabby?"

Nothing.

"I'm coming in," he said, perspiration beading on his brow. He stepped inside to find it empty.

He raced out to the nurses' station, praying they'd taken her somewhere—perhaps for testing.

"Gabby Rowley?" he said, his breath catching in his throat.

"Sir?" The woman looked up from the nurses' station.

"She's not in her room. Was she moved?"

"Not that I'm aware. Let me check with Pam." She picked up the phone and dialed. "Hey, Pam, did Gabby Rowley go for tests? She's not in her room."

Finn held his breath.

She hung up. "Pam's on the way. She said Gabby wasn't moved anywhere."

The hallway spun, and Finn raced back to Gabby's room, searching for any clue of where she might have gone.

Pam rushed in, her eyes wide. "I don't know where she is. I have the nurses checking all the rooms. She may have woken disoriented and got out of bed to wander. We hadn't changed her into a gown yet, so she might not be easily noticed as a patient in her clothes."

He flashed his badge. "I need the hospital sealed off immediately. Call security and get it done. Tell them I'm coming down now." He ran for the stairs, not willing to wait for the elevator. His heart racing with his pace, he flew down the stairs, and he dialed Caleb as he sped down the hall for the security office.

"Eason?"

"Gabby's gone."

"What?"

"They can't find her, and its possible someone took her. Noah asked her to wear a tracker in her locket after her last escapade. It should be tracking from his phone, which is in his car at the marina lot. I need you to get it ASAP."

"On it," Caleb said.

"Have Logan take over with Mo and press him hard. We need answers *now*."

Finn rushed into the security office, and the two guards stood. He flashed his badge. His breath coming in short spurts, he blurted out the pertinent information.

SEVENTY-THREE

Gabby woke to utter darkness. She blinked. Had the snakebite taken her vision? Her pulse quickened.

She moved her arms, but something fastened them behind her back. She tugged against the restraint as it bit into her wrist.

Some kind of plastic strap?

She shifted her head, and fabric chafed her cheek.

Her chest tightened.

Someone had her.

A car engine roared beneath her. She jostled in the seat as the car sped over railroad tracks.

She swallowed, her throat constricting.

Shock riddled through her once again that Paul was the man behind Litman Limited. Had he intercepted Kenzie's car? Where was her sister now?

"She's awake," a man said, his voice familiar. From the warehouse. The tall man with dark hair. "The Collector will be pleased. It's far more exciting killing someone who's awake."

Finn paced back and forth in front of the hospital's security screens replaying the footage from the past hour.

Pumping his hands in and out of fists, he waited for Caleb's call. What was taking so long to retrieve Noah's phone?

"There," he said as a dark sedan caught his eye. "Can you zoom in on the license plate?"

"You got it." Pete, the security guard running the footage, did as he'd asked.

Finn studied the plate. It was the same sedan that had picked Fletcher up at the hospital.

He checked his phone again. No missed calls. His leg bounced. *Come on, Caleb.*

Pete resumed scrolling through the footage, and Finn's chest seized as an unconscious Gabby was rolled out the ambulance bay door by a tall, dark-haired man.

The driver of the sedan got out, and both looked to be sure no one was watching. The dark-haired man lifted Gabby up and shoved her into the car's backseat. Kenzie rushed into the footage.

He swallowed, his jaw clenching. Not Kenzie too.

The driver pulled his gun out of his shoulder harness and aimed it at her. She raised her hands, and the man shoved her toward the car. Then he slammed his elbow into her neck, knocking her out, and shoved her limp body in the car beside Gabby.

The car screeched out of the lot.

His muscles coiled as the car with Gabby and Kenzie disappeared from view.

His cell rang, and he nearly dropped it in a rush to answer.

"I've got a location," Caleb said. "But I have no clue what's out there."

Finn's brow pinched. "Out where?"

"It looks like the location is at the tip of Tangier Island, where it juts out into the ocean."

"There aren't any houses or other buildings that far south, are there?"

"Not that I'm aware of."

Finn clutched the phone. Had they, whoever they were, taken Gabby and Kenzie out in the middle of nowhere to kill them?

He swallowed the bile burning up his throat.

"I'll direct everyone to those coordinates," Caleb said.

"Roger that." He turned to Pete. "Thanks for your help. I'll be back for the footage."

"I hope you reach them in time," Pete said, his voice trailing off as Finn rushed for the parking lot and Rissi's car, which she'd been kind enough to leave for him.

Keys jangled in his grip as he bolted for the red Fiat.

Please let me reach them in time, his soul cried.

A hand closed around Gabby's upper arm in a viselike grip, digging into her flesh.

The man dragged her from the car. She pitched forward, her face colliding with hard-packed earth. A sea breeze riffled her hood. She was near the water, but where?

The man hauled her to her feet and shoved her forward.

"Both of you, walk!"

Both? Heat rushed up her neck despite the cool air. *Please don't let it be Kenzie.*

She couldn't do more than grunt with the thick tape across her mouth.

A female grunt sounded back.

Her head spun. What had she gotten her sister into?

SEVENTY-FOUR

Light flooded her eyes as the fabric was nipped from her head.

She blinked to find Paul standing in front of her.

She lunged for him, but someone grabbed her from behind, jerking her back. His hands clamped on her arms.

"I told you she was a feisty one."

Fuentes?

He walked into her line of sight. "Hello, Gabrielle. I told you that you'd pay for what you did." He tore the tape off her mouth in one painful swipe, but she refused to cry out.

"What *I* did?" she said, her gaze landing on the crystal chandelier overhead. Chandelier? Marble statues lined the hall, along with . . . She squinted. Was that a Degas?

Kenzie murmured behind her, and Gabby spun around. A man held her hard against his chest, his 9mm pressing into her ribs.

She swallowed the heavy lump in her throat. "Kenzie!" She struggled to break free of the man's grasp.

Kenzie's hood was still on, but she recognized her sister all the same.

Paul lifted his chin, and the man gripping her sister tore off her hood.

Kenzie's wide, tear-filled eyes locked on Gabby.

If I have to die, so be it, but please not Kenzie.

A smug smile curled on Fuentes's face, a jagged scar running along his right cheek.

Gabby lunged at him.

"Enough!" Fuentes roared, backhanding her with blistering force, jarring her back.

The back of her head collided with the man's jaw behind her.

An expletive escaped his mouth as he released his hold.

She rushed for Kenzie but, losing her footing, splayed onto the marble floor. Her cuffed hands prevented her from breaking her fall as she face-planted onto the cold tile.

Pain shot through her cheekbone, a splintering *crack* reverberating through it.

Warm liquid slithered down her face, rolling over and dripping off her chin. The splattered blood was a stark contrast to the cream-colored floor.

Fuentes grabbed a fistful of her hair and yanked her to her feet.

A whimper escaped her lips.

"That's more like it." His smile widened. "I want to hear you suffer."

"You've got me. Now let my sister go."

"No can do," Paul said. "She's seen me."

"We see you all the time in the Coffee Connection."

"As Paul, not as the Collector."

Thoughts tossed through her mind as she scrambled to put all the pieces together.

How did Fuentes and the Collector—as Paul referred to himself—know each other? Had they been working together?

"So who works for whom?" she asked, her heart racing, throbbing in her ears. Her gaze darted between the two men bent on killing her, searching for any means of escape. Tears smarted in her eyes.

"Neither," Fuentes said. "The Collector contacted me when he dug into your background, and we discovered we shared a common nemesis."

She'd never been called that before. "So Paul broke you out of prison?" She tried stalling for time, but from the gleeful expression on Fuentes's face, time was running out.

"No." Fuentes laughed. "I did that on my own, but he invited me down to his turf for a fresh start. Because thanks to you, I'm a fugitive."

She narrowed her eyes, studying Paul's stoic expression. She highly doubted a man of such power would seriously help Fuentes out of the goodness of his nonexistent heart.

"Don't you see what he's doing?" she taunted. "Paul is using you as a scapegoat. Everyone knows you're out to kill me. If anything goes wrong, you're to blame."

"Shut your mouth." Paul belted her across the face, knocking her to the ground—her knees taking the brunt of the force this time. Her cheek still throbbing, she looked up at him, defiance burning through her.

Kenzie's muffled cry broke past the duct tape still across her mouth.

"You took from me." Fuentes's voice shook. "Now you pay while your sister watches her impending fate."

Gabby tried to scramble to her feet, but Fuentes grabbed her neck.

The air caught in her lungs as he squeezed. She twisted away to loosen his hold, but he only pressed harder.

So this was how she was going to die.

SEVENTY-FIVE

Gabby gasped for air that wouldn't come.

"Enough," Paul hollered.

Fuentes paused and glared up at him. "You said I could kill her."

"And we will, but I have a far better plan. Trust me."

His hands slipped from her neck and snagged on her locket, pulling it to the floor. Swallowing gulps of air, she fell to the side, covered the locket, and slipped it into her back pocket. They had a chance. Surely Finn and Noah would be looking for them.

Paul hauled her to her feet. "Bring the sister," he said.

"No!" Gabby wrestled in his hold.

His hands clamped tighter around her upper arms, his fingers pinching into her flesh. "You can blame yourself for your sister's death. You brought this on her."

Hot tears streamed down her face, mixing with the blood trickling across her chin. Her split lip stung as she spoke. "Where are you taking us?"

"To see my babies." He shoved her toward the outside door.

Babies? Paul didn't have kids as far as she knew, but clearly, she didn't know him at all.

The outside door swung open. Paul pushed her down a root-filled dirt path. "What about Smitty?" she asked, wondering about his involvement in all this. Was he waiting to watch her die too?

"What about him?" Paul said.

"Your comments to Noah at Dockside made us look at him. How is he involved?" She saw a rugged shoreline ahead, illuminated by the rising super moon. How could it be night already?

Paul laughed. "That idiot has no clue what's going on. I thought CGIS might be starting to look at the Coffee Connection, so I shifted the suspicion to him. Figured I'd just dispose of him if the need arose."

He halted at the dark water's edge. "Speaking of disposal." He lifted his chin, and the dark-haired man switched on a flood lamp, its light directed at a steel cage attached to a small crane.

It looked like a shark cage, but it couldn't possibly be. The width of the openings would easily allow the bull sharks teeming off the coast to enter.

Gabby's stomach flipped as Kenzie sobbed beside her. Surely Paul was not so sadistic as to . . .

She swallowed as she studied the cage, bile burning up her throat.

Were those human remains?

"I believe you knew Dennis Fletcher and Marv Lewis? They, unfortunately, became liabilities I couldn't afford."

"Let me guess," she said, her knees shaking as she tried to stall for time. Prayers that Finn and Noah would find them flooded up to heaven. "Fletcher and Seavers provided you with Coast Guard patrol schedules so you could run drugs without getting caught." Her words slurred, her bottom lip swelling and tender.

"Very good," Paul said. "Xavier told me you were a smart one."

"And Mo and Marv . . ." The treasure in the hangar sparked to mind. "I'm guessing they found a wreck containing treasure and looted it for you. And John Layton let your stolen goods through customs. But I'm betting he kept a piece for himself." Based on the Rembrandt Rissi and Noah had found.

"Yes." Paul's grip around her arms tightened. "And he paid for it."

"Mo killed Layton?" she said, believing Marv had failed underwater, so Mo finished the job, then covered his tracks with the explosion, sinking the evidence to the bottom of the sea.

"Yes, I don't accept failure or tolerate loose ends. Now, enough chatter." With a lift of Paul's chin, two of his men grabbed hold of Gabby and Kenzie, shoving them toward the cage.

Gabby wrestled in the man's grasp as Kenzie lunged against the man holding her back. They ripped Kenzie's duct tape off.

"More satisfying to hear her scream." Paul chuckled.

"Please let her go. You have me. Let her go," Gabby pleaded.

Her pleas were only met by wide smiles on Paul's and Fuentes's faces.

Kenzie sobbed, "I didn't get to say good-bye to my babies. To tell them how much I love them."

Hot tears streaked down Gabby's cold cheeks. This was all her fault. If anyone was going to die, it should be her and *only* her.

The men shoved them in the cage. The crane attached to it hovered a few feet over the water's surface.

To Gabby's shock and confusion, the men slid oxygen tanks on their backs and goggles over their heads before cuffing their wrists into the shackle-style handcuffs overhead.

The men shoved regulators in their mouths.

What kind of sick game was this?

"The killing is much more pleasurable when victims are given opportunity to consider their fate. You have an hour's worth of air. I keep my babies well fed, so we'll see if they eat you first or if you run out of air and drown," Paul said. "Then we'll toss Xavier in."

"What?" Fuentes said as one of Paul's men seized him. "We had a deal."

Paul lit a cigar, took a puff, and released the smoke in a smooth trail, highlighted in the floodlight's glare. The last thing she saw before they lowered the cage was Fuentes's panic-stricken face.

Cold water rushed in, swirling around Gabby's ankles, over her knees, up her thighs, hips, and waist.

Her goggles fogging from the moisture of her tears, Gabby blinked, trying to see in the darkness engulfing them.

The light above shifted and angled toward them, streaming through the depths. The floodlight. He really wanted them to see what was coming.

Please, Lord, calm me so I can think of a way out of this. We need to conserve air. Please direct Finn and Noah to us in time.

Hot tears spilled from her eyes, further fogging her goggles. *Please, Lord.*

The silhouette of a bull shark swam at the edge of the floodlight's beam. Kenzie started jerking beside her as a second and then a third shark approached, flicking their tails. They circled closer and closer until they were nearly upon them.

Please, Father.

If Gabby could just get the cuffs off, it would be a start. She stared up at them—separated, as the chain had been slipped through two different openings in the cage roof and held in place by a large metal ring.

She needed to get her hands closer together, needed to reach the bobby pin she'd tucked in the loose hair under the braid at the base of her neck.

Wrapping her fingers through the chain links, she kicked, swimming her way up to the cuffs. With an understanding only siblings shared, Kenzie positioned herself under Gabby's rear, supporting her with her shoulders and providing the leverage

Gabby needed to gain traction. The slack in the chain was now enough for her to loop it around her hands, allowing her to pull up with her arms as she used her feet to climb up the cage slats. Finally reaching the top, she stuck her feet in the highest slat. She lay back, arching to reach the cuffs. She used her right hand to pull out the bobby pin and worked the right cuff free, then the left one.

Suddenly Kenzie flailed backward against the far side of the cage.

Gabby looked down, her muscles seizing.

One of the sharks had rammed the cage, searching for an opening. He rammed a second time and then a third.

Wrapping her fingers in the chain links as Gabby had, Kenzie bent her knees and swung herself back and forth, kicking her legs out in a forward motion, then bending them back.

The shark found an opening, and Kenzie kicked forward, the force of her movement propelling her feet into its snout.

Shaking its head, it swam away, then returned. Kenzie wasn't fast enough, and it took a chunk out of her calf. Her scream reverberated in the water, rising with the air bubbles.

Gabby swam down. She wrapped her arm under her sister's shoulder as the shark circled back. Her heart pounding in her chest, she kicked for the top of the cage.

Blood pooled like a cloud in the heightening tide of the super moon—the killing tide. Water swirling in with pummeling force pulled them toward the front of the cage.

Please, God!

Just as Gabby felt all was lost, the crane creaked overhead. The cage rose up.

She clutched her sister's hand. What were they about to face?

Her breathing hurried, she tried to calm herself before she hyperventilated. She needed to remain composed for Kenzie.

The floodlight pierced her eyes as they breached the surface, Kenzie clinging tightly to her side.

She blinked, trying to make out the silhouette of the man standing before her.

He rushed to the cage. "I've got them," he yelled.

Finn.

The adrenaline coursing through her abated in a shaky release—her arms and legs trembling. Tears sprang to her eyes, fogging her goggles. She pulled them off and yanked the rebreather from her mouth as Finn unlatched the cage.

She rested her hand under Kenzie's arm, helping to stabilize her.

Red emergency lights spun in the distance. A fire truck's whirring siren drew near.

Finn reached for her. "Come on, honey. I got you." Those three words rivaled his declaration of love—holding just as much meaning. He had her. Next to God, he was her rock and shield.

He extended his reach. "Come on, Gabby."

"Take Kenzie first. A shark bit her leg." She gripped Kenzie's waist to help hoist her up.

"On three . . ." he said.

Gabby tightened her grip, steadying Kenzie as she wobbled, unable to put weight on her left leg.

"One, two . . ." He waved the paramedic over.

"Three."

He looped his hands under Kenzie's arms, lifting as Gabby heaved upward.

"I got her," Finn said. Lifting her the rest of the way up and turning, he rushed to meet the paramedic. "You're going to be all right," he assured Kenzie.

Using the slats as leverage, Gabby slipped her foot in one of the openings and pushed up. Working her way up and out of the cage, she bent to catch her breath. After handing Kenzie off, Finn turned back to Gabby. Midway to her his eyes widened, his gaze fixed on something behind her.

An arm snaked about her waist, and without pausing to think, she jabbed her elbow back, the bone colliding with the man's ribs.

An expletive spewed from his mouth and she stiffened. *Fuentes.*

The muzzle of a gun pressed to her temple.

"Back away or I shoot," he hollered.

Finn halted, the color draining from his face.

"You're my way out," Fuentes whispered, his breath sickeningly moist and hot against her ear.

He pulled her with him as he moved for the dock, her back pressed flush against his chest.

Finn followed, paramedics keeping their distance, police officers swarming in.

"Everyone stay back or she dies!"

"Stay back," Finn yelled, his hands in the air.

Everyone froze where they stood.

Fuentes's sweaty face rubbed against hers.

Reaching the dock, he kept her between him and Finn, backing onto the boat. Her foot caught on the side, and she fell back, knocking Fuentes down in the process. His gun fired, and a vise clinched around her heart.

"No!" Finn rushed forward.

Fuentes wriggled beneath her, and she turned her head to see the bullet hole in the boat's port side.

Thank you, Jesus.

She rolled onto her side. The gun had knocked free from Fuentes's hand, and he struggled underneath her, trying to reach it with the tips of his fingers.

Her breath tight, heat coursing through her veins, she lunged forward, kneeing him in the process.

He swore, curling into a ball as her hand gripped the gun.

She shifted onto her side again, and his hand clutched her wrist. As they wrestled for hold of the gun, it retorted. Fuentes jerked back onto his knees, then stood clasping his chest.

META

He stumbled back, tripping over a cooler, then over the side of the boat, water plumming up in his wake.

She scrambled to the edge of the boat, searching.

Finn raced to her side. "Are you hurt?"

"I'm okay." She kept her gaze on the dark water.

"We need a floodlight over here," Finn called, and Caleb obliged.

It illuminated the surface of the water for several square feet, but there was no sign of movement other than shark fins bobbing above the surface, then dipping back under.

It seemed a fitting fate—Xavier Fuentes dying the way he and the Collector intended to kill her and Kenzie.

"My sister?" Her pulse quickened.

"Is on her way to Wilmington General. She's in good hands."

"But will she be all right?"

"From what I saw, definitely."

"Where's Paul?"

"Handcuffed in the back of Caleb's car. He claims Smitty lured him out here, that he had a gun on him and several of the men called him Boss."

"No, it's Paul. He calls himself the Collector. I saw him at the warehouse."

"So . . . Co for Collector?"

"No, Coffee Connection."

Finn sank back on his knees, hugging her against his chest. "I can't believe it was Paul this entire time."

A paramedic approached and bent down to look at Gabby. "Ma'am, we're ready for you."

She stiffened. "Ready for me?"

"You endured some trauma." He gently pointed at her face.

"Oh." She touched her cheek and winced at the tenderness.

Finn smoothed her wet hair back from her face. "Who did this to you?"

"Fuentes and Paul."

"Then Paul's lucky Caleb got to him before me."

"Miss?" the paramedic said. "We really should take a look at you."

She nodded, then looked to Finn. "You coming?"

"Darling, I'm never leaving your side again."

She smiled. That sounded pretty good right about now.

SEVENTY-SIX

Gabby plopped on the bed, her head spinning. Finn had suggested she stay in his guest room, but with Paul Barnes, aka the Collector, in jail and Fuentes dead, she could finally breathe freely. And with the feelings she and Finn had for one another, it seemed more appropriate for her to stay in her own place, even if it was on his property. Now they just needed to decide what to do with their feelings.

She loved Finn and didn't want to be separated from him, but what about her job in Raleigh? She loved her job, but she loved Finn. It came down to which she loved more, and deep down she knew the answer.

She moved for the bathroom, needing a hot shower. She'd had a blanket draped over her since the paramedics checked her out, but her clothes had yet to fully dry and . . .

She winced as she looked in the mirror, studying her bruised and scraped face. It looked as if someone had nailed her with a cricket bat. She moved for the shower, turning it on. Grabbing a towel off the stand, she hung it on the hook by the shower door.

Steam filled the room, warmth rushing over her. She bent and slipped off her wet socks, tossing them in the hamper. The bathroom door creaked open, and she stilled. "Finn?"

She must not have fully shut it. No way Finn would enter her bathroom without knocking and calling out first.

She padded along the cool tile floor, her feet leaving a trail of wet prints behind her. She froze when she saw a second, much larger set of wet prints, leading from the entrance to behind the now fully open bathroom door.

Her chest muscles compressed, the weight making it hard to breathe.

She tiptoed past the door, but before she could clear the doorframe, the door swung at her, knocking her to the ground.

Her eyes wide, her heart pounding in her chest, she turned, and Fuentes stepped around the door.

He staggered forward, his white shirt clinging to his bloody chest, an ax raised above his head.

"You're going to pay, witch."

She scrambled back, grabbing her purse and pulling out her gun. She fired once . . . twice, and the ax clattered to the floor. His body slumped lifelessly on top of it.

"Gabby." Finn rushed into the loft, straight to her side, lifting her into his arms. "You okay, baby?"

She nodded, clinging to him.

SEVENTY-SEVEN

Two days later, Finn held the door open for Gabby as she stepped into Noah's hospital room carrying a basket of his favorite treats. No doubt he'd appreciate the Doritos and jerky far more than flowers.

"Looks like we're the last to the party," she said, her gaze tracking over everyone. Nana Jo sat in the chair angled and facing her son. Kenzie sat on the edge of the bed. Fiona attempted to teach Owen how to play Chutes and Ladders on a blanket spread across the floor.

She set the basket of goodies on Noah's tray table.

"Yum." He smiled. "Thanks, kid."

"Really?" Nana Jo shook her head. "He needs real food, not that stuff coated in flavored powder."

"Doritos!" Fiona hopped to her feet and skipped over to her uncle. "Can I have some, Uncle Noah?"

"Of course." He smiled, handing her the bag.

"Ritos." Owen waddled to his sister's side.

"Be sure you share, Fiona," Kenzie said.

"Yes, Mom." She ripped the bag open, popped one in her mouth, and handed one to her brother.

"We've got some news," Gabby said as Finn wrapped his arms around her from behind.

She leaned back into his hold, and he rested his chin on the top of her head.

337

"I'll take the kiddos to get a drink," Kenzie said.

"Thanks," Noah said.

No need for them to be present for shoptalk.

Kenzie scooted them from the room with the promise of soda. "Caffeine free, of course," she said, looking back at them. "The last thing these rug rats need is more energy."

"So what's the latest?" Noah asked.

Finn looked to Gabby with a smile, giving her the go-ahead to fill Noah in.

Gabby sighed. Where to begin?

"Hadley determined that Layton was strangled to death, causing burst blood vessels in his brain. Mo copped a deal for a lesser murder sentence, and both he and Jacobs also copped deals for their roles in the smuggling ring—both providing more than enough information to put the Collector away for a very long time. All three were arraigned and are set to stand trial."

Gabby could hardly believe this next bit herself. "But Paul Barnes, owner of the Coffee Connection, was just an alias and cover."

Noah arched a brow. "For?"

Finn lifted the file he'd dropped on the side table and handed it to Noah. "We have Logan and Em to thank for this. They ran his prints, and it turns out his real name is Raul Gomez."

Noah opened to the eight-by-ten FBI Most Wanted flyer.

"That doesn't look like Paul," Noah said.

"Turns out Raul Gomez was the head of MS 13 in El Salvador. He disappeared right before the local authorities raided his compound. It appears he fled the country and underwent massive plastic surgery to change his appearance. Then he set up shop right here in Wilmington. He utilized the sleepy off-the-grid ports to smuggle goods in and used Layton at the airport to do the same. Layton handed them off to Jacobs, who delivered them to Raul via one of his men."

"And Fletcher and Seavers?"

"With both dead, we can't know for sure if they actively smuggled drugs or gave up Coast Guard patrol schedules. My guess is both," Finn said. "I hate to think Will could have been involved in either, but we can't overlook the facts."

"Did you tell Tess?"

Finn shook his head. "It didn't seem necessary to make her suffer more. Especially since she's told us everything she knows."

"Agreed." Noah nodded. "What's being done with the salvaged treasure Mo and Marv found for Gomez?"

"The FBI is handling all of the art and treasure. DEA is handling the drugs. Looks like they are about to seize millions."

"They are searching Paul's—or should I say, Raul's—properties, as well as combing through all Litman Limited's financials," Gabby said, shaking her head. "I can only imagine what they'll find."

"So it's over." Noah sat back, relief settling on his face.

"Thankfully." Finn smiled.

Noah looked to Gabby. "And you?"

She glanced back at Finn. "I'll keep you posted."

He nodded with a smile.

The next morning, Finn carried a breakfast tray and a bouquet of wildflowers up to the loft. "Knock, knock," he said.

"Come in."

He opened the door to find her packing.

His stomach dropped. Was she leaving?

"We should talk," she said. "Why don't we sit down?"

He nodded, his body tensing, and set the tray on the desk. "Thanks, that looks amazing."

He forced a smile. "No problem."

She wore yoga pants, an Annapolis T-shirt, and her hair was up in a ponytail. Her face looked shiny and fresh with no makeup on. "You look amazing," he said, taking a seat on the edge of the bed, while she pulled the desk chair up.

"Thanks." A soft blush crept across her cheeks. She took a deep breath. "I've been thinking about things—us—and I'm staying."

He inhaled, never having heard more beautiful words. "But your career . . . I've been thinking too. You were born to be a reporter. You come alive when on a story. As much as I'd love for you to stay, I love you too much for you to give up reporting."

Her brow furrowed. "What are you saying? You want me to leave?"

"No." He leaned across the small distance separating them and clasped her hand. "Of course not. I never want to be apart again, which is why I'll move to Raleigh."

"You'll what?"

"I'd be happy to go to Raleigh, so you can continue with the paper you love."

Tears filled her eyes. "But . . . I've already handed in my resignation."

"What? But you love your job."

"I love you more."

Heat rushed through him. "I love you too."

"But I haven't given up reporting." She smiled. "You're looking at Wilmington's WGAR-TV station's new investigative reporter."

"Seriously?"

"Yep. Lawrence called when he heard about the capture of the Collector and Fuentes's death. He wanted to make sure I was all right. I told him I was fine but I wouldn't be returning to Raleigh, and he totally understood. In fact, he offered to call a colleague at WGAR. Based on his introduction and their knowledge of my work, they called me about the job, and I accepted last night."

"But you're packing."

"I found an apartment in town. Noah has a friend who's leasing a place while he's overseas for a six-month stint. I figured if we're dating, it'd be more proper if I was in my own place."

She was staying. Permanently, by the sound of it.

Love raked through him. "But I don't want to date."

Her face slackened. "You don't?"

"No."

She swallowed. "I don't understand."

He sat forward, taking her hands in his. "I don't want to date because I want so much more."

"You do?"

"I do," he said, dropping to his knees and pulling a ring out of his pocket, his hands steady. This felt beyond right in his heart and his soul.

Her eyes widened. "Baby . . ." Tears slipped from her eyes.

"Gabby," he began, then exhaled any nerves away. As long as she said yes his whole world would be right. "I give you my word that I'll always do right by you. You know that, right?"

"Of course." She nodded. She pulled her hand from his and cupped his cheek, caressing it. "I know *you*. And you have my word that I'm never going anywhere. This is where I belong . . . with you."

"You're sure that's what you really want? That I'm who you want?"

She smiled. "I've never wanted anything or anyone more. I promise."

He inhaled the pleasure those words flooded through him. "I can't tell you how happy that makes me."

Her lips twitched into a smile. "Then why don't you show me?"

He smiled back. "Yes, ma'am." He leaned forward, bringing his lips to hers.

She wrapped her hands around his neck, spreading her fingers through his hair as he deepened the kiss.

Thank you, Father.

SEVENTY-EIGHT

TWO WEEKS LATER

Noah signaled Rissi to his desk. Unable to stay away from work, he'd chosen desk time over rest time. "We just got a call. I need you to investigate an accident at sea."

"You think foul play might be involved?"

"It could be."

Noah looked to the parking lot, and Rissi saw a black '67 Chevy Impala pulling in, its motor rumbling in the way vintage muscle cars did.

"Right on time," Noah said, straightening the papers on his desk and standing.

"Who is?"

"Our new teammate."

"The new dive investigator?"

"Yep. Why don't you go greet him, since you'll be working together on this case?"

"Of course." She still wasn't anywhere near over Sam's loss, but she understood the team's need for a new member.

She rounded the corner and stopped short. Her gaze locked on a boy she'd once known.

She blinked as her breath caught. *It can't be.*

Her gaze tracked over his rugged jaw and the scruff trimmed close on his face. His shoulders were broader, and he had to be at least six-three now. But it was him.

Mason.

His captivating green-gray eyes widened. "Ris? Is that you?" His deep voice resonated through her chest and vibrated along her limbs.

It *was* him. All grown up. She swallowed, finding her voice. "Mason?"

He raked a hand through his spikey, dark blond hair, and relief at her remembrance of him washed over his ruggedly handsome face. He smiled, and she forgot to breathe.

She was suddenly aware of her hands fidgeting at her sides, aware and in tune with her entire body. It wasn't unease raking through her. It was more like she'd sunk back into her real, full self—the one she'd kept tucked safely away—for the first time in years. The sensation was startling and yet refreshing. But she had no clue what to do with her restless hands, so she combed them through her hair, twisted a strand around her finger. "Wh-what are you doing here?"

"Mason?" Noah said, striding up behind her and extending his hand. "Noah Rowley."

Mason clearly had to force his gaze to shift from her to Noah, and he shook his hand. "Pleased to meet you, sir."

Rissi swallowed, gaping between the two. What was happening?

"Ris, meet the newest member of our team, Mason Rogers."

Acknowledgments

To Jesus—none of this would happen or matter without you. Thank you for your equipping, provision, and gracious love.

To Mike—for being my hero every day. I love you beyond measure.

To Kayla—for all your love, help, and kindness.

To Ty—for always keeping life interesting.

To my grandbabies—for filling my life with joy.

To Dave—for everything you do. I'm blessed to work with you. Here's to ten novels!

To Janet—for your guidance, support, and friendship.

To Crissy, Amy, and Joy—for being my cheerleaders, encouragers, and biggest supporters. I so appreciate your amazing creativity and generosity.

To Debb—for your great heart!

To Kate—for the fantastic job of making me look like a better writer than I am. I appreciate you.

To Noelle and Amy—for everything you've done this past year. You went above and beyond to support me, and I so greatly appreciate it.

To Lisa—my heart sister. I love you.

To Dee—for your creativity, for sharing God's abundant love with me, and for your enduring friendship. I thank God upon every remembrance of you.

To Dr. Weinman—for your compassionate care, brilliance, and wonderfully inventive story ideas. I'm extremely grateful for you.

Praised by *New York Times* bestselling author Dee Henderson as "a name to look for in romantic suspense," **Dani Pettrey** has sold more than half a million copies of her novels to readers eagerly awaiting the next release. Dani combines the page-turning adrenaline of a thriller with the chemistry and happy-ever-after of a romance. Her novels stand out for their "wicked pace, snappy dialogue, and likable characters" (*Publishers Weekly*), "gripping storyline[s]," (*RT Book Reviews*), and "sizzling undercurrent[s] of romance" (*USA Today*). Her Alaskan Courage series and Chesapeake Valor series have received praise from readers and critics alike and spent multiple months topping the CBA bestseller lists.

From her early years eagerly reading Nancy Drew mysteries, Dani has always enjoyed mystery and suspense. She considers herself blessed to be able to write the kind of stories she loves—full of plot twists and peril, love, and longing for hope and redemption. Her greatest joy as an author is sharing the stories God lays on her heart. She researches murder and mayhem from her home in Maryland, where she lives with her husband. Their two daughters, a son-in-law, and two adorable grandsons also reside in Maryland. For more information about her novels, visit www.danipettrey.com.

Sign Up for Dani's Newsletter!

Keep up to date with Dani's news on book releases and events by signing up for her email list at danipettrey.com.

More from Dani Pettrey

In college, Griffin and his three best friends, Luke, Declan, and Parker, planned to live out their futures side by side in law enforcement. But then Luke vanished before graduation and their world—and friendships—crumbled. Now years later, their lives become entwined once again as they reunite to solve mysteries, encounter dangerous criminals, and find love.

CHESAPEAKE VALOR: *Cold Shot, Still Life, Blind Spot, Dead Drift*

More Gripping Fiction

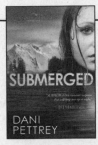

The close-knit McKenna siblings run an adventure outfitting shop in Yancey, Alaska—and have a knack for landing themselves in dangerous situations. Each book in this thrilling series features a new mystery, exciting exploits in the wilderness, and the heart-tugging love story of one of the siblings.

ALASKAN COURAGE: *Submerged, Shattered, Stranded, Silenced, Sabotaged* by Dani Pettrey
danipettrey.com

In the wake of WWII, a grieving fisherman submits a poem to a local newspaper asking readers to send rocks in honor of loved ones to create something life-giving—but the building halts when tragedy strikes. Decades later, Annie returns to the coastal Maine town where stone ruins spark her curiosity and her search for answers faces a battle against time.

Whose Waves These Are by Amanda Dykes
amandadykes.com

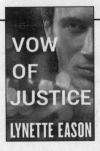

When Allison Radcliffe is killed, FBI Special Agent Linc St. John goes after her killer with a vengeance until he discovers she's been in hiding. He must put aside their unfinished business before she becomes the next victim.

Vow of Justice by Lynette Eason
BLUE JUSTICE #4
lynetteeason.com

BETHANYHOUSE

You May Also Like . . .

FBI profiler Kaely Quinn visits Nebraska to care for her ailing mother. She can't help but notice suspicious connections among a series of local fires, so she calls on her partner, Noah Hunter, to help find the arsonist. Together they unwittingly embark on a twisted path to catch a madman who is determined his last heinous act will be Kaely's death.

Fire Storm by Nancy Mehl
KAELY QUINN PROFILER #2
nancymehl.com

Once lost to history, the Book of the Wars has resurfaced, and its pages hold ancient secrets—and dangers. Former Navy SEAL Leif Metcalfe has been tasked with capturing the ancient text, but a Bulgarian operative snatches it, determined to secure her freedom. When a series of strange storms erupt, they must form an alliance to thwart impending disaster.

Storm Rising by Ronie Kendig
THE BOOK OF THE WARS #1
roniekendig.com

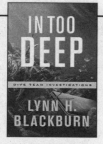

When the Carrington dive team discovers an encrypted laptop with a connection to an open murder case, detective Adam Campbell turns to the only person he can trust—but what they find may require a choice between loyalty and the truth.

In Too Deep by Lynn H. Blackburn
DIVE TEAM INVESTIGATIONS #2
lynnhblackburn.com